Lipstick and Lies

Debbie Viggiano

Lipstick and Lies © Debbie Viggiano 2012

Published worldwide 2012 © Debbie Viggiano

ISBN 978-1-291-24514-1

www.debbieviggiano.com

www.debbieviggiano.blogspot.com

Cover design by Robert Coveney

Formatting by Rebecca Emin

For all the lovely people who asked me to write a sequel to *Stockings and Cellulite*, this is for you. Enjoy xx

Chapter One

I heaved a sigh from the bottom of my Ugg boots and ground to a halt in Tesco's baby food aisle. Delving into the enormous holdall that doubled as both handbag and baby travelling case, I sifted through milk pads, nappies and wipes until Eddie's spare dummy was located. Quickly, I popped it into his gummy mouth.

'Hush darling,' I soothed.

Eddie glared at me mutinously. Please God that my six month old son wouldn't spit the damn thing out and howl to be put to the breast. Not here. Not now. Not on New Year's Eve in this packed superstore with a trolley stuffed with frozen food.

I fiddled anxiously with my maternity bra. My bosoms twanged within their hammock-like constraint, nipples like nuclear missiles on standby lest Eddie's cries put them on full-scale alert. This mothering lark was exhausting. Eleven years ago I'd given birth to twins no less. But somehow, looking back, it seemed a doddle compared to this time around. On my fortieth birthday, believing I was simply menopausal, it had come as one hell of a shock to find myself three months pregnant. And today – my forty-first birthday as it happened – I knew for sure my energy levels weren't what they used to be.

But perhaps I was being too hard on myself. After all, I wasn't just mother to my twins Livvy and Toby. I also had two full time step-children, Petra and Jonas. Exactly one year ago today I had remarried. Yes, today was not only my birthday but also my first wedding anniversary. Twelve months ago I had stood under a Bahamian sun, a radiant bride. Turquoise waves had lapped a shoreline of white sand as I'd exchanged vows with the man of my dreams, the love of my life, my second husband Jamie.

I sighed again. The difference between this time last year and right now didn't compare. The only radiant thing about me these days was my figure – still blooming away despite shedding its surprise load several months ago. If only I didn't feel so knackered. I was constantly on a short fuse thanks to sleep deprivation. Especially with the older children. It didn't help that they all seemed to be hitting pre-teen mood swings and mouthiness. Add a fractious, teething infant into the equation, was it any wonder my energy levels were at zero?

Eddie's eyes began to glaze as the dummy worked its magic. Thank heavens for small mercies. Now if I could only muster the wherewithal to finish this shop – preferably before my aching breasts resorted to emptying themselves and soaking my cotton top. I really should start weaning. Although goodness knows what my boobs would look like once the milk dried up. They hadn't exactly been a picture of perkiness before my surprise pregnancy. A chanting rhyme hovered at the corners of my memory as I recalled Livvy and Petra recently catching me naked. They'd stood wide-eyed and incredulous before guffawing with laughter. The girls had clutched each other with mirth as they'd sung:

Do your boobies hang low?

Do they wobble to and fro?

Can you tie them in a knot?

Can you toss them in a bow?

Do you get a funny feeling

When your boobies hit the ceiling–

'Thank you very *much* girls,' I'd snapped, snatching a towel about my person. Not for the first time had I wished they'd *knock* before barging into my bedroom. Heavens, on the one occasion I'd dared to do the same to them I'd been subjected to a week's worth of door slamming.

All right Cass, all *right*. Meanwhile just get a move on!

With a renewed burst of energy, I headed away from the shelves of baby food and zoomed toward Beers and Wines. I was under strict instructions to buy champagne for the Hardings' party tonight. I screeched to a halt by the bubbly and began shoving bottles between pizzas and lamb chops. What else? I scanned the shopping list. Milk, milk, mustn't forget milk. Hastening to the dairy aisle, I grabbed hold of a six pint jobbie. Right. Time to get out of here. I trolleyed smartly towards the checkout.

Eddie's eyelids had succumbed to gravity. Yes! With a bit of luck I'd have everything scanned, packed, loaded and home before my son awoke and demanded another feed. Sometimes I wondered who my body belonged to – me or my baby? Even my husband looked deprived whenever he caught a flash of my maternity bra. Sexy satin push-ups had been off the agenda the moment the ink had dried on our marriage certificate. Poor Jamie. I really should wean our son and return my boobs to my woefully neglected husband. And maybe one day I could have them back? When everybody else had finished with them, of course.

I parked the trolley next to a whirring conveyor belt. Quickly, I began unloading. The clock was ticking. It was a race against the moment my son's eyes pinged open. In record time I stood at the other end of the checkout clutching a Bag for Life.

'Want any help packing love?' asked the checkout lad.

'I'll be all right thanks,' I smiled anxiously. Come on man. Hurry up!

And we were off. *Blip, blip, blip* went the scanner. Consumables tumbled into the stainless steel packing area.

'Not so fast!' I puffed as champagne bottles clanked alarmingly.

'You've got a problem love.'

'Oh?' my hand hovered over a packet of oven chips.

'Yer milk's leaking.'

'My milk's leaking?' I repeated stupidly.

'Yeah. Look. It's all over the place. Everywhere.'

Appalled, I dropped the oven chips and clutched my bosoms. Bugger. I should have changed my milk pads before coming out. And now my milk had leaked, in front of this queue of customers. How embarrassing.

'I'll mop it up shall I?' The lad brandished a roll of paper towelling.

'I don't think so!' I snatched the roll. Clutched it possessively to my breasts.

'Shall I get you some more?'

'More what?'

'Milk. Six pints wasn't it?'

'Oh!' I dropped the paper towelling.

'Are you all right love?'

'Yes.' You berk Cass. 'Six pints. Thanks.'

'Oi, Maureen! Over 'ere. This customer's milk is knackered.'

I gazed at my dry sweater in relief. I would definitely start weaning now. That had been a narrow escape. To hell with my son's refusal to take the bottle. It would be my New Year's Resolution!

I finished the packing, paid the cashier and glanced at Eddie. He was stirring. My pulse rate quickened. No! Don't wake up! I pointed the trolley toward the automatic doors. Eddie spat out his dummy. And gave a belch from the depths of his navy-blue booties. Unfortunately some of his earlier feed got caught up in this windy extraction. It exploded forth and caught the side of my face. Oh joy. As the sour smell of regurgitated milk shot up my nostrils, I eyed my son beadily.

'One day my darling I'm going to get my own back on you. Just when you're introducing the woman of your dreams, rest assured I too shall regurgitate – all the embarrassing things you've put me through in your short little life thus far.'

Eddie gave a squeal of delight. And then a frown of concentration. As rampant farting filled the air, I marvelled how something so small could make such noise. And smell. The whiff of baby pooh abounded as a contented look fell upon my boy's face. Mission accomplished. I sighed wearily as the trolley bumped towards the car. Men. They were all the same. Even at six months old. Give it another year and Eddie would be picking his nose and scratching his balls like the rest of his gender.

I drove home as quickly as I dared. The digital speedometer nudged twenty-five miles per hour. Behind me, a queue of traffic grew. That was another puzzle since becoming a mother for a second time. I might be forty-one years old, but would I ever drive at forty-one miles per hour again? Being responsible for the conveyance of my baby from A to B was a daily nightmare. I drove as if my cargo were fragile porcelain. It wasn't quite so bad if it were just the older children in the car. But the moment Eddie's baby seat was strapped in, changing into fourth gear was a non-event. Which didn't endear me to fellow motorists. I challenged myself to go faster. As the speedometer climbed through twenty-six and twenty-seven, a muck sweat broke out under my arms. The smell inside the car was dreadful. Puke, shit and body odour assailed my nostrils. I buzzed down the window to let out some of the reek. In the rear view mirror, a red Astravan was almost touching my bumper.

'Bully,' I muttered.

Why didn't the DVLA introduce an M plate? There were L plates for learners. P plates for drivers who'd passed their tests. An M plate for 'new mother' would be perfect. A simple badge to inform the frustrated motorists crawling in my wake that I wasn't an incompetent female driver, simply a new parent getting back into the swing of things.

As I rounded a bend, the road widened. The Astravan swung out to overtake. As he drew alongside me, he slowed down. What was the guy playing at? I risked a glance. The driver had opened his passenger window. Clearly he was intent on an exchange of words.

'Bleedin' snails go faster than you!' he yelled.

'Oh bog off!' I bawled back.

'You silly tart.'

'Prat.'

'Twat.'

'Well *really* there's no need–'

But my words were drowned out by the van's horn. I jumped like a scalded cat. The driver roared past giving a middle-fingered salute. Lunatic. He must have been doing at least thirty-five miles per hour.

Shaking slightly, I eased my foot off the accelerator. Watched the speedometer fall to twenty. Now that the road had broadened out, a steady stream of traffic was overtaking. Eddie began to whine with displeasure at his dirty nappy.

'It's all right little man,' I soothed, 'we'll soon be home.' Eddie's grizzling progressed to full scale objection. 'Hush now my darling. Mummy will sort you out just as soon as–'

I paused. By the time I'd changed my child's stinking nappy, put him to the breast and finally managed to wash my face, the shopping would have defrosted. If I shoved thawed food in the freezer, food poisoning would be on the agenda. A sensation of not being able to cope rose to the surface. My eyes welled with tears. Stop it Cass. Stop it right now! But there was a definite lip tremble coming on. Yes, there it was again. Chin wobbling all over the place. By the time the car had crawled along Lavender Hill and skirted the lush common that our house overlooked, both Eddie and I were in full flow. As I trundled through the electric gates of Lilac Lodge, our large Victorian home, it was debatable whether it was me or Eddie making the most racket.

Jamie came out of the house, ready to assist.

'Hello darling,' he pulled open the driver's door. 'I was expecting you home ages ago. Oh! Whatever's the matter?' My husband took in my tear-stained face before taking a step backwards. 'Pooh. What a stink!'

'Eddie v-vomited on me,' I sobbed. 'And I can't drive fast anymore.'

'Go and have a bath and get ready for the party. I'll see to Eddie.'

'But– '

'Just do it Cassie. Go on – in!' Jamie strode around to the other side of the car. He reached in for Eddie. 'Hello little fella. How's my – oh phew!'

'Eddie's nappy– '

'I'll see to it. Mum's arrived, so she'll sort out the shopping.'

My heart sank. Oh no, my mother-in-law was here already? I couldn't bear the thought of Edna going through all the shopping. Silently regarding the convenience foods. Counting tins of mandarins instead of fresh ones. She'd never actually said anything about my microwave cookery, or my distinct lick-and-promise style of housework. But I always judged myself to be sorely lacking when making comparisons with my mother-in-law. In a nutshell, she was perfect. When we'd first moved into Lilac Lodge, Edna had been a Godsend. Albeit a Godsend that ever-so-slightly jarred. She'd unpacked china, hung curtains and filled the old-fashioned pantry with homemade pies and fruitcake. When the baking was done, she'd removed her pinny, donned a pair of overalls and appropriated Jamie's power tools. In no time at all, the children had desks for homework and extra bookcases. And just when I thought her talents were finally exhausted, she'd produced a set of screwdrivers and wired in our new light fittings. Oh there was no limit to Edna's capabilities. Couldn't figure out flat pack furniture? Call Edna. Couldn't help with your daughter's homework? Ring Edna. Couldn't find the wherewithal to unpack your shopping? I groaned inwardly as Super Gran hastened towards the car.

'Hello Cassandra,' my mother-in-law said. 'I won't kiss you dear as I can see you need to have a clean up.'

'Hi Edna,' I cranked up a smile. 'Thank you. I won't be long.'

'You take your time dear. Go and have a nice bubble bath and get ready for Matt and Morag's party. Jamie's seeing to Eddie. I've fed the children. Everything is under control.'

And that was probably the rub. Because Edna always made me feel so very *not* in control. Right now I should be bounding up the stairs, enthusiastically greeting the children, exclaiming with interest at their latest musical download, effortlessly recalling the mathematical formula for trigonometry, and offering an informed opinion on whether black nail polish looked better than green.

Instead I drooped up the stairs to the master bedroom, peeled off my stinking clothes and wandered listlessly into the en-suite bathroom. Standing over the tub I contemplated the plug hole. A couple of grey pubic hairs lay forlornly to one side, not having been washed away by the previous occupant. They were probably mine. How depressing. Even my pubes were going grey.

I flattened the pop-up plug. Blasting hot water into the bath, I added a dollop of foaming Radox. Leaving the water to run, I turned to study my reflection in the full length mirror. Dull hair. Pasty skin. The boobs looked surprisingly good, but that was due to them being full of milk. I turned sideways and sucked in my stomach. Now *that* looked good. I exhaled. My midriff promptly dropped like exhausted knicker elastic. The hips were generous. And the bottom – I jiggled around – well the less said about that the better. When I'd been pregnant with the twins I'd been lucky to escape stretchmarks. No such luck second time around. Silvery lines snaked across my abdomen as if a child had gone berserk with a gel pen.

I'd just lowered myself into the tub when there was a knock at the door.

'Who is it?' I squeaked. I didn't want the girls catching me out again or mocking my figure.

'Room service.'

I sank under the bubbles. It was debatable which was worse – the girls seeing my nakedness or my husband. I couldn't remember the last time I'd undressed with the light on. Or the last time we'd made love. A hundred years ago? Oh we'd attempted it of course. Many a time we'd nipped upstairs on the pretext of an early night, only to have plans scuppered by Eddie bawling lustily. Once we'd even got as far as stripping completely naked – in total darkness of course – and enjoyed a passionate thirty second grapple. But Eddie's colic had ended the shenanigans. We'd fared no better in the mornings either. Invariably one of the children would barge in demanding clean jodhpurs or wanting to know if I'd laundered their precious ponies' numnahs.

'Can I come in Cassie?'

'I'm not decent.'

'Good.' Jamie elbowed the door open. He was holding a tray. On it were two flutes of champagne and a single red rose. 'Happy birthday my darling. Also, happy first wedding anniversary.' He dropped a kiss on my head. 'And finally, here's to a very Happy New Year!'

My eyes welled. I loved this man so much.

'What a lot of happiness!' I blinked back the tears. Gave a watery smile.

'Why so glum?' Jamie knelt down by the side of the bath and passed me a champagne flute.

'Probably my hormones. They're still all over the place. Damn things. But I'm determined to phase out the breast-feeding and get my body back to normal.'

I glugged some champagne. Once Eddie was weaned, I'd be able to indulge without guilt. My good friend Morag had frequently lamented – during our respective pregnancies – about the enforced alcohol deprivation. Especially when she'd been ambushed by PMS. Or Pregnancy Mood Swings to the uninitiated. Upon visiting one day I'd found her prostrate over the kitchen table, sobbing her heart out but at a loss to understand why.

'What's the matter with me Cass?' she'd sobbed into a fistful of Kleenex. 'All I ever wanted was a baby. Now look at me! Finally pregnant, but blubbing like a wimp.'

It was true that Morag wasn't usually ambushed by tears. A formidable solicitor, she was also feisty, outgoing and gregarious. Uncontrollable weeping just wasn't her style.

'Talk about manic mood swings. I'm hanging off the chandeliers half the time. Matt doesn't know whether he's coming or going. One minute I'm all over him, the next I'm threatening to pack my stuff.'

I'd giggled. 'You've just given the definition of PMS – Pack My Stuff. Not to mention Pardon My Sobbing!'

'That's quite good Cass. What about,' she'd puckered her brow, 'I know! Pass My Shotgun!'

'Y-e-s. Not bad. How about Psychotic Mood Shift? Even better, Perpetual Munching Spree?'

'Provide Me with Sweets!'

'Ah, but Pimples May Surface.'

'And we'll get a Puffy Middle Section. Although we already have that,' she'd pointed at our respective baby bumps.

'No problem. Simply Pass My Sweatpants.'

At that point, her husband Matt had stuck his head around the kitchen door. Returning from the busy equestrian centre he ran so lucratively, he'd taken in the scene of hilarity. A look of relief had passed over his face.

'Feeling better my darling?'

Whereupon Morag's head had rotated one hundred and eighty degrees and she'd snarled, 'Plainly Men Suck.'

But all that was many months ago. Morag and I were now the proud mothers of our baby boys, although sometimes the pair of us were still laid low with Pissy Mood Syndrome. Would it ever go away?

'Cassie?'

'Hmm? Sorry darling. I was miles away.' I stared vacantly at my gorgeous husband, a dead ringer for Brad Pitt in his heyday.

'I was asking if I could wash your back,' my husband said huskily.

Suddenly the champagne was hitting all the right places.

'Indeed.' I looked up at him under my eyelashes. 'And if you do a good job, you can wash my front too.'

'Is that so?'

My empty champagne flute was whisked away. Seconds later a huge soapy sponge was whizzing over my back. As Jamie's breath whistled around my neck, I realised it wasn't just the sponge that was getting in a lather.

'Turn out the light darling,' I cooed.

'Don't be daft Cassie. You're in the bath.'

'Yes I know, but I don't want you seeing me—' I broke off in surprise. 'Jamie, what are you doing?'

My husband had dumped the sponge and was now urgently shedding his clothes.

'You don't need the light off,' his t-shirt flew through the air and landed in the washbasin, 'because you aren't getting out of the bath.'

'What are you talk–?'

'*I* shall get in the bath with *you*.' A pair of socks had now been balled up and tossed over one shoulder. They sailed through the air. And disappeared down the toilet.

'Don't be daft you can't– Oh!'

A tidal wave cascaded over the side of the bath as Jamie joined me. As his mouth glued to mine, my insides turned to mush. Seconds later we came up for air.

'I love you Cassie,' he roared into my armpit.

'And I love – *argh* – you but – *ouch* – you're squashing my boobs. They're still awfully tender.'

'Sorry, sorry,' Jamie panted. 'No problem. You get on top.'

Jamie wriggled within the bath's confines, manoeuvring my position. This was entirely unacceptable. Under no circumstances was he having a daytime audience with my baby tummy or overhanging view of my face which – when in the grip of gravity – gave a whole new meaning to the word *gobsmacked*.

'No!' I protested, as my body went from horizontal to vertical. Gallons of water splashed onto the floor.

'Yes! Yes!' Jamie insisted feverishly. He pulled me down on top of him. And instantly disappeared under a landslide of mammary tissue. Maybe this wasn't so bad. My spare tyres had gone unnoticed thanks to my husband being blinded by bosoms.

By the time things had come to a bathroom-wrecking crescendo, I had just twenty minutes to dry my hair and apply party makeup.

As I hurriedly blasted the hairdryer over my tingling scalp, I vowed that in my next life I would be a man. They had it so easy! A few strokes of the razor and a splash of aftershave, and they were done. No messing about with flat irons or mascara wands. Unless they were transvestites or drag queens. Or simply thoroughly vain. An image of my ex-husband sprang to mind. I was ninety-nine per cent certain Stevie was on intimate terms with the hair dye. Shade *Elvis Presley*. I also had a horrible feeling he might be at the party this evening. Since our separation and subsequent divorce, he'd somehow managed to charmingly crowbar his way into my new circle of friends. It wasn't as if we were at loggerheads with each other – those days were long gone – but surely it wasn't the done thing to be on the same social circuit with one's *ex*. Whatever outrageously flirty antics Stevie got up to this evening, thankfully it no longer concerned me. Unlike two years ago to this day. Still married to each other, we'd been guests at another New Year's Eve party. I'd inadvertently walked into our host's bedroom to find a porky middle-aged woman bonking the living daylights out of him. That memorable little episode had been the concluding chapter of our turbulent marriage. The pleasure of keeping Stevie in check now fell upon the much younger shoulders of his current live-in beau, Charlotte. She was a stunning twenty year old with sharp eyes and an even sharper tongue.

I applied some glossy lipstick. Thank God for my Jamie, loyal and true.

'Nearly ready darling?' Jamie stuck his head around the bedroom door. 'Wow. You look beautiful. I love the dress.'

I turned to face him. 'It was a bit of a squeeze getting into it.' Material strained at the seams. Beneath the plunging neckline, my boobs jostled for space. 'You don't think it's vampy?'

'Yes. But compared to whatever Morag will be wearing, it's positively demure.'

I giggled. This much was true. Morag was not afraid to flaunt her chest, the measurement of which put Katie Price in the shade.

'Just to let you know, the taxi is here. See you downstairs.'

'Okay. Won't be a mo.'

I quickly threaded some dangly earrings through my earlobes. Then, padding across the bedroom to my wardrobe, found my party stilettos and rammed my feet in. Whoa! It had been a long time since I'd worn shoes like this.

Teetering out of the bedroom, I crossed the landing. I couldn't leave without saying goodnight to the children. I also wanted to check Jonas's bedroom for an illicit stash of vodka. I gave a cursory knock on his bedroom door, then barged in before contraband could be stashed. But my step-son wasn't there. I had a quick peek in his wardrobe. A jumble of clothing fell out. Shoving it back in, I peered under the bed. Festering trainers. No booze. Good. I shut his door quietly. Tiptoeing over to Toby's room, I avoided the squeaky floorboard and cupped an ear against my son's door. It instantly flew open. Party poppers exploded in my face.

'Happy New Year Mum!' my son laughed uproariously.

'Oh for goodness sake Toby!' I snapped irritably. 'You frightened the living daylights out of me.' I plucked a tangle of streamers off one shoulder.

'That was the general idea,' Toby shrugged.

'I'm off in a minute. Where's Jonas?'

'Here.' A tousled head appeared from the other side of Toby's bed. Seconds later an arm followed. A Wii controller was clasped firmly in one hand.

'Okay boys. I'll see you both in the morning. Be good for Nanny Edna. Happy New Y–'

The door slammed in my face. Charming. Not. A little chat about manners was overdue. Downstairs the taxi beeped its horn. Yes, yes, all right.

I stood outside Livvy's bedroom. Knocked tentatively. No response. Sticking my head around the door, I surveyed a neat and tidy bedroom. But no daughter. I turned on my heel and ventured over to my step-daughter's bedroom. Mumbling could be heard from within. I flattened my ear to the door. The girls were together. They were discussing somebody. Or some*thing*. A dipstick. A pink dipstick. No. A pink *lip*stick.

'Come in Cass,' called Petra. How did she know I was ear-wigging?

'We can see the shadow of your feet Mum!' Livvy laughed.

I elbowed the door open. The girls were sitting on Petra's bed. They were surrounded by girly paraphernalia.

'I've just come to say goodnight.'

'You look amazing Cass!' Petra looked genuinely surprised.

'Do you like it?' I gave a little twirl.

'It's definitely an improvement on your usual attire.'

'Yeah,' Livvy agreed, 'ancient tat covered in baby puke.' She shifted off the bed and came over to me. Her arms entwined around my neck. Ah. Still my baby girl at heart. I dropped a kiss on her head just as the taxi emitted a series of urgent toots.

'See you later girls.' I blew a kiss to Petra, before hastening downstairs.

In the kitchen I found my mother-in-law. She was spooning mashed potato and flaked cod into Eddie's mouth. Naturally

Edna had made her grandson's dinner from scratch. Okay, it was hardly coq au vin. But it definitely wasn't Mr Heinz. Another inadequacy on my part.

'Hi Edna,' I smiled, instantly ashamed. Who was I to pass judgement on Edna's menu for Eddie when she'd agreed to babysit five children on the biggest knees-up of the year?

'You look nice Cassandra,' Edna said politely. Her eyes avoided my billowing chest. The taxi gave another round of agitated tooting. 'You'd best be off dear. Have a wonderful evening and don't hurry home.'

'Thanks Edna. For everything.'

I hovered. Debated whether to risk kissing Eddie. An unappetising mixture of fish and dribble slid down his chin. Opting to wave instead, I scampered out to the cab.

When Matt greeted us the party was well underway.

'Hello!' he yelled over the thumpity-thump of disco music. 'Come in and make merry. My wife certainly is. Ooh, champers. And lots of it. Lovely!'

'Cass! Over here,' called Morag. She'd been buttonholed by an admirer and was signalling, discreetly, for rescue. The man had his back to me, but I'd have recognised those shoulders anywhere. Stevie. My ex-husband. Predictably he was flirting. When he turned to greet me, it was evident he was in a fluster. But then that was hardly surprising given Morag's outfit. Her tiny dress was little more than silver bands criss-crossing around her body. Two scraps of material were struggling to support her bust. Her back was entirely bare. The remains of the dress just about covered her bottom. She looked like a badly wrapped bandage. Albeit a very glamorous one.

'Hi Cass,' Stevie pecked my cheek. 'You're looking very Rubenesque. The additional pounds you're carrying suit you.'

'Thank you,' I inclined my head graciously. 'You too are carrying your extra weight very well.' Stevie threw his head back and laughed. Turning to Morag, I embraced her warmly. 'You look amazing,' I said truthfully. She was slimmer now than before her pregnancy, and twice as toned. 'Do share your secret!'

'Protein shakes. And lots of sex. Beats the gym every time.'

'Sexercise!' Stevie laughed throatily. 'Great idea, Morag. Anytime you want a bit of help with the workout, give me a shout.'

Morag waggled a finger playfully. 'And does Charlotte know you are volunteering naughty services?'

'Talk of the devil,' I muttered. A young girl, her beautiful face marred by irritation, was shoving her way through the throng.

'Ah. Excuse me girls. I'll catch up with you later.' Stevie went to greet his long-suffering girlfriend.

'He doesn't change,' I sighed.

'No regrets?' Morag asked slyly.

'Don't be ridiculous,' I spluttered. 'The man's an absolute tart.'

'Yes,' Morag agreed, 'but sexy nonetheless.'

I gaped at my friend in astonishment. 'You're not tempted by the likes of him are you?'

'I'm a happily married woman Cass. But if I wasn't, then I wouldn't say no. Thankfully I have a gorgeous husband who revs me up perfectly.'

'Still taking your aphrodisiac jollop?'

'Of course. And so should you. Sex is important.'

'I'm too tired half the time. Plus we nearly always get interrupted. You have no idea what it's like in our household.'

'No different to mine surely?' Morag arched an eyebrow. She had a point. My friend was the *fourth* Mrs Harding and had inherited a large readymade family. 'Baby Henry has more brothers and sisters than I can remember.'

'And where is my divine godson this evening?' I asked, anxious to steer conversation away from my sex life.

'Upstairs with Joanie.' Joanie was Matt's eldest daughter, and an absolute sweetie. 'I'll pop up in a bit and give him his bottle. Isn't it about time you got Eddie off the tit and onto the silicone?'

I prickled slightly. 'As it happens, it's my New Year's Resolution.'

'Good. And then you can start getting yourself back into shape.' Morag cast a critical eye over my hips and chest. 'You've been carting those udders around for far too long.'

My friend was never backward in coming forward.

'Well my *udders* – as you so eloquently put it – haven't looked this good in decades. I'm not particularly looking forward to losing them when the milk dries up. How come yours haven't dropped?'

'Ah, well that's another type of silicone.'

'Eh?'

'They're not real Cass.'

'You have implants?' I squawked.

'*Sotto voce*,' murmured Morag.

'But in all the time we've known each other,' I hissed, 'you've never said a dickey bird!'

'Well now I have. And it's our little secret. If you want to treat yourself to a pair one day, I'll give you the telephone number of my surgeon. He's excellent.'

'Flippin' heck Morag. In the last few minutes you've told me to sort out my sex life, my figure, and have a boob job. It's a good thing you're a mate.'

'Don't be silly Cass.' Morag waggled a finger. 'All I'm saying is, just because you've bagged yourself a handsome hubby, you don't want to take your eye off the ball. That's all.'

'I haven't!' I protested indignantly. 'Jamie is more than happy with my curves, adores my *udders* and our sex life is incredibly adventurous!' The fact that our most recent of rare couplings had taken place in the bathtub surely qualified that statement.

'Excellent news,' said a familiar voice. Aghast, I turned to see Matt. He was snorting with laughter. 'Is my wife winding you up Cass?'

'Just a bit,' I snapped.

'Take no notice. She's always jack-booting around telling everybody what to do. My back's covered in heel marks where she stomps all over me.'

'And don't you just love it,' Morag quipped.

'Yeah, I do actually,' Matt grinned disarmingly. 'Come on Cass. Let's have a dance.'

Chapter Two

Matt led me off to the centre of the room which was heaving with gyrating bodies. He gave my hand a squeeze. 'Morag doesn't mean to ruffle feathers. She's just a natural bossy boots.'

'I know,' I sighed.

Matt smiled and changed the subject. 'So, what do you think of Jamie's business plans?'

'To expand? Oh that was always on the cards. Thank goodness it's all going so well.'

Jamie had left the police force at the start of the year to go into partnership with Ethan Fareham, an old colleague. Ethan had spotted a hole in the market at the right time. The result was a consultancy service in the City. Together the men kept pace with technology in order to stay one step ahead of criminals and hackers. The business had flourished – no mean achievement in recession. Ethan and Jamie had worked long hours, sometimes not leaving clients until midnight. It had only been a matter of time before they cast their net looking for an assistant.

'And what do you think of the new recruit?' Matt asked as he twirled me under his arm.

'I haven't met him yet.'

'Her,' Matt corrected.

'Really?' I had a misty recollection of Jamie attempting to discuss the matter. He'd come home late, hollow-eyed with tiredness. Our paths had crossed briefly on the landing, just as I was about to give Eddie his last feed for the night.

'We must talk Cassie,' Jamie had said. 'Ethan is adamant we need an assistant. You're never going to believe this but–'

'Not now darling. Eddie will wake the others if I don't see to him in the next ten seconds.'

By the time I'd settled our son and returned to Jamie, he was in bed fast asleep. I looked at Matt.

'Let's hope she's not a whiskery old boot. Anybody prepared to invest such long hours clearly doesn't have a family.'

'You're absolutely right, Cass. I once met the lady in question, and can confirm she is indeed unmarried and childless.'

'Oh dear. So she *is* a whiskery old boot,' I giggled.

'Au contraire. In fact I'd go so far as to say she's positively stunning.'

I had a sudden sense of foreboding. I paused mid-whirl. 'You've met her? How come?' But somehow I already knew the answer.

'She used to date Jamie.' Matt was suddenly alive to my appalled expression. 'But it was a long time ago,' he assured hastily.

'What's her name?' I whispered.

'Um, Selina I think.'

The floor lurched beneath me. I felt dizzy with horror. Hell's bells. Selina. She wasn't by any stretch of the imagination a tweedy spinster. Nor did she have a surplus of facial hair. With her dark mane, sexy pout and chiselled cheekbones, she bore more than a passing resemblance to Angelina Jolie. Selina had been madly in love with Jamie. Her fury had been second to none when I'd come along and mesmerised him with my so-so looks and absence of chiselled anything. I would just like to mention at this point, I was not the *other woman*. Selina's relationship with Jamie ended long before he asked me out. However, unbeknown to Jamie, Selina had harboured plans to woo him back. When Jamie hadn't responded, she'd taken to harassing him at work. And when that had failed, she'd switched her attention to me. I'd been subjected to anonymous telephone calls at home. When the dropped calls had started at work, I'd really freaked out. Selina had gone on to instigate a situation whereupon I'd turned up at a restaurant to discover her and Jamie apparently having a romantic candlelit dinner. Naturally I'd jumped straight to adulterous conclusions. All hell had broken out. I clenched my teeth at the unhappy memory. Selina! What was Jamie playing at?

'Darling, there you are!' my husband appeared by my side. He wrapped an arm around my waist and pulled me to him. 'Thank you for looking after my wife Matthew, but I would like her back now.'

'That's all right matey. I have one of my own. Speaking of which, I'd better go and rescue her.' Matt nodded in Morag's direction. We followed his gaze. Stevie was back in situ and in earnest conversation. Although he seemed to be addressing Morag's chest, rather than her face.

'Why on earth did you invite the man?' I asked Matt in amazement.

'I didn't,' Matt said, genuinely surprised. 'I thought you did.'

'Me? Why on earth would I do that? God, talk about bloody gate-crashing.'

'And Charlotte's looking mutinous,' said Matt. 'I'd better get over there, before she starts chucking the champers about.'

Jamie hugged me tight. 'Thank goodness you're not like Charlotte, throwing your weight and bad temper about.'

'Well I haven't had cause to,' I regarded my husband coolly, 'up until now.'

'What do you mean – up until now?' Jamie looked puzzled.

'Is it true you've recruited a certain ex-girlfriend as a business colleague?' I demanded.

Jamie frowned. 'You mean Selina?'

'No,' I said sarcastically, 'I mean Mandy Micklewaite from Year Six at primary school. Of *course* I mean Selina!' My lip seemed to have curled back, teeth bared like a savage dog.

'Yes,' Jamie said patiently. 'I told you about it the other night.'

'What other night?'

'Gosh, I don't know Cassie – not specifically anyway. Three nights ago? Four nights? Don't you remember?'

'No, I do *not* remember.'

'Well Cassie I can't help it if you fall asleep while I'm talking to you.'

'And I can't help being exhausted all the time,' I roared. 'Why the hell didn't you tell me when I was awake and had my wits about me?'

'Cassie, in our household there is rarely a quiet moment. You think I'm going to talk about important work decisions over the cornflakes? Shout across the cereal bowls as the kids row about which judge should be booted off X-Factor, or Eddie screams blue murder because Petra won't let him play with her iPod? Or perhaps you'd prefer it if I left you a note eh? Dear Cassandra: please be advised that as from next month Fareham & Mackerel will be employing a female I once dated for all of five minutes, yours sincerely James Mackerel, PS any chance of lamb chops for dinner tonight?'

'But didn't you realise I'd fallen asleep when you didn't get a response?' I persisted.

'But you did respond!'

'How?'

'You pulled the duvet over your head and mumbled, "Whatever", which pretty much brought the topic of conversation to a close.'

Had I? Oh God, that sounded so typical of me.

'But why Selina?' I argued. 'There are surely umpteen suitable candidates out there.'

'I have already explained this, but clearly my words made no impression on you whatsoever.'

'Because I was asleep!' I shrieked.

'Okay, I'll go over the whole thing again with you now. Firstly, I didn't *recruit* Selina, as you put it. Ethan did.'

'Well surely you had some say in it – you're his business partner!'

'The situation is sensitive in this case because–'

'What do you mean *sensitive*?'

'Because Ethan is co-habiting with Selina.'

I gaped at Jamie. 'You mean they're living together? As in bonking each other?'

'Correct. Ethan isn't aware of all the funny business we had with Selina–'

'*Funny business*,' I spluttered. 'That woman behaved like a lunatic. Is he aware he's shacked up with a fruitcake?'

'It's quite obvious he's totally enthralled with Selina and deadly serious about her. What am I meant to say to him,

Cassie? "Oh by the way Ethan matey, did you know that your woman once had the hots for me? That she wouldn't take no for an answer, and spent weeks harassing me and my wife?"' Jamie raked his hair. 'The man is dotty about her. But if it helps Cassie, Selina is dotty about Ethan.'

'Oh right. And pigs fly,' I spat.

'Darling, *please*. Stop giving me a hard time. Hear me out. Ethan had told me his girlfriend had moved in with him, but I never made the connection who she was. Why would I? He refers to her as *Lena*. He hadn't introduced her at that point. Ethan said he'd like me to meet Lena with a view to us employing her. When Selina bowled into the office, I was speechless. She acted like we'd never met. Formally shook my hand. It was all terribly civilised. Then Ethan took a telephone call and left us together. Selina begged me to not say anything. She apologised profusely for her previous behaviour–'

'Oh she did, did she?' I gnashed my teeth.

'Selina said everything was water under the bridge and–'

'Not for me it isn't!'

'And that she wanted to leave the past where it belonged – in the past.'

My mouth worked but nothing came out.

'Her entire focus was on Ethan. In fact, she acted like a woman deeply in love. When Ethan asked me outright if I would agree to *Lena* joining us, there was no professional reason to object. Whether I like it or not, she has the perfect working background and the right knowledge to progress our company.'

'I don't trust her Jamie. What if Selina wants to reignite things with you?'

'What, you mean try something on when she's already loved up with Ethan?'

'Well, put like that no, but–'

'Darling, let's not argue. It's New Year's Eve. We are enjoying a rare night out together. I want to dance with my beautiful wife. Tell her I love her. Hold her close. I don't want to regurgitate old girlfriends who never meant anything, and who I mean nothing to either. And if I can turn a blind eye to your ex-husband leering at you–'

'Stevie was leering at Morag,' I corrected.

'And you too Cassie. So if I can be pleasant to Stevie and not get my boxers in a twist, can you do the same about Selina?'

Fuckity fuckity fuck! I blew out my cheeks, and then shrugged in resignation. Jamie had never been in love with Selina. And whilst she might have once been in love with him, it had been a long time ago. Clearly she'd moved on. Moved on and moved in with Ethan Fareham. Well good for her, I thought magnanimously. I'm sure they made a splendid couple. The fact that Ethan was one of the plainest men I'd ever met was neither here nor there. It was probably his charm that had knocked Selina for six. Although I couldn't exactly remember him ever oozing charisma on the few occasions I'd met him. Well perhaps it was his amazing intellect. Yes, that was probably it. All that confidential hush-hush intelligence filed away in his computerised brain. All terribly *Ssh Secret Squirrel* which was clearly a babe magnet. I sighed. And Selina was most definitely a babe.

'Are we done with this conversation now?' Jamie sounded brow-beaten.

'I guess so. You're right. I shouldn't have let myself get worked up about it.' I wound my arms tightly around my husband's neck. Hugged him hard. Good heavens, we *all* had old flames lurking in our backgrounds. It didn't mean anything at all!

This was all Morag's fault. Banging on about my figure and taking my eye off the ball. She'd momentarily knocked my confidence. Unsettled me. Well we'd soon see about that. Starting from tomorrow I was going to re-invent myself. Definitely. I'd pop round and see Nell, my old neighbour and dear friend. Get reacquainted with her mad Red Setter, Rocket. Together my canine chum and I would pound the pavements, toning up and working out like the good old days. I would also book myself a long overdue appointment at Fairfield's swish hair salon. And whilst there I would make use of the vast number of designer boutiques that littered the sidewalks. Finally, I'd book myself an appointment with Morag's Chinese herbalist. Pop a few aphrodisiac pills. And then stand back everybody. A brand new Cassandra Mackerel would emerge – slimmer, blonder and so damned *hot* there would be smoke trails coming out of her Agent Provocateur knickers. Eye off the ball? Not likely.

I gazed at my husband winsomely. Little did he know that when this fabulous creature emerged, he would be bonked vigorously every single night. Bonked until he could bonk no more. He'd be all bonked out. So if Selina *did* have any secret designs on my husband, he'd be impervious to her pouting charms on the grounds of – well, he'd be impotent. Yes! Brilliant idea Cass. And he'd flop into bed every night, too exhausted to do anything other than give a chaste kiss on the cheek. Bingo! And we'd both have a good night's sleep. Sex free forever more. I frowned. Was that what I wanted? An impotent husband? Well no, of course not – not indefinitely anyway. Just temporarily. Until Eddie stopped giving me broken nights. And Selina was safely married off to Ethan. And vast with child. And then another child. Twins. Make that triplets. And couldn't *possibly* return to Fareham & Mackerel ever again on account of the fact that she too was now an exhausted mother. Naturally she'd have changed over this period of time. Turned into a total frump. Frightfully mumsy. Long bobbly sweater pulled down over her jeans to hide thunderous thighs. And an enormous bottom.

'That's better Cassie,' Jamie smiled at me approvingly. 'You have a gleam in your eye again. Are you thinking naughty thoughts, you little minx?'

'More than you realise darling,' I snuggled into my husband's chest as smoochy music suddenly poured out of the speakers.

All around us couples were slow dancing. Some – a little worse for wear – treading on toes as they gazed at each other. My eyes snagged on Stevie nearby. He was looking over Charlotte's shoulder, an expression of longing on his face. I followed his gaze and glimpsed Morag in all her unabashed glory. She had her mouth welded to Matt's and appeared to be sucking the life out of him.

And suddenly it was midnight. Someone put the television on. The volume was so loud it was as if we were right there – on the London pavements in the cold night air – listening to Big Ben chiming in the New Year. The small hairs on the back of my neck lifted as the poignancy of it all threatened to overwhelm me. Suddenly I was choking up with emotion. The twelfth note was drowned out in rowdy cheers. Party poppers exploded, and colourful streamers sailed through the air. Arms linked as revellers bellowed out *Auld Lang Syne*.

'Happy New Year darling,' Jamie folded me into his embrace. Suddenly I was being kissed very thoroughly.

'Ooh I'll have one of those!' Morag lurched over and thrust her mouth at Jamie.

'No tongues,' I warned my friend, as Jamie deflected the kiss to his cheek.

'Spoilsport,' she pouted.

'Morag!' Stevie materialised by her side. 'If you're after a bit of Froggie,' he waggled his eyebrows suggestively, 'try me for some French snoggy.' He stuck his tongue out optimistically and wiggled it from side to side.

'Ooh you are a naughty boy,' Morag cooed.

'And you're a naughty girl,' Stevie bandied back.

'And you're a fucking bastard,' screeched Charlotte zooming in with a balled fist. She caught Stevie a resounding smack on the chin. Everybody turned to look at the commotion. Morag melted away. There was a collective gasp as Stevie staggered backwards and fell into the Christmas tree.

Jamie steered me into the hallway. 'Time to go I think,' he murmured. 'Ah Matt! Fantastic party. Wonderfully entertaining. As ever.'

Behind us all hell was breaking out.

'Take care folks,' Matt kissed me on both cheeks and pumped Jamie's hand several times. 'Best go and see what's happening in there. Clearly somebody's had enough,' he rolled his eyes.

Only Charlotte, I thought sympathetically.

'You okay?' asked Jamie in the back of the taxi.

'Sort of,' I winced.

'What's wrong?'

'It's these,' I pointed to my milk-laden breasts. They'd gone rock hard. 'They're killing me.'

Chapter Three

'Hello?' I bawled down the telephone. Eddie, on my hip, drowned out the caller with his lusty cries. 'You'll have to SPEAK UP!' I clamped the receiver between shoulder and ear and tried not to garrotte the pair of us – we'd yet to go cordless. Freeing one hand, I grabbed a bottle of formula milk from the worktop. Eddie stepped up his howls. I tried slotting the silicone teat into my son's mouth. He took one look at it and knocked the bottle right out of my hand.

'Cass?' a familiar voice squawked.

'Hang on!'

I flung the receiver down and put Eddie in his playpen with a rusk. To hell with the mess. Anything for a civilised conversation. I picked up the bottle, dumped it in the sink and retrieved the phone.

'Nell!' I beamed into the mouthpiece. It was always a joy to talk to my old neighbour and loyal friend. 'Happy New Year!'

'You too Cass. Can you talk for five minutes?'

'I most certainly can. The children are at the stables, and Jamie is with Matt. He's helping clear up after last night's revelry.'

'That's why I was calling. How was the party? Did I miss a great night out?'

'No,' I lied. 'Anyway, it's far more important to keep your feet up.' Nell was in the final stages of a very difficult pregnancy. She was taking no chances after a miscarriage the previous year.

'So tell me all about it. Bit by bit. Blow by blow.'

'There were a few of those actually.' I glanced at the clock. Time for elevenses. I siddled towards the kettle, stretching the telephone cord to its limit. A beverage break was essential when gossiping. 'Morag looked amazing. And Stevie was being utterly outrageous with her. Offering to give her a tonsillectomy with his tongue. That sort of thing.'

'Oh God. Didn't Matt mind?'

'I think Matt is actually quite proud of having a wife other men lust after.' I poured boiling water into the mug. 'And Morag, for all her flirting, worships the ground Matt walks on.'

'So where was Stevie's girlfriend?'

'Oh Charlotte was there. She stayed long enough to black Stevie's eye and shove him into Morag's ten foot Christmas tree.'

'So I *did* miss a good party,' Nell sighed. 'What were you wearing? I bet you looked ravishing.'

'Hardly. But talking of ravishing, guess whose name popped up last night?'

'Gosh, I don't know.'

'Come on Nell, you can do better than that. I'll give you a clue. Long dark swishy hair. Pouty lips. Drop dead gorgeous.'

'I don't know anybody like that.'

'Used to go out with Jamie,' I prompted.

There was a pause. 'Not Selina?'

'The very one and same.'

'Why were you discussing her? She's history.'

'Apparently not.' I slurped some coffee. 'Would you believe Selina has shacked up with Jamie's business partner?'

'No!'

'Yes. And what's more, she's joining Fareham & Mackerel.'

'You've got to be kidding.'

'Sadly not. Ethan wants her to join the consultancy. Selina has begged Jamie not to mention what happened previously. Said she's mad about Ethan. Or words to that effect. So as from tomorrow, she's on the payroll.'

'Well!' I heard Nell puffing out her cheeks. 'How do you feel about it Cass?'

'Truthfully?'

'Of course.'

'Peed off. I'm absolutely dreading our paths cross–'

Just at that moment, Eddie let out a screech. He'd finished his rusk. A dribbly mess trailed down the front of his sleep suit. Why hadn't I put a bib on him? His fingers, covered in gunge, were now travelling over his head. Downy hair was sticking up all over the place. He looked like an irritable duckling.

'Nell, I'm going to have to go. My darling boy has made the most stupendous mess. You wouldn't believe what one little rusk can do.'

'Well I pretty much remember from the first time around with Dylan. Although granted that was now several years ago. However, I can't wait to go through it all again,' Nell chuckled.

'You won't say that six months down the line. You'll be knackered, up to your armpits in endless baby laundry, and have Ben complaining about a non-existent sex life.'

Eddie's sticky fingers tangled in his hair. His face registered pain, and then crumpled. The previous squawk turned into a howl.

'Go see to Eddie,' Nell shouted over the din. 'Love to Jamie.'

'And love to Ben and Dylan,' I yelled back.

Hanging up quickly, I picked up Eddie and clasped him to me. I was back in my uniform – yet another pair of Smart Price joggers and matching t-shirt in Regulation Grey. As Eddie snuggled into my chest, I felt as if we'd morphed into a human sandwich, the congealed rusk acting as the butter between us.

'There, my darling. Hush.' I patted Eddie's back rhythmically. Bit by bit, his cries subsided. 'I think we'd better clean you up. And then Mummy will pop you into another romper suit.' My son, like his mother, had his own scaled-down uniform. But in various shades of blue.

By the time I'd changed Eddie, administered Calpol for sore gums and spooned a jar of Mr Heinz into him, it was mid-afternoon. With a baby, time went nowhere. I strapped my son into his rocker chair, and turned my attention to stacking the dishwasher. Minutes later, Eddie had zonked out. Laying a crib blanket over him, I moved the rocker into the lounge. Resisting the temptation to curl up on a nearby sofa, I went back out to the kitchen to start on a tottering pagoda of ironing.

I'd barely set up the ironing board, when the cat flap opened. A black feline head poked through. It was Wallace. His green eyes were the only distinction between him and his yellow-eyed brother, Gromit. He minced into the kitchen. I ignored him and continued running a hot iron over a pair of jodhpurs. With four pony-mad kids in the house, they went through riding breeches almost as quickly as Eddie did romper suits. Wallace weaved around my ankles, yowling pitifully.

'Oh for goodness sake,' I banged down the iron. 'If it isn't kids demanding attention, it's cats. I suppose you want feeding?' Wallace regarded me adoringly, purr box bursting into life.

'Couldn't you have picked something up on the go? A mouse? Or a bird?' I opened the cupboard under the sink. Hunkering down, I peered amongst dusters and paraphernalia for cat food. Wallace head-butted my elbow with impatience. There was a noise behind me. I turned just in time to see Gromit leap through the cat flap. 'Ah. Heard your brother demanding food, did you? Another lazybones who can't catch his own din–'

The words died on my lips. I had an overwhelming urge to climb into the cupboard. And shut the door. Sandwiched between Wallace's jaws was a huge blackbird. As Wallace meowed a greeting, the bird fell to the floor. But instead of keeling over, claws up, it found its feet and regarded me with beady eyes. Jesus. It was still alive. I had to get it out. Before it took flight inside the house – where, no doubt, every internal door was wide open. I paled at the thought. At that precise moment both cats, in perfect synchronisation, pounced. The blackbird, shocked but still capable, launched itself upwards. Wallace and Gromit promptly head-banged each other. Livid, they fluffed up like porcupines. As I went to stand up, my foot connected with one furry tail. Gromit's. Screeching with pain, he twisted his body and raked his claws down my legs. Sharp needles stabbed through the thin material of my joggers. I yelped in agony. There was a moment of pandemonium as both feline and human limbs entangled, and then both cats sprang after the bird. I stumbled awkwardly. As the floor rushed up to greet me, I struck out with one wrist. Unfortunately this connected with the ironing board's legs. I looked up fearfully. A hot iron, imitating the cats with its hissing and spitting, rocked precariously. Before I had even registered that the iron was about to topple, my reflexes kicked in. In a nano-second my arms had propelled my body away. The iron slammed down to the floor, cable looping around the ironing board. Moments later there was a second crash as metal hit marble. The noise was deafening. From the lounge, Eddie let out a startled cry.

'It's okay darling,' I croaked. 'Mummy's just being a bit noisy.'

Gingerly, I picked myself up. Nothing broken. Apart from the iron. I unplugged it, and picked up a bit of plastic. Directly overhead were some ominous thumpity-thumps. Clearly Wallace and Gromit were charging about in Petra's bedroom. I collapsed the ironing board and leant it against the wall. Eddie was grizzling now.

'Coming darling,' I hobbled into the lounge. Sounds of mad scrabbling persisted. It was getting closer. I had a mental vision of Wallace and Gromit skidding on two legs around the banisters. I bent down, unstrapped Eddie and scooped him up just as the terrified blackbird flapped into the room. Both cats were in hot pursuit. I screeched, ducked, and flung one hand over my head. The bird landed on an overhead light fitting and instantly let forth a volley of crap. Blobs of gunk landed in the spaces between my fingers. Eddie's grizzling changed to squeals of delight. The cats had leapt onto a cabinet, intent on hurling themselves at the light fitting. Both sofas were pebble-dashed with bird shit.

'You *bloody* cats,' I screeched.

My shouting only served to further unnerve the bird. It spread its wings and took off from the light-fitting – straight toward the cabinet. Wallace, practically hanging off by his tail, swiped front paws through the air. His aim was spot on. Suddenly the room was filled with feathers and flying fur as both bird and cat crashed to the ground.

Out in the kitchen, a voice could be heard. Who was that?

'Cassandra?'

'Help! I'm in *argh–*'

I let out a bloodcurdling cry as Gromit – unsure how to get off the cabinet – leapt straight onto my head. Scrabbling wildly, claws impaled into my scalp and forehead. Desperate to protect Eddie, I held my son out at arm's length. Eddie wasn't at all perturbed. Indeed he was clearly thrilled to bits to see Mummy wearing a cat on her head and pulling funny faces. As Gromit swayed about, Eddie gurgled with laughter.

'Help!' I screeched again, as claws dug perilously close to my eyes. I charged towards the kitchen, baby aloft, cat akimbo, straight into my mother-in-law. Of all the hero rescuers in the world, why did mine have to be a pint-sized version of Nanny McPhee?

Edna instantly assessed the situation and took charge. Grabbing Eddie, she whipped him over to the playpen and out of harm's way. Seconds later a tea towel landed on my head. Gromit was swaddled and removed. At that moment Wallace, bird in mouth, strolled into the kitchen. He gazed at Edna. Recognising a superior being, he placed the bird reverently at her feet. She bent down, palm open. The bird, moth-eaten but still alive, hopped onto her hand. Edna opened the kitchen door, and the bird flew off to freedom. Just like that.

She went to the sink and scrubbed her hands.

'Forgive me for letting myself in Cassandra dear, but Jamie telephoned me. He wants me to babysit again. Tonight. He said Ethan Fareham has invited both of you to have dinner with him and his fiancée.'

I stared at Edna stupidly. 'Fiancée? Ethan's proposed to Selina?'

'Sit down Cassandra. You look very pale. And those scratches are nasty. Quite swollen. Let me find some antiseptic.'

'I can't possibly go out to dinner,' I said. But I was talking to thin air. Edna had taken herself off to the bathroom medicine cabinet.

The telephone shrilled into life. I reached out a shaky hand. The skin was peppered in scratches. I frowned at them. My face was starting to throb. 'Hello?'

'Cassie, it's me,' said Jamie from his car. 'The kids have finished at the stables and I've picked them up. We're on our way home. Has Mum told you about tonight?'

'Yes, but the house is covered in pooh,' I replied.

There was a pause. In the background the kids sniggered with laughter.

'Are you okay Cassie? You sound a bit spaced out.'

'I've had a bit of an accident.'

I could hear Toby roaring with laughter. 'Oh my God. Mum's poohed herself. All over the house.'

Edna returned with a bottle of TCP and some cotton wool. She took the phone from me.

'Jamie dear, Cassandra has been badly scratched by one of the cats. A bird got into the house and has made a bit of a mess. I want all the children to pull together and help me get this place ship-shape.'

'Edna,' I interrupted, 'I can't possibly leave you and the children to clean–' I gasped as, with her free hand, she doused my wounds in TCP. Geez, it stung.

'See you in a couple of minutes,' she said to Jamie before hanging up.

'Edna, I really can't–'

'Of course you can. And must. This is important. It's business.' She finished dabbing. 'Here. Take these painkillers. Now go and have a bath. Put Eddie in with you while I start on the cleaning.' My mother-in-law was already rolling up her sleeves.

And so for the second night running I found myself sharing the bathtub. This time with my baby son and a brightly coloured army of plastic ducks. They bobbed around in the bubbles as Eddie, wedged between my thighs, splashed in delight. In the background I could hear all sorts of activity going. Beds were being stripped of soiled linen, surfaces washed and floors mopped. Jamie and the children had taken one look at me and been horrified. Toby, appalled for laughing earlier, had hugged me tightly.

I picked up a sponge and soaked my hair before gently rubbing in shampoo. My scalp was stinging like blazes. What an absolute fiasco the afternoon had been. And as for tonight. I sloshed water over my head and rinsed away the lather. I really could have done without it. After last night's bombshell that Selina was joining Fareham & Mackerel, I knew we'd meet again one day. But at no point had I reckoned on it being just twenty-four hours later. What on earth were we going to talk about? *Hi there Selina! How ARE you (gush gush)? The last time we met I flung a glass of wine in your face. Would you like another for old time's sake?*

Eddie began to beat a tattoo with his palms against the water. The bath was far cooler than I'd have liked on account of him being in it with me. In fact, I was starting to feel a bit shivery. I finished rinsing my hair, then turned my attention to Eddie. Hauling myself out of the water, I wrapped us both in a big bath towel. Thanks to the cats' antics, Eddie had missed out on a decent afternoon nap. He was now struggling to keep his eyes open.

Ten minutes later my baby was fast asleep in his cot. I checked his alarm was on, that no cats were in the room, and quietly shut his door. Time to get to work with my hairdryer. That was the easy bit. Attempting to do the same thing with my face wasn't so straightforward. My forehead looked as though havoc had been wrought with a sharp fork. All around my eyes were tiny puncture wounds. The swelling had subsided slightly, but everything looked red and angry. Liquid make up was out of the question. I stroked some mascara onto my eyelashes and opted for a bright red lipstick. Hopefully this would draw attention to my mouth, rather than my forehead.

Smells of home cooking drifted upwards. I sniffed the air appreciatively. It certainly wasn't my culinary special – beans on toast. My relationship with the vast range in our kitchen was a standoffish one. I didn't ask too much of it, and it didn't give me much in return. Whereas Edna would have all the ring burners blazing, double ovens stoked, and – before you could say Jamie Oliver – produce a week's worth of home cooking.

I riffled through my wardrobe. What would Selina be wearing? Something fabulously chic and tailored? Or smart-casual? I swished coat hangers this way and that, appraising everything with a critical eye. I swept half a dozen pairs of identical joggers to one side and considered a red velvet dress. I'd bought it in the Sales last year before discovering I was expecting Eddie. By the time an opportunity to wear it had come along, my baby bump was well and truly established. I removed the dress from its hanger and let it slither over my head. It was a snug fit, but not enough to restrict breathing. I stood in front of the mirror. Not bad. Not great, but definitely not bad. Rummaging around in the wardrobe, I found a pair of shiny black boots and a matching clutch bag. They would do. I finished off with a liberal squirt of perfume. If nothing else I might just manage to *smell* nicer than Selina.

Jamie came into the bedroom. 'That's a lovely dress darling. Give me thirty seconds in the shower, and I'll be ready to go.'

I smiled. 'See you downstairs.'

I grabbed a coat and walked across the landing. The aroma of furniture polish and cleaning fluid jostled with cooking smells. The house was positively sparkling. I found the children in the TV room, glued to some ridiculous reality programme.

'Hey kids.' They glanced my way. 'Thanks for helping clear up all that mess.'

'That's okay Cass,' Petra smiled. 'You clear up after us all the time.'

'We didn't mind doing it,' said Toby, 'but don't expect me personally to do it again. It's a woman's work.'

Just eleven years old and my son was already a chauvinist.

'Where are you going Mum?' asked Livvy.

'Out to dinner with Ethan and his fiancée.'

'Oh yeah. That's ironic,' Jonas snorted. 'The fiancée used to go out with Dad.'

'Did she?' Petra's brow furrowed. 'What's her name?'

'Sabrina.'

'Actually, it's Selina,' I corrected.

'That's right,' said Jonas. 'I remember her. She was a milf.'

'A what?'

'Jonas!' Petra chided.

'What's a milf?' I asked, perplexed.

Livvy and Toby had gone a bit pink.

'It's, um, a sort of modern compliment,' said Toby.

'Enlighten me,' I said. On the screen a woman with fake breasts and a mouth like Donald Duck was talking about her life being incomplete unless she had bum implants. 'Jonas? Spill the beans. What's a milf?'

Jonas shifted uncomfortably. 'I can't remember exactly. But it's, well, like Toby said, a sort of compliment. But a bit, you know, racy.'

'Racy?' I eyed my step-son. Not quite thirteen but definitely waking up in the puberty department. He was already six feet tall, albeit built like a piece of string. Only last week, when vacuuming his room, I'd picked a forgotten magazine off the floor. It had been full of naked women. I'd taken a black marker pen to it. Drawn dresses and one-piece swimsuits on all the busty ladies. Sensible ones too. No plunging necklines or high-cut legs. And then I'd warmed to the task. Given them accessories. Harry Potter spectacles. Handlebar moustaches. One or two blacked-out teeth. And then I'd carefully placed the magazine back on the floor. Jonas hadn't said anything. And neither had I. But I knew that he knew that I knew that he knew and I knew that he knew it too.

'Daddy was never that keen on her though. And neither were we Cass,' said Petra loyally.

I smiled. 'Thank you, sweetheart.'

Jamie bounded down the stairs. 'Told you I wouldn't be long. Come on then Cassie. Bye kids. School tomorrow so don't be late to bed please.'

Out in the kitchen Edna stood before the range, oven mitts on both hands. She bent down and removed a huge terrene of coq au vin. All the ironing had been done. To one side, on the worktop, freshly laundered and folded sheets were neatly stacked. How did she do it? And so effortlessly. They were questions I'd asked myself so many times.

'Cassandra dear,' my mother-in-law carefully set the terrene down. 'Those puncture wounds look very sore. How are you feeling?'

'Much better thank you Edna.' My stomach growled with hunger. I hoped we'd be eating something equally scrumptious tonight. 'Thanks so much for coming to the rescue.' At this point any other daughter-in-law might have hugged her mother-in-law. Unfortunately our relationship was not a touchy-feely one. Rather it was more employer/employee. With me definitely in the employee role.

Edna inclined her head. 'It was no trouble. Hurry along now. Have a nice time.'

'I'm sure we will Mum,' said Jamie. 'We'll try not to be too late.' My husband turned to me. 'Ready?'

'Yes darling,' I pasted on a bright smile. As ready as I'd ever be for this dreaded meeting.

Chapter Four

'Your car or mine?' I asked Jamie.

'Mine,' he said picking up his keys.

As we walked out of the house, a cold wind whipped up my hair. I stuffed my hands in my pockets as Jamie pressed his key fob's remote button. The central locking sprang open on the BMW X5. It was a company car, and pristine. The kids rarely travelled in it. Instead their muddy riding boots, sweet wrappers and rubbish detritus graced the inside of my car – a seven seater Citroen affectionately known as The Muck Truck.

'So,' I folded my legs into the BMW and sank back against the leather, 'which restaurant are we off to for this evening's fun foursome?'

Jamie ignored my sarcasm. 'No restaurant Cass. We're going to Ethan's apartment in Greenwich. I believe Selina insisted on it. She's doing the cooking.'

'Well she'd better not poison me. I want it on record, right here, right now, that if I'm ill later it's her fault.'

'Darling, don't you think you're being a bit childish?'

The electric gates slid open, and Jamie eased the Beamer out onto the road.

'Childish? *Childish*! That woman is a nutter! You know it. I know it.'

'Cassie, I know this is hard for you–'

'You have no idea how hard it is for me!'

'Yes, I do! And it's just as difficult for me too.'

'Well you're very calm about it. You've evidently taken the whole situation in your stride. I'm still struggling to get my head around everything. I don't know why you can't tell Ethan straight. You'd be doing the bloke a favour. How would he feel if he knew his girlfriend – correction, *fiancée* – had once harassed his business partner? And not just at work, but home too? Not forgetting all her dropped phone calls to me. *And* at my place of work too. Talk about freaking me out.' I was aware that my voice had risen. 'That woman was hell-bent on making out you were having an affair. She set you right up. I can still see her. Sitting opposite you in that restaurant. Looking oh-so-smug. Telling me, "Sorry you had to find out this way."'

I could feel my stomach knotting with bad memories – me chucking wine at Selina, stuffing a handy bread roll into Jamie's shirt, and then legging it before an army of waiters turfed me out.

'Look, we've gone over this. Ethan would be devastated, Cassie. You know that. Quite apart from anything else, you are forgetting that Ethan is the Senior Partner. He's the one who put the dosh into the company. Ultimately the overall decision is his. And he wants Selina working for us. I have told you several times now that Selina has emphasised the past is over and done with. As far as she's concerned, it's all water under the bridge. She's potty about Ethan. And she's very sorry about what happened.'

'Well she's not apologised to me.'

'I'm sure she will this evening.'

'Unlikely.'

'Why?'

'Because Ethan will be there of course.'

'Look Cassie, I'll say it again. I'm powerless. We're going round in circles discussing it.'

'I know, I know,' I wailed. 'And I'm sorry. But I'm just not happy about it. I'm not happy about it at all.'

The BMW accelerated down a slip road and onto the duel carriageway to London.

'Cassie, if I could change things, I would. You know that. If Selina's joining the firm means you are going to be utterly miserable, I'll tell Ethan I can't work with him anymore. Is that what you want?'

'Now you're boxing me into a corner.'

Jamie reached across the handbrake. He caught hold of my fingers.

'Listen to me. You're my wife. Your well-being and happiness is important to me. I'm not boxing you into a corner intentionally. There are two options here. Either I work with Ethan – and in this case Selina too – or I don't. I could go back to the police force. Be a cop again.'

'I don't want to be worrying about you in a job like that. Apart from anything else, we can't afford our current outgoings on a policeman's pay.'

'Agreed. We'd have to move. Downsize in order to reduce bills.'

I bit my lip. And move into what? Even a four bedroomed property – a luxury for many families – would be a squeeze for us. The children wouldn't have their own rooms anymore. And where would Edna sleep? She often stayed for extended periods of time. Due to fortuitous financial circumstances, we owned our beautiful home outright. Lilac Lodge was a six bedroomed Victorian pile overlooking Lavender Common. It would be a wrench to leave it. And then there were the kids' horses to think of. They were stabled at Matt and Morag's equestrian centre. Keeping horses in pony nuts and New Zealand rugs was an expensive business. And thanks to Katie Price pointing a manicured nail at the equestrian industry, it had become even more expensive. Just this very Christmas Petra had insisted Honey, her chestnut mare, simply *had* to have a raspberry rug complete with coronet motif. It would be pink hoof oil and mane extensions next.

'I know! Tell Selina to turn the job down! Insist on it. Tell her to concoct some excuse to Ethan. She owes you. And me. End of problem.'

'Don't you think she's already tried that?'

I turned to face Jamie. 'Has she?'

'Yes! She started off telling Ethan that the line of work didn't interest her. Then she voiced concern over them both living *and* working together – that it might ruin their relationship. She's trotted out every excuse under the sun. Ethan won't take no for an answer. He wants her working for us. And professionally there's no reason why she shouldn't.'

I sighed. Turned to look out the window. My face reflected back at me. Anxious and pinched.

Jamie gave my fingers a reassuring squeeze. 'Why don't we take things one step at a time, eh? Let's see how this evening goes. You never know, you and Selina might end up good friends.'

'Good fr–?'

The words died on my lips. Men had no understanding of women's friendships. None whatsoever. People like Nell and Morag were good friends. Selina could never fall into that bracket. The rest of the journey passed in silence, both of us with our own thoughts.

Twenty minutes later we shot into the underground car park of a swanky building overlooking the Thames. Jamie reversed into a space next to Ethan's Mercedes.

'The lift's over there.'

Jamie took my hand as we walked across the car park. Our heels echoed. The noise made me shiver. This might be a super-dooper address, but the location wasn't my cup of tea.

'What floor is Ethan's?' I asked.

'Right at the top. The penthouse.'

The most expensive. Naturally. I wondered how much his place was worth. I was pretty sure Selina was the sort of woman who checked out such things. Ethan had left the police force long before Jamie. He'd branched off into another area. Computers. And being a nerdy type, he'd devised some sort of software that had halted the illegal shenanigans of a geek group. The geeks had been running their own software. Making fake digital money, and then converting it into real money. Ethan had traced an entire network of computers running into thousands – at banks no less. The Governor of the Bank of England had declared such activity had had the potential to destabilise the world economy. Certainly Ethan's pockets were now lined with gold. And the banks had opened their doors to him. Ethan was – as my mother would have said if still alive – a *catch*. And clearly Selina had caught him.

As we stood outside Ethan's front door, I could feel my heart rate increasing. I made myself take some deep breaths. The door opened and Ethan stood there. Tall, thin, and totally bald. But not in an *I-only-shave-my-head-because-I'm-trendy* kind of way. Rather *No-I-really-don't-have-any-hair* kind of way. His intelligent blue eyes regarded me behind rimless spectacles.

'Welcome,' Ethan smiled. 'Do come in.' He shook Jamie's hand, and then mine. All frightfully formal. 'Lena's in the kitchen putting the finishing touches to something extraordinary. So I'm told anyway.'

This was a major stab at humour for Ethan. Jamie and I laughed politely as Ethan took our coats.

'How are you Cass?'

'I'm good thank you Ethan,' I said, feeling anything but. Where was she? As Ethan hung up our coats, my eyes darted around the hallway.

'Come on through. Let me get you both a drink.'

'I'll have a soft drink,' said Jamie. 'I'm the driver tonight. However, I'm sure Cass won't say no to a G & T,' my husband winked at me.

'That would be lovely,' I smiled tightly. Preferably a quadruple. I needed something to soften the blow of this evening.

We followed our host into a vast ultra modern room. A cathedral-type ceiling soared above our heads. The entirety of one wall was glass. A feature balcony wrapped itself around the penthouse. The City's twinkling lights filled the room. It was an amazing living area. I looked around. The room appeared to combine lounge, dining room and – my eyes travelled to the far end – a kitchen. It looked like something out of NASA. And there, setting out food on a granite worktop the length of an airport runway, was Selina. She looked up, and gave a dazzling smile.

'Well hello!' She skirted the runway and came towards us, hands outstretched in welcome. 'Good to meet you again Jamie.' She kissed him soundly on both cheeks, continental style, before turning to me with wide eyes. 'And you must be Cass.'

I glared at her. If she attempted to kiss me, I wouldn't be responsible for my actions. I had an overwhelming urge to shove her back into the space-age kitchen, press a button and launch her into oblivion.

'That's right. I must say,' I couldn't resist winding her up, 'you look awfully familiar. Have we met somewhere before?'

Selina feigned consideration. And then shook her head. 'No. I never forget a face. Or a frock,' she indicated my red velvet dress. 'That is sooooo fab. I remember seeing it in the Sales at Harvey Nicks last year. I was desperate to buy one. Regrettably they only had the extra large sizes left.'

Bitch!

Jamie caught my expression, and hastily took up the reins of conversation.

'Cheers!' he raised his glass. 'A very Happy New Year. And congratulations on the engagement – fabulous news!'

Selina took a drink from Ethan. 'Thank you, sweetheart.' She held her glass aloft. 'Cheers all!'

'My wife is such a romantic. I'm sure she'd love to know all the details of the proposal, wouldn't you darling?'

I bared my teeth in response.

'Oh Cass, it was just dreamy. Wasn't it honey?' Selina beamed at Ethan. He inclined his head graciously. 'We wrapped up nice and warm, went out on the balcony – with champers naturally – and watched the City below. So many people! And in such high spirits. The atmosphere was electric! And then, literally seconds away from midnight, Ethan dropped down on one knee and asked me to be his wife. Well I didn't hesitate. Did I sweetums? Just said, "Yes! Yes-yes-yes-yes-yes!" And then my voice was drowned out by all the fireworks exploding. Next thing is we're ripping each other's coats and clothes off, and making mad passionate love! Right there,' she waved an arm at the balcony, 'in front of millions of people,' she tinkled with laughter, 'who naturally couldn't see us! But it was terribly thrilling nonetheless. Not to mention invigorating. There's nothing like cold air and hot sex! Ethan always makes the earth move for me but, by golly, it was positively shaking with all those fireworks exploding!' She rolled her eyes theatrically. 'I love starting New Year with a bang – if you catch my drift, ha ha!'

Was she for real? Ethan appeared unembarrassed by this recital of his balcony bonk. His face was expressionless, as if Selina had merely been talking about grocery shopping. He cleared his throat.

'Lena and I would very much like to extend belated Happy Anniversary wishes to you both. Wasn't it a year ago yesterday you wed in the Bahamas?'

'Indeed it was,' Jamie put an arm around me and gently kissed my punctured forehead.

'Oh do let me see your ring Cass,' Selina pretended to be interested.

I held out my hand.

'Gosh, isn't your diamond *sweet*,' she beamed. 'I wanted one as small as that but Ethan gave me no choice in the matter, did you darling? Just presented me with a box with this socking great rock in it,' she waggled her hand under my nose. *Socking great rock* was indeed an accurate description. I was amazed she could lift her hand. 'Do you like it?'

I pretended to study the diamond. 'Jamie wanted to buy me something similar but I said, "No darling. In this case size *isn't* everything." So I opted for classiness.'

Selina's smile froze. An unspoken current passed between us. The gloves were off.

'I simply can't help noticing your forehead Cass. If I were you I'd sue the beautician who did that Botox job.'

'Botox? Um, no. My cat scratched me.'

Selina gave another of her tinkling laughs. It was starting to grate on me. 'Oh is that what you say to everybody. Don't worry Cass,' she winked, 'your secret is quite safe with me.'

'Another drink Cass?' asked Ethan.

'Yes please,' I snapped.

'And I just love your black boots Cass. Wonderfully shiny. And those big buckles are perfect.'

I stared down at my footwear. Where was this conversation going? I didn't have long to wait.

'Yes, they co-ordinate beautifully with the red dress. Especially at this time of year. You look like Mrs Christmas! You've even got a jolly tummy like her hubby. Ho, ho, ho!'

Dear God. Where was this woman's off button?

'Gosh you are funny Selina,' I chortled. 'Actually I've had more compliments wearing this ensemble than hot dinners. Only this evening I was told I looked like a milf.'

Jamie choked on his lemon slice, Ethan was doing some rapid blinking behind his specs, and Selina's mouth formed a perfect O. Ah, that had caught her attention hadn't it!

'Are you sure darling?' Jamie spluttered.

'Of course I'm sure. Edna told me so.'

'My mother called you a milf?' Jamie's eyebrows shot off his forehead.

'Don't look so shocked darling. Your old mum is perfectly up to date with modern lingo. A very hip-hop-and-happening lady is my mother-in-law,' I nodded sagely at Selina.

'Ah ha ha ha,' Jamie forced a laugh. 'Well I must say dinner smells absolutely delicious!'

'I can't smell anything,' I muttered.

Selina smoothed down her dress. 'Yes, let's eat. Everything is ready.'

We followed her over to the granite runway and climbed onto some tall stools.

'Lena is very creative in the kitchen,' said Ethan.

'I'm creative everywhere darling,' she smirked. A starter of raw mushroom soup was set before us. 'I think you're going to enjoy this Jamie. You look like somebody who cares about their figure.' She paused. Gave me a moment to digest the message that I didn't care about mine. 'Ethan and I recently discovered the raw food diet. It's wonderful. Super healthy. Low fat. And leaves you fizzing with energy.'

I stuck my spoon in the bowl of pale gunk. What was wrong with hot soup?

'It's all very well working out in the gym, but you need to look after what's under the bonnet too,' Selina prattled on. And on and on.

Nobody else got a word in edgeways as we worked our way through raw Pad Thai Salad, raw 'Burrito' lettuce wraps, raw broccoli covered in 'Alfredo' sauce and raw Asian-style crunchy salad with sesame vinaigrette. By the time I'd finished munching and crunching, my jaw ached. It was a wonder none of us had turned into Bugs Bunny.

'And finally,' she chirruped, 'Carob nut cookies. You just won't believe how yummy these are.'

'Thanks but I'll pass,' I pushed my plate away. 'I'd love a coffee though.'

'Oh no, Cass. No coffee. Or tea. Not in this house. However,' she disappeared briefly inside the enormous fridge to extract a large jug, 'I do have some absolutely delicious raw cashew milk.'

My stomach chose that precise moment to let out an ominous rumbling noise. It wasn't a rumble of hunger. More an intestinal protest. Dear Lord. What had her menu done to my insides?

'Could you tell me where the bathroom is please?'

'Back through the hallway,' Ethan smiled kindly. 'First door to your left.'

My tummy now sounded like a washing machine in the grip of a final spin. Suddenly it was of paramount importance to be in that loo.

'Won't be a mo,' I squeaked. Leapfrogging the granite runway, I charged off to the bathroom. Whisking up my dress, I lowered my throbbing bottom. I gasped as a spasm of wind twisted my intestines. An explosion echoed around the toilet bowl. Dear Lord. I'd never made a sound like that in my entire life. Beads of perspiration formed on my upper lip as another spasm took hold. I leant forward, hugging my knees as a series of blasts rocked the porcelain and threatened to vandalise the plumbing.

A quarter of an hour later I dared to stand up – backside sporting a toilet seat imprint – and staggered off to the washbasin. I had surely dropped three dress sizes. My Father Christmas tummy had totally disappeared.

'Are you all right?' Ethan asked as I staggered back to the table. 'You look very pale.'

'I'm just a bit tired,' I smiled apologetically. 'The joys of having a six month old baby and broken nights.' Not to mention being disembowelled by your fiancée's choice of menu.

Jamie stood up. 'I think we'd best be making tracks home. Thanks for a fabulous evening guys.'

We said our farewells before taking the elevator back to the underground car park.

'Well done,' Jamie squeezed my hand as we walked to the car. 'You handled it very well.'

'I just want you to know,' I gingerly lowered my derrière onto the passenger seat, 'that I am never, ever socialising with that woman again.'

Jamie sighed as the engine turned over. 'Hopefully you won't have to. Not for a very long time anyway.'

Chapter Five

The following morning the household was up early. The Christmas holidays were over. Work beckoned for Jamie, and the kids were back to school. My brood piled into The Muck Truck, with Jonas complaining bitterly about an impending maths lesson.

'Well at least you don't have physics first thing,' grumbled Petra. 'What's the point in studying a subject like that? It won't benefit my chosen career. When I leave school I want to be a riding instructor!'

'I quite like physics,' Livvy blushed.

'That's because you've got a crush on Mr Brown,' said Petra.

I put the car into reverse. 'Oh yes? And what's Mr Brown like?'

'Pukey,' Toby laughed.

'No he's not!' Livvy protested, blushing again.

The banter continued all the way to Boxleigh Grammar.

'Have a good day all of you,' I trilled as they piled out, doors slamming after them. I turned to Eddie. 'Looks like it's just you and me kiddo.' My son gave a gummy smile. 'And Nanny Edna,' I added.

Edna had briefly returned to her own home only to reappear trailing a full-size suitcase of clothes. Clearly she was staying a few days. My mother-in-law had now taken over the pull-out bed in the study. She had also appropriated the workshop at the rear of the garage. An awful lot of sawing seemed to be going on.

Sure enough, as I pulled up on the driveway, the whine of a planer could be heard. Leaving Edna to it, I let myself into the house. I put Eddie in his playpen and made a start on the laundry. The phone rang. It was Jamie.

'Hi Cassie. I'll probably be very late this evening. We have a potential new client. The proposals promise to be very lucrative. It calls for a bit of wining and dining. So if you don't mind, I'll be passing on your finest beans on toast supper. Instead I'll have to try and force myself to eat a horrible filet steak. With all the ghastly trimmings.'

I laughed. 'My poor husband. The things you suffer for your craft. So, where are you and Ethan taking them?'

'Ethan won't be there. In fact, as we speak, he should be half-way to America. He's meeting with the client's sister company. How about that eh! Soon it could be Fareham & Mackerel International!' I could sense Jamie rubbing his hands together.

'That's fantastic. Okay darling, I won't wait up.'

'Tell the kids I'm sorry not to see them this evening and that I love them loads.'

'Will do. Don't work too hard.'

'We won't.'

We?

'Don't wait up Cassie. Must go.'

'Jamie?'

But he'd already clicked off. I stood there for a few moments. Held the whirring receiver with one hand. Clutched the kitchen worktop with the other. My brain digested the conversation. He'd said *we*. Oh for goodness sake Cass, it was *we* as in Jamie and the client! But might Selina be there too? She was, after all, now working for the company. Wrong again Cass! Right now she was thirty-five thousand feet up in the air. In an aeroplane. Sitting by Ethan's side. I exhaled slowly, my heart banging about a bit.

For the remainder of the day I couldn't shake a sense of foreboding. When the children came home from school, their chatter went straight over my head. I felt distracted.

A little before midnight I went to bed. But sleep evaded me. I lay there, troubled but without really knowing why. Eventually I snapped on the bedside lamp. Stared at the telephone. After a moment's hesitation, I picked up the receiver. Withholding my number, I dialled Ethan's apartment. The apartment he now shared with Selina. I held my breath as the line connected, and began to ring. Below my ribcage, my heart had started to beat in time to the ring tone. Immediately my conscience began clamouring. What the devil are you playing at Cass? Just because your first husband was a philandering Casanova, it doesn't mean all men are the same. This is *Jamie* for heaven's sake. Your wonderful husband! He's with a client. In the City. And Selina is in America. Any second now the answering machine will pick up your call confirming that nobody is home and–

'Hello?' said a voice. It was Jamie.

Shocked, I dropped the phone. It smacked against the bedside cabinet before bouncing over the edge like a bungee jumper. The receiver rotated mid-air, dangling from the stretched cord. I stared at it, horrified, before carefully retrieving it.

'Hello? Hello!' Jamie sounded very irritated.

What the hell was my husband doing there? Clearly Selina was not on a plane to America. Don't jump to conclusions Cass. Perhaps Jamie was simply wrapping up an exhausting evening with a coffee. But then, why not have a coffee at home? Unless – I gasped – unless there was more than a coffee on offer? I gulped. Instead of Selina asking Jamie if he'd like one lump or two, perhaps completely different lumps were being offered. After all, there wasn't much sex to be had at home was there? One could even say Jamie was starved of it. Sex-starved. How peculiar to see the significance of that expression only now. Stupid. Had I interrupted feverish foreplay? Had the pair of them been getting all hot and sweaty, tearing at each other's clothes, buttons pinging off as they panted–

'IS THERE ANYBODY THERE OR NOT?' roared my husband.

'Who is it darling?' I heard Selina ask.

Darling! Bloody *darling!* Bloody hell. Bloody bitch. Bloody man. Enraged I slammed the phone back into its cradle with such force the handset split in half. Bugger. I snatched it up, shoved it together and, with a trembling hand, put it back in its cradle.

I flopped back on the pillows and stared at the ceiling. Morag was right. I'd taken my eye so comprehensively off the ball, my husband was now being baited by a woman I couldn't begin to compete with. Selina. I whimpered, rolled over and stuffed the pillow in my mouth.

Okay Cass, think. Think! What to do, what to do? Confront him? Wait for him to put his key in the door and then hurl myself at him, fists flying? Or – better still – woo him back!

I leapt out of bed. Rushed off to the bathroom. And spent twenty minutes applying full makeup before dousing myself in perfume. Hot-footing back to the bedroom, I riffled through my bedside drawers until I found what I wanted. Stripping off my practical but unsexy pyjamas, I slithered into a satin negligee. I was just fluffing up my hair when headlights lit up the drive.

Jamie was home. I slid back under the duvet, arranging it so my plunging neckline was showcased.

Moments later the landing floorboards squeaked. As Jamie crept into our bedroom, he looked genuinely surprised to see me bathed in the glow of lamplight and wide awake.

'You still up?' he came over and kissed me on the forehead.

'I've been waiting for you,' I said huskily.

'That's nice.' He shrugged off his suit and dumped it on a chair. 'I'm too tired to hang it up,' he said apologetically. 'Ah bed!' Jamie groaned with pleasure. 'I *lurve* my bed. Turn out the light.'

Turn out the light? Wasn't that my line?

'Darling,' I tapped him on the nose coquettishly, 'I've been *waiting* for you!' I leant over and wobbled my chest in front of him.

Jamie groaned again. But not in an aroused way. 'Oh Cassie,' he passed a hand wearily over his forehead, 'sorry to disappoint you. But I'm absolutely shagged.'

I froze. Shagged? Since when did Jamie ever use a word like that? Never! So why use the expression now? Well maybe – a small voice in my head piped up – it was because he'd just been shagged?

For once Eddie slept all the way through the night. And wasn't it just the Law of Sod that I, instead, should lay awake until the small hours torturing myself. Why had Jamie answered Selina's telephone? Why had she called him *darling?* And why had he used the expression *shagged?* It seemed as if I'd barely nodded off when the bedside telephone exploded into life. I shot upwards in shock as Jamie stretched out a hand. Picking up the receiver, it promptly fell apart.

'What on earth–?' he stared at broken plastic and a small explosion of wiring. 'What happened to the phone?'

I sank back against the mattress and kept quiet.

'Hello?' Jamie clamped the telephone remnants against one ear. 'Can you hear me?' Tiny red and black cables bounced against his nose. 'Sid! Good morning to you too. No, no trouble at all. I was getting up anyway. Sure, no problem. I'll be with you in an hour or so.'

'Who's Sid?'

'The guy I was with last night.'

Suspicion swept over me. Had that really been someone called Sid? Or had it been *her*?

'Cassie, do you know anything about the state of this phone?'

'No.'

'I guess our little babe is the culprit. Don't let him play with the telephones darling. The flex could be dangerous.'

I knew exactly what I'd like to do with the flex, and to whom.

'If you get a moment today, buy some decent digital handsets.'

'Okay.'

'Now before I reluctantly leave this bed, I want to hold my wife. Like this,' Jamie pulled me roughly into his arms, 'and tell her how much I love her.'

I stared at my husband. If I hadn't been lying down, I would have swooned. Blue eyed. Honey-blond. Great body. If you liked that sort of thing – and I most certainly did – you'd consider him extremely good looking.

'I love you too,' I whispered. My lip wobbled slightly.

'Is something the matter Cassie?'

Ask him! Ask him now!

'How did last night go?'

'Extremely well.'

What – the meeting with the client or the meeting at Selina's place?

'Where did you go?'

'Le Gavroche.'

'Anywhere else?'

Jamie chuckled. 'If you're referring to a place like Stringfellows, then no. The guys aren't the sort of clients who expect you to pick up the tabs for lap dancers. We said goodnight and then went our separate ways. Then I gave Selina a lift home, changed an awkward light bulb for her that Ethan wasn't around to do, before finally coming home and hitting the pillow.'

I hadn't realised I'd been holding my breath until it whooshed out of me. Oh thank you God! Thank you, thank you, thank you.

'And much as I love being in bed with you, I'm now going to haul myself out and take a quick shower.' Jamie planted a perfunctory kiss on my cheek before bounding off to the en-suite.

'Will you be home early tonight?' I called.

'Hope so,' Jamie's voice was drowned out by the blast of the shower.

I sighed. I'd speak to Morag about Selina being back on the scene. Pick her brains on how to handle an ex-girlfriend. I glanced at the broken handset. First, we needed new telephones.

An hour later, after dropping the children to school, I drove through the usual traffic of commuters and mothers finishing the school run. Arriving at Currys, I wheeled Eddie's buggy around the aisles searching for cordless phones. After a mere ten seconds of cogitation, I selected what appeared to be a good deal. Nothing like shopping with a baby to speed up decision making. As I headed towards the checkout, my mobile rang. It was Morag.

'You'll never believe what Henry's just done!' she shrieked.

Like most first-time mothers, Morag was convinced her baby son was a genius.

'Do tell,' I shoved the receipt and small change into my purse.

'He just said Mama!'

'No! Fancy that.' Henry was four months old.

'Come over for coffee. You can hear him speak for yourself.'

'Will do. I was on my way to see you anyway.'

'Oh?'

'I need your advice.'

'I'm putting the coffee on now. Don't be long.'

Twenty minutes later I walked into Morag's bright sunny kitchen. Disentangling Eddie's fists from my hair, I popped him into Henry's playpen.

'Hello sweetie-pie,' I cooed at my godson. Henry was lying on his back under a plastic mobile.

'Mwah-mwah,' he gurgled happily.

'You see!' Morag said ecstatically. 'Mama!'

'Amazing! Henry is clearly destined for great things.'

Morag smirked. 'You don't need to tell me Cass – I already know that.'

It was a good thing I loved Morag. She wasn't everybody's cup of tea with her overpowering personality. I sat down at the table. She sashayed over with steaming mugs.

'Any bickies?' I asked.

'Certainly not,' replied Morag primly. 'If you want something to nibble, I can cut you up some carrot sticks.'

'Thanks, but I'll pass.' I'd had enough raw food to last me a life time.

'So. What's up?'

'Ah,' I stared morosely into my mug.

'Ah what?'

And suddenly all my fears tumbled out.

'So what do you think?'

'Cass, this is *Jamie* we're talking about. He is one of the most honourable men I have ever met. In fact,' she furrowed her brow, 'I'd go so far as to say he's the *only* honourable man I've ever met. Apart from Matt of course,' she added as an afterthought.

'So why was Selina asking my husband to change light bulbs for her at midnight?'

'Because she's a helpless female?'

'Huh!' I took a sip of coffee. 'And why did he answer her phone?' I raked a hand through my hair. 'Don't you think that's odd? If your phone rang right now, you wouldn't expect me to answer it would you! And don't forget I heard Selina call him *darling*. What do you make of that?'

'Just being friendly?'

I gave Morag a withering look.

'This is ridiculous. Selina just needed a bit of male help. That's all.'

'You think so?'

'Yes!' Morag cried. 'Don't you think you should tackle the obvious Cass?'

'The obvious what?'

'Well clearly your own love life is not ticketty-boo, otherwise you wouldn't doubt Jamie's intentions with Selina. Firstly, you need to get bedroom time back on track.'

'But I'm knackered,' I groaned. 'And anyway, I tried last night and *he* was knackered.'

'Well he had been working late! Look, most of the time you're the one that's exhausted. You have been for months. So you're not thinking straight. First things first, start with a sleep plan for Eddie.' The palm of her hand shot up like a traffic cop. My protests stopped in their tracks. 'Enough of this nonsense about feeding on demand. Eddie isn't a newborn anymore! Cut out the night feed. And start a controlled crying sleep plan. I promise you, within one week Eddie will have stopped disturbing you.'

I shook my head. This was feisty Eddie we were talking about. Not placid Henry. Morag placed a photocopied article on the table.

'Do it. Within days you'll be having seven to eight hours of regular sleep. Every night. Then you'll have some energy for horseplay. Secondly,' Morag arched an eyebrow, 'sometimes nature needs a helping hand. Like herbal supplements.'

'Oh no–'

'Oh yes.' She rattled a little bottle at me. 'One hundred per cent guaranteed to put fizz in your fanny.'

'The last time I popped some of your pills I ended up a panting nymphomaniac.'

Morag held up a hand again while the other scribbled out the name and number of her Chinese herbalist. She slapped the piece of paper on top of the photocopied sleep plan.

'And finally,' she gave me a frank look, 'sort out your appearance. It's no good looking at me like that Cass. I'm your friend. What are friends for if they can't be a little honest?'

'A *little* honest. Crikey, if I had balls right now I'd be clutching them in agony.'

'You're an attractive woman Cass. But *look* at you! Anybody would think you deliberately set out to try and look as awful as possible. Did you actually bother to brush your hair this morning? Or do you simply favour the bedraggled look?'

'Bleeding hell Morag–'

'And look at your sweater! Covered in Farex or similar muck. Change is due. And you can start right now,' she picked up her mobile, 'by seeing my hairdresser.' She touched the mobile's screen and selected a number.

'Morag I can't just up and go to a hair salon. Eddie will go bananas sitting on my knee for three hours.'

'You can leave Eddie with me while you– ah, hello? Is that Dominique? Damn. When will she be back? Oh I see. Well I have a friend who's having a major hair crisis. It needs urgent attention. No, I don't know Chloe and Miguel. Are they any good? Okay. I'll send my friend along now.' She ended the call.

'Morag, no!' I protested.

'Why not?'

'Because the children will need picking up from school–'

'In five hours.'

'And I haven't got Eddie's lunch with me–'

'Stop making excuses. I'm quite sure Henry won't mind Eddie pinching a jar of Heinz. Now get a move on. Here's the address.'

I stood up. 'But–'

'Good-bye,' Morag gave me a little push towards the door.

'Oh for goodness sake,' I snatched the piece of paper from her hand.

'Don't forget all your other bits,' Morag popped the sleep plan and herbalist's number in my handbag. 'You can read the article and make the herbalist's appointment while you're covered in tin foil.'

Half an hour later I found myself seated in a high-end salon. The entire staff were drop-dead gorgeous.

'Hi, I'm Chloe,' said a tall waif. 'I'm your colouring technician,' she ran her fingers through my lank tresses. 'Your friend has instructed me to give you – and I quote – *a bucket of golden highlights*. Is that okay with you?'

'I guess so.'

Forty-five minutes later I looked like a pale Rastafarian with foil dreadlocks.

'Okay,' said Chloe. 'I'll leave that to take. Can I get you a coffee?'

'Please.'

Chloe strode off. With legs that long she should be on *Britain's Next Top Model*. I stared after her. What I would give to have a figure like hers. And wear a tiny cropped top. Show off not just a flat tummy, but abs. Which reminded me, I'd completely forgotten my New Year's resolution to reinvent myself. Well thanks to Morag's bullying, I was now in a swish hair salon. Not the one I'd originally planned on visiting. But same result. The only matter outstanding was a date with Nell's dog. Rocket. A canine gym machine. I ferreted around in my handbag ignoring Morag's sleep plan and the herbalist's telephone number.

'Nell, you old bag!' I greeted my friend affectionately. 'How's Bump?'

'Still a bump. I'm two days overdue. But never mind that, how's you? Has *you-know-who* started work with Jamie and Ethan yet?'

'Yes.'

'How's it going?'

'Now isn't the time to tell you. But I'm putting everything right–'

'Putting what right?'

'Things,' I answered vaguely, 'and I need Rocket to help me.'

'You need my dog to help you put everything right?'

'My figure for starters. It's one vast wobble. I think that's why Jamie stayed out so late last night.'

'Because he didn't want to see you wobble?'

'On account of *her*,' I hissed into the handset. 'She tried to poison me you know and then he answered her phone and I was so mad I broke ours but I bought a new one and Morag says I must see a herbalist with a sleep plan so I'm having my hair done and now I need Rocket.'

'Cass I didn't understand one word of that,' Nell replied faintly. 'But you are very welcome to see Rocket.'

'Excellent,' I purred into the handset. 'I'll pop by after the school-run tomorrow.'

I ended the call just as Chloe materialised by my side with the coffee and a pile of magazines.

Forty minutes later, she was back. 'Time to be shampooed Mrs Mackerel. And then Miguel will be taking over with your re-style.'

In due course Miguel minced over. 'What would Madame like me to do?'

'Make me look amazing.'

'My name is Miguel. Not Jesus. But I'll do my best.'

An hour later I walked out of the salon not entirely displeased. When I went to collect Eddie, Morag complimented me on the transformation.

'Did you read the sleep plan?'

'Yes,' I lied scooping up Eddie.

'Good. Start it today. No time like the present. And did you ring the herbalist?'

'Yes,' I lied again.

'And what did he say?'

'He said I could see him tomorrow.'

Morag folded her arms across her jutting chest. 'Why are you lying?'

'How do you know–?'

'Because *he* is actually a *she*. And there is at least a week's lead time on appointments. I'll bet you didn't read that sleep plan either.'

'Morag stop nagging me.'

'I'm not the one moaning about my husband keeping the company of another woman,' she pointed out.

'I should think not!' said an indignant voice. Matt came through the door, grinning away. He reeked of horses. 'Hello Cass. I won't kiss you on the grounds of being a bit whiffy. So, spill the beans. Whose naughty hubby is having an affair?'

I shot Morag a warning look. 'We were simply hypothesising.'

'Ah. Then I'm out of this conversation. I don't even know what hypothesising means.''

'Idiot,' I grinned at him before turning to peck Morag on her proffered cheek. 'I promise I'll read the sleep plan tonight. And I'll sort out the herbalist appointment first thing in the morning.'

All I had to do now was devise a way to see off Selina.

Chapter Six

That evening we ate without Edna. She'd been invited to dinner by an elderly gentleman she'd met in B&Q.

'Aye aye, my mother's landed herself a toyboy,' Jamie had informed me earlier.

'Who is he?' I'd asked in amazement.

'Some chap she met in the paint aisle. He's five years younger than her. Transpires he's making a rocking horse for his grandson. Just like she has for Eddie.'

'Fancy that.'

'I think she does,' Jamie had chortled.

Sitting now around the dinner table eating a rather adventurous chicken stew I'd managed to throw together, the children regaled us with their woes. Their complaints centred on teachers setting overly large amounts of homework.

'Mrs Peterson is a right old bag,' announced my step-son. 'She gave me an A minus in French when it should have been an A star.'

'Stop showing off Jonas,' my step-daughter chided good-naturedly. 'We can't all be brainboxes like you.'

'Speak for yourself Petra,' Toby shrugged.

It was a fact that both our boys were academically gifted, whereas Petra and Livvy had to work hard to achieve good grades.

'Okay kids, if you've finished you may be excused,' Jamie said.

There was a moment of noisy chair scraping followed by a mass departure.

'So, with the exception of our little boy, I have you all to myself,' Jamie stood up. He moved around the table and pulled me into his arms. I melted against him. 'I don't believe I've yet complimented you on your hair,' he kissed the top of my head. 'It's stunning. You look like you used to. When I first met you.'

'Before I became a mother again,' I said ruefully. I wound my arms around my husband's neck and gazed up at him adoringly. How could I have doubted Jamie wanting to spend time in Selina's apartment for any reason other than being helpful? The expression on his face said it all. The look of love.

Jamie released me and went to Eddie's highchair. I began to clear the table. 'By the way,' he said, undoing Eddie's safety straps and lifting our son out, 'I have something to tell you. Something you're not going to like.'

I froze, the casserole pot suspended in my hands.

'Is it to do with Selina?'

Jamie gave a rueful look. 'Yes.'

'Go on.'

'She's coming to dinner tomorrow evening.'

'She's *what*?' the colour drained from my face.

'Well she kept going on and on about how lonely she is. You know, while Ethan's in America. And banging on about going home to an empty apartment. Hating her own company. That sort of thing. She dropped so many hints about fitting one more around our table – which incidentally I ignored – that in the end she asked me outright.'

'Asked what outright?' my heart refused to follow this conversation, even though my brain already knew the answer.

'She asked if she could join us for dinner.'

'To which you replied *No I'm very sorry you cannot.*'

Jamie gave me an apologetic look. 'She also said how much she wanted to see you again. Said she really likes you.'

'*Likes* me? Are you mad? I swear she tried to poison me.'

'Oh don't be daft Cassie. Now you're being melodramatic.'

'Funny how it was only me pinned to the toilet after eating her food. I can't believe you've allowed yourself to be coerced.' I put the casserole pot down. Before I flung it at my husband. Instead I set about clearing plates and cups, banging and crashing things about. How dare Jamie agree to that woman coming here! How dare he! And how dare she ask! Impudent cow.

'Well she knows we've had Ethan here a few times for kitchen supper. What am I meant to say?'

'Yes, but he was on his own back then!'

'And currently Selina is on her own. Ethan would be very pleased to know we're looking after her. I've told you before that he's tremendously keen for our women to bond.'

'I'll never bond with that woman. Not in a million years. And nor do I *want* to bond with her.'

'Cassie calm down,' Jamie wiped Eddie's mouth and put him in his playpen. 'I know you don't want to see Selina–'

'You promised me I wouldn't have to suffer her again for ages!' my voice was rising. I couldn't seem to stop it. I sounded like one of Alvin's chipmunks in the grip of hysteria.

Jamie raked his hair. 'The woman invited herself and–'

'Well she can bloody well uninvite herself! Tell her our cooker has blown up. Or the house has imploded. Use your imagination.'

At that moment the back door opened. A gust of cold air curled around my ankles as Edna came into the kitchen.

'Are you okay Cassandra?' My mother-in-law shook out an umbrella and took off her coat. 'I could hear you outside dear.'

'I'm fine Edna,' I said through gritted teeth. 'Totally hunky-dory.'

'I was just explaining to Cassie that my business partner's fiancée is joining us for dinner tomorrow.'

Edna turned a pair of blue headlamps on her son. 'The fiancée is coming *with* the business partner?'

'No. He's in America.'

'Cassandra dear, don't distress yourself. I'll do the cooking for you. It will be my pleasure.'

'That's very kind of you Edna, but that's not why I'm upset.'

'I am sensitive to the situation dear. I haven't forgotten the problems this young lady caused you both. However, these are tenuous circumstances. She's the fiancée of Jamie's business partner. And Ethan *is* the Senior Partner. So don't let this person spoil things.'

I gazed at my mother-in-law. She was astute. And her message to me was clear. Refusing Selina could jeopardise Jamie's partnership. So don't upset the apple cart.

I rubbed a hand over my forehead. Perhaps I was being a tad over-reactionary. I could understand Selina being lonely while Ethan was away. I remembered how lost I'd been when I'd first split from Stevie. Once the twins had gone to bed it had been me and the four walls. Although I'd kept myself busy with the many things a mum always had to do. Having a family meant there were always chores to keep up with. I'd been glad to immerse myself in washing filthy football kit, scrubbing muddy boots, or staying up until midnight sewing name tags in uniform. It had been a welcome distraction. Whereas Selina didn't have children to dilute the loneliness. She didn't even have to clean the apartment or do the ironing because Ethan employed a home help. And Jamie was right. Ethan had, from time to time, joined us for supper. It didn't escape me either that if Selina and Ethan were a permanent fixture, I'd have to get used to her visiting periodically in the future. Give me strength.

'Right,' I said sourly. 'Selina will join us tomorrow.'

'I think that's very wise Cassandra dear,' said my mother-in-law. 'Now, if you'll excuse me, I know Livvy has some Physics homework she needs help with.'

I stacked the dishwasher while Jamie played with Eddie. If only I wasn't so tired perhaps I wouldn't be so paranoid about Selina. Chucking a powder tablet into the machine, I switched it on and then went off to find Morag's sleep plan. It wouldn't hurt to have a read. And maybe give it a whirl.

Five hours later, the entire house was asleep. Apart from me and my puce-faced screaming son. With nerves stretched to breaking point, I consulted my watch. In one more minute the plan permitted Mummy to return to baby's cot, make reassuring noises, then smartly exit before marking another five minutes on the clock. If baby was still awake after one hour of controlled crying, the plan should be abandoned. Whereupon Mummy must keep baby awake for precisely one more hour before starting all over again. As the second hand on my wristwatch concluded its fifth revolution, I padded back into Eddie's room. Of all the babies in the world, I'd known mine would be the infant to turn the sleep plan on its head.

'Hush Eddie, there's a good boy,' I whispered. Leaning into his cot, I scooped him up. After one hour of squawking, he was almost hoarse. The noise tore at my heartstrings as I jiggled him about, patting his little back. And somehow we had to now stay awake for another hour. As I blearily wondered how the hell I was going to achieve this, Eddie crashed out on my shoulder. Well bugger me. Carefully I returned him to the cot, laying him gently on his back. His long lashes swept across the pillows of his cheeks. My heart contracted into a tight little knot. Suddenly I was gulping back the tears.

A shadow fell across the open doorway. 'What's up?' whispered Jamie tip-toeing into the room. 'Why are you crying?'

'Oh Jamie,' I sobbed, 'I can't bear the thought of Eddie getting married and leaving home.'

'Darling for goodness sake, that's about twenty years from now. By which point we'll be dragging women off the street, and begging one of them to take Eddie off our hands.'

'Never,' I dissolved into fresh floods. 'No woman will ever be good enough for my little boy.'

'Of course they won't, of course,' Jamie pulled me to him. He began patting my back. Not unlike how I'd patted Eddie's. It was strangely soothing. I could see why Eddie liked it so much. Maybe Jamie could pat my back more often. Perhaps I should patent the idea. To Mothercare. Design a soft fluffy contraption that patted babies to sleep at night. I sniffed. In the absence of a tissue, I wiped my wet face on the back of my dressing gown sleeve. Jamie led me back across the landing and into our bedroom.

'Come on. Bed.' Jamie tucked me in. 'Go to sleep.' He stroked my forehead. Ah, lovely. His hand caressed my weary brow. Again. And then again. Fantastic. My eyelids drooped. Scrap the idea of patenting a back patter. Instead I would design a baby bonnet with inbuilt head massager. Brilliant idea Cass. Ten seconds later I was fast asleep.

When my alarm went off the following morning, I realised Eddie had slept through the remainder of the night – after his initial sleep plan rebellion. I wasn't convinced we'd cracked things on the first attempt. But it was a positive start. The baby alarm emitted a rustling noise followed by a reedy cry.

Two minutes later I crept downstairs, babe on my hip. It would be another twenty minutes or so before the other children were up and about. I fed Eddie and then popped him into his playpen. I was just scrambling a mountain of eggs when Edna came into the kitchen.

'Good morning Cassandra.'

'Hi Edna. How are you?'

'I'm very well dear.'

'You didn't tell me how your date went,' I smiled.

Was it my imagination or was my mother-in-law blushing? She busied herself with the kettle.

'Pleasant,' she nodded. 'Like me, Arthur is making a rocking horse. Although his is on a far more elaborate scale. But it's nice to chat with somebody who has similar interests. Very nice actually.'

'So where did he take you?'

Edna's eyes lit up. 'To a tool fair.'

'Wow.' This Arthur clearly hadn't a clue about romance.

'It was most informative. We saw all the latest tools being put through their paces. And for lunch we had a very passable bacon butty. And right at the end of the day we were both given a free t-shirt. Mine says *Power Drills Do It Best.*'

I boggled into the scrambled eggs. 'I see.'

'Now Cassandra dear,' Edna poured boiling water into a teapot and added four teabags. 'I know this evening is going to be a little taxing for you.'

'Ah, yes.' I'd momentarily forgotten about Selina gracing us with her presence.

'I insist you let me take care of dinner tonight.'

I transferred the scrambled egg into an oven dish to keep it warm.

'Okay. Thank you. That will be a great help.'

I set about loading an industrial sized toaster with bread.

'Is there anything else I can do?'

'As it happens Edna, I'd love to take Nell's dog for a run this morning. I was going to drive to Nell's straight after the school run. Could I leave Eddie with you for an hour or two?'

'Of course dear. He's no trouble at all.'

'Thank you so much.'

Whilst I sometimes grumbled about Edna taking over, this was one time when I was tremendously grateful for her doing so.

In due course the children and Jamie came down. There was a frantic five minutes as hands whipped across the table grabbing scrambled egg and demolishing a tottering pagoda of toast.

Kissing Jamie good-bye, I waved to Eddie in Edna's arms, and then loaded the kids into the Muck Truck. I was just about to reverse out of the driveway when my mobile rang. It was Morag.

'I'm bored.'

'How can you possibly be bored with a four month old baby to look after? Not forgetting all Matt's children and step-children that seem to prefer living with the pair of you, rather than their biological parents.'

'That's just it. They've all naffed off.'

'Where?'

'Uni. Or abroad. One's gone on World Challenge with their school. Another is doing a student language exchange. The only daughter at home right now is Joanie. And she's bundled Henry up and taken him down to the yard in his buggy. She absolutely dotes on him. Joanie told me to go shopping. So I wondered if you were up for a trip to Fairview?'

'You know me. Always up for a bit of retail therapy. However, this is one morning I can't. After I've finished the school run, I'm seeing Nell. Albeit briefly. I'm going for a workout with her mad red setter.'

'Ooh, I'll come with you.'

I made a snorting noise. 'Since when did you ever do exercise?'

'I exercise every night!' said Morag indignantly.

'I don't meant that sort of exercise,' I hissed into the handset, 'and watch what you're saying because I'm about to switch you to loudspeaker. Four sets of ears will be wiggling away. As of now.'

Hands free, I reversed the car through the electric gates.

'I'm perfectly capable of going for a run,' Morag sounded indignant. 'In fact I've just bought a new sports bra. It's excellent. My boobs don't even wobble in it.'

The children snorted with suppressed laughter as we headed off.

'It's Morag,' whispered Toby to Jonas. 'She's got massive boobies.'

'I know,' Jonas whispered back, 'but they're not as big as Miss January's. I've got a naughty calendar in my room. I'll show you later.'

'Just a moment Morag,' I looked in the rear view mirror at my step-son. 'Where's the naughty calendar Jonas?'

'What naughty calendar?'

'The naughty calendar you just told Toby about.'

'Oh *that* naughty calendar. It's in the dustbin.'

'But you just told Toby it was in your room.'

'Um. No. You misunderstood.'

'Mum it's perfectly normal for boys of Jonas's age to look at smutty photographs,' said Livvy, 'we've been debating this in PHSE.'

'Normal or not, I don't like it. Nor do I want that sort of thing in the house. Okay Jonas?'

'Please don't bin it Cass. It's not mine.'

'Well who does it belong to?'

'Harry's dad. Harry nicked it out of his dad's office. I've got it on loan. It cost me two packets of chewing gum.'

'Well you can tell Harry from me I think he's out of order.'

'Dirty Harry,' said Morag coming back into the conversation. 'Now Cass, never mind pubescent children and Miss January's–'

'Yes *thank* you Morag,' I spluttered.

'So you'll be at Nell's in, what, twenty minutes?'

'Yep.'

'I'll see you there.' Morag clicked off.

Five minutes later I parked up by Boxleigh Grammar. The kids piled out of the car without so much as a backward wave, never mind a kiss or a hug. I'd learnt long ago that it was uncool to be demonstrative in front of their peers. Indeed the only thing I was permitted to do at this stage of the drop off was to sit silently and look straight ahead. Even playing the radio was a no-no.

'But what's wrong with listening to music?' I'd once asked in exasperation as Petra had leant over my shoulder and stabbed the off button.

'Nothing Cass. It's just that you have a habit of jerking your head in time to the music. It looks a bit spazzy.'

Livvy had agreed. '*And* you sing the wrong lyrics.'

'I do not!' I'd protested.

'Groove Armada do not sing about shaking their arms Mum,' Livvy had looked pained.

As soon as I was on my own, I hit the play button. Music flooded the car. I drove off jerking my head in time to its rhythm. It wasn't just teenagers who had the monopoly on rebellion. And the fact that it was one of Eddie's nursery rhyme CDs was irrelevant.

I had just parked up on Nell's driveway when Morag arrived. The natty little sports car she had owned pre-Henry had been replaced by a sensible Ford Galaxy. As a nod to still being a girl-racer, the Galaxy had *don't-mess-with-me* low profile tyres, state of the art interior and rear passenger privacy glass. It had yet to reach the slobby levels of my own car, but all in good time.

'Good morning Cass,' Morag greeted me looking like she was off to do a photo shoot. She was in full make-up and pristine joggers. A cosy fleece stretched across her ample bosom.

Two doors down a man in a pin-striped suit emerged from his house. He took one look at Morag and tripped over a cat that had been patiently waiting on his doorstep.

'Good morning!' I gave her a hug.

We were momentarily distracted by the sound of a spitting kitty. Pin-stripe had the grace to look embarrassed. He slung a briefcase in his car and hastily drove off.

'Where's this mad dog of Nell's then?'

'Brace yourself. I don't think Rocket has had any exercise of late due to Nell's enforced bed rest.' I rang the doorbell. 'Expect to be carted along at ninety miles per hour.'

As Nell opened the door, a red blur shot out.

'Heel!' Nell commanded. Rocket goosed Morag before crashing back through the front door. 'She's very excited about going for walkies. Hello Morag. Here's her lead Cass. I'll give you Rocket's coat, just in case she feels cold.' Nell peered at the sky anxiously. 'The weather forecast said there might be snow later.'

'She's already wearing a fur coat Nell,' Morag pointed out.

'Well I'd like you to take it nonetheless. And here's a bottle of water in case she gets thirsty.'

Morag took the bottle of Evian. 'What does she do? Hold it in her paw and swig?'

'Don't be silly. You pour it into the palm of your hand, and then let her lap.'

'But she's all slobbery.'

'All babies are slobbery,' Nell smiled benignly.

I gave Morag a meaningful look. She opened her eyes wide. I nodded. Rocket might be canine, but she enjoyed the same status as a daughter.

Nell straightened up. She looked fit to burst.

'No contractions yet?' I asked sympathetically.

'Not a twinge.'

'If you want to bring on labour, you should have sex,' said Morag.

'Isn't that an old wives' tale?' I asked.

'Not at all. Sex releases oxytocin. It's a hormone. It causes the uterus to contract. Also semen contains prostaglandins, which help to soften the cervix.'

'Is that how you triggered your own labour,' asked Nell, 'by getting Matt to bonk you?'

'Of course. Actually Henry was a bit prem. Possibly from too much bonking. But you know me. A bonk a day keeps the mistress away.'

I grimaced as a sudden vision of Jamie – who was not even having a bonk a week – flashed through my mind. Ah yes. There he was. At work. With Selina by his side. Leaning across him. Letting her hair brush against his cheek. Passing a biro. Making sure her hands touched his. Wafting perfume. Trying to intoxicate him.

'Ben's at work,' said Nell, 'so right now sex is out of the question. Even if I wanted it. Which I don't. We haven't had sex for ages. It's just too uncomfortable when you're this big. And apart from anything else, Ben isn't wildly turned on by my stretchmarks and swollen ankles.'

'No problem,' said Morag, 'how about a bit of nipple twiddling instead?'

'Certainly not!'

'Nipple stimulation helps to bring on labour much the same way as sex does. It gets the oxytocin going.' Morag paused. Frowned. 'Hmm. Might take a bit more effort than the sex though. How about Cass doing one nipple and me doing the other?'

'Geddoff,' Nell slapped Morag's hand away. 'I don't want sex and I don't want my nipples twiddled. I'll let Mother Nature see to it. Now are you taking my girl for a run or not?'

Chapter Seven

'You weren't kidding when you said this dog was a lunatic.' Morag grimly hung on to Rocket's lead while I puffed along behind her.

'She's like her name. A missile.'

'When we get to the park, can we let her off the lead?'

'Yes. It's well away from the road.'

We jogged along for another fifteen minutes. It was a chilly, damp morning. Despite the cold, I was absolutely wet through with perspiration. Morag hadn't so much as broken out in a sweat.

As we entered the park, Morag unclipped Rocket's lead. The setter took off, nose down, tail up. I ground to a halt.

'Give me some of that water,' I gasped.

'I thought it was for the dog.'

'Rocket won't mind. She drinks from puddles when she's thirsty.'

I glugged from the bottle. It was one of those moments when water tasted like nectar. Wiping my mouth, I handed the bottle back to Morag. We set off again, power walking this time, and took a picturesque path through towering oaks. Bare branches soared into a sky the colour of milk. Rocket threaded her way through the trees, stopping every now and again to wee on piles of wet leaves.

'You really are very unfit Cass.'

'I can't believe you're not out of breath. You don't exercise. Not properly. And don't give me all *sexercise* talk. That's a load of baloney.'

'Ah, but it depends where you do it,' Morag smirked.

'What do you mean *where* you do it? The bedroom. Like normal folk.'

'The bedroom is for boring people.'

Oh God. Wait for it. I was about to be regaled with stories of legs akimbo on dining tables or jumping off wardrobes. And there was me thinking my bathtub bonk had been avant-garde.

'Well if we want a really good workout, we go to the stables.'

'Are we still talking sex? Or horse riding?'

'Sex of course. We leave Joanie babysitting Henry, and slip away on the pretext of checking the horses. And then we pop into the indoor riding school, and Matt puts me on the lunging rein.'

'You do realise the pair of you are totally kinky?'

'Of course we're not kinky Cass. It's a perfectly straightforward piece of cardiovascular exercise with a bit of pleasure thrown in. I slide out of my coat, and toss it onto the side rails. I'm naked. Naturally.'

'Oh naturally. It's the most normal thing in the world to be in an indoor riding school late at night totally starkers. Not to mention freezing.'

'Oh I don't get cold. Not at all. It's straight into a brisk trot and concentrating on being schooled. Last week I was put through my paces and learnt how to tackle a series of cavaletti.'

I boggled at an oak tree.

'And what about Matt? Isn't he a bit, you know, chilly around the nether regions? Just standing there while you trot around him in circles?'

'Oh no. He's a very fair instructor. He always jogs beside me.'

'I see. So, let me get this straight. Together you run around the indoor school naked and leap over jumps?'

'Yes.'

'I'm still not understanding the sex in this.'

'I'm getting to that. Well because my cavaletti technique has improved, last night Matt put up a small triple and a wall.'

'I see.' I didn't.

'Now a refusal – three faults – means a light flick of the whip. Whereas knocking down a jump – four faults – means having your bottom gently smacked. But if you get a clear round, then you not only have a big pat – all over the chest – you get a chance to go to the stud farm.'

'Don't tell me. Matt's the stud farm.'

'Well of course he is. If anybody else was the stud farm that really would be kinky. And last night Matt covered me over the wall. It was brilliant. Although we did incur four faults.' I arched a questioning eyebrow. 'Quite a lot of the bricks fell down,' Morag explained. 'So how's your own sex life coming along?'

'Superb.'

Now it was Morag's turn to arch a questioning eyebrow. 'How many times have you done it since New Year's Eve?'

'Oh for heaven's sake Morag. We don't keep count you know.'

'I thought so. Nil. Have you telephoned my herbalist yet?'

I scowled. 'I've had other things to think about.'

'I see.' We emerged from the tree lined path and crossed a sweeping stone bridge. Beneath us the local river rushed by. Elegant swans and Canadian geese bobbed about on water the colour of a night sky. 'And do these *other things* in fact translate as *other person*? A female whose name begins with S?'

I scowled a bit more. 'As it happens, yes.' And suddenly, like the river we were walking over, I was gushing forth about Selina and her unwelcome return in our lives. 'And to crown it all she's invited herself to kitchen supper with us tonight.' My trainer connected with a squashed cola can. I kicked it viciously.

'Cass I know this woman was a bit of a fruitcake at one point, but let's stop and analyse the situation. Selina is now engaged to Ethan. And Jamie is convinced she's nuts about the guy. It's Ethan who is pushing for his fiancée to work within the partnership. Selina's trying to make the best of it. She's invited you into her home. Welcomed you at her table. The upset tummy is just a coincidence. And she's told Jamie she likes you and wants to be your friend. Let's face it Cass, your hubby is earning big bucks. You have a great lifestyle. Don't let a tiny fly in the ointment spoil things. No hear me out–' Morag put up a hand to silence me, 'you don't have to *be* her friend, just *tolerate* her.'

'I *am* tolerating her. Why do you think she's coming into our home tonight? But that doesn't mean I'm happy about it. I don't trust her Morag. Not one little bit. I know Jamie isn't going to be charmed by her. He's no Stevie thank God. But where Selina is concerned,' I tried to find the words to explain my foreboding, 'I just can't put my finger on it,' I finished lamely. 'Fruitcakes don't change their currants.'

'Talking of fruitcakes, where's that daffy dog gone?' Morag stopped. Putting up one hand to shield her eyes against the low winter sun, she scanned the horizon.

Suddenly there was a commotion of cackling and hissing. A group of swans and geese on the riverbank scattered as Rocket shot out of some bushes and pounced on them.

'Rocket!' I yelled. 'Heel! Do you hear me?'

A man on a bicycle appeared. He was peddling furiously towards us. 'Is that your dog down there? It's a ruddy menace. It chased me along the tow path. Put it on a lead or I'll wallop it with my bicycle pump.'

The swans and geese had now gathered as one. Wings were flapping. Beaks pecking. Rocket immediately went into reverse and charged towards us.

'Good girl, come to Aunty Morag!' Morag held her arms wide. Rocket, tongue lolling, ears flapping, galloped towards us – and then whooshed straight past. Her destination appeared to be the cyclist.

'Oh no!'

Behind us the air turned blue. Angry swearing was punctuated by the frantic rings of a bicycle bell.

Morag chewed her lip. 'What shall we do?'

'Run,' I advised.

We fled.

'Oh God,' snorted Morag as we belted along the tow path, 'I know it's not funny Cass, but I can't help it.'

'Me neither,' I gasped, hair flying. 'Have you ever seen a dog trying to bonk a bicycle?'

'Never. I didn't think lady dogs were like that.'

'Me neither. Perhaps Rocket is bike-exual.'

'Oh don't,' Morag wheezed, 'I can't laugh and run.'

A children's playground loomed. We vaulted over the perimeter fencing, pounded up a ladder and hid in a playhouse on stilts.

'Get your head down,' Morag whispered hoarsely, 'Bicycle Bill is coming this way.'

'No!'

'Yes. And Rocket is in hot pursuit.'

'Oh buggerations. What are we going to do?'

'Try not to laugh,' said Morag, and promptly convulsed.

'Oi you bloody women,' hollered the cyclist. 'I know you're both there somewhere. You haven't heard the last of this. I'll be reporting you to the police. Along with your dog.'

Morag inched up slowly and peered over the wooden sill. 'Rocket's jumped the fence,' she whispered wiping tears from her eyes. 'She's now running around the playground. But I think Bicycle Bill has gone.'

From down below we heard whimpering followed by scrambling noises. I poked my head cautiously around the door opening. Rocket saw me and let out a series of joyful barks.

'You naughty girl,' I admonished.

'Come on,' said Morag, dropping to the ground. 'Let's get the hell out of here.' She grabbed Rocket's collar. 'And as for you young lady. Your mother's going to have plenty to say about this when we see her.'

Rocket emitted a few more baritone barks as I snapped on her lead.

'My legs are like jelly.'

'Well sharpen them up because we're not lingering,' said Morag. She gave a furtive look left and right, then beckoned with one hand. 'This way.'

I didn't need telling twice. Pounding after Morag, we fairly flew back along the tow path, over the bridge, through the oaks and towards Nell and sanctuary. By the time we walked into Nell's cul-de-sac, we'd been gone for the best part of two hours. I rang the doorbell.

'I can't wait to get home and have a shower,' I sighed. 'And I might be totally decadent and have a whopping slice of choc–'

The front door flew open.

'Help,' bleated Nell. Her stricken face said it all. 'The baby's coming.'

'Oh my goodness, I'll call an ambulance.' I ferreted through my pockets looking for my mobile phone.

'Don't be daft,' said Morag, 'it's quicker to take her in the car.'

'Okay. We'll go in mine,' I jingled my car keys.

'I'm not going anywhere in your car Cass,' panted Nell, 'it's full of rubbish. What if my baby makes a swift entrance into the world? I'm not having it delivered on a pile of McDonald cartons.'

'Okay, we'll go in Morag's car.'

Morag looked horrified. 'I'm not sure I want a baby being delivered on my back seat. Henry did a pooh when he was born. There was black meconium everywhere. I don't want to be scrubbing that off the upholstery.'

'Well go and get a towel out of the airing cupboard,' I huffed.

'Don't come into my house with those muddy trainers on,' screeched Nell. 'I've been cleaning this place rigorously for the last week. It's spotless.'

'Well you've got a muddy dog in here.'

'She's different,' snapped Nell, 'she's my boofles.'

'Well I think we'd better get your boofles out the way.' I pushed past Nell and led Rocket into the kitchen. Shutting the door firmly after her, I turned to Morag. 'I think you and I had better wash our hands very thoroughly. Just in case.' I went into the downstairs cloakroom.

Nell shut the front door. 'I need to call Ben. He wants to be present at the birth. And I also need to call my mother and let her know she'll have to pick up Dylan from school. And then I need to call the school and let them know–'

'Yes, yes. I'll get your mobile,' said Morag drying her hands. 'Where is it?'

'It's–' Nell broke off and doubled over. 'Argh!'

I rushed to Nell's side. 'Look in the kitchen,' I flapped an arm at Morag. 'It's usually on the table.' Nell leant on me heavily. 'Breathe!' I instructed.

Morag pushed her way into the kitchen. Rocket instantly bounded out.

'Get back in here you bloody dog!' yelled Morag.

'Don't talk to my boofles like–' Nell screwed up her face. 'ARGH,' she screeched even louder. There was a funny popping sound. 'Oh no, I think I've wet myself.'

Suddenly amniotic fluid gushed all over the laminate flooring. Rocket began lapping up the puddle. Morag clapped a hand over her mouth.

'Your dog is seriously gross. I think I'm going to throw up.' She flung herself into the downstairs loo.

'I want Ben,' Nell wailed. 'It hurts. I don't remember it hurting like this when I had Dylan.'

'Stay there.' I propped Nell against the wall and charged into the kitchen. Her mobile phone wasn't on the table. My eyes swivelled around the room. There it was, next to the kettle. I grabbed it and raced back to Nell. Shoved it into her hands. 'Ring Ben. And as for you,' I grabbed Rocket's collar, 'out!' Rocket promptly keeled over making it extremely difficult to move her.

'Go with Aunty Cass,' Nell implored the setter.

Rocket was now lying on her back, all four paws up in the air. I dragged her by the collar backwards. Bit by bit she slid down the hallway and into the kitchen. I opened the back door and hauled her unceremoniously into the garden. Shutting the door firmly behind me, I set about finding a mop and bucket. Morag emerged from the downstairs loo looking very pale.

'I feel ill.'

'Oh for heaven's sake Morag. I thought you were made of sterner stuff than this.'

'I was fine when Henry was born. But then again, I didn't look. Just kept my eyes shut throughout the whole thing until it was over.'

'Go and distract yourself. Make us some coffee while Nell's doing her phone calls.'

'I don't want coffee,' Nell cried, 'I want Ben. Ooooooh, I think I need the loo.'

I put the mop and empty bucket down. 'Come on,' I led her toward the downstairs toilet.

'No,' gasped Nell. 'There's not enough room in there for my bump between the loo and the wash basin. I'll have to go upstairs.'

'Right. Fine.' I reversed us back along the hallway and headed towards the stairs. Nell was stabbing her mobile's touch screen as we puffed our way upward.

'Hello?' she squawked into the handset. 'Ben! It's me. I'm in labour. Yes of course I'm sure. My waters have broken. What do you mean you're in Cambridgeshire? Well never mind Mr Bodwin's emergency. There's a far bigger emergency going on right here in your own home.'

I steered Nell into the bathroom and left her to it. Back downstairs I filled the bucket and began mopping.

'Coffee's ready,' said Morag putting mugs on the kitchen table. 'Where does Nell keep the biscuit tin? I think I need some carbs to settle my tummy.'

'On that shelf above you.'

There was a crash as Rocket planted two paws either side of the back door. A red shaggy head appeared in the windowpane. She clapped eyes on the biscuit tin and began licking the glass.

'That dog is a head case,' Morag declared. 'How on earth does Nell think she's going to manage a newborn with that mutt bouncing all over the place?'

'I'm sure she's got it sussed,' I said, not entirely convinced. I finished mopping the hallway and then whizzed the squeegee mop around the kitchen floor. When the last of Rocket's paw prints were eradicated, I tipped the dirty water down the loo, put away the mop and bucket and washed my hands again. I took some hurried sips of coffee, scalding my mouth in the process. 'Are you all right up there Nell?' I bellowed. A series of groans filtered down by way of response.

'I really do think we should get her to hospital,' said Morag.

'You're right. Come on. Drink up.'

We took the stairs two at a time and made our way to the bathroom.

'Can we come in?' I called through the door.

'Ooooh,' Nell said by way of response. I levered down the door handle. Nell was on all fours rocking around the bathroom. 'Somebody rub my back,' she bleated. Morag crouched down and began massaging. 'Harder! Faster!'

'Is Ben on his way?' I asked.

'Yes,' Nell gasped, 'and I've sorted out Dylan with both my mother and the school.'

'We need to get you to hospital Nell. Come on, get up.'

'No. I can't move.'

'You can. And must. I'm going to get a towel and then we'll get you into Morag's car. And you'd better text Ben to meet you at the hospital rather than here.'

'I can't stand up,' wailed Nell, 'it hurts too much.'

'Then stay like that.' There followed a very iffy ten minutes of getting Nell down the stairs and out to Morag's car whilst on all fours. 'You go on ahead,' I said to Morag. 'I'll just let Rocket back in and lock up.'

'I haven't got my overnight bag!' cried Nell.

'Where is it?'

'Down by the side of my bed.'

'I'll grab it and bring it along in my car.' I helped Nell onto the back seat of Morag's car. Slamming the door shut I banged the roof. 'Go!'

The Ford Galaxy catapulted off the driveway with Nell swaying on the back seat and very red in the face. At that moment I could see an uncanny resemblance between her and Rocket.

Forty-five minutes later, Nell was gowned and in a delivery room. A monitor was strapped to her bump. A midwife assured us that everything was going swimmingly.

'A few more hours and baby will be here,' she beamed. 'Where's your birthing partner Mrs Lambert?'

'Stuck in a ten mile tailback thanks to a closure on the M25,' Nell snarled. 'When he finally gets here, I'm going to kill him.'

'Ben is doing his best,' I soothed. 'Meanwhile you have Morag and me to hold your hand.'

'Sorry girls, but I'm going to have to go,' said Morag. 'There's only so long I can take advantage of Joanie, and I've been away for hours.'

'Fine, fine,' Nell waved a hand.

'Morag, can you do me a favour and divert past my house. Let Edna know what's happened.'

'Sure,' she gave me a good-bye hug. 'Let me know the news as soon as it's all over. Good luck Nell,' Morag kissed Nell on the forehead, nearly knocking her out with her chest. 'Go cervix go!'

Nell smiled weakly.

Four hours later there was still no sign of Ben. But Nell was beyond caring. She was now in the grip of full blown labour.

'I can feel the baby's head crowning,' she gasped. She looked like she was stretching her body to breaking point.

The mid-wife peered between Nell's legs. 'You're doing really well dear. I can see hair!'

'Ooooh, I want to see my baby's hair. Cass, get me a mirror.'

I cast around the delivery room looking for a convenient compact mirror.

'Here you are,' said the mid-wife producing the sort of mirror one usually finds in a hair salon.

'Short back and sides?' I joked. My laughter turned to an agonised yelp as Nell grabbed one of my hands and crushed it within hers. 'Bloody hell,' I gasped, 'I think you've broken all my fingers.'

'Aaaaaaah,' Nell wailed.

'A really good push dear and this baby will be born,' said the midwife.

Nell screwed up her face and turned the colour of beetroot. Making a noise like Tarzan, she pushed as if her life depended upon it. The baby shot out into the midwife's hands. A few tugs on the cord and the placenta was delivered.

'It's a girl!' I whooped with joy. And promptly burst into tears.

The mid-wife lifted the baby onto Nell's breast just as Ben burst into the delivery room.

'Oh my God,' he swooped down on his wife and new daughter. 'Oh my darling! Oh my baby!' And then he caught sight of the placenta. Suddenly he turned the colour of putty, his eyes rolled backwards and he crashed down to the floor.

Half an hour later I was behind the wheel of my car and beetling home. Nell and baby Rosie were doing fine. And so was Ben. He and his concussion were in the next ward. All I wanted to do now was get home, see my own beautiful brood of children and have a nice hot bath. Wouldn't everybody be amazed to hear my story of being Nell's birthing partner. What a fantastic feeling. I was high as a kite!

I shot through our electric gates, parked the car and, with a spring in my step, bounded up to the front door. Just as my key was poised, the door opened. And suddenly my bubble of elation burst like a pricked balloon. For there, standing on my Welcome mat, was Selina.

Chapter Eight

I stared at the vision haloed in the doorway. *My* doorway. Selina looked more like Angelina Jolie than ever – elegant and poised. I presumed she'd come straight from work. Her slim frame was dressed in a smart trouser suit. On her feet she wore expensive leather boots. The long dark hair was loose and shiny, and the pumped up lips glossed to perfection. In contrast, I looked a wreck. My hair was still stuck to my head from the earlier workout with Rocket. My joggers were splashed with amniotic fluid. And as for my trainers. I kicked them off irritably. Our nostrils twitched as whiffy insoles made their presence known.

'Cass!' Selina's face lit up. 'How lovely to see you.' Either she was a damned good actress or genuinely ecstatic that our paths had crossed again so soon. Personally I suspected the former. 'Do come in.' For one surreal moment I felt as though I were being invited into *her* home. 'You've missed mains but we're enjoying the most delicious pudding cooked by your charming mother-in-law. She's an absolute poppet.'

'Well don't let me interrupt your meal.' Dear God, now I sounded like a visitor. 'I mean, carry on.' Where was Jamie? Why wasn't he greeting me?

'Jamie's just changing Eddie's nappy,' Selina said, as if reading my mind. 'We're in the kitchen. Come on through.'

There! She was doing it again – inviting me into my own home! Somehow I ended up following her through the hallway, for all the world like a guest. In the kitchen an unfamiliar sight greeted my eyes. Four children sat around the table, elbows in, backs ramrod straight, eating apple crumble with impeccable manners. Not a scraping spoon, nor a slurped drink, and definitely no rowdy conversation.

'Good evening kids,' I smiled at them all. They beamed back.

'Good evening Mummy,' said Livvy politely before turning to her step-sister. 'More custard on your crumble Petra?'

'Thank you Livvy.'

'I'll have the custard jug after you please,' said Toby to Petra. 'Thank you. Jonas, would you like some too?'

'I've had sufficient thank you Toby.' Sufficient? Since when did anybody in this house say *sufficient*? 'I wouldn't mind finishing off the cream though.' Jonas paused, and instantly looked contrite. 'So long as nobody else wants any,' he added.

'No, no, that's fine, go ahead,' the other three graciously urged Jonas to pig out with a carton of double.

My eyes flicked from face to face. I had an overwhelming urge to whip out a thermometer and take temperatures.

'Charming children,' Selina murmured at my elbow.

'Yes. They've been brought up to be,' I couldn't resist pointing out. Frankly I hadn't a clue who these children were. They might look like Livvy, Toby, Petra and Jonas, but they weren't. The real Livvy, Toby, Petra and Jonas should be noisily chatting about school, arguing about who had the biggest measure of custard, eating with their mouths open, knocking drinks over and spilling crumble down their clothes.

'Ah, Cassandra dear,' Edna came into the kitchen with Eddie on her hip. 'Jamie's just this second taken an international call from Ethan. He's shut himself in the study. I'm afraid he could be a while.'

'Oh well. Business is business,' I cranked up a smile.

'Sit down. I've kept your dinner warm.'

'Thanks. I'm absolutely famished.' Famished? Was that the right sort of word to use in the company of a woman like Selina? I couldn't imagine her sitting down and saying, "Feed me, I'm famished" before tucking into a plate of raw cauliflower. I held out my arms to Eddie. 'Hello beautiful boy. Come to Mummy.'

'You eat your dinner Cass,' Selina immediately swooped on Eddie. 'I'll look after this little fellow.'

And suddenly my baby was in her arms. My heart jumped into my throat. I had an overwhelming urge to snatch Eddie away – as if to protect him. Every nerve in my body screamed *hands off*. But I could do nothing about it. Edna had plonked a hot plate in front of me. The food was steaming. I could hardly eat with Eddie on my lap – his little fingers had a habit of going everywhere and I didn't want him getting burnt. Edna caught my eye.

'You must tell us all about Nell's new baby dear.'

'Gosh, yes!' Selina smiled. 'How exciting! I gather you ended up playing mid-wife.'

'Well, it wasn't quite like that,' I forked up some chicken, 'but I held Nell's hand and gave her lots of encouragement while Rosie was being born.'

'I can't wait to have a family,' Selina smiled and began to bounce Eddie on her knee. He gave a delicious chuckle of laughter. She turned to me with wide eyes. 'I want at least six children. These five will do nicely for starters.'

Any casual onlooker would have believed Selina's words to be complimentary. But I was on red alert.

'They're already spoken for,' I said coldly.

Selina flushed. 'Well of course. I simply meant–'

'–and I'm sure you'll make a very good Mummy one day,' said Livvy coming to Selina's rescue. My daughter flashed me a dirty look. Now it was my turn to flush.

'Well you can be my Mum any time,' Toby gave Selina a cheeky wink. Dear God. Was my son attempting to flirt? Aged eleven but already revving up to follow in his father's womanising footsteps? I was irked that my own children should be enthralled with this woman. My appetite fizzled and died. I put my knife and fork together.

'If you'll all excuse me,' I stood up, 'I'd like to have a shower and get out of these clothes.'

Edna whisked my plate away. The cats meowed around her feet, clamouring for the leftovers.

'Perhaps you'd like some crumble later on Cassandra dear, when you've had a chance to unwind?' Edna's message was clear: when Selina had gone and my knotted guts had unravelled.

'That would be great Edna. Thanks.'

I went out into the hallway. Selina's voice floated after me. She had now turned her attention to Edna.

'You are such a wonderful mother-in-law to Cass. One day I want to live in a house just like this one, with a mother-in-law just like you.'

I grimaced. Not content with making a play for my kids, Selina was now sucking up to my mother-in-law. Cow. Passing the study I could hear Jamie within talking to Ethan. I stuck my head around the door. He looked up. Smiled. Gave me a thumbs up. I blew him a kiss and shut the door.

Upstairs in our bedroom, I set about running a bath in the en-suite and peeled off my clothes. With a bit of luck, if I strung it out, Selina might have gone home by the time I was done.

Feeling a smidgen happier, I hopped in the water and tipped shampoo over my head. Half an hour later I emerged from the bathroom wearing a bath towel and turban. I nearly dropped the bath towel when I saw Selina sitting at my dressing table. She had her legs elegantly crossed. Her manicured hands were folded in her lap. I glanced at the bedroom door. Shut.

I immediately went on the defensive. 'What are you doing up here?'

Selina spread her hands wide, palms open. A gesture of coming clean. 'I wanted to talk to you in private.'

'What about?'

'Look Cass, I feel that we've got off to a bad start.'

Was she for real? 'You don't say!' I feigned surprise. 'Now why on earth could that be? Let me think,' I frowned theatrically. 'Hang on. It's coming back to me. Yes, yes, that's right. Something to do with a series of intimidating phone calls at my home. Oh, *and* place of work. And lots of whispering down the phone, that I was a bitch and you hated me. And let's not forget the little matter of dragging me off on a wild goose chase to The Planet Restaurant where – lo! I stumble across you apparently having a romantic dinner with Jamie and trying to make out there's a passionate affair going on. Sorry, what was that you were saying about us getting off to a bad start?' I stood there blinking very rapidly. Any moment now I'd whisk off my wet towel – to hell with lack of modesty – and thrash her with it.

'Cass, try and see things from my perspective. After all, you were *the other woman*.'

'I most certainly was not!' My chest heaved with indignation.

'Well it seemed that way from my side of the fence,' Selina said evenly. 'There I was, dating my dream man, happy as a lark. Yet wherever we went, you'd show up. My God, you were even skiing in the same place as us. Of all the mountains in the world,' Selina's voice cracked, 'there you were crashing into my boyfriend on a red run in Risoul.'

'Hold it right there lady. Yes, through a series of unfortunate coincidences our paths did cross a few times. But at no point did I set about to steal Jamie from you. The first time I met Jamie I was newly separated and barely functioning. And later –*much* later,' I added, 'I was involved with somebody else.'

'Oh yes. I seem to remember he belonged to another woman too – married no less.' My mouth dropped open. How the bloody hell did Selina know that? 'I was there. In the restaurant,' she looked at me knowingly. I gazed at her, suddenly wrong-footed. 'What was the place called? Ah yes, Cavendish's. Jamie was meeting me there to celebrate my birthday. Due to work detaining him, he didn't see the showdown. But I did. You caused quite a rumpus, didn't you? When that guy's wife marched in, one couldn't see the space around your table for flying ice buckets and dinner plates.'

'I didn't know Euan was married,' I whispered.

Selina made a tutting noise. 'Don't trot out that old line Cass.'

I sucked in my breath. 'It's true! But actually I don't care whether you believe me or not. Frankly it's none of your damn business.'

'You're right. It's none of my business. However, Jamie *was* my business. Until you came along.'

'Jamie had finished with you months before I started seeing him.'

'So you say. Not sure I believe you though.'

'Tell you what. Why don't I get Jamie up here? Sod his international business call to your fiancé,' I made to go to the bedroom door, 'let's listen to the facts – straight from the horse's mouth.'

Selina stood up. 'There's no need for that Cass. It's all in the past now.'

'Well obviously you still have an axe to grind, otherwise we wouldn't be having this conversation – in my home,' I added, 'where you invited yourself as a guest. Unwanted by me. And frankly I'd like you to now leave.'

Selina smoothed an imaginary crease from one leg of her trouser suit. 'When I came up here to see you, the intention was to have a friendly one to one with you. I didn't mean for us to end up being hostile with each other.'

'Things already were hostile – don't flatter yourself.'

'What I'm trying to say,' Selina took a deep breath, 'is sorry. I'm sorry for everything that happened.'

I glared at her. 'Okay. So now you've said sorry. I still want you to leave.'

'Cass, whether you like it or not, I'm engaged to Ethan and working with your husband. I just want to wipe the slate clean. Start again. It would make things so much easier if we could do that.'

I narrowed my eyes. 'You mean make it easier for you.'

'No. I mean make it easier for you actually.'

'I don't think so. If I told Ethan about your past behaviour and what you'd done, he'd drop you like a hot cake.'

'He wouldn't Cass. Because he wouldn't believe you.'

'No?'

'No. I've since told Ethan that I once dated Jamie.'

That flummoxed me. 'And what did Ethan say?'

'As far as my fiancé's concerned, I finished with Jamie.'

'Oh don't give me that.'

'But it's perfectly plausible. Ethan believes I could no longer deal with Jamie's emotional baggage. That Jamie was one thoroughly mixed up man following the death of his first wife. Ethan totally believes my story. However, if you give me a hard time Cass, I'll tell him that Jamie wouldn't take no for an answer. That for quite a long period of time he was an utter pest. Made nuisance calls. Stalked me,' she gave a twisted smile, 'and that the real reason why I needed persuading to work for Fareham & Mackerel was because of Jamie's previously unstable mind.'

My mouth dropped open. 'You wouldn't dare!'

'Wouldn't I? Who is Ethan going to believe? The woman he loves and can't wait to marry? Or a man who lost his marbles after his first wife died? And look at it from another angle too. Who is the most expendable? Me – the woman Ethan wants to spend the rest of his life with? Or Jamie – a junior partner who can be replaced? This is a nice house you have Cass. Very grand. High maintenance. Not to mention five children to feed, clothe and keep in ponies and iPads.'

'You really are round the bend,' I spluttered.

Selina smiled. 'No. I was once. When I was heartbroken about Jamie. But not any more. I'm trying very hard Cass to be your friend now. I've apologised. And I'll apologise again. But in my defence, at the time I was in a bad place. I was devastated. And suffering. It affected me. Yes, I went a bit loopy. But I'm good now. Sorted my brain out. I'm better. I have Ethan, and a future again. I want to make the best of it. Can't you sympathise, just a little bit? Your first husband treated you badly. Didn't you ever have a moment where you felt you'd lost your mind?'

I stared at her. My mouth momentarily had lost the power of speech. A part of what Selina was saying struck a chord. Stevie had sent me to hell and back. I'd always suspected he'd been unfaithful but Stevie had repeatedly denied it. He'd made me out to be some sort of over-possessive basket case. And then I'd caught him out. Literally. I had a flashback. Walking in on Stevie. Seeing him welded to Cynthia Castle, a neighbour no less. It had been the talk of our cul-de-sac for weeks. Hadn't I gone a bit potty for a while? My mind had certainly worked overtime dreaming up revenge tactics. Popping a bit of superglue in Stevie's condoms. Giving Cynthia's car a top coat of paint stripper. Needless to say I hadn't done either of those things, but it had been a close call. Unlike Stevie's current girlfriend – Charlotte – who only a few months ago had spectacularly lost the plot and trashed his entire house. Losing in love was a soul destroying experience. Was it any wonder that sometimes there were casualties?

'Okay,' I let out a shaky breath. 'I can identify with some of what you're saying.'

Selina nodded. 'So, truce?' She extended a hand. I stared at it. I really didn't want to take it. 'You don't have to like me Cass. You just have to tolerate me.'

Tolerate. That word again. Only this morning, while walking in the park, Morag had said the very same thing. "You don't have to *be* her friend, just *tolerate* her." Everybody had said it. Jamie. Edna. Nell. Morag. And now Selina herself. There was so much to lose. And everything to gain. I had my husband's career to think of. And my children's future. They were growing up fast now. Before I knew it they would be wanting driving lessons. Cars. Money to pay for university. More money to pay for digs. And then there was Eddie's schooling. Only a little while ago Morag had been talking about enrolling Henry in an exclusive prep school for boys. "There's a three year waiting list Cass. The education is second to none. Just think how wonderful it would be to give Eddie such a golden opportunity to fulfil his potential. Our boys could go on to Eton! They might even be Prime Minister one day!" And whilst I was pretty damn sure my baby boy wasn't going to be walking in David Cameron's shoes, I understood Morag's fundamental reasoning. All mothers want the best for their children. And if there was any way of guaranteeing the best for one's child, what mother wouldn't go the extra mile? Could I go that extra mile now? It was a no-brainer. Selina's hand remained proffered.

'I'll never be your friend,' I told her, 'but I will tolerate you.'

And then I took her hand.

Chapter Nine

After Selina had taken herself off downstairs, I gave my hair a quick blast of the dryer, pulled on some jeans and a clean sweater and then went to find Jamie. He was in the kitchen giving Eddie a bottle while chatting to Edna. My mother-in-law immediately excused herself on the pretext of wanting to watch a DIY programme on the television.

'How's my hubby?' I kissed Jamie on the mouth and pulled up a chair next to him.

'I'm good. And what about Florence Nightingale?' he teased. 'I hear you've started a new career in midwifery.'

I grinned. 'Mother and baby are doing fine. And Ben too – after his bang on the head. What a performance,' I tutted. 'But never mind that for now. I've hardly seen you this evening. You were on the phone for ages. Any progress with Ethan's business trip?' I leant forward and stroked Eddie's hand while he was glugging. His chubby fingers gripped mine.

'Ethan is flying home tomorrow. He's delivered! The American bank is officially our client. This is going to open so many more doors Cassie. I can't tell you what a great feeling it is,' Jamie exhaled with relief.

'That's fantastic news,' I smiled. 'So the hard work is paying off.'

'And some.'

I looked around. Dropped my voice an octave. 'Has Selina gone home?'

'No. She's in the study talking to Ethan. I must take her home when she's finished the call.'

I straightened up. 'Didn't she drive here?'

'Her car is at the garage. Some mechanical problem. She took a taxi here.'

'So let her take a taxi home.'

Jamie pulled a face. 'It would be rude not to offer her a lift.'

I could do rude. 'Greenwich isn't just around the corner Jamie. And you're tired.' The doorbell rang. Eddie was almost asleep in Jamie's arms. 'Who can that be?'

'Maybe it's my mother's admirer,' Jamie waggled his eyebrows.

'Ooh yes. Amorous Arthur. With a bouquet of spanners.' I stood up.

'I'd like to meet this chap. Mum was doing quite a bit of mentionitis while you were upstairs. Arthur strokes his planer this way. Arthur prefers screwing to banging. I had great trouble keeping a straight face.' The doorbell rang again. 'You see who it is while I take this little fellow up to bed.'

But when I opened the front door, I wasn't greeted by a pensioner with a big tool and a twinkle in his eye. Instead my ex-husband stood there, his face partially shadowed thanks to the angle of the porch's courtesy light.

'Hi Cass. Sorry to turn up unexpectedly,' Stevie smiled apologetically, 'but your mobile was switched off and the landline seems to be constantly engaged.'

'Ah yes. Someone is indeed using our phone at the moment. And I switched my mobile off earlier because I was at the hospital. Nell's finally had her baby. A little girl. Oh my goodness – I clean forgot to tell Morag. I must text her.'

'That's great news about Nell. Give her and Ben my love.'

'I will. Anyway, come in out of the cold.' I shut the door on the freezing night air. 'Would you like a cup of coffee?'

'Sure. Why not.'

Stevie followed me through to the kitchen. I picked up the kettle. Empty. 'Is everything all right?' I asked. Shoving the kettle under the water spout, I hit the tap too hard. Water droplets sprayed across my sweater.

'Yeah,' Stevie slid out of his jacket and hung it over the back of a chair. 'I was just missing the kids and thought it would be nice to say hello.' He sat down near the range, rubbing his hands together for warmth.

'I'm sure they'll be thrilled to see you. Do you want to take them out for an ice-cream or something?'

On the whole, my ex and I were on reasonably good speaking terms. And where the children were concerned, we'd made sure there had never been conflict. The twins' emotional well-being was of paramount importance to us. Despite Stevie's womanising, I'd never bad-mouthed him to Livvy and Toby. Whatever Stevie's faults as a husband, he'd been a good father. Withholding access as a means of revenge – like some women – had never been my style.

'It's a bit cold for ice-cream,' Stevie chuckled. 'Anyway, it's a school night so I don't want them being late back. They'll be with me this weekend so there's time for ice-cream then. I just wanted to give them a hug.'

'I'll call them down.' As I made the coffee, I couldn't help noticing how tired my ex-husband looked. The corners of his mouth were uncharacteristically turned down. 'What's up? You look like the weight of the world is on your shoulders.'

'Oh,' he shrugged, 'this and that.' He accepted the coffee and stirred in some sugar. 'Actually, Charlotte and I aren't seeing eye to eye at the moment.'

'What's new,' I grinned. Charlotte had been Stevie's live-in lover for the best part of a year. Give or take a month here and there when she packed her bags and stalked off home to Mother. A statistician would surely have put the odds on Charlotte – stunningly beautiful and half Stevie's age – as being the one to give *him* the run around. And whilst young lads did occasionally beat their chests and vie for her attention, for some bizarre reason she only had eyes for my ex. There was no denying Stevie was in good shape for his age, and he had a silver tongue when it came to charismatic chat-up lines. But at the end of the day, no matter how you dressed his personality up, he was still a cad with a wandering eye. He never said no to an extra-curricular leg over. A psychologist might have diagnosed Stevie as suffering anxiety over the aging process – that he was a man worried about the shelf life of his pulling power. After all, everybody's sex appeal had a sell-by-date. But for Stevie it was a struggle to come to terms with. Hence the tom cat behaviour. Even Charlotte's parents despaired of their daughter not wising up and dumping Stevie permanently. Perhaps it boiled down to the *treat 'em mean keep 'em keen* mentality. But Stevie's relationship was no business of mine. I was just relieved to be free of the shoes Charlotte now walked in.

'She wants a baby,' Stevie rubbed his forehead wearily.

'Ah,' I pulled out a chair and sat down opposite him, 'and you don't.'

'Definitely not. I've been there. Done that. And in all honesty Cass, much as I love our kids to bits, I look back and sometimes wonder–'

'What?' I prompted.

'Well. You know. I wonder if we'd still be together if we hadn't become parents. Blokes like me – I'm not making excuses for my past behaviour – but when your partner is big with child and then subsequently knackered with a newborn,' he shrugged. Took a sip of coffee. 'It can put the best of relationships under pressure.'

'Jamie and I have had a baby. Eddie is wonderful. We certainly have no regrets.'

'Yes but Eddie isn't the glue in your relationship. You and Jamie were good in the first place. Charlotte and I have never been solid.'

'Then you'll have to tell her straight I guess.'

'Mmm. I did. She took it badly,' Stevie looked sheepish, 'which is another reason why I've come out this evening. The air at home is poisonous.'

'Oh dear.'

At that moment Toby came into the kitchen looking for a TV snack to take up to his room. 'Dad!' he put his arms around Stevie and gave him a hug. 'Jonas has Paranormal Activity on DVD. Want to watch it with us?'

'Is that suitable viewing?' Stevie asked.

'Probably not,' Toby grinned. He extricated himself from Stevie and palmed a family sized bag of crisps from the larder.

I checked my watch. 'You can have an hour's viewing Tobes, but then I want all four of you in the shower. School tomorrow remember.'

'Sure.'

At that moment Selina came into the kitchen. 'Sorry to hog your phone for so long Cass.'

'That's quite all right,' I said stiffly. Stevie clocked my body language. He gave me a curious look as he stood up to follow Toby. 'Selina, this is Stevie. Toby and Livvy's father.'

She held out a hand. 'How do you do?'

'I do very well thank you Selina,' said Stevie switching on the charm as he shook her hand. He held it a fraction longer than necessary.

'I'm a colleague of Jamie's,' Selina explained.

'Lucky Jamie,' Stevie winked.

'And Selina is also the fiancée of Jamie's business partner,' I added.

'He's lucky too,' Stevie grinned.

'We're watching Paranormal Activity,' Toby said to Selina. 'Would you like to see it too?'

'I absolutely adore scary films,' Selina clapped her hands together, 'and crisps,' she added.

'Cool. You can sit next to me Selina,' said Toby. He puffed his chest out importantly. Clearly my son was thrilled to bits knowing he'd have Dad on one side and crumpet on the other. I stared after them as they piled out of the kitchen. Well don't mind me. Do make free with my house. And my bags of crisps. I stood up to shut the larder door. When was that wretched woman going home?

Wandering into the lounge, I picked up the remote control. Snuggling down with a cushion, I found myself watching a repeat of *The Real Hustle*. A little while later Jamie came in.

'There's all sorts of shrieks and screams coming from Toby's bedroom,' he said as he sat down next to me. 'I just stuck my head around the door and it's like a cinema in there. I see Stevie's here,' Jamie put an arm around me, 'and batting his eyelashes at Selina.'

'I wonder if she'll flirt back.'

'Unlikely. I've told you before. She's nuts about Ethan.'

'Yes, she went to great lengths to expound that fact when she paid a little visit to me upstairs earlier on. She apologised profusely for all the past behaviour. Assured me she was a born-again sane person.' I gave Jamie a re-run of the conversation.

'You see,' he squeezed me reassuringly. 'I told you she was sorry. Give her a tiny bit of credit for having the bottle to talk to you.'

'Huh,' I rolled my eyes.

'What are you watching?' Jamie went to take the remote control from me, a sure sign that channel hopping was about to take place. I clung on to it possessively.

'I'm watching unsuspecting members of the public being duped by con artists. I can't believe people can be so gullible.'

'That's because conmen can be convincing. It happened to you once,' Jamie gave me a sidelong look.

'What *are* you talking about?' I spluttered.

'Do you remember the time those two guys rang the doorbell and wanted to use our phone?'

I screwed up my face in concentration. Flipped backwards through pages of memory. 'Y-e-s. They'd had a puncture, and neither of them had a mobile phone.'

'That's right. And you were more than happy to invite them in to use our telephone.'

'Where is this leading to exactly?'

Jamie whipped the remote out of my hand and turned the volume down. 'Do you also remember one of them asking to use the toilet while the other made his phone call?'

'I do as it happens. I directed him to the loo down the hallway.'

'Well I never told you this Cassie, but the guy came into our kitchen – where I happened to be sitting at the table quietly reading the newspaper. He looked quite shocked when he walked in and saw me. He clearly thought it was just you at home that day.'

'Credit me with some sense Jamie. I wouldn't have invited strangers into the house if you hadn't been around.'

'Yes, but the point is they were opportunists. And they took a chance you might be on your own.'

'So what happened when this bloke saw you sitting there?'

'Oh he made some spurious excuse about mistaking the kitchen for the cloakroom. So I re-directed him and waited outside while he went through the motions of flushing the chain, before leading him back down the hallway. His mate finished his pretend phone call, and then I waved them both off the premises.'

'So how do you know they weren't legitimate?' I frowned.

'Did you see a flat tyre on their vehicle?'

'Gosh I don't know. Not as such no. I didn't go out there and demand to inspect the puncture if that's what you mean. It's not something anybody would do is it?'

'Exactly. And none of their tyres were flat. And as they drove off I made a note of the registration number. It turned out the van was stolen.'

'No!' I gasped. 'Why didn't you tell me this at the time?'

'You were pregnant with Eddie and I didn't want to frighten you. But I'm telling you now. So be warned Cassie. Be vigilant and have your wits about you at all times.'

'Good heavens,' I muttered faintly.

The sound of footsteps coming down the stairs could be heard. Stevie and Selina appeared in the lounge doorway.

'Thanks for letting me see the kids Cass,' said Stevie. 'I'll be off now.'

'I must go too,' said Selina.

Hurrah. At last.

'Can I call you a taxi?' I asked quickly, before Jamie could volunteer his services.

'That's very kind Cass, but no thank you. Stevie is going to pop me home.' Selina gave Stevie a winning smile. 'Are you sure you don't mind? I don't want to take you out of your way.'

'No trouble at all,' Stevie assured, as if *popping* twenty miles to Greenwich and then twenty miles home again was nothing more than a five minute round journey.

'Well don't let us keep you,' I trilled. Standing up I steered them into the hallway. 'And no problem seeing the twins, Stevie. Anytime. You're always welcome.' I didn't follow through with a similar assurance to Selina. Hopefully she'd twig my subliminal message. Jamie stood up too and followed everyone to the front door.

'Well good-bye,' Selina hovered, unsure whether our truce might include pecks on cheeks. They didn't.

'Good-bye,' I opened the door to usher her out. She stood her ground. Looked at Jamie.

'I'll see you at the apartment in the morning.'

'Sure,' Jamie nodded.

Selina gave me a look. I could have sworn it was one of triumph. 'My car,' she said by way of explanation.

Ah yes. The car with an abundance of mechanical problems. How convenient. It occurred to me that in the space of just a few hours this woman had achieved both my husband and ex-husband running around after her. Stevie placed the palm of one hand in the small of Selina's back and guided her out into the night. There followed a few more goodnights and words of thanks before they finally took their leave. I shut the door after them.

'What's the matter Cassie? You look like you've swallowed a wasp.'

'That woman.' I drew in a breath. 'She doesn't fool me for one moment.'

'What are you talking about now?' Jamie gave a sigh of exasperation.

'You've just finished giving me a pep talk about conmen. Instructed me to have my wits about me at all times. Well frankly, darling, you should heed your own advice.'

'How do you work that one out Cassie?' Jamie took me by the hand as we walked back to the lounge.

'Because I can't shake the feeling that Selina is conning the lot of us.'

Chapter Ten

The letterbox clattered as it spewed forth a new day's delivery from the Royal Mail. Envelopes fell in an untidy pile on the doormat. I bent down and gathered everything up. Walking into the kitchen, I nearly tripped over Wallace and Gromet. The cats were waiting patiently for their breakfast, tails folded primly over paws. As soon as they saw me, they began a cacophony of yowling. Wallace stood up and weaved around my ankles. I frisbeed the post onto the kitchen table, and got on with opening a tin of cat food. Jamie came into the kitchen, Eddie in his arms.

'Our son slept through the night!' he declared in amazement.

'Indeed.' I plonked whiffy meat down in front of the cats, and then busied myself mixing milk and cereal for Eddie. 'All thanks to Morag and her sleep plan.' I shoved the bowl of gloop into the microwave. 'And due to her incessant nagging about weaning, my boobs are back to normal. Look,' I patted my deflated chest. 'Soft again.'

Jamie squeezed my left breast. 'So they are. I've a good mind to whisk you straight back upstairs Mrs Mackerel, and give your chest a thorough examination.'

My mother-in-law walked in. 'What's the matter with your chest Cassandra dear? I couldn't help noticing you didn't have enough layers on for your jog in the park with Rocket yesterday. I hope you haven't caught a cold.'

The microwave pinged. I turned to open the door, hiding a smile. 'You're quite right Edna. I promise to wrap up more warmly next time.'

Jamie caught my eye and winked. 'Let me have that,' he took the baby cereal, 'and have the pleasure of feeding our little boy before I race off to Greenwich.'

Ah yes. Princess Selina. Not only lonely in her penthouse turret but apparently stranded too. I pursed my lips but refrained from saying anything. Instead I busied myself laying the table with plates and cutlery while Edna whisked up fluffy pancakes for the children. They piled into the kitchen seconds later demanding maple syrup and jam. Jamie shovelled porridgey mix into Eddie's eager mouth while I poured juice into cups. I then started on the mail. The electricity bill was *how much*? I stuffed the offending paperwork back into its envelope. I could see why Jamie was so keen for his business partnership to continue, and avoid going back on a bobby's beat. There was a clatter of knives and forks being put down. I looked up.

'All finished kids? Right, I'll just get your little brother out of his pyjamas and we'll be off to school.'

Jamie lifted Eddie out of his highchair and handed him over to me, before disappearing upstairs to shave for work.

'I'll clean up properly later Cassandra dear,' said my mother-in-law as she dumped the frying pan in the sink. 'I promised to meet Arthur at nine.'

'Leave everything Edna. Really, I don't expect you to tidy up after us. I'll see to it when I'm back from the school run.' Curiosity got the better of me. 'What have you and Arthur got planned?'

'Well,' Edna's blue eyes were suddenly ablaze with a light I'd never seen before, 'we've almost finished our respective rocking horses, so we've decided our next project will be a joint one.'

'How lovely,' I smiled indulgently. 'What have you both in mind? A sledge? I do believe snow is forecast.'

'Gracious no, Cassandra dear. I can knock up one of those anytime. We're going to make a boat.'

'A boat?' I stared at her stupidly. 'A toy boat?'

'No. A proper boat. With a cabin. And then we're going to sail it.'

'Right,' I said, slack-jawed. And by *sailing*, did she mean gently pottering up and down the Thames or Around the World in Eighty Days?

'Cool, Nanny Edna,' said Toby clapping his hands with glee. 'Can we go in it too?'

'Of course, Toby dear. And now I really must get a move on. Have a good day at school children.'

Moments later Jamie charged into the kitchen with his briefcase.

'I'm going to be late. Have you seen my car keys?'

'Your mother's building a boat.'

'Excellent, excellent,' Jamie began riffling through drawers in the ritualistic morning hunt for his car keys.

'She's going to sail it. With Arthur.'

'Couldn't be more thrilled. Ah, there they are,' Jamie plucked them from the fruit bowl. 'Bye kids.'

'Bye Dad,' a hasty kiss was deposited by Petra as both Toby and Jonas shot under Jamie's extended arms and out through the open doorway.

'Bye Jamie,' Livvy stood on her tiptoes to peck her stepfather's cheek. He tweaked her ponytail in response.

'See you about half seven darling.' Jamie turned to me and brushed his lips against mine.

There was a last minute delay thanks to Eddie having a bowel evacuation just as we were piling into the Muck Truck.

'Can't you change him when you get home Mum?' asked Livvy.

'No darling. Apart from his nappy whiffing the car out, he'll whine like billy-ho. Won't be a sec.'

Being a *sec* wasn't strictly true. By the time I'd cleaned up my wriggling infant and wrestled him into a clean nappy, a good fifteen minutes had elapsed.

'We're going to be late Cass,' Jonas complained.

'No we won't,' I assured. I reversed smartly out of the driveway and shot off along Lavender Hill at...ooh...a good twenty miles per hour. A collective groan rippled around the car. Needless to say, it was gone nine by the time the children ran through the school gates.

'Tell your teachers I'm very sorry,' I called after them as they flew across the playground.

When I arrived home Morag was waiting on the doorstep for me, Henry on one hip. She looked incredibly put out.

'I was just about to strap Henry back into his car seat and drive off. Where on earth have you been?'

'Sorry,' I said, extracting Eddie from his own car seat, 'school run.'

'But it's nearly ten o'clock!' she exclaimed. 'I wasn't sure if you'd naffed off to Fairview to do some shopping.'

'You could have phoned me to check my whereabouts!'

'Unfortunately I've come out without my mobile. I took a chance on you being home. Earlier on I picked up your text about Nell. Have you recovered from your midwifery stint?'

'Just about,' I hauled Eddie onto my shoulder and locked the car. 'Baby Rosie is beautiful.'

'I can't wait to see her. When do you think we can visit Nell?'

'Well, perhaps we should let them have a couple of days to sort themselves out – Ben did have concussion remember. And they'll probably just want to be on their own with Dylan too, and bond with the new family member.'

'Good idea. Well come on, let's get inside. I have something to tell you.'

'Ooh, that sounds promising. Gossip?' I slotted the house key into the front door.

'Naturally.'

'Come on through to the kitchen. Oh dear,' I stared around me in dismay. 'I'll just clear up the breakfast things and then I'll put the kettle on. Promise.'

'Honestly Cass, you are such a slob,' Morag chided. 'Why don't you tidy up as you go along?' Morag took Eddie from me and hopped into the playpen with both boys. I quickly loaded up the dishwasher and wiped down floury surfaces, while she played peek-a-boo with our babies.

Fifteen minutes later we sat companionably at the table, coffee mugs by our sides and a plate of Hob Nobs between us.

'I shouldn't be eating these,' said Morag helping herself, 'but lately chopped up carrot sticks have lost their appeal.'

'Hardly surprising. I'd rather have a Nob than a stick any day.'

'Don't be smutty.'

'Why not? You usually are!' I dipped a biscuit in the hot liquid before letting it crumble over my tongue. 'Mmm. Delish. So what's this gossip?'

'Well,' Morag took a deep breath, 'yesterday evening I was in Tesco's and bumped into Charlotte.'

'Charlotte as in Stevie's Charlotte?'

'The very one and same,' Morag took a sip of coffee, 'and she wasn't looking so hot.'

'Stevie was here last night. He mentioned they'd had a row and he'd come out to distance himself.'

'Well from now on there will be permanent distance. She told me she's left him.'

'Oh Charlotte is always saying that. She'll run home to Mummy for a day or two and be back in situ by the weekend. You'll see.'

'Not this time. She told me she'd packed her bags and was in Tesco's picking up a few things for her journey. Apart from anything else, I think your ex has already moved on.'

'You're wrong,' I dunked another Hob Nob in my mug. 'This time–'

I stared in dismay at my coffee. Half the Hob Nob had over-soaked and fallen into the mug. It was so annoying when that happened. I stood up to make a fresh one.

'I'll have another coffee too please Cass.' Morag waved her empty mug at me.

'Currently their relationship has hit a wall,' I took Morag's mug, 'because Charlotte wants a baby, and Stevie isn't in agreement. And I heard that straight from the horse's mouth.' I poured scalding water into the two mugs.

'Well if that's true, then I'm sorry for Charlotte. However, there's more to this than just refusing to have a baby. Stevie rang the stables early this morning. I'd popped down to the yard to give Matt a message and then got side-tracked talking to one of the stable girls in the office. So I just happened to be there when Stevie's call came through. He booked a hack for this Sunday.'

I put the fresh coffees on the table. 'Gosh, he's not ridden a horse for a good few years. His legs will be as stiff as a board.'

'Well I privately thought that might not be the only thing to get stiff,' Morag arched an eyebrow, 'because it transpired he'd booked two horses,' she waited for this to sink in, 'for him and A.N. Other.'

'Now *you're* the one being smutty,' I tutted. 'Well the second nag is obviously for Charlotte.'

'Nope,' Morag shook her head.

I took another Hob Nob. This time dunked it carefully. 'This isn't good gossip Morag,' I shook my head. 'I thought you were going to tell me something riveting. My ex-husband's social life is of no interest to me.'

Morag ignored me and ploughed on. 'Five minutes later Stevie rang back. And this time *I* answered the phone.'

'And?'

'And after exchanging pleasantries, Stevie went on to say that regrettably he had to cancel the double hacks because his *lady friend* – please note no mention of Charlotte's name – wanted to use a different stable.'

'God he's so tactless,' I spluttered.

'Yes he is. But the point is, when I went to cross out his booking in the diary, I noticed the name next to his. And it wasn't Charlotte's.'

'So whose name was it?'

'A woman,' Morag rolled her eyes theatrically, 'called Selina.'

My entire Hob Nob splashed into my coffee. 'Bloody hell.' I fished out the biscuit and deposited the mess on the table. 'I'll wipe that up in a minute. Right now I need to main-line on sugar.' I took another biscuit. 'Are you absolutely sure about this Morag?'

'Of course I'm sure! Although to begin with I thought it was a massive coincidence. I couldn't understand how on earth Stevie knew *that* Selina. But you've since answered the question by telling me he dropped in on you last night. And I know you had a certain person in your house who'd invited herself over for kitchen supper. So you don't have to be Einstein to work out that the two of them met and clearly took a shine to each other.'

'Stevie was putty in Selina's hands. She managed to wangle a ride home from him – all the way to Greenwich no less. Goodness knows what time he got back to his place last night.' Morag and I looked at each other as realisation dawned. 'If he went home at all of course. Ethan isn't due back from America until later today.'

Morag let out a low whistle. 'Selina must have asked Stevie to change stables for their horsey afternoon to avoid running into Matt who she met when she dated Jamie.'

'Well quite,' I said, spraying biscuit crumbs across the table, 'and of course it's possible all the kids would have spotted her too. They will be there this weekend riding their own ponies.'

'Exactly. And Matt would have told Jamie he saw his ex-girlfriend–'

'And then Selina would have had an awful lot of explaining to do as to why she was out horse riding with Stevie when she's so *in lurve* with Ethan. What time did you get the first phone call?'

'It was early. About half past seven. Don't forget stable life starts at six in the morning. Mucking out and wotnot. It's not unusual to have the phone ringing at that hour.'

'And you say Stevie called again minutes later.'

'Yup.'

'So by my reckoning, at that point they must have been in her apartment together – Ethan's apartment as it so happens – discussing their next rendezvous. "How about a bit of fun?"' I mimicked Stevie, '"a bit of chilly winter horse riding and then back to mine to warm up?", and then Stevie ringing the stables and organising everything before Selina thought *hang on, I've been to that yard before*. And then she probably tossed back her hair,' I threw back my own head and shook my hair about, 'and declared, "Oh Stevie honey-buns. Change of plan. Horsey-shenanigans will have to take place elsewhere. We can't risk bumping into your kiddie-poohs and–"'

'I'm sure she doesn't talk like that Cass. You sound like a retarded Hollywood actress.'

'And talking of kiddie-poohs, she made a comment about the children last night that got right up my nose. It was almost like she wanted to *steal* them off me.'

'And now you've lost yourself in a dire Hollywood drama. Honestly Cass, sometimes your imagination is something else. Let's stick to the facts–'

'Fact One,' I put down my Hob Nob and ticked off on one hand. 'Stevie spent the night in that apartment – *Ethan's* apartment. Fact Two, Selina has started an affair with him. Fact Three,' I floundered. There must be a third thing.

'Fact Three,' Morag leant forward. Looked me in the eye. 'If Selina dumps Ethan and marries your ex-husband, she will be step-mother to your children.'

'Over my dead body,' I growled. 'This is one occasion where my ex-husband's love life suddenly does interest me. That woman is driving me nuts. Wherever I turn, she's there. In my face. I can't have Stevie falling for Selina.'

'Oh don't upset yourself so. Stevie turns women around faster than conveyor-belt sushi.'

I stood up. Took some deep breaths. 'You don't understand Morag. I've had a bad vibe about Selina ever since she reappeared in our lives. That woman is bad news,' I thumped the table to emphasise my point. 'You mark my words. She's trouble. With a capital T.'

It was no good. I needed to speak to Stevie.

After Morag had left, I tried ringing my ex at his place of work. The telephonist told me he was out of the office and on site. I called his mobile. It went to voicemail. So I busied myself stripping beds, and tried not to shred pillowcases in frustration. Finally, at lunchtime, I tracked Stevie down to a watering hole just off Leicester Square.

'Hey Cass,' Stevie shouted above the noise of music and City chatter. I had a mental picture of him perched on a tall chrome stool popping an olive in his mouth between sips of white wine spritzer. 'Everything okay? Nothing wrong with the kids is there?'

'Everything is fine Stevie.'

'Ah, so this is a social call.'

'Um. Sort of. I just wondered if everything was now okay at home with Charlotte? I mean,' I studied my fingernails, 'it must have been quite late by the time you drove back from Greenwich. Was Charlotte cross?'

A pause. 'She was asleep. In the spare room.'

'But you did see her?'

'Well no, not last night. As I said, she was in the spare room. And I didn't want to disturb her. By the way, your new best friend is very charming. Selina,' he added. Not that any explanation was needed.

'Selina is not my best friend.'

Stevie chuckled. 'Well she's clearly under the impression she is. Holds you in very high esteem. It was *Cass this* and *Cass that*. Banged on and on about what a fabulous person you were, what a great house you lived in, and what fantastic kids you had. Two of which are mine of course.'

Clearly Selina's flattery was all part of buttering Stevie up.

'Well never mind that. Getting back to Charlotte. You saw her this morning?'

Another pause. Slightly longer this time. 'Um. Yeah. But briefly. She was very frosty with me.'

The first lie. God I was so glad Stevie was no longer my life partner. No wonder Charlotte had finally naffed off. Clearly Stevie just hadn't realised this as yet. Oh well. He would tonight. When he *really* went home.

'Well I hope things settle down soon.'

'Thank you Cass. I didn't know you cared about me so much.'

'I don't. But I do about Charlotte. Toodle-oo.' I hung up. Stared at the mobile thoughtfully. Stevie hadn't mentioned anything about seeing Selina again. But thanks to Morag's gossip, I knew the pair of them would indeed be hooking up. I wondered which yard they'd go to. Why did Selina want to dally with the likes of Stevie when she had a golden future all mapped out? Why risk jeopardising it all?

I spent the rest of the day working my way through chores as quickly as a six month old baby permitted. Edna came home just as I was about to set off for the school run. She breezed through the door looking like Mrs Doubtfire after a stint with a bottle of sherry. Cheeks very flushed.

'Cassandra dear,' she beamed. 'Leave Eddie with me. You'll be able to drive a bit faster without him.' She took my babe and gave him a resounding kiss on the cheek, before twirling him around a few times. Eddie squealed with joy. I wasn't used to my mother-in-law being so openly demonstrative. Or doing happy jigs. Or grinning foolishly.

'Okay,' I smiled at my mother-in-law, 'thanks. That would be very helpful.' I needed to get back into the kids' good books after making them so catastrophically late this morning. 'Did you have a good meeting with Arthur?' I ventured. 'Discuss lots of, um, boating stuff?'

Edna stopped dancing about for a moment. 'Yes, thank you Cassandra dear. In fact, I wanted a word with you about our project.'

'Oh?'

'I was going to go home tomorrow night, but–' she hesitated.

'What is it Edna?'

'Well Eddie's little rocking horse is pretty much finished. Just a final bit of paintwork and then it can sit in his nursery ready for him to grow into. Arthur and I would very much like to get started on the boat. It would be wonderful if we could use your garage. It's so big. An ideal working space.'

'Of course you can Edna. Jamie and I never bother putting our cars away. Use it for the duration.'

'That's marvellous. Thank you dear. And would you mind terribly if I stayed a few more nights. Just while Arthur and I start the ball rolling so to speak.'

'Not at all.' I paused. Would this mean Arthur would be staying here too? I had a sudden vision of Edna and a silver-haired gentleman tucked up together on the pull-out bed. My expression must have been an open book. Edna immediately went to great lengths to point out that Arthur lived only two roads away, and could be here in minutes, whereas her own house was a good hour away.

'Well I'd better get my skates on,' I picked up the keys to the Muck Truck. Turning to Eddie I kissed the top of my son's head. 'Be a good boy for Nanny.'

On the drive to Boxleigh Grammar, my thoughts strayed back to Stevie and Selina. Should I tell Jamie? He would probably dismiss it in the first instance as nothing other than gossip by Morag. Which of course it was. But, I frowned, if Jamie *was* concerned, might he not feel that he should tell Ethan? Was it fair to put him in a potentially invidious position? And would Ethan appreciate being told? Would he not be embarrassed that his business partner knew he was being cuckolded? I sighed and leant back in the driver's seat. For all Morag's talk, I needed hard evidence. Something a little more definite than a crossed out entry in a riding school's diary. I signalled right and drove into Boxleigh Road. I wouldn't say anything to Jamie for now. I'd do a bit of detective work first. Like finding out the nearest riding school to Matt and Morag's equestrian centre – and maybe paying it a visit this Sunday.

Chapter Eleven

'Ooh, something smells interesting,' said Jamie. He sniffed the air cautiously as he came through the front door. A blast of wintry air whipped around the hallway.

'Shepherds pie,' I smiled. 'All my own work.'

'Jolly good. I'm absolutely starving.'

I could sense my husband trying to muster enthusiasm as he shrugged off his suit jacket. He slung it over the banister. It landed on a pile of kids' coats. This family seemed to have a total allergy to pegs, coat hangers and wardrobes. I made a mental note to put them all away at some point, and followed Jamie through to the kitchen. He washed his hands at the sink, before parking his bottom on a chair at the kitchen table.

'Am I too late to eat with the family tonight?'

''fraid so darling,' I rummaged around in the range and extracted a plated meal. 'We had dinner at six.' I set the steaming food before my husband. 'You're late tonight. I thought you said half seven. It's gone eight.'

'Sorry. Ethan will be back on Monday, so things will be a little easier.' Jamie regarded the meal before him. Sock-grey mince, dubious mash and anaemic peas. He picked up his fork gamely.

'I thought Ethan *was* back from America.' I pulled up a chair and sat down.

'He is. But jet-lagged. So he spent today working from home. We've been on the phone to each other throughout the day. By the way, Ethan wants us to celebrate the American success. So we're out to dinner with him and Selina tomorrow night. Oh Cassie don't look at me like that.'

I exhaled slowly. Counted to ten. 'Right,' I said lightly. 'I shall look forward to it. What are we eating this time? Raw turnip and sprout crudités?'

Jamie put down his fork. Took my hand. 'You will be very pleased to know we shall be eating out. A posh restaurant this time. The Oxo Tower.'

My mouth dropped open. The Oxo Tower! For the uninitiated, this is a restaurant that is quite simply the bee's knees. Owned by Harvey Nicks, slotted into a prime spot on the South Bank of the River Thames, this would be a whole new experience in arty farty dining. And knowing I wasn't going to be subjected to Selina's raw food offerings, the menu would most definitely be arty rather than farty.

'Can I presume from your bemused expression that you are feeling somewhat happier?' Jamie asked.

'Oh yes,' I nodded, 'much, much happier.'

'Thank God for that,' Jamie closed his eyes, apparently offering a prayer of thanks upwards.

Before I could make any further comment about Selina and the impending restaurant date, the kitchen door opened. Gusts of cold air swirled around our ankles as Edna came in. Hello. Somebody was following in her wake.

'Good evening my dears.' She ushered a tall silver-haired man into the warmth of the kitchen. 'I'd like you both to meet Arthur.'

For the second time in as many minutes I found my mouth dropping open. Jamie immediately stood up and greeted Arthur properly. The men pumped hands chummily.

'A pleasure to meet you Arthur. We've heard a bit about you, haven't we darling?' Jamie turned to me. I stood up too, scraping my chair noisily.

'Hello Arthur.' I also shook his hand. Arthur's grip was firm. Clearly a no-nonsense person. Like Edna. 'I'm Cassandra. But do call me Cass.'

'Good evening to you both,' Arthur smiled warmly. 'Don't let me stop you from having your meal Jamie. Please, carry on.'

Jamie's smile faltered. 'Um, I think I was just about finished actually.' He turned to me. 'That was absolutely delicious darling.'

I whisked the plate away. 'Do sit down Arthur. Can I get you coffee? Or tea? You both look frozen.' I transferred Jamie's leftovers into a cat bowl. Perhaps Wallace and Gromet would eat it. Reaching for the kettle, I blasted in some water.

'A cup of strong coffee would be delightful Cass,' said Arthur. 'After you, Edna my love.' He pulled a chair out for my mother-in-law to sit upon.

'Why, thank you Arthur. Always such a gentleman,' Edna simpered, before sitting down.

I boggled into the kettle. My mother-in-law, usually made of incredibly stern stuff, was behaving in a way never witnessed before. Like a teenager. In the grip of a schoolgirl crush. I risked a glance at Jamie. He was looking slightly bemused. He caught my eye. His look said it all. *I'm totally unprepared for this.* I turned my attention back to the kettle, popped its lid down and flicked the switch.

'So!' Jamie rubbed his hands together in a matey way. 'I hear there are plans to build a boat. Is that right?'

And Arthur was off. He joyfully told Jamie about his seafaring days in the Merchant Navy, his position as Master Mariner, and worldwide travels on the waves. I slid mugs in front of them, and silently took my seat. Edna was adding her tuppence worth too – talking excitedly about the shell of a boat they'd found at a yacht club. Plans were afoot to add to the framework, and then refurbish. Now back to Arthur who was waxing lyrical about the pros and cons of diesel engines against petrol. Jamie's eyes were on stalks. Now Edna again, gabbling about somebody loaning a trailer to transport this twenty footer to Lavender Hill where it would be transformed into a cabin cruiser; back to Arthur now thanking Jamie for agreeing to lend our well-proportioned garage for the duration – I avoided Jamie's gaze as he gawped incredulously at me – but once again Edna had picked up the reins of conversation and was rattling on about sailing routes that encompassed the Isle of Skye, Ireland, the Isle of Man, and sailing down the west coast, before once again Arthur picked up the conversational thread and told us about their even bigger plans to eventually do a continental trip. Judging from their blissful expressions, both of them had mentally reached Nirvana. Dear God. This couple were in their seventies. What was wrong with a retirement spent in front of the telly wearing his 'n' her bobble slippers? Just at that moment there was a cry from the baby monitor.

'Please excuse me,' I murmured, before slipping away. I don't think Edna and Arthur even noticed me go. They were lost in an exciting world of ocean adventure. I padded into Eddie's nursery. 'Hello little man. Why have you woken up? Oh pooh!'

I picked Eddie up, laid him down on his changing mat and unbuttoned his romper suit. Nothing like a stinky nappy to remind one that life wasn't all sailing boats and sunshine. As I set to work with wipes and Sudocrem, I wondered if Nell might be doing the very same thing now she was back home with baby Rosie. I would telephone her. Just as soon as I'd strapped my son into this clean nappy.

'Keep still for Mummy, there's a good boy.' Eddie energetically kicked his plump little legs and knocked the nappy out of my grasp. 'Oh no! Stop!' My son chuckled with laughter as pee shot straight up in the air and arced over my sweater. Marvellous. Start again.

By the time I'd settled Eddie and changed my top, Arthur had gone and Edna had taken herself off for a bath. I tracked Jamie down in the lounge, slumped in front of the television. Toby and Jonas were either side of him, their sprawling bodies aping that of my husband. He looked up as I stood in the doorway.

'You don't mind if I catch a bit of footie do you?'

'Only if you don't mind me holing up in the study with the phone for the next hour. I want to chat with Nell.'

Jamie waved a hand. 'Take as long as you like. Me and the lads are fine.'

'Boys, isn't it past your bedtime?' I asked.

'Aw Mum, please let us stay up and watch the football. It's Friday. No school tomorrow.'

'Oh okay,' I sighed. It was easier to give in. I had a quick check on Petra and Livvy. They were both in their respective bedrooms and on their mobile phones. It transpired they were talking to each other. Nothing like wasting their contract minutes. I shook my head in disbelief. Again it was easier to give in than moan. Once back downstairs, I barricaded myself into the study and picked up the phone.

'Nellie-Wellie!' I grinned into the handset. 'How's it all going?'

'Cass?' my friend squawked. In the background, all hell seemed to be breaking loose. I could hear Ben rumbling furiously at Dylan who in turn was answering back in a pre-teen slang that I could barely understand. This was followed by a blood-curdling yell fit to perforate eardrums. The sound of a newborn's wails joined the cacophony. Nell promptly burst into tears.

'I-I can't cope,' my friend sobbed. 'I'm totally out of my depth. Should never have had another b-baby. Dylan is jealous. And Ben's as much use as a boil on the b-bum. And R-Rosie won't feed.'

'Stay right there. I'm coming over.'

'Cass, it's nearly ten o'clock. I can't drag you out. You have your own baby to see to.'

'Eddie is fast asleep. I also have a hands-on husband and a mother-in-law at the helm.' Although Edna would be transferring to a boat's helm in due course, but no matter. We would survive. That's why Mr Heinz had invented baked beans. To save families like mine from the dubious culinary skills of mothers like me. 'See you soon.' I rattled the phone down and picked up my car keys.

When I went into the lounge to tell Jamie about my imminent departure, he and the boys were doing a war dance up and down the sofa's edge.

'They scored darling!' Jamie beamed before high-fiving Jonas and Toby.

'I couldn't be more thrilled,' I replied. Football left me cold. A lot of men rolling around in mud, one minute snogging each other, the next sitting on top of each other. Or was that rugby? Either way, I was immune. 'Nell's having a crisis. I may be a while.'

'Oh dear. Baby blues?'

'Possibly. Listen out for Eddie.'

'Will do. Give Nell my love. Oh no ref! That's a foul!'

I left them to it. Removing my coat from the heap over the banister – I really *must* put this little lot away – I went out into the freezing night.

When I pulled up outside Nell's house, I could hear the rumpus within from the driveway. Neighbours' net curtains were twitching. I rang the bell. After a minute or two, Ben flung the door open. To say he looked harassed was an understatement. He was sporting a deep gash on the forehead after fainting in the hospital delivery room.

'Adjusting to the impact of a new addition?' I smiled.

'Cass!' Ben rubbed one hand over his forehead and promptly winced. 'Dear God. It's like World War Three in here. Nothing I do is right. And Dylan's playing up. I'd have thought an eleven year old wouldn't be resentful, but guess I got that wrong too.'

'I'm not jealous,' a voice snarled. I looked beyond Ben to see Dylan standing on the bottom stair. His face was chalk-white, eyes puffy from crying. Dylan was in the same class as Liv and Toby. Unlike my twins, puberty had paid an early visit. A fine down of dark hair covered his upper lip. He'd shot up almost overnight and was a good head taller than Toby. His pyjama bottoms were about five inches too short. He made an incongruous sight, the boy-man in his Star Wars pyjamas.

'Hi Dylan,' I pushed past Ben who closed the door after me. 'What's up?' I watched as Dylan wrestled with his emotions. He'd known me all his life. We were very fond of each other. But clearly he was struggling to switch off the Rude Button.

'You're no better than him!' Dylan jerked his head towards his father. 'Having babies,' he enlightened me. 'It's disgusting. I know all about sex Cass! We've had the lessons at school. There's no way people of your age should be–' Dylan floundered while his brain sought the appropriate word to convey his revulsion.

'Okay,' I shrugged off my coat, 'thanks for sharing your opinion Dylan. Very thoughtful of you. Meanwhile, where's Mum?'

'Upstairs,' Dylan spat, 'trying to shove her tits into Rosie's mouth.'

'Good God!' I feigned shock. 'It shouldn't be allowed should it? Whatever shall we do?'

'Buy formula milk!' Dylan howled.

'Absolutely,' I agreed. 'And presumably you'd do the same if Rocket had puppies?'

Dylan looked perplexed. 'What are you talking about Cass? Rocket is an animal. It's nature for mammals to suckle their young.'

'So it is. You're absolutely right Dylan. I'll leave you with that thought while you make me a cup of coffee. Oh, and two Hob Nobs please. The dinner I made earlier was absolutely ghastly and I'm feeling somewhat peckish.'

I marched past Dylan and took the stairs two at a time. I found Nell in the master bedroom perched on the edge of the bed. One of her boobs hung redundantly out of her nightie, rejected by Rosie. Both mother and daughter were bawling heartily. Next to the bed sat Rocket, a picture of trembling concern. I was reminded of Nana, the dog from Peter Pan, gamely attempting to look after her family. Nell glanced up as I walked in.

'I d-don't know what to do,' she wailed.

'Oh Nell. You big silly. Of course you know what to do.' I went over to my friend and put an arm around her shoulder. 'Put your boob away and let Rosie calm down. Give her to me for a minute.' I took the tiny infant from Nell. Crumbs. I'd forgotten how weeny a newborn was. It made me realise how much Eddie had grown. He was like a heffalump compared to Rosie's fragility. I placed the baby over my shoulder, and gently rubbed her back. 'Hush little one, hush,' I crooned. Nell re-arranged herself, and then reached for some tissues by the bed. She blew her nose noisily.

'I'm bleedin' knackered. Ben's absolutely useless at putting meals on the table. He hasn't even walked the dog today.'

'Well he is recovering from concussion Nell. That cut looks nasty. Couldn't Dylan have taken Rocket out for you earlier on, after school?'

'Dylan!' Nell snorted. 'He's too busy telling us how disgusting we are for *doing it*. Like we're dinosaurs or something.'

'But he must have known for ages you and Ben still *do it* – unless he's spent the last nine months totally oblivious to your bump. Did he seem upset about it when you were pregnant?'

'No. Not at all. Quite the opposite. He was delighted to be having a little brother or sister. Kept telling me he couldn't wait to help. It's so hurtful hearing him talking like this. I can't understand what's come over him.'

'I'll have a chat with him in a minute. Meanwhile, your darling daughter has gone very quiet.' I transferred Rosie into the cradling position and peered at her. She was almost asleep. 'Here. Try putting her to the breast now. See what happens.'

Nell took the drowsy infant. Within seconds Rosie had latched on. She began to suck contentedly.

'You're a genius!' Nell gave a watery smile.

'It's a trick I used when Eddie was initially refusing to nurse. I think sometimes anxiety can run high on both sides. When they're almost asleep, it removes the fretfulness.' I smiled at the sight before me. 'In six months time you'll be begging my help on weaning. Back in a bit. Let me find your son.'

In fact I nearly tripped over Dylan as I left Nell's bedroom. Clearly he'd been ear-wigging.

'Your coffee's ready,' he growled.

'Thank you. Come on,' I led the way, 'we need to talk.'

'I have nothing to say to you Cass.'

'That's fine. But I have plenty to say to you.' I steered Dylan into the kitchen. 'Sit down.'

Dylan sat. His back was rigid, jaw set. For a moment his face worked furiously, but he remained silent. I could hear the football on in the lounge. Ben had absented himself and was clearly watching the same match as Jamie.

'So,' I dragged a stool out and perched opposite Dylan. 'What's it all about eh?'

'What's what all about?' Dylan scowled.

'Oh come on Dylan.' I took a sip of coffee. 'I'm talking about this attitude. This,' I gestured with one hand, '*anger*. Why? Only a few days ago you couldn't wait to welcome the baby. Said you wanted to push the buggy around the park. Help Mum with nappies. You even hinted at getting up in the night to Rosie – not that your mother would allow that, she doesn't want you tired for school. So what's changed all that?'

Dylan visibly slumped. 'You don't understand,' he mumbled. A tear suddenly rolled down one cheek. It plopped onto the table. He sniffed noisily.

'Try me,' I said gently.

Dylan took a deep breath. 'I'm being teased. At school. Ridiculed.'

'In what way?' I was baffled. Nobody had given the twins a hard time when Eddie had been born.

'It's Richard Clegg. The class bully. He's a prat. He overheard me saying how I couldn't wait to help Mum. With the baby. You know – stuff. Like bathing Rosie. I was talking to Katie Wells about it. And Katie was being all girlie and saying things like, "How cute, I'm so jealous," and then I told Katie that I'd saved up my pocket money and bought a teddy from Mothercare. Next thing I know is Richard Clegg – on my way home from school – scooping up a load of wet leaves and shoving them down the back of my neck,' Dylan took a shuddering gasp, 'and there were some worms caught up in the leaves Cass and–' he faltered. Looked embarrassed. 'I don't like worms. I went mental.'

'What, mental as in punching Richard Clegg's lights out?'

'No,' Dylan looked ashamed. 'Mental as in having a hissy fit like one of the girls. I began screaming. Grabbing at my back. Trying to pull everything out, but too frightened to touch the leaves in case my hand came in contact with worms.' Dylan paused. His face wrestled with emotions while he struggled for composure.

'Weren't you walking with anybody? Someone who could have helped you?'

'No. I was on my own.'

'So what did you do next?'

'I had no choice but to strip off down to my waist. In front of all the passing traffic. Richard Clegg thought it was hysterical. He and his mates – the class Chavs – cracked up. And now they all call me gay. Tell me I'm like a big girl and want to be a Mummy because I bought something at Mothercare. And he's started calling Mum and Dad names. Disgusting names. Because they still,' he broke off, 'you know.'

'Have a love life,' I concluded.

Dylan nodded. Studied his fingernails. 'It's embarrassing Cass. *I'm* embarrassed. If Mum and Dad hadn't had Rosie, if things had stayed as they were,' he shrugged, 'then I wouldn't have been excited about it. Wouldn't have got caught out about Mothercare. Wouldn't have had muck shoved down my back or behaved like a cry-baby. Wouldn't now be listening to daily filth–' he broke off. Steered the conversation down a different route. 'Seeing Mum struggling to feed Rosie,' Dylan closed his eyes, 'just set Richard Clegg's voice off in my head. Horrible words. I can't tell you Cass.'

'Do Livvy and Toby know about this?' I asked. 'Have they seen you being bullied?'

'No. Nobody sees. Apart from Richard Clegg's mates. He's clever. Picks his moments. Makes it look like we're having fun. Being *boys*,' he spat.

'Well you must report him Dylan.'

'I can't do that. It would just make things worse.'

'You must be twice the size of Richard Clegg. Can't you beat him up?' Heavens Cass, what are you suggesting here? I blanched. Is this the sort of advice a sensible adult should be handing out to an eleven year old?

'I'd love to beat him up. And yes I am miles taller than Richard Clegg. But he's wider. And heavier. He'd flatten me Cass. Please don't tell Mum about it. She'd only worry. Or Dad. He'd tell the school and then things would go nuclear.'

I nodded my head slowly. 'Okay. But I *am* going to tell my bunch. I want them sticking to you like glue Dylan. Don't allow yourself to be alone with this bully. All right? And no more walking home either.'

'I don't want Mum picking me up,' Dylan looked horrified. 'Richard Clegg might shout out foul names to her.'

'All right. In which case *I'll* drop you home.'

'But that will take you out of your way Cass.'

'Only by a few minutes. It's not a problem.'

'Can this be our secret?'

I hesitated. If the boot were on the other foot, would I want Nell not telling me? The answer was categorically no. However, Nell was currently hormonal, knackered and adjusting to life with a newborn. 'It can be our secret only if you promise to let me regularly know what is happening and to allow Liv, Toby, Petra and Jonas to help. If things get worse though, then obviously I'll have to speak up. Okay?'

Dylan nodded. 'Okay,' he mumbled. 'I feel a bit better having shared the problem with you.'

'Good,' I leant across the table and ruffled his hair. 'A problem shared is a problem halved. Meanwhile, how about you go and say sorry to your Mum and Dad while I finish my coffee and biscuits.'

Dylan gave me a watery smile. 'Thanks Cass.'

He disappeared out of the kitchen leaving me to munch thoughtfully on a Hob Nob. Why were children sometimes so cruel to each other? And what was going on in Richard Clegg's life that made him feel the need to be such a toe-rag to Dylan?

Ben wandered in, hands stuffed in pockets. 'Footie's finished. Liverpool Won. Scouse gits.'

'Charming.'

Ben shrugged. 'Where's Lord Voldemort gone?'

'Upstairs to see Nell. He'll be back down in a tick to see you too.'

'Not sure I'm up for any more hysterics,' Ben pulled out a stool and sat down heavily.

'Go with it Ben. Dylan has a lot on his plate at the moment.'

'And I don't? Christ. I nearly miss my daughter being born. End up in Casualty with concussion. Have a hysterical wife telling me she can't cope. A demented son behaving like the villain in a Harry Potter film. A newborn that I can't touch because Nell tells me I'm a rubbish dad. In the last twenty-four hours I've come this close,' Ben held a thumb and forefinger millimetres apart, 'to packing a suitcase and sodding off.'

'You're not a rubbish dad,' a voice piped up. Nell stood framed in the doorway, Dylan by her side. They had their arms around each other. She released Dylan and walked over to Ben. 'Sorry if I've been a bitch. I love you.' Ben reached up and pulled Nell onto his lap.

'I love you too,' he kissed his wife. 'And how are you now Dylan?' Ben looked across at his son. Extended a hand. Dylan walked over and took it. Allowed himself to be pulled onto Ben's other knee.

'Sorry Dad. For everything. Of course I'm pleased about Rosie. I just lost my cool.'

'But you're cool now?'

'Yeah.'

'Good,' Ben hugged his son hard.

I stood up. 'Right folks, I'd best be off. Is Rosie asleep?'

'Absolutely sparko,' Nell smiled wearily. 'I'm going to get my head down too. While the going is good.'

'That sounds like a wonderful idea,' Ben tipped Nell and Dylan off his knees. 'Thank you Cass for coming over and restoring calm to this household.'

'You're welcome,' I smiled and walked out to the hallway.

'I owe you,' Nell said as she opened the front door.

'Indeed. And I will call in the favour Sunday morning.'

'Why's that?'

'Because something is happening tomorrow night. Something I'm not particularly looking forward to,' I paused on the step.

'Oh?'

'I'm out. At the Oxo Tower no less.'

Nell gasped. 'You lucky cow! Oh for a husband like Jamie. To be wined and dined in such style.'

I smiled thinly. 'Also with Ethan and his delectable fiancée. Selina.'

'Oh. Ouch.'

'Yes. Ouch indeed. So Sunday morning, coffee and Hob Nobs at yours. I'll be needing to bend your ear and vent my spleen.'

Nell rubbed her hands together gleefully. 'I shall look forward to it. Tell Morag to come along too.'

I stepped out into the cold night air. 'It's a date.'

Chapter Twelve

Swishing back the curtains the following morning, I gasped with delight. Jack Frost had visited. Lavender Common sparkled like a glittery Christmas card. A couple of Saturday morning dog walkers were puffing along one of the steeper inclines, their warm breath clouding the cold air. A robin landed on the window ledge completing the post-Christmas festive look. I sighed with happiness. On mornings like this it was so damn good to be alive. I raised my eyebrows in surprise at such an acknowledgment. I'd felt so half-dead with tiredness these last few months, it struck me that my life had turned a corner. A better corner. A place where optimism reigned. Where energy levels were restored. Where achieving anything was possible. All because my darling baby boy had once again slept through the night and – I cocked an ear towards the baby monitor – was still apparently sleeping! It was amazing what a few hours of uninterrupted slumber did to the human body. And libido. My eyes flicked to Jamie, snoring soundly on his side of the double bed. He still made me go weak at the knees. Even with his mouth hanging open and making sounds like a farrowing pig. I padded over to my side of the bed. Peeling off my nightclothes, I slid under the duvet.

'Oh lover boy,' I cooed. My fingers walked across the flat sheet to my husband's body. 'Wake up Jamie. Your slave is here,' I murmured, 'your *sex* slave. Come to service you.' My fingers made contact with Jamie's torso. And began to travel down.

Suddenly my wrist was caught in a vice-like grip. 'Ah ha!' Jamie shot upright and pinned one hand over my head. 'Sex slave eh?' He found my other wrist and whizzed that one over my head too. 'So, wench. You've come into my bed offering to do all manner of debauched things.' He regarded me. 'And what be your name, fair maiden?'

Jamie seemed to have launched into a pirate accent. I had an overwhelming desire to laugh. And then I thought of Morag. No doubt she'd instantly throw herself into some role playing. Absolutely relish it. I mentally squared up to the task. If Morag was happy to hop over horse jumps and visit imaginary stud farms, then I was pretty damn sure I could immerse myself in a spot of sea-faring shenanigans.

'Oh kind sir, be gentle with me now.'

'Ah harrrr! You should have thought of that before you disturbed the Cap'n from his slumber. I ask again. Your name?'

'Penelope sir.'

'Pen–?'

'Penelope Cruz. And I'm *hot* for you Cap'n Depp. Oh aye, ooh-arrrr. Hot for being spanked, hot for walking the plank, hot for–' I hesitated. The only word that came to mind was *wank*. What else went on in a pirate's world? '–some hanky-pank.'

'What–?'

Using all my strength I pushed my wrists upward and rolled my body to the right. Jamie flipped over and suddenly I was astride him. I gazed down at him.

'I'm gonna show you the real meaning of Jolly Roger.'

The ensuing romp was feisty to say the least. Well, on my part. I don't think Jamie knew what had hit him – a Force Ten gale or a wrestle with a wannabe actress re-enacting Pirates of the Caribbean. Five minutes later it was all over. My husband staggered off to the en-suite looking not so much rogered as wrecked. I lay back on the rumpled bed covers feeling pretty damn smug. Morag eat your heart out.

An hour later, we all piled into the Muck Truck. Jamie drove us to Matt's equestrian centre. The four older children peeled off to the stables to spend the day mucking out, riding their ponies and cleaning tack. Later they would return smelling of manure and sporting nails the colour of a blackboard. I shoved such thoughts away as Matt, on his return to the house, buttonholed Jamie.

'Mac!' he greeted my husband by the nick-name he'd called him for years. 'I'm absolutely frozen,' Matt rubbed his hands together and stamped his feet. 'Come on in and have a coffee with me. Hello sweetheart,' Matt pecked my cheek, 'Morag will be overjoyed to see you. She's been itching to have a shopping session. Why don't you two girlies go to Fairview for a bit?' he fished in his pocket for the front door key.

'Good idea,' said Jamie, 'you could buy yourself a nice dress for tonight.'

'Is he wining and dining you, Cass?' asked Matt with a grin.

'As such, yes,' I smiled back, 'although the boss and his fiancée will be there too. So it won't be romantic.'

'Ah!' said Matt. His tone indicated he understood the delicacy of the situation – that Selina would be there. 'And where is the venue?'

'The Oxo Tower,' said Jamie. 'So you make sure,' my husband turned to me, 'that you buy yourself a rocking frock, okay? Nothing but the best for Mrs Mackerel.' My husband fished in his back pocket for his wallet, and pulled out a wad of notes.

'Thanks darling.' I took the money, and kissed my husband's cheek.

'Oh God,' Matt inserted his key into the lock, 'don't tell Mrs Harding or I'll never hear the end of it.'

The front door opened before Matt could turn the key. 'Never hear the end of what?' asked Morag.

I smiled. 'I'm going shopping. Want to come?'

Morag snorted. 'With Henry and Eddie? Not likely. If I'm going shopping I'll want to try on dresses, and have a civilised coffee in John Lewis. Not spend my time charging in and out of assorted mother and baby rooms, suffering one interruption after another.'

'The boys can stay with us,' said Matt.

I looked at Jamie. 'Is that all right with you?'

'Of course. Go on. Take the money and run.'

'What money?' asked Morag beadily.

'Here you are,' Matt sighed and pulled out his wallet. 'That's the livery money for Snowden's stabling. Don't spend it all at once.'

'I will,' Morag blew Matt a kiss. 'Come on Cass. Freedom beckons.'

Minutes later we were in Morag's spotless Ford Galaxy heading along the motorway to Fairview. On the way I brought Morag up to speed regarding the impending dinner date with Ethan and Selina.

'I'm sure everything will be fine,' Morag soothed.

'And I'm sure it won't,' I gazed stonily out the window. We were overtaking a red Astravan. At that moment, the driver glanced sideways. Flashed a puzzled look. I stared back. Frowned. He looked familiar. Morag edged the Galaxy past. 'I've said it before,' my neck swivelled slightly as I held the driver's gaze, 'and I'll say it again. I don't trust Selina as far as I can throw her.'

Morag grinned. 'All the same, I can't wait to hear how the evening goes!'

The Astravan appeared to now be accelerating, closing the distance between our respective vehicles. 'By the way,' I continued staring at the driver, 'we're meeting at Nell's tomorrow morning for Hob Nobs and a post-mortem on the evening.' The van driver and I recognised each other at exactly the same moment. He levelled alongside the Galaxy. A synchronised buzzing down of windows took place.

'Nice to see you've given up driving,' he shouted.

'Nice to be overtaking you,' I yelled back.

'Cass?' Morag risked taking her eyes off the road. 'What the devil are you playing at? Put the window up. You're freezing my tits off.'

'You're a silly tart!' yelled the van driver.

'And you're a stupid fart.'

'Bitch!'

'Bastard!'

'Right you fucking cow – I'm coming after you!'

'CASS! PUT THE FRIGGING WINDOW UP!' Morag roared just as the van driver panned the floor and pulled out on us. Morag swerved to avoid a collision. Fortunately there was nothing travelling close behind us. 'For Christ's sake Cass, what the hell's going on?'

'Shit. I wasn't expecting him to do that.'

'Who is he?'

'Somebody I had an exchange of words with on New Year's Eve. He gave me a mouthful when I was driving home from Tesco too slowly.'

'Great. So now I have to deal with a road rage lunatic in front of me. Why did you have to answer him back?'

'I guess I was a bit fired up talking about Selina.'

'Well isn't this just fab,' Morag growled as she hit the brakes, thus avoiding crashing into the back of the van. 'He's now playing stop-start silly buggers. Right. He's winding me up now. Enough.' She tooted her horn. The van blared back. 'Time to ditch this guy.'

Morag edged out enough to be seen in the van driver's wing mirror, and then indicated right. The van immediately pulled out to block her from overtaking. Whereupon Morag checked her rear-view mirror for traffic coming up behind. There was none within striking distance. Still indicating right, she instead chucked a sharp left. We took off down a slip road leaving the motorway altogether. The Astravan sailed on. Furious that he'd been outwitted, a horn filtered back to us.

Morag took her foot off the accelerator. The Galaxy's speedometer instantly dropped.

'Geez Cass. These days, whenever I'm with you, I seem to be running away from burly men.' Morag checked some signs at a roundabout before turning left.

'Nonsense,' I could feel myself bristling.

'Yeah? I seem to remember it was only five minutes ago we were holed up in a Wendy House on stilts in a kids' playground.'

I sighed. 'That wasn't my fault. It was Rocket's.'

'Yes, but you were in charge of her.'

'Correction. *We* were in charge of her.'

'Well if you could just stay out of trouble for five minutes while we go shopping, I'd quite like a civilised few hours.'

'Sorry,' I huffed.

'Forgiven.' Morag guided the Galaxy into one of the many car parks at Fairview. 'And stop sulking.'

'I'm not sulking!' I sulked.

'I'll buy you coffee if you drop the strop.'

'Okay,' I perked up.

We made our way into Fairview, and immediately headed to Costa's.

'So we're meeting at Nell's tomorrow morning?' Morag stirred a sweetener into her black coffee.

'Yes. We'd better buy a new baby gift for Rosie while we're here.'

'Good thinking. I must say, I'm looking forward to seeing little Rosie and having a cuddle. I've been feeling quite broody lately.'

I stared at Morag aghast. 'You've got to be kidding. How can you feel broody when you've barely given birth?'

Morag shrugged. 'I don't know. I guess it's my hormones. Apart from anything else, I don't want a big age gap between Henry and the next one.'

'Henry is only four months old. I thought you'd wait at least a couple of years before even thinking about nappies and broken nights again.'

'We'll see. Anyway, getting back to tomorrow. I'll pick you up. I want to be sure that if we bump into Mr Van Driver again, *I'm* behind the wheel.'

'Are you implying I'm no good at driving?' I spooned the foam up from my cappuccino.

'Let's just say you'd never make a great getaway driver.'

I shrugged. My days of being a girl-racer were long over. However, my days of being able to rev up in other areas clearly had some mileage left on the clock. I grinned to myself as I thought of this morning's bedroom antics with Jamie.

'Why are you looking so secretive all of a sudden?' demanded Morag.

I blushed. 'Nothing.'

'Don't give me that. You're all pink in the face. It's to do with sex isn't it?' Morag peered at me. 'Did you have a bonk this morning?'

To our right, a pair of permed pensioners threw Morag a disapproving look.

'Morag, *please*!' I whispered.

'I was right!' Morag crowed. She banged the table with the palm of one hand. 'Come on, spill the beans. There's obviously something to tell.'

'Oh all right,' I lowered my voice. 'Jamie pretended to be a pirate.'

'A pirate?' Morag frowned.

'Yes. You know. Johnny Depp.'

'Don't you mean Jack Sparrow?'

'Him too. And I was Penelope Cruz. His sex slave.'

'I'm not sure Jack Sparrow had a sex slave, Cass.'

'Well this morning Jack Sparrow DID, okay!' This time it was my turn to slap my palm down on the table. The permed pensioners looked in danger of swallowing their dentures.

'Okay. Keep your cutlass on,' Morag snorted into her coffee.

'You shouldn't be making fun of me,' I wiped coffee froth off my upper lip, 'I'm taking a leaf out of your book. Using my imagination for once. Getting my eye back on the ball, like you told me to do. And all without the aid of herbal sex jollop!' I cried.

The permed pensioners had had enough and were creaking off, backs as rigid as their walking sticks.

'Well I'm very glad to hear you have your mojo back. Meanwhile drink up Penelope. Retail therapy beckons.'

We set off to John Lewis and in no time at all had made short work in Glass and China buying a gift for Rosie. Hopping on an escalator, we alighted in the Designer section. I stopped dead in my tracks. Grabbed Morag's arm.

'Look!' I pointed. 'There's a little black dress over there with my name all over it.'

'You're right Cass. I can see you in that. Go and try it on.'

Inside the dressing room, I eyed my reflection with delight. What a superb piece of tailored engineering. Thanks to an in-built bra and girdle, wobbly bits had been moulded and re-positioned. My boobs looked like they'd been blown up with a bicycle pump and were actually on my chest, rather than my navel. And as for my backside – I turned sideways and preened – definitely Jennifer Lopez and not Danny DeVito.

Morag stuck her head around the curtain. 'How are you doing? Oh yes! Very glam Cass. What a transformation. A good dollop of slap and you'll look like a celebrity when you walk into the Oxo Tower tonight.'

I beamed with pleasure. 'And I see you've found something too,' I nodded at the sparkly fabric adorning Morag's shoulder. 'Let me see the rest of it.'

Morag swished the curtain all the way back, and joined me in my changing cubicle.

'Not too short is it?' she twirled this way and that, admiring her reflection in the mirror.

'Wow,' I sucked in my breath. The hemline seemed to be just below Morag's bust. 'Are you sure it's not a top?'

Morag continued to twist left and right. 'No, definitely a dress.'

'I don't think it does you justice,' I said carefully.

'You're right. I think I'll try on the purple bandage dress I saw on the Whistles rail. Won't be a mo.'

Several hours later, having finally exhausted our cash, we beetled back along the motorway, and in no time at all were at the stables. I transferred my shopping bags into the back of the Muck Truck, found Jamie and Eddie and, after another very quick coffee with Matt and Morag, we gathered the rest of the children up and headed home.

But as we drew close to Lilac Lodge, the driveway was blocked by a transporter. Perched askance, in all its ramshackle glory, was a boat. Although from this angle it looked more like an ocean liner. Edna and Arthur stood on the driveway, feet planted wide. Arthur gave the driver the thumbs up as the vehicle cleared the gatepost by a millimetre.

'Bloody hell,' I muttered.

'I don't think that's going to fit into the garage,' Jamie said faintly.

I slid out of the car. 'I'll leave you to assist them darling. I must crack on and get the kids fed. I want time to get ready for this evening.'

And so it was that a couple of hours later I found myself once again slipping into Jamie's BMW X5, and heading towards Greenwich. We were to leave our car in Ethan's underground car park, and then transfer to a taxi which would take us to the South Bank of the River Thames. For once I was pleased with my appearance. The cat's claw marks on my scalp and forehead had healed enough for a coating of foundation. My skin actually looked flawless. My recently highlighted hair fell like a waterfall over my shoulders. And, thanks to a dress that had cost an eye-watering amount of money, I appeared to have a bootylicious figure.

'By the way,' said Jamie interrupting my thoughts, 'I just want to say that I'd like you to wear that dress all the time. Morning, noon and night.'

'Why's that?'

'Because you look so damn good in it,' Jamie grinned.

'It wouldn't last five minutes with Eddie on my hip. I hope Edna doesn't feel too put upon with all this extended babysitting she's doing.'

'Of course she doesn't,' Jamie said dismissively.

'I'm not so sure. She looked like she was itching to roll up her sleeves and start on the boat restoration.'

'Ah yes. The boat. I didn't realise Mum and Arthur had got themselves a scaled down version of HMY Britannia.'

I giggled. 'It's a good thing our garage is the size of an aircraft hangar.'

'You're not kidding. Here we are,' Jamie slowed down and indicated right. An oncoming car gave way and flashed him to proceed. Suddenly the X5 was purring into the familiar underground car park. As if on cue, Ethan and Selina appeared from the lift and strolled over. I realised that a private taxi was

already parked and waiting for us. After initial greetings –
reserved on Ethan's part and overly enthusiastic on Selina's –
we settled into a Mercedes. Ethan plumped for the front
passenger seat. I found myself wedged between Selina and
Jamie in the back. It wasn't a comfortable ride. In more ways
than one.

Chapter Thirteen

I was glad to leave the confines of the Mercedes. Selina had been wearing a cloying perfume that had intoxicated my senses, but not in a pleasant way. It reminded me of a fragrance from long ago. Poison. The irony of the name wasn't lost on me.

We took the scenic lift – a mix of mirror and glass – to the restaurant. As it slowly crept up the iconic art-deco tower, I caught my breath at the view of the City spread below. The Capital's lights twinkled warmly. Up on the eighth floor, the restaurant was packed. Three white walls showcased one that was entirely of glass. For miles, diners could see the banks of the River Thames, and historical landmarks like Big Ben, Saint Paul's Cathedral and the immense London Eye. A team of waiters, dressed in black trousers and blue shirts, were working flat out. Conversation was buzzy, and everybody seemed to be having a good time. I hoped our party of four would loosen up a little, because conversation in the taxi had been stilted. A waiter showed us to our table. It was set with white linen, silver cutlery and a centrepiece candle. Throughout the restaurant a blue light pervaded, lending ambience to the atmosphere. The waiter pulled out blue leather chairs, and we sat down.

Ethan picked up a wine list. I ran my eye over it and nearly fell off the chair. The dessert wine wouldn't give much change from a hundred pounds.

'Champagne?' Ethan looked around the table.

'Definitely,' said Selina. 'I like my fizz.'

I didn't dare look at the price. 'Lovely,' I smiled. Personally I would have preferred to hoover up a gin and tonic. But then again, this wasn't our local pub serving chicken in a basket on a ring-stained table.

A minion handed out menus with much bowing and scraping, before hastening off to fetch the bubbly. Ethan cleared his throat.

'I'd just like to say thank you Cass for inviting Lena over for kitchen supper while I was in America. I really appreciated you looking after her, and extending such warm hospitality.'

'Not at all,' I inclined my head graciously, jaw rigid.

The waiter reappeared with the champagne, popped the cork and – to dutiful oohs and aahs – filled long-stemmed flutes.

'Cheers,' Ethan raised his glass. 'A toast to a triumphant business move – and here's to many more successes.' We all clinked glasses, and there was a pause while we sipped. 'Although it's nice to be home,' Ethan turned to Selina, 'and be with my beautiful fiancée again. Did you miss me darling?'

'Of course, hunny-bunny,' Selina pouted.

'Poor Lena hates her own company,' Ethan took another sip of champagne.

'Make the most of it,' I smiled and picked up the menu, 'before the children come along.' The champagne was delicious. Obscured by the *carte du jour*, I took a few more nifty glugs.

'Lena was so lonely the night before I came home, she stayed overnight with a friend,' said Ethan, 'didn't you angel?'

'Yes. Laura.'

I frowned. That wasn't right. The night before Ethan returned to the UK was when Stevie had driven Selina back to Greenwich. 'Really?' I asked.

'Yes,' Selina said again. 'After a little while I couldn't bear the four walls of the apartment. So I took a taxi round to an old school friend's place.'

'Given the lateness of the hour, that must have been one very accommodating school friend,' I murmured.

'She is,' Selina gave me a level look. Was it my imagination, or was she pissed off?

'Well at least you managed to ditch Stevie without any trouble,' said Jamie. 'I was half expecting him to do a number on you,' my husband guffawed with laughter. Nobody else joined in.

'Who's Stevie?' asked Ethan. The question was said in a mild enough tone, but there was an undercurrent of surprise that an unknown male had escorted his fiancée home.

'My ex-husband,' I informed Ethan helpfully. 'He turned up without warning while Selina was with us. He said it would be no trouble to pop Selina home afterwards.'

An expression of relief passed across Ethan's face. 'Then you must thank him for me Cass. Lives local to Greenwich does he?'

'No,' I smiled cheerfully, and disappeared behind my menu. In my peripheral vision I was aware of Selina giving me a murderous look. Good. Serve you right after inviting yourself into my home, sucking up to my kids, flirting with my mother-in-law and cuckolding your kind fiancée while you bonked my love rat of an ex-husband. I was aware the champagne was now hitting its spot very nicely. I'd better watch my consumption. It was all very well making Selina edgy, but I didn't want my mouth giving me away. Jamie had no idea about Stevie ringing Matt's stables for a horsy day out with Selina tomorrow, or later cancelling it to go riding elsewhere. Nor did Selina know that she'd been rumbled by Detectives Harding and Mackerel. I put my glass down, and pretended to study the menu. Selina leant across the table to inspect the cocktail list. Her wrist caught the end of my champagne flute and it wobbled precariously.

'Oops, sorry.' She righted the glass.

'No harm done,' I said coolly, before taking the drink from her. 'So did you have a good time at Laura's?'

Selina met my gaze head on. 'Great thanks.'

I wondered how Selina was going to ditch Ethan tomorrow in order to see Stevie. I didn't have long to find out.

'Laura and I go back a couple of decades. She's between husbands at the moment, so has loads of free time on her hands. She gets pretty lonely herself. In fact,' Selina turned to Ethan, 'I completely forgot to mention it darling, but Laura is very keen to see me again tomorrow.'

'Are fiancés included?' Ethan attempted playfulness.

'Of course,' Selina beamed. 'Laura is absolutely longing to be introduced. After all, she's heard so much about you.'

Calling Ethan's bluff, eh? My forehead muscles clung on to my eyebrows, lest they shot off my forehead. Clever move Selina. I focussed on the Starters. But would inviting Ethan along be a gamble that paid off? As I waited to find out, my eyes roved across the menu without absorbing a single dish.

'Another time,' Ethan patted Selina's hand. 'I'm still feeling pretty jet-lagged and would much prefer to veg out at home. You go and have fun'

'Only if you don't mind sweetums,' Selina squeezed Ethan's hand, 'because I wouldn't want you to feel abandoned.'

'I won't,' Ethan assured. 'Spend as long as you like with Laura. Just so long as you're home for me to tuck you up in bed.'

I stared grimly at some blurb about a lamb dish. The frilly description and niceties of buttered cabbage completely bypassed me. Watching Selina duping Ethan was sickening to witness. What a manipulative bitch.

'I'll definitely be back for bedtime,' Selina giggled, before leaning into Ethan. She whispered something in his ear, and he visibly melted. Putty in her hands. Where had I seen that before? Ah yes, when Stevie had been around her.

'So,' I put the menu down again, 'what do you and Laura have on the agenda for tomorrow?'

Selina looked taken aback that I should be so interested in her plans, but rallied. Clearly she was under the impression I was making an effort at being friendly. *Tolerating* her.

'Oh, this and that,' she shrugged, but failed to expand.

'I love Sundays,' I enthused. 'Indeed I plan to be out all day tomorrow. Lots of fresh air!'

Jamie looked slightly alarmed. This was news to him. 'Er, darling, I don't know what you have in mind but there's a very important football match I'd like to catch up with tomorrow–'

'No problem,' I waved my hand airily. 'I'm meeting up with Nell and Morag, so your footie is quite safe.'

'Oh good,' Jamie visibly relaxed. 'So what's Nell going to be doing with you and Morag in the Great Outdoors?' my husband looked perplexed. 'After all, she's just had a baby.'

'I'm borrowing Rocket. My friend's loopy red setter,' I added looking at Selina. 'Morag – my other friend – wants to walk the dog with me. She's very big on exercise. Rides horses too.'

'Does she?' asked Jamie in surprise.

'Well no, not yet. But she's learning. At night school.'

'Night school?' asked Selina.

'Yes, just to get to grips with the basics.'

Selina looked confused. 'Without a horse?'

'Yes. It's a sort of advanced stable management course. Except in the arena. At night. She's up to date with lunging. Perfected her trot and canter. Even been doing some cavaletti jumps. She jumped a whole stack of them the other night, including a small triple and wall.'

'All on her own two feet?' Selina's voice was dripping with sarcasm.

'That's right. She's going to be amazing when she finally gets into the saddle.'

Jamie seemed to be concentrating very hard on his hands.

'Are you sure you have the right sport?' Ethan appeared flummoxed. 'Your friend Morag sounds more like she's training to be a hurdle jumper.'

'She's doing that too,' I nodded. I reached for my champagne. Tossed it down my neck. This conversation needed redirecting. 'Do you run Selina?'

'Yes. On pavements.' Selina gave me a look reserved for the educationally subnormal. 'I do, however, ride horses from time to time. As it happens, Laura and I are horse riding tomorrow.'

'How marvellous! Where?'

'Where what?'

'Which yard?'

Selina gave me a curious look. An expression flickered across her face. Suspicion?

'Only you don't want to go to Pearson's,' I gabbled. 'I've heard all their hacks are ex-racehorses and completely hyped up. They can't trot past a hedgerow without trying to jump it.'

'Better introduce your friend Morag to them,' Selina remarked dryly, 'sounds like the perfect equine partnership.'

'Oh, very good Selina! Ah ha ha ha! And don't go to Glebe Farm because all their horses have one hoof in the grave. Not to mention ringworm. And lice.'

'Right,' Selina said faintly. 'Well Laura and I certainly won't be experiencing any of those problems. We're going to Maxwell's Equestrian Centre. They have a superb selection of pristine horses and ponies for all skill levels. More champagne Cass?'

'Thanks,' I slumped over the menu, verbally exhausted. Maxwell's. I had a rough idea where it was. Certainly Morag would know. I picked up my refilled glass and sucked greedily, just as a waiter zoomed over. He was clearly affronted that Selina had poured the champers rather than himself.

'I think we're ready to order,' Ethan said.

Were we? I'd spent so much time talking nonsense, I hadn't a clue what to have. I scanned the menu hastily.

'I'll have the wild mushroom and celeriac lasagne to start with,' Selina said.

'Excellent choice Lena,' Ethan nodded approvingly. 'I think I'll have the same. What about you Jamie?'

'The sweet potato waffle with the goat's cheese mousse sounds–' Jamie broke off. 'Are you all right Cass?'

I nodded. Although my head suddenly felt a bit peculiar. Clearly too much champagne on an empty stomach.

'Would Madame like some water?' asked the waiter.

'Yes, I think she would,' Jamie spoke for me. The waiter signalled to another to fetch a glass of water.

'And what would Madame like to start with?' asked the waiter.

'Just give me a moment,' I smiled, eyes glazing as I desperately tried to concentrate on the writing. I made an arm gesture. 'Perhaps everybody could order their Mains while I peruse.' There was a resounding silence. Had I suggested everybody order brains and booze? I shook my head again.

'Roast suckling pig for me please,' Ethan was the first to speak.

I zoned out while the waiter took the remaining orders. A second waiter appeared with the water. I picked up the glass and banged it painfully against my teeth. I couldn't remember the last time I'd felt so catastrophically drunk.

'Is Madame ready now?' asked the waiter.

I nodded and picked up the menu. Stared at it. The words danced before my eyes. I stabbed with an index finger. 'I'll have this, this, this and this.'

The waiter's face remained passive. 'So that's cheesecake, followed by poached pears, apple soufflé and spinach on the side?'

I gave him the thumbs up. Should one stick one's thumbs up at the Oxo Tower? I cast about to check. Apparently not. But alarmingly several diners did appear to be eating their dinner at some very strange angles. Perhaps the floor was tilting? I did feel incredibly giddy. Had our table, perchance, turned sideways? I clung on to the sides of my chair lest I slip off. Cautiously I looked down. Good Lord. What had happened to the floor? It was miles away. I swayed on my seat.

'Cassie darling, are you okay?' Jamie peered at me. His nose zoomed in and out of my face. Good heavens. I'd never noticed before the size of his breathing apparatus. It was huge. Vast.

Certainly put La Streisand's hooter in the shade. I stared at it in fascination. And it was growing! Oh my goodness. My husband had turned into Pinocchio. Any minute now, that nose was going to jab me. Possibly even stab me. Suddenly the table top rushed up to greet me. Cutlery, champagne flutes and wine glasses went flying.

And then everything went black.

Chapter Fourteen

'Ah. You're awake.'

I opened one eye. It was too much effort to open both of them. Morag appeared to be sitting at the end of my bed. She was balancing Henry and Eddie on both knees. My eyelid slammed down again. For a while I floated in a dark place. Eventually a persistent knocking on my forehead had me zooming towards wakefulness. This time I managed to open both eyes. Morag was still there, but no longer with Henry and Eddie.

'Why were you knocking on my forehead?' I mumbled.

'Don't be silly Cass. You clearly have a stonking great hangover.'

I hauled myself upright. Blinked owlishly. 'Where are Henry and Eddie?'

'Having a snooze. They've had a very busy morning debating the best teething toys on the market, discussing the price of baby food and whether to take a kip in either the playpen, or Eddie's cot with musical mobile.'

'Isn't it a bit early for them to take a nap?' I massaged my temples gingerly. A herd of elephants seemed to have taken up residence in my brain.

'Not really. It's gone noon.'

'What?' I glanced at the bedside clock. Ten past twelve. How could that be? 'Where is everybody?'

'Well, when I arrived your mother-in-law was greeting a silver haired chappie by the name of Arthur. Seemingly he turned up a minute or two before me. Edna and Arthur were dressed in his 'n' hers matching overalls. Moments later they headed off to your garage. Edna was clutching a portable CD player. I ventured in there about an hour ago with a cup of coffee for them both.'

'Right. I suppose they're working on the boat.'

'That and singing.'

'Singing?'

Morag nodded. 'Rod Stewart. Sailing.'

I groaned and swung my legs out of bed. Right now water was a high priority. Both to drink and wee. Not necessarily in that order. 'Excuse me a minute.' I hauled myself to my feet, and staggered off to the en-suite.

'Do you always go to bed in your best clothes?' Morag called after me.

'Don't be ridiculous,' I snorted as I hoiked up my cocktail dress. I froze. Stared at the crumpled material in horror. Last night rushed back to greet me. My headache threatened to go into overdrive. I slumped down on the toilet seat. The Oxo Tower. Dinner. With Ethan and Selina. But I hadn't eaten any dinner. Had I? I'd looked at the menu. Had a feeling I'd ordered. Something. What? I couldn't remember. Doubling over I rested my head on my lap while my bladder did its stuff. Flushing the chain, I peeled off my dress and stepped into the shower. I'd drink the water at the same time as washing myself.

When I came out of the bathroom with a towel wrapped about me, Morag had pulled the bed together. She'd also lain out a fresh regulation uniform and made some toast and coffee.

'Give that to me,' she took my crushed dress. 'What a way to treat such a sacred garment.' She smoothed the creases before delving into my wardrobe for a hanger.

'I didn't go to bed fully clothed on purpose,' I protested.

'Clearly you were off your head,' Morag pursed her lips.

Annoyed, I rummaged in a drawer for some underwear. How dare my friend go all sanctimonious on me! I snatched up the freshly laundered joggers and stuck one leg in. 'Oh do drop the face Morag,' I rolled my eyes. 'There have been plenty of times you've been plastered.'

'Sure,' she swished clothes along the rail to make room for my Little Black Dress, 'but not in front of my husband's business partner. There's a time and a place to get paralytic Cass.'

'But I wasn't paralytic!' I pulled the long-sleeved t-shirt over my head. 'I barely drank two glasses of champagne.'

Morag shut the wardrobe door and turned to face me. 'Cass, two glasses of champagne wouldn't have you head banging a table.'

'I didn't head bang anything!' I protested. My hammering skull begged to differ. I sat down on the bed. Reached for the coffee.

'Not according to Jamie.'

'What? When did you talk to Jamie?'

'He was busy getting the kids out of the house. He didn't tell me much Cass. Just the basics. The bones of the evening. Delivered through clenched teeth.'

I gulped. Nothing ever ruffled my husband's feathers. He was always calm. Capable. In control. He was my rock. Since when had Jamie ever held a conversation through *clenched teeth*?

A wave of nausea washed over me. Perhaps I'd drunk more than I'd realised. The truth was, I just couldn't remember. I put the toast down. 'So, do tell all.'

'There isn't much to tell.' Morag perched on the bed next to me. 'We were meant to be heading over to Nell's this morning to have a post-mortem about last night. It's meant to be *you* telling *us* what happened.'

I picked up the toast again. 'Just spill the beans Morag,' I bit into the soggy bread. 'Tell me what Jamie said.'

'Well,' Morag took a deep breath, 'he shooed the kids into the car and made sure Edna and Arthur were out of earshot. Clearly the family is none the wiser about what happened.'

'Go on.'

'You drank too much, and made a complete ass of yourself. Told everybody I was training to be an Olympic hurdler. Ordered a ridiculous number of desserts. Swayed on your chair as if riding a motorbike at Brands Hatch. Finally you nose-dived into all the glassware on the table. It's a wonder you've not cut yourself. Jamie said there was broken glass everywhere.'

I shook my head. This wasn't true. It simply couldn't be. 'And then what happened?'

'The entire restaurant ground to a halt. Jamie carried you out. Ethan ordered a cab. Home you came, apparently out cold all the way.'

'And where is Jamie now?'

'At the stables. I took Eddie off him, for which he was grateful. He said he thought he might stay with the kids for the day, and do a bit of hanging out with Matt too. Something about a football match this afternoon. He didn't look at all happy Cass. In fact, I'd go so far as to say he looked absolutely furious.'

Furious? My Jamie? I was silent for a moment. 'Sorry,' I stared at the soggy toast and tepid coffee. 'I can't finish this.'

Morag sighed and took the cup and plate from me. 'Can't you remember anything about last night?' she asked gently.

'Bits. But not properly,' I shook my head miserably. 'I'd better ring Jamie. Apologise. And Ethan. Oh God,' I put my head in my hands, 'Selina too. Presumably she witnessed everything.'

'I think that goes without saying.'

'I can't bear it Morag. It's bad enough Ethan seeing me in that state. But her! That wretched woman! Of all the people to make a prize prat of myself in front of–'

'Look Cass. Can I make a suggestion?'

The baby monitor crackled into life as a wail went up. Eddie. I took my head out of my hands. 'What?' I asked, as second wail began to duet with the first. Henry.

'Let Jamie calm down. Give him some space. Matt will jolly him up. And if their footie team wins the match this afternoon, Jamie will perk up even more. With a bit of luck, you'll just get your wrists slapped.'

'As opposed to Jamie divorcing me.'

'Don't be silly. Jamie worships the ground you walk on.' The wails turned to outraged bellows. 'Come on. Let's sort the boys out, then get over to Nell's.'

'She was expecting us hours ago.'

'Nell has a new baby Cass. Her daily schedule has just been tipped upside down. I can assure you she'll have lost complete track of time.'

Half an hour later our sons had been bottled, burped and changed. They were now sitting docilely in their car seats as we drove to Nell's. Morag was behind the wheel. Her insistence on driving had nothing to do with van drivers suffering road rage, but everything to do with me being potentially over the limit. I gazed glumly out the window. Even listening to the happy sounds of Henry and Eddie blowing raspberries failed to lift my mood. Eventually we turned into Nell's cul-de-sac. Transferring the boys from car seats to hips, we rang the doorbell.

'Have you got baby Rosie's present?' I asked, as we waited for Nell to come to the door.

'Yep. Safe in my handbag.' Morag patted the vast hold-all draped over one shoulder.

Nell greeted us in her nightie and dressing gown.

'See?' Morag turned to me. 'I told you Nell's routine would have gone to pot.' Morag leant in and gave my old neighbour a big hug. 'Phew. You smell a bit stinky.'

'Hello Morag,' Nell grinned wanly. 'Nice to know you haven't lost your sense of tact. And that's not me personally smelling whiffy. It's my darling daughter's puke on this dressing gown. I must buy some muslins. Hi Cass,' Nell squeezed me. 'You look a bit peaky. Can't wait to hear about last night. Good one by the looks of your eyeballs.'

'So good I can't remember anything,' I shut the door behind us.

'Where's Rosie?' asked Morag.

'Asleep upstairs. Go and have a peek.'

'I'll be right back,' said Morag tip-toeing up the stairs with Henry.

I followed Nell into the kitchen. Chaos reigned. The dishwasher lid was down and the bottom shelf pulled out. It had been emptied of some clean crockery, but abandoned half way through. The sink was piled high with dirty dishes waiting to be stacked. Congealed saucepans and empty sauce jars littered the worktop. A plastic wicker basket was stationed next to an open washing machine from which clean laundry spilled. Next to it was a pile of dirty laundry awaiting attention. Tucked into the corner of the kitchen was a dog basket. Rocket was curled up within. She wagged her tail, but didn't get up.

'Your dog's very subdued,' I said. 'What's the matter with her?'

'She's tired, bless her.'

Since when had *tired* ever figured in Rocket's doggy vocabulary? The dog was usually bursting out of her skin with energy.

'Rocket has been doing the night shift with me,' Nell beamed. 'Every time Rosie wakes up, Rocket is right there by my heels. She keeps me company while I feed the baby. She's even learnt to fetch me the nappy pack when I change Rosie. She's amazing.'

'Thank goodness she's not jealous.'

'If Rocket could talk she'd ask to have Rosie in her basket, wouldn't you boofles?' Nell cooed at the setter.

Rocket thumped her tail, but didn't move. I'd never seen her like this before. But then again I'd never seen a dog with bags under its eyes before either.

'Rosie is absolutely gorgeous!' Morag came into the kitchen. 'I can't tell you how broody I feel just looking at her. She's so tiny. So exquisite. I want another baby. That's it. I've decided.'

'Well before you pin Matt down and get big with child again, let's put the kettle on,' said Nell. She stared vaguely around the kitchen. 'If I could only find it.

'Where's Ben?' asked Morag.

'Out for the afternoon. Taken Dylan off for some *father and son* time. Ah, there it is!' Nell shoved some bottles out the way. 'Oh, it's empty.' She stared from the kettle to the congested sink. 'I'll just pop into the downstairs loo and use the tap in there.'

Morag turned to me. 'Take Henry from me Cass. I can't stand this muddle. Trust Ben and Dylan to naff off and leave a bombsite. Some men just haven't a clue.'

Nell returned with the kettle and plugged it in.

'Here,' I thrust Eddie and Henry at Nell. 'Take the boys into the lounge and let me help Morag. We'll soon have the place ship-shape. There are some baby toys in my hold-all to keep them entertained.'

Fifteen minutes later, order was restored. Machinery whirred. The tumble dryer was humming with wet laundry, the washing machine was sloshing the next load, the dishwasher had started a fresh cycle, empty glass jars had been rinsed and taken out to the recycling box in the garage, and surfaces shone like a new pin. Morag made the coffee and, finding an unopened packet of Hob Nobs, took everything through to the lounge.

'I'll put the drinks here,' she said setting a tray on the occasional table, 'away from the boys.'

The babies were laying on their tummies, heads up and bobbing about. Henry was rocking his little body in a desperate effort to move around. Eddie, two months older and that much bigger, was actually attempting to crawl. Another week or two and he might have mastered it – and then I'd really have my work cut out keeping an eye on him.

'Thank goodness Rosie is still sleeping,' Nell said. 'Hopefully she'll stay down long enough for me to enjoy this.' She leant back in her armchair, and lifted a mug to her lips.

'And while you're enjoying five minutes peace and quiet, you can open this,' Morag rummaged in her hold-all. 'This is for Rosie, from me and Cass with our love. She's too young for it now, but will appreciate it later.'

Nell took the parcel and tore at the wrapping paper. 'This is beautiful girls.' She smiled in delight at the Wedgewood Peter Rabbit Dinner set. 'Thank you.' She set the china carefully on the occasional table and once again leant back in her armchair. 'So come on Cass. What happened last night?'

'Apparently I behaved in an embarrassing and outrageous fashion.'

'However much booze did you ship?' asked Nell.

'Well that's just it. I didn't. Not really. Two glasses of champagne at best. But clearly enough to render me virtually unconscious until noon today.'

Nell went very still. Her expression was solemn. 'Cass, people don't pass out on two glasses of champagne. This smacks of having your drink spiked.'

'Don't be silly,' I laughed, 'who would do such a thing–'

We stared at each other.

'Selina,' Morag said.

'B-But why?' I asked bewildered. I knew there was no love lost between us, but surely she wouldn't do something like that. 'Apart from anything else – how could she have? I was sitting opposite her!'

'Well it's obvious how,' Nell puffed out her cheeks. 'She nobbled your champers. Did she touch your glass at any point?'

Like forked lightning, a dollop of memory flashed through my brain. 'Yes!' I squeaked. 'She reached across the table to pick something up.' A cocktail list? I frowned in concentration.

'She almost knocked my glass over, but caught it in the nick of time. And later she poured me more champagne. But nobody else.'

'Sorted,' said Nell. 'She slipped something in when she righted that glass. And she topped up your glass to speed up the effect of the Mickey Finn. This happened to a colleague of Ben's a few months ago – a bloke would you believe. He went away on business, and later had his drink spiked in the hotel's bar. The police suspected the barmen did it. And when this chap was carrying on all drunk and peculiar, the barman and another member of staff put him to bed. In the morning he woke up to find his wallet gone, along with his mobile, laptop and the keys to his car. And when he finally got home, he'd been burgled. No prizes for guessing who'd robbed him.'

'If this is true,' said Morag, 'then I feel perfectly dreadful. I for one have urged Cass to tolerate this woman. Not just for the sake of Jamie's business partnership, but for the family and the whole–' Morag swept an arm wide, 'lifestyle thing.'

'Well we've all urged Cass to tolerate this woman. But hang on a minute,' said Nell, 'there is no proof it was actually Selina who did this. I mean, could it have been the waiter?'

'Why would the waiter put drugs in my drink?' I asked.

'Was he, you know,' Nell winked, 'batting his eyelids at you. Giving you the come on. Hoping to lure you away from the table?'

'From under her husband's nose?' asked Morag. 'I hardly think so.'

'We have no proof I was drugged,' I massaged my temples. 'Can a test be done?'

'Yes. A urine test,' said Nell. 'However, even if we could do such a test right now, it wouldn't prove anything. These date rape drugs can leave the system in as little as eight hours. That time has long since elapsed.'

'You're going to have to tell Jamie,' Morag took a sip of coffee.

'Do you really think he's going to believe me?' I cried. 'We have no *proof*. Only supposition. And what would be Selina's motive? Just to get some sort of vicarious kick out of seeing me spread-eagled across a table in a top London restaurant?'

'Yes,' replied Nell calmly.

'She'd have to be off her trolley to pull a stunt like that,' I breathed.

'Well she's been off her trolley before,' said Morag. 'We know that from the past when she stalked you, and tried to frighten you off when you hooked up with Jamie. Perhaps she's always been off her trolley.'

'She told me she'd been in a bad way at one point. But she also assured, thanks to counselling, she was better.'

'Clearly Selina isn't better,' said Nell. 'Let's look at what we know so far.' Nell put down her coffee cup and began to tick off on her fingers. 'Firstly, you've been anxious about this woman from Day One. Secondly, Selina was definitely once a fruitcake. So it might well be that she still *is* a fruitcake. Thirdly, she's very conveniently wormed her way into Ethan's life, managed to get engaged to him *and* work with him thus impacting on yours and Jamie's lives. Coincidence? Maybe. But let's continue. Fourthly, because of this whole scenario, Selina can now even come inside your home and potentially make mischief.'

'Selina incensed me when she invited herself for kitchen supper,' I nodded. 'She informed me that she wanted at least six children, and my five would do for starters. Then she flattered Edna, and said one day she wanted to live in a house like Lilac

Lodge with a mother-in-law just like mine. Finally Stevie turned up to see the twins, was bowled over by Selina, and Morag and I have reason to believe she has started an affair with him.'

Nell's jaw dropped open. 'So finally,' Nell ticked off her little finger, 'what Selina really wants is your life. And if she can't have your current husband, by the looks of things she'll settle for your ex-husband.'

'This is ridiculous,' Morag piped up. 'We sound like three frustrated housewives with nothing better to gossip about. Even if Selina did want Cass's life, realistically that's not possible.'

'So the drink spiking could be some sort of petty revenge,' Nell put her head on one side and considered. 'But as you say Cass, we need proof. We can't get proof of the drink being spiked, but might it be possible to prove Selina is bonking Stevie?'

'Yes!' I hissed. 'Thanks to Stevie having his brain lodged in his boxers, he slipped up and rang Matt and Morag's riding stables. Booked a hack for himself and a woman called – wait for it – Selina! Moments later he rang back and cancelled. And then last night Selina told us all she's going horse riding today. At Maxwell's Equestrian Centre. But she lied and said she was going with an old chum called Laura.'

'For *Laura* read *Stevie,*' breathed Nell.

'Why didn't you tell me earlier about this?' demanded Morag.

'Because it's only just come back to me!' I cried.

'Well what are we waiting for?' Morag leapt to her feet. 'Let's get over to Maxwell's now. I know exactly where it is. Swanky as you like. Let's hope we catch Stevie and Selina together. You can film them on your mobile phone Cass. If nothing else, you'd then have proof to show Jamie that lies were told about being with a woman called Laura. That has to count as some sort of starting point, before putting the cat amongst the partnership pigeons.'

I looked at my watch. 'It's nearly half past three. Stevie and Selina have probably long gone from Maxwell's.'

'Well we won't know if we don't check it out.' Morag grabbed her car keys.

'What about the boys?' I leapt up, but dithered. Looked anxiously from Morag to our babies.

'Leave them with me,' said Nell, 'they'll be fine. Go!' Nell heaved herself out of the armchair and shooed us to the front door. 'Don't forget your mobile phone Cass,' she pressed it into the palm of my hand, 'and make sure you keep me updated. Gosh, this is quite exciting. I'll have to call you both Cagney and Lacey!'

'Showing your age there Nellie-Wellie,' I gave her a grim smile, and hastened after Morag.

Chapter Fifteen

Morag's Galaxy didn't take the corner of Nell's cul-de-sac on two wheels, but inside the vehicle it certainly felt like it. As soon as we hit the M25, Morag floored the accelerator.

'Where exactly is Maxwell's Equestrian Centre?' I asked anxiously. We had now merged on to the A21, and appeared to be heading towards Hastings.

'Sevenoaks. Don't panic. We're not going that far. That was rather clever of Selina, booking somewhere off the beaten track. So Detective Cagney, how are you feeling after your foray into the world of drugs?'

'The headache has gone. Although my forehead,' I touched it gingerly, 'feels a bit tender, thanks to the table bashing.'

'Yes. Next time you get out of it, stick to table dancing.'

'It's not funny Morag. In fact, the more I think about it, the more furious I feel.'

'I wonder what she slipped you,' Morag pondered. 'Do you know, in Pharmacology drugs have two names – a trade and a generic name. For example, the trade name of Amoxil is also called Amoxicillin. And Advil is also called Ibuprofen. I heard,' Morag swung the Galaxy past a lorry, 'that Big Pharma has been looking for a generic name for Viagra.'

I gave Morag a sideways glance. 'Are you being serious?'

'Perfectly. After careful consideration, a team of government experts has settled on the generic name of Mycoxafloppin.'

'Oh ha ha. Very funny. Not.'

'Other considerations were Mycoxafailin, Mydixadrupin and – of course – Mydixarizin.'

'Morag this is no time to joke, I could have died!'

'But you *must* joke about it Cass. It's therapeutic. If you don't, you'll go barmy.'

I stared out the window. Morag had a point. I couldn't change what had happened. Laughing it off was a coping mechanism.

'Well for your information, I actually read that Viagra will soon be available in liquid form.'

'Really? Are *you* joking?'

'Straight up. No pun intended. Pepsi Cola are going to market it as a power beverage mixer. So it will literally be possible for a man to pour himself a stiff one.'

Morag snorted with laughter. 'In which case they will no longer be able to call it a soft drink.'

'Exactly,' my lips twitched, 'gives a whole new meaning to cocktails and highballs.'

We both convulsed as the Galaxy shot off down a slip road. Suddenly we were in very green belt. We whizzed along winding roads, passing farms and bleak fields. I began to think our foray into Sevenoaks was nothing more than a wild goose chase. The winter afternoon was rapidly turning to dusk. Before our very eyes a feeble sun was sliding behind stark trees. Pale light was greying with every passing second.

'This is Maxwell's.' Morag swung an abrupt left, and we bounced down a dirt track.

'Geez,' I muttered, nearly hitting my head on the Galaxy's roof, 'I thought you said this place was swanky.'

'It is. The road is pot-holed for safety purposes. Maxwell's don't want cars whizzing along here and cannoning into their horse riders. See! Look at those riders ahead,' Morag nodded at two large bay horses trundling back to the yard. 'If I'd been going fast I could have crashed straight into those horses' hocks and–'

'It's them!' I shouted. The colour drained from my face. 'That's Stevie.'

Morag dropped a gear. The Galaxy was now virtually crawling. 'Are you sure Cass? Both riders are wearing hard hats and have their backs to us.'

'I spent more years than I care to remember being married to Stevie. I'd recognise those shoulders anywhere. And note his riding companion is female. The person might have a hard hat on, but observe the long dark hair.' I pointed at the woman's locks trailing down her wax jacket. 'I would bet my last lottery pound that is Selina.'

Both riders had now reverted to single file, allowing us to overtake them.

'Stevie doesn't know my car, so I'm okay to pass them,' Morag said. 'However, I'd rather not risk them recognising us. You'd better jump in the back Cass. The rear passenger privacy glass will hide you. Hang on,' Morag touched my arm, 'before you leg it, have a quick rummage in the glove box. There's a baseball cap in there, and a pair of sunnies. I need to hide my face.'

I scrabbled frantically in the glove box, found a pair of Ray-Bans and pulled out a Burberry baseball cap. The Galaxy was almost at a standstill. The horses most certainly were. Stevie's hack was swishing its tail impatiently. I prayed he wouldn't look over his shoulder. Morag shoved the cap on her head, rammed the Ray-Bans on her nose, and pulled down the Galaxy's sun visor for good measure. I launched myself over the handbrake and landed in a heap on the floor.

'Stay down,' Morag hissed. The Galaxy lurched forward again. 'And you forgot this.' She tossed my mobile after me. 'Get ready to film.'

I reached for the mobile. Oh bloody hell. I'd never even used the camera on my Android phone, never mind the video. I stabbed the screen randomly. No I did not want to set up a Google Account. Nor use the calculator. What the hell was a Cardock? The screen was now requesting me to turn on my Wi-Fi and connect to a network. I gnashed my teeth in frustration. Livvy had ridiculed me for wanting a Smartphone.

'You'll never learn to use it in a million years Mum,' she'd guffawed.

Rebelling furiously, I'd upgraded and told myself I *would* catch up with technology. Tomorrow. Or the day after tomorrow. But most definitely next week. None of which had ever come to pass.

The Galaxy was speeding up again. I bounced around in the back feeling slightly motion sick.

'I'm going to do a three point turn in a minute Cass, and then head back the other way. Are you ready to film them passing us head-on?'

'No! I mean, yes!' I sighed with relief at an icon labelled *Camcorder.* God's sake. Why couldn't they have labelled the button *Video* for the likes of technophobes like me? Suddenly I was all fingers and thumbs. The screen changed and the phone instantly displayed the Galaxy's floor mats. Hoo-flippin'-ray. Lights, camera, action.

'Camera's rolling,' I squeaked and hauled myself up. 'Oh Lord.' My bowels lurched as Selina appeared to look straight at me. 'Are you sure they can't see me.'

'They might be able to make out your shape, but that's all. Apart from anything else, the daylight is rapidly receding. Even if I wasn't wearing my sunnies and cap, I don't think they'd see my features that clearly. Are you managing to pick them up okay on that phone?'

'Yep. The picture is a bit grainy, but good enough.' I held the mobile up and let it play over Selina's face, then let the picture drift to Stevie. They were both talking to each other. Selina was laughing about something. One could detect the sexual chemistry between them at five paces. I clung on to the phone, terrified of dropping it. I didn't want to miss this golden opportunity of catching out my nemesis. The filming continued to roll without incident. The Galaxy bumped past the horses, and suddenly they were both behind us. I let out a shaky breath and hit the red button. 'It's a wrap.'

'Well done.' Morag whipped off the cap and sunglasses and chucked them back in the glove box.

'Geez, I'm shaking like an aspen.' I clambered back into the passenger seat. 'I thought I was going to crap myself with nerves.'

'You're not alone,' said Morag. She lifted one buttock and noisily broke wind.

'Oh for–' I flapped the mobile phone about, fanning the air between us.

'Sorry,' Morag apologised. 'The adrenalin caught up with me – nervous tummy.' She buzzed the window down to let in fresh air.

I snapped my seat belt on. 'Mission accomplished Lacey. Let's hurry back to Nell's, and pick up our boys.'

By the time we arrived at Nell's, my old neighbour was looking a little frayed around the edges. Both boys were grumpy and grizzly, plus Rosie was awake and wanting attention.

'Thank Gawd you're both back,' sighed Nell. 'I don't know how mothers cope with triplets. So, was it a successful venture?'

'Oh yes,' I said smugly. 'One hundred per cent. It's all on here,' I tapped my mobile. 'I'm looking forward to sharing this with Jamie. If nothing else, I will prove Selina is a liar and a cheat.'

By the time we were back at Morag's, both boys were hungry and complaining loudly.

'Come on in Cass,' said Morag as she unstrapped Henry from his car seat. 'Give Eddie a jar of Mr Heinz. I'm pretty sure our men are still watching their football match.'

'Okay.' I slung my hold-all over one shoulder and lifted Eddie onto my hip. Wrestling with the rear seat-belt, I pulled the baby seat out of the Galaxy. Taking a step backwards, I was just about to use my foot to slam the door when Morag shrieked with horror.

'Cass! Do not even *think* about shutting my car door like that.'

'Oh for the love of–' I swung around and reversed my backside against the door instead. It clunked shut. Weighted down, I staggered into Morag's hallway just in time to hear Matt and Jamie erupting at the television.

'What a load of RUBBISH!' Jamie shouted.

'DISGRACEFUL!' Matt bellowed his agreement. 'The lads at the local primary school can play better than that lot.'

I deposited Eddie's car seat in the hall, and followed Morag into the lounge.

'Ah, hello my angel!' Matt hastily removed his feet from the coffee table. He stood up and began plumping cushions. Gone were the days when his house was littered with muddy riding boots, or had grubby saddles leaning up against the French doors. Now that Morag was Mrs Harding with her feet firmly installed under the fashionably distressed kitchen table, Matt's house was like something out of the pages of Country Living magazine.

'Hi,' Morag went over and kissed Matt full on the mouth. 'Take Henry while I get a bottle for him, and then I'll sort out dinner. Jamie, would you and Cass like to join us? The kids are welcome too.'

Jamie eased himself out of an armchair. 'Thanks Morag. That's sweet of you. But we'll be heading home.'

'As you like.' Morag headed off to the kitchen.

'Cassie,' Jamie nodded at me. 'How are you feeling?'

Since when had my husband ever nodded at me by way of greeting?

'Hello darling,' I smiled. Jamie didn't smile back. 'I'm fine. Sound as a pound.' I stared at my husband. He was acting very strange. Quiet. I'd never seen him like this before. Matt suddenly seemed very alive to the shift in atmosphere.

'I'll just see how Morag is doing with that milk,' he said tactfully. He almost bolted from the room, such was his discomfort.

'And you?' I asked.

'Me what?'

'Well, how are you of course?' What an awful conversation. So stilted.

'Tired.'

'Oh dear. Didn't you sleep well last night?'

'Funnily enough, no.' A nerve was going in Jamie's cheek.

'Why?' I asked in a small voice.

Jamie finally crossed the room, but only to take Eddie from my arms. 'Hello my handsome boy,' he kissed the top of Eddie's downy head. 'And what have you been up to today?' Jamie was rewarded with a gummy smile.

'Why?' I asked again.

'We'll talk at home Cassie.'

'Oh but I was just about to give Eddie a jar of–'

'Make it quick,' Jamie handed Eddie back to me. 'The children are still down the stables. I'll round them up. We'll be waiting in the car.' And with that he turned on his heel. 'Catch you later guys,' he called out to Matt and Morag. Their voices floated back in unison. Jamie picked up Eddie's car seat and let himself out.

'Right then,' I said to Eddie. 'Let's be having that jar of baby food.' I forced a bright smile. But as I set off to the kitchen, my stomach was in knots.

Chapter Sixteen

On the drive home to Lilac Lodge, Jamie was very quiet. His somewhat solemn mood made me feel edgy. Even the children seemed subdued. Only Eddie made any noise, happily blowing bubbles to himself.

As the Muck Truck swung through the electric gates, my gaze fell upon Arthur coming out of our garage. He put up a hand and waved. Jamie waved back.

'Here comes Captain Birdseye,' Jamie murmured.

I giggled, relieved that the tension between us had broken.

'And there's his first mate,' I nodded at Edna who appeared a moment later. She was wiping her hands on an old rag.

We piled out of the car and into the house. The delicious smell of home cooking pervaded the air. Edna followed us in. She washed her hands at the sink and then set about laying the table.

'Something smells scrumptious,' Jamie stooped to kiss his mother on one floury cheek.

'Nothing amazing I'm afraid. I left a chicken chasseur and some jacket potatoes to slow cook in the oven. We've been working on the boat all day. Cassandra dear, if you want to bath Eddie before dinner I won't be dishing up for another twenty minutes.'

'Yes, okay. Thanks Edna.' Yet again I was being organised in my own home, but as my headache was making a comeback, I batted away such irritation. My stomach let out a growl of hunger. It had been a long time since the coffee and Hob Nobs at Nell's. Food, especially cooked by Edna, would be most welcome.

'I'll give you a hand,' said Jamie following me.

'Oh that's all right darling, I can man—'

I stopped as I caught the expression on my husband's face. Ah. Clearly I had been wrong about the tension between us being broken. I turned on my heel and went out to the hallway, pausing only to shrug off my coat and sling it over the banister. Jamie did likewise before following me up to the family bathroom. He shut the door, and bolted it for good measure.

'It's pointless locking it. I need to get Eddie a fresh romper suit and nappy from his nursery. What's the matter Jamie? Why are you looking at me like that?'

Jamie unbolted the door. 'Go on then. Go and fetch Eddie's stuff. Give him to me while you're faffing about in his room.'

'Faffing about? Since when do I *faff about*?'

'All the time Cassie,' said Jamie taking Eddie from me.

'Well really, there's no need to be—'

'Just. Go.' Jamie gave me a prod.

I went. Jaw rigid. Back stiff. Opening Eddie's wardrobe, I selected a babygro and cardigan. Sliding out a drawer, I whipped out a vest then plucked a nappy off the overhead shelf. Faff about. As if. Chance would be a fine thing. I'd been far too busy filming his rotten ex-girlfriend up to no good. Faff about indeed. I'd soon have Jamie eating his words when he saw the results of a *very* productive afternoon. I gathered everything into my arms, and went back out onto the landing. Where was my phone? Ah yes. In my coat pocket, over the banister. I hastened down the stairs.

'The bathroom is this way Cassie,' Jamie's voice floated after me.

'Yes I know, I'm just—'

'Faffing. This is exactly what I'm talking about.'

I grabbed my coat and pulled. It shot off the banister dislodging umpteen wax jackets piled on top of it. 'Why does nobody in this house hang up their coats?' I howled.

'Cassie, will you just leave them and get back up here now please. You don't need your coat to bath Eddie. I want to talk to you.'

'I'm coming!' I stomped back up the stairs, arms full, coat trailing in my wake. 'If you just stopped harassing me for one moment,' I brushed past Jamie, 'there's something I want—'

'I've run Eddie's bath,' said Jamie. He grabbed the plastic changing mat propped up against the wall. 'I've spent the bulk of the day with the kids and Matt, taking deep breaths of country air to stop me hyperventilating with anger.'

'Anger?'

'Yes, Cassie.' Jamie laid Eddie down on the changing mat. His fingers deftly attended to the romper suit's poppers. He looked up at me. 'Mind telling me what last night was all about? Every time I think about what happened, I squirm with embarrassment.'

'Oh you do, do you!' I glared at my husband. 'In a nutshell, it was Selina's fault.'

Jamie's eyes widened. 'Oh Selina,' he nodded, 'yes of course, how silly of me. I should have known that she was entirely responsible for your ridiculous conversation. All that rubbish about Morag show jumping without a horse, and then ordering yourself three desserts. Were you trying to be funny Cassie?'

'Of course not,' I could feel myself growing pink with indignation. 'How do you think I feel, knowing that I passed out in front of Ethan?'

'So you do remember passing out?' Jamie balled up Eddie's romper suit and lobbed it at the laundry basket. 'You're sure it wasn't Selina holding you down on the table and demanding you behave like an incoherent drunk?'

'How dare you!' I hissed. 'That woman spiked my drink!'

'Oh, for heaven's sake. I've heard it all now.' Irritably, Jamie removed Eddie's nappy.

'But it's true! Why won't you believe me?'

'Because,' Jamie bagged the nappy before scooping Eddie up, 'you were drinking too much, too quickly, on an empty stomach. Also, there were witnesses that Selina did no such thing. And why the heck would she even want to?'

'Because Selina hates me!'

'She doesn't hate you Cassie.' Jamie lowered Eddie into his bath seat. 'The woman wants to befriend you. And has tried to. Repeatedly. You both shook hands on it. Remember?'

'Selina is clever. Manipulative. She obviously wants to put me in a bad light.'

'Why?' Jamie sighed.

'Revenge. She was adamant I was *the other woman* and lured you away from her.'

'Look, this conversation is getting us nowhere.' Jamie filled a sponge with water and let it trickle over Eddie's shoulders. 'What happened between me and Selina is in the past. And she knows that. She's dotty about Ethan, and with every good reason. The guy is loaded. He keeps her in designer clothes and jewellery. She has a great job working alongside him. Then there's the big wedding being planned right now as we speak. And you can bet the babies will arrive soon afterwards. Selina is totally loved up.'

'Oh is she?' I sneered.

'Yes. Of course!'

'Remember how she was telling us all about her friend Laura? The one who she spent the night with after Stevie dropped her home?'

'Yes. What about it?'

'Laura might well exist, but she didn't keep Selina company while Ethan was waiting to fly home from America.'

Jamie sighed. 'Cassie, listen–'

'No!' I put up a hand. 'You listen to me. That woman is having an affair and–'

'Cassie I'm starting to get really annoyed now. Selina is not having an affair. And even if she was, I couldn't care less. What she does in her private life is exactly that. Private. It's no business of mine or yours who Selina goes to bed with. And nor am I interested to know. What is this obsession you have with Selina?'

'Obsession? Me?' I pointed to my chest, face now puce with fury. 'You've got it wrong. Selina is the one obsessed with *me!*'

'I can't see that Cass.' Jamie tipped some baby shampoo into the palm of one hand. 'All I can see is my wife behaving in an increasingly erratic fashion.' He massaged the liquid into Eddie's baby curls. 'When we went to Ethan's apartment, you dismissed yourself from the dinner table for the best part of twenty minutes. It came across that you were bored, and couldn't be bothered to be civil.'

'I was indisposed, thanks to that woman doing something to my food!'

Jamie ignored me. 'And then you made a big fuss about her coming to dinner at our house – which was quite needless. She spent most of the time talking to Ethan on the phone, before holing up with Stevie and the kids to watch television.'

'Well if Stevie hadn't shown up, it would have been *you* entertaining her – not to mention taking her home – which was totally unaccept–'

'And then finally,' Jamie cut across me, 'we have you in a top London restaurant spouting a load of garbage, drinking too much and passing out in the most public way possible.'

'I keep telling you,' I shouted, 'she spiked my drink!' The yelling startled Eddie. His little lip began to wobble. 'Oh, my darling. I'm so sorry.' I swooped down and kissed his chubby cheeks. 'Don't get upset sweetheart.' I adopted a sing-song voice. 'It's just Mummy being silly.'

'That's an understatement,' Jamie muttered. He began rinsing Eddie's hair.

'And Daddy not listening to Mummy,' I grinned at our son, and pulled some funny faces. Eddie began to chuckle. I sighed with relief and rocked back on my heels. 'Believe me Jamie. Please. Selina put something in my drink. *And* she's having an affair with Stevie.'

'Stevie!' Jamie crowed. 'Oh my God, this is the icing on the cake.' Grabbing a white fluffy towel, he lifted Eddie out of the bath and wrapped him within its soft folds. 'How on earth have you implicated your ex-husband into this incredible fantasy?'

I smiled thinly. 'Watch, listen and learn.' I removed my mobile phone from my coat pocket, and shoved it under Jamie's nose. Touching the arrow, the screen burst into life. The picture swung about crazily. Morag's car seats whooshed into view. 'I was down on the floor to begin with,' I spoke over the excited chatter between Morag and myself, 'but any minute now you're going to have the biggest surprise of your life.' The bathroom was instantly filled with the sound of rampant farting. I stared at the screen in disbelief. And cringed as Morag's apology rang out, clear as a bell, followed by me addressing her as *Lacey*. 'I can explain.'

Jamie stared at me incredulously. 'Can I just say Cassie, that you're not just coming across as neurotic, but certifiable.'

'Oh thanks a bunch. You're my husband and should support me. Nell and Morag believe me.'

'Nell has just had a baby and – much as I love her – she makes Daffy Duck look like Einstein. And as for Morag, I think she's missing work and courtroom drama. I can think of no other explanation for getting caught up in your imaginings. I don't want another word on the subject of Selina.' I opened my mouth to speak, but Jamie put up a hand. 'I mean it Cassie. And just to let you know, the bank is holding its annual ball next Saturday at a swanky venue in Oxfordshire. We're invited. All four of us. And I want you behaving in a way that makes me proud. Understand?' And with that Jamie plonked Ethan in my arms, and stomped out the bathroom leaving me mouthing like a goldfish.

Eventually, I went downstairs with Eddie on my hip. I kissed his damp hair. He smelt divine. In the kitchen, Edna was presiding over the Chasseur with a huge ladle. Steam spiralled upwards. Everybody was sitting up.

'Perfect timing Cassandra dear,' said Edna.

'I hope you don't mind me joining your family Cass,' said Arthur, as I popped Eddie into his playpen.

'Of course not!' I took my place at the table. 'The more the merrier!' I risked a look at Jamie. He was mashing butter into his jacket potato, and didn't look up. 'So,' I took a dinner plate from Edna and set it before me, 'what work did you do to the boat today?'

Arthur rubbed his hands together gleefully. I had a feeling that Edna would have done the same, had she not been setting plates before the children.

'Well today we've thoroughly acquainted ourselves with our lovely new seafaring friend. And we've started on the floor. To begin with, we stuck our screwdrivers into some cracks which pushed through the wood like a wet paper bag.'

'The wood was totally shot,' said Edna sitting down. 'So we ripped up fibreglass around the cracks, and that came off fairly easily. But when we realised the extent of the rotten wood, we just grabbed the power saws and went to town.' My mother-in-law picked up her knife and fork. 'But it's not all bad news. We were able to salvage one half of a support to give a template of the curve of the bottom of the boat.'

'How fascinating,' I nodded. It was gobbledegook to me. And even if I understood what they were talking about, it struck me as mind-numbingly boring. Thank God my husband didn't have an urge to mess about with boats. Or power saws. I spooned up some chicken. He messed about with power houses instead. Like banks. I cut into my jacket potato and loaded up my fork. Powerful banks that held annual events. I swallowed the potato and felt it stick in my throat. Black tie events. With women like Selina and myself attending. Yet again circumstances were pushing the two of us together. I stared at my dinner miserably. I didn't want to go to a ball with that woman. What would she do to me next time? Kill me? I pushed some chicken around my plate. Jamie's words echoed in my head. Was I really neurotic? Certifiable? Was it perhaps just an unhappy coincidence that her raw food diet had upset my tummy? Was it really just possible I had drunk too much? After all, it was only Nell's supposition that had come up with my champagne being spiked. Nell was no pharmacist. The only thing I could be sure of was Selina spending the day with Stevie. And as Jamie had said, it wasn't our business. What upset me more than anything though, was Jamie requesting I behave in a way that made him proud. I forked up another bit of chicken. As opposed to *ashamed*. I gulped. I'd humiliated my husband in front of his boss. And not just his boss, but an entire restaurant. Mortification washed over me. I'd make it up to him. Stop behaving like a fool. I was forty-one years old for heaven's sake. It was time to stop hiding in playgrounds from irate cyclists, or having road rage with red van drivers, or chasing around the Kent countryside filming two unmarried people up to no good with each other. I couldn't even get the filming right. And even if I had, so what? It was still none of our business.

'So I guess you'll be using plywood for the floor then?' Jamie was asking.

'I think,' Arthur considered, 'that we'll probably end up applying a fibreglass cloth, and epoxy a few inches up the side.' He put his knife and fork together and turned to Edna. 'That was absolutely delicious Pumpkin.'

Pumpkin? I boggled at my jacket potato. Edna smiled coyly by way of response. Clearly there was a lot more than just affection between Arthur and my mother-in-law. They'd known each other for all of five minutes, yet they'd bought a boat together, and were billing and cooing like a pair of turtle doves. I wondered if they'd fallen in love. I knew from my own experience with Jamie that it was possible to fall in love instantly. Morosely, I wondered if one could fall out of love as speedily. I glanced up at Jamie to find him looking at me. But as our eyes met, he quickly looked away.

I spent the rest of the evening alternating between quietly seething, and sinking into depression. I had an urge to scribble a picture of Selina and stick voodoo pins all over it. The earlier distance between Jamie and me had turned into a yawning chasm. At this rate, his cold shoulder was in danger of giving me frostbite. Never in all our time together had I known him so livid. And much later, when the household was asleep, I crept into bed to find Jamie's back to me. My hand reached for the bedside light. As the room plunged into darkness, I hoped Monday morning would see things right.

Chapter Seventeen

When the alarm went off the following morning, Jamie's side of the bed was empty. My eyes swivelled over to the en-suite. Was he in the bathroom? The door was shut but there was no tell-tale light spilling through the gap where tiles met carpet.

I flung back the duvet. Reaching for my dressing-gown, I crossed the landing. The house was still slumbering. Creeping downstairs, I discovered the kitchen light on. A lone cereal bowl was on the table, a few soggy cornflakes clinging to the porcelain's side. Outside a car engine started. I made for the hallway, nearly tripping over Wallace and Gromet who had silently materialised and were waiting for breakfast. By the time I'd yanked open the front door, Jamie's car was bouncing along the potholed road. I watched in dismay as the tail lights lit up the still dark morning.

I couldn't bear going through the day without some sort of harmony being restored between the two of us. Reaching for the hall telephone I rang Jamie's mobile. His voicemail immediately clicked in. Oh for heaven's sake. Who could he be talking to at this hour? I listened to my husband's voice inviting me to leave a message.

'Hello!' I warbled. 'It's me. Um. I missed not seeing you this morning. And I'm just phoning to say that I'm really sorry. *Really* sorry. About everything. Drinking too much. Filming Morag farting. It won't happen again. The drinking. Not the farting. And I promise to make you proud at the ball this Saturday,' my lip wobbled a bit, 'and, um, I love you.' My voice cracked. 'A lot.' I replaced the handset and drooped back into the kitchen. I'd just set some Whiskas down for the cats, when the phone shrilled into life.

'Hello?' I answered tremulously.

'Sorry Cassie, I was on the phone to Ethan when you called. Selina is off sick today so the pair of us will have to make up for her absence. I could be home a little on the late side tonight.'

'Okay.' I was determined not to make any comment about Selina. Oh no. From now on her name would be erased from my vocabulary. 'Did you get my message?'

'Yes you silly goose. And I love you too,' said Jamie. I clutched the handset in relief. 'And I know you'll do me proud at the bank's ball.'

'I will, I will,' I gabbled.

'Good. You'll need a long dress for the occasion. Better take yourself off to Fairview and buy one eh?'

'Really? Ooh thank you darling!' I hugged my body in delight. My husband wasn't cross with me anymore!

'You can thank me properly tonight Mrs Mackerel. Catch you later.'

'Bye!' I replaced the handset feeling a million times happier. My husband still loved me. He wanted me to buy an evening dress. And I was going to make sure he *was* the proudest man at the ball.

I almost skipped over to the range as I set about frying eggs for the children. Edna came into the kitchen just as Eddie's wails sounded through the baby alarm.

'Let me do that Cassandra dear, you see to Eddie. I'll put some bacon in a pan too.' My mother-in-law was dressed in yesterday's overalls. Ready for action on every level.

There was a knock at the kitchen door. Through the glass I could see Arthur. He gave me the thumbs up. I pulled my dressing gown a bit tighter around me as I set about unlocking the back door. Arthur for dinner last night. Arthur for breakfast this morning. Arthur in our garage all day. Wouldn't it just be easier if Arthur moved in?

'Morning Cass!' Arthur chirped. The cats minced over and weaved around his legs. 'By golly something smells good,' he rubbed his hands together.

'Hi Arthur,' I smiled. 'Come in and have some breakfast.' I stepped to one side as he came through the door. A pale sun was rising over the tree tops lighting up the winter morning. Bird song filtered into the kitchen. There was the unspoken promise of a chilly but bright day. I put my foot up the cats' backsides and shooed them out the door.

'Good morning Arthur dear,' Edna trilled.

Arthur went over and pecked Edna on the cheek. All very chaste. She blushed delicately. I left them making small talk and took one of Eddie's pre-prepared bottles from the refrigerator. As I popped it into the microwave for a thirty second blast, the children filed into the kitchen. Toby was holding up his PE bag.

'My plimsolls are missing,' he whined.

'They're probably under your bed,' I said.

'No they're not. I checked. I bet that bloody Richard Clegg took them.'

'Don't swear Tobes.' The microwave bleeped. 'Richard Clegg?' I removed Eddie's feed. 'I know that name.'

'Do you?' Toby looked surprised. 'How come?'

'Dylan happened to mention him. Said he'd had a spot of bother with this boy. In fact,' I shook the bottle, 'As far as Richard Clegg goes, I was going to ask you all to keep an eye on Dylan.'

'He's a pain in the arse,' said Toby. 'Richard that is. Not Dylan.'

'Yeah, and a chav too,' added Jonas.

'Sorry,' I rolled my eyes apologetically at Arthur.

Arthur took a loaded plate from Edna and sat down. 'Why don't you simply ask him to kindly return your plimsolls?' he suggested amiably.

'Because,' Toby explained patiently, 'Richard Clegg is built like a brick sh–'

'Toby!' I warned. 'Just all stick together. Get the plimsolls back and look after Dylan.'

Jonas pressed an index finger against the side of his nose and winked. 'I get your drift Cass. Consider it done.'

'Marvellous,' I sighed. 'And I'll be dropping Dylan home so he doesn't have any problems with this bully after school. Now I must get upstairs to Eddie and sort him out. Meanwhile Jonas–' I rummaged in a drawer, 'here are my keys. See you all in the car in fifteen minutes.'

I hastened up the stairs. Eddie had pulled himself upright, little fists clinging onto the bars of his cot. He gave me a dribbly grin.

'Hello little man!' I beamed. 'Oh phew. Somebody has a stinky nappy. Here. Take this. Mummy will be back in two minutes.'

I left my smelly son happily guzzling from his bottle and charged off for the quickest wash and change in history. One day I might get around to wearing make-up on a school day. For now a dash of lip gloss would have to do. I tore back into Eddie's nursery just as the last dregs of milk were going down the hatch. Picking my son up, he rewarded me with a huge belch. Five minutes later my baby was topped, tailed and dressed. I swung Eddie onto my hip and hastened back down to the kitchen.

Arthur was already out in the garage. Edna was loading up the dishwasher.

'I'm popping into Fairview after the school run,' I said, removing another of Eddie's bottles from the fridge and chucking it into my super-sized Mummy holdall. I spun round and grabbed a couple of Heinz jars from the larder for good measure. That should keep Eddie's hunger pangs at bay for a while.

'Now worries Cassandra dear. Arthur and I will be out on the boat for most of the day. And don't worry about dinner tonight. I put a large steak and kidney pie in the freezer just before Christmas. We can all enjoy it this evening. There's plenty of veg in the fridge too.'

'Great stuff.' Having a mother-in-law virtually living with us did have its benefits. 'Well I'll see you later then.' I checked there were sufficient nappies in my hold-all along with my purse, then grabbed my coat and went out to the car where the children were waiting.

After the usual customary crawl to school, I was just about to set off in the direction of Fairview when my mobile rang. It was Stevie.

'Hi Cass. Can you talk a minute?'

'Yes. I'm parked up at the moment. Just watching the kids go through the school gate.' A small lump lodged in my throat. These days the children rarely seemed to want much input with me. I felt almost defunct as a mother in the cuddly sense. Most of the time I seemed to be a cash machine, a taxi service or a personal maid. The days of children rushing out to greet me clutching wet paintings had long passed. Nor did they want to confide in me. Instead they confided in each other. Or their friendship groups. On the one hand it was lovely they were so independent. I wanted them to flourish and grow into confident young adults. But on the other, boy did I miss those days where Mummy was the centre of their universe.

'Are they okay?'

'Yes,' I sighed. 'They are very okay. And you?'

'Ah. Well, that's one of the reasons why I was ringing actually. About this weekend's access. Not that it really makes much difference to the twins, but if you could let them know that Charlotte and I are no longer together.'

'Really?' I feigned surprise. Stevie wasn't to know that Morag had bumped into Charlotte at Tesco's and already banged the jungle drums to me about Charlotte's departure. I was surprised it had taken Stevie so long to mention it. Surely he'd been home somewhere between his ex-girlfriend's departure and the horsey day out with his new amour? Was it only now that he'd spotted a *Dear Stevie* note in Charlotte's handwriting propped up on the mantelpiece?

'Silly girl,' Stevie tutted, 'but it's probably for the best. All that baby business. Not for me.'

'Yes, I remember you saying.' The children disappeared around the corner of a building and out of sight. I started the engine up. 'So, you don't mind being single again?' I indicated and pulled out.

'Oh no. Not at all. It's quite a relief actually. From now on I want a relationship with no strings. Preferably with a married woman. Or one that's about to be married. That would do very nicely, ha ha!'

'Does that mean you've met one?' I asked.

'Met what?'

'A woman that's about to be married?'

'Cass you really are incredibly nosey.'

'I'll take that as a yes then.' In the background I heard Stevie's doorbell ring. 'Are you still at home?' I asked.

'Yeah,' Stevie sounded cagey, 'bad back. Must go. My masseuse has arrived.'

'God Stevie, you don't change. Have fun in your sick bed.'

My ex-husband chuckled and rang off. Interesting. He was pulling a sickie. And according to Jamie, Selina was off sick today too. Still, it was none of my business. From now on, the two of them could get on with it. They could bonk each other senseless. I felt immensely sorry for Ethan, but was hardly in a position to enlighten him. And Jamie thought I had an over-active imagination. So that was that. I drove to Fairview with my mind firmly on evening dresses and the impending ball banquet. This time I was going to have my wits about me. Oh yes. My plate and wine glass would be a million miles away from Selina's butterfly hands.

In due course I arrived at Fairview. Pulling Eddie's buggy from the boot, I strapped him in, made sure my hold-all was hanging over one of the handles and then set off. Shopping with a baby wasn't ideal. The moment you found something you wanted to try on, it would be the Law of Sod that baby would cry and demand your attention. I'd done the *ignore it and carry on* thing but unfortunately Eddie had copied me. As in the *carry on* bit. And the game of wits had been won by my son, especially as by that point I'd had other shoppers casting the sort of dark looks that clearly conveyed I was a negligent mother. So when I cruised into John Lewis, glided up an escalator and discovered a pale pink evening dress begging to be tried on, I was totally prepared for Eddie's blood-curdling screams to start.

'There, there darling,' I grinned at my howling son, 'Mummy has something nice for you to chomp on while she goes into the changing room.' I rummaged in my hold-all and withdrew a Rusk. 'Mmmmm,' I rolled my eyes in an *I've-just-died-and-gone-to-heaven* way. 'Look what Mummy has for Eddie!'

With peace briefly restored, I hastened into the changing room. In mounting excitement I stripped off my regulation grey joggers and long tee and let the gown slither over my head. The colour was perfect with my complexion. The dress clung to my curves beautifully. Although – I glanced down at the hem puddling over the floor – it would need some incredibly high heels. No problem. I slipped the gown off. Shoe shop next.

By mid-afternoon I was pretty much done. I free-wheeled the buggy out to the car park with not just a carefully packed evening dress in the shopping tray, but also a boxed pair of pink satin killer heels and matching evening bag. I just hoped Jamie didn't have a fit when he received the credit card bill. I set about strapping Eddie into his car seat and dismantling the buggy. Placing the shopping bags carefully on top of the pram, I slammed the boot down, jumped into the driver's seat and started the car up. Eddie was due his afternoon nap. Although, I glanced in the rear view mirror at my son, it was apparent he was on the verge of crashing out any...second...now. His eyelids fluttered down, dark lashes sweeping rosy cheeks.

I popped the gear into reverse and was just edging out, when I nearly stalled the engine in shock. For there, walking right behind my car, was Stevie. He didn't see me. Nor did his companion. I paused, feet depressing the clutch and brake pedals, and watched slack-jawed as the pair of them sauntered over to a bright green Mazda MX-5 convertible sports car. Oh very nice. Clearly Fareham & Mackerel were paying a pretty penny for this particular employee to drive around in *that*. Stevie was carrying a couple of M&S shopping bags from the food hall. Selina was carrying a pale pink boutique bag adorned with a fancy logo. I recognised it as that of a hideously expensive lingerie shop. Whatever lay within that bag would be black or red, incredibly wispy and extortionately expensive. Selina's key fob popped the central locking. Shopping was chucked carelessly into the boot. Moments later the engine burst into life and the car reversed out of its parking space. I released the clutch on the Muck Truck and did likewise. And then I did what all good detectives do. I followed them.

Chapter Eighteen

As Selina's nifty little sports car edged out of the car park and accelerated off, I realised I needed to change my mindset about speed. Immediately. Gulping hard, I clutched the steering wheel and applied pressure to the accelerator. The car's engine rose and I changed gear. Third. Now fourth. Okay Cass. You can do this. You can drive at – I peered at the speedometer – forty five miles per hour. I was now in fifth gear. This was unchartered territory with my baby in the car. My eyes darted to the rear view mirror and sought out Eddie in his car seat. He was fast asleep, head lolling to one side. I gripped the steering wheel tighter and sped after Selina. For a while it appeared the lovers were heading for Boxleigh. Certainly I had assumed they were both going back to Stevie's house. But in due course Selina filtered on to the A2 heading towards Greenwich. Surely she wouldn't be taking Stevie back to Ethan's apartment? That would be far too risky now Ethan was back in the UK. For a while we simply cruised. I glanced nervously at the speedometer. We were up to sixty miles per hour. Water was trickling down my sides. Were my armpits leaking? I risked taking one hand off the steering wheel and flicked the air con on. So what if the outside temperature was only five degrees. Right now, inside my long tee, there was a heatwave going on.

Eventually the Mazda filtered off the carriageway. We were heading towards Blackheath. Ah yes. I seemed to remember Jamie saying that Selina had an apartment in this area. Had she not sold it before moving in with Ethan? I had a feeling I was about to find out. We bounced along several residential roads before Selina indicated left. Slowing down, I watched as the Mazda swung through a pair of towering twin gateposts topped with concrete lions. I crawled past. Whichever apartment was hers, it was part of an elegant Grade II listed building. I indicated and pulled over, parking two wheels illegally on the pavement. Craning my neck round, I watched as Selina and Stevie – now carrying the shopping bags – went through the imposing front door. They'd had a morning bonk, done a bit of sexy shopping and were no doubt all set for more sex with sex food on the side. I shook my head. What a way to spend a day. Scanning the building, I deduced there were three flats. Basement, ground and top floor. Very smart. Very expensive. The lobby door closed behind them. For a moment I wondered what to do next. Jamie would be apoplectic if he knew I'd gone spying. I couldn't possibly tell him. Nor would it do any good trying to convince him Stevie and Selina were having an affair. It would make his position with Ethan untenable. And if I confronted Stevie, what would he say? Probably, 'Mind your own business Cass.' Which, come to think of it, was more or less what Jamie had said when we'd bathed Eddie last night.

I glanced at my watch. Time to be thinking about the school run. And not a moment to lose, because no way was I roaring back to Boxleigh Grammar at nearly sixty miles per hour. Forty minutes later I was parked outside the school gates. Eddie was starting to stir. He opened his eyes and grinned with delight when his siblings piled into the car.

'Hi Cass,' Dylan slid in behind Toby. 'You don't need to give me a lift in future. Everything is fine with me and Richard Clegg now.'

'Is it?' I waited for the back passenger door to close, indicated and pulled out.

'Are you now the best of chums then?'

'Hardly!' Dylan scoffed. 'You told me to beat him up. Remember?'

'Don't be ridiculous,' I spluttered, 'fighting talk is one thing. To actually start a fight is something totally different.'

'No,' Dylan furrowed his brow, 'you pointed out that I was twice the size of Richard Clegg and asked if I couldn't beat him up?'

'Well I meant hypothetically. Not literally!'

'And also,' Jonas chimed in, 'you more or less told me the same thing this morning – to get Toby's plimsolls back and look after Dylan.'

I had a sudden recollection of Jonas pressing an index finger against the side of his nose, telling me he'd caught my drift and to consider it a done deed.

'Oh terrific,' I thumped the steering wheel. 'So what did you both do to Richard Clegg?'

'It was really cool Mum,' said Toby. 'The three of us followed Richard Clegg into the loo at break time–'

'And then I leant against the door,' said Dylan, 'to stop anybody else being able to follow us in–'

'And I grabbed hold of Richard Clegg's neck,' Jonas said cheerfully, 'and threatened to stick his head down the toilet if he didn't return Toby's plimsolls and stop harassing Dylan. He cried like a baby.'

'Bullies always do when they're on their own,' Toby nodded sagely.

'So all's well that ends well,' agreed Dylan.

'Right,' I said faintly as the Muck Truck pulled up outside Nell's house. 'Well I hope there are no repercussions.'

'Nah,' Jonas swaggered, 'Richard Clegg asked if he could join our gang. Said his last gang was too puny for warfare. We said we'd think about it.'

'Thank you very much Jonas, but there will be no more talk of gang warfare. The last thing I want is Miss Jenner calling me up and asking for explanations on why I told my children to stick a boy's head down the toilet.' That was all I needed. My children would be snatched away before you could say Social Services.

'Anyway,' said Dylan, 'not a word to Mum, eh Cass?'

'Definitely not,' I assured. I wasn't quite sure what Nell would make of her oldest friend organising school terror tactics of which her son was an active member.

That evening Arthur once again joined us for dinner. There was more endless chatter about boat restoration. I found myself discreetly yawning into my steak and kidney pie. How on earth could such a project interest Edna? But clearly it did for her eyes were alight. In fact everything about my mother-in-law seemed to be glowing. And I wasn't too sure it was just boat conversation thrilling her to bits. The more I studied Arthur and Edna, the more convinced I became that a completely different set of undercurrents were going on.

I didn't have to wait long for confirmation either. Sometime after Eddie and the children had gone to bed, Jamie and I were watching television when Edna put her head around the living room door.

'I'm just popping over to Arthur's,' Edna said, for all the world as if saying she was just off to Sainsbury's. Except it was ten o'clock at night. 'For a nightcap.'

Jamie's head swivelled and his mouth dropped open. 'Can't he have a nightcap here Mum?'

'No dear,' said Edna briskly. 'There are some things we want to discuss.'

'Can't you discuss them tomorrow?' Jamie frowned. 'After all, you spend all day together. Surely you could have discussed whatever it was earlier on?'

'Jamie dear,' Edna was now belting up her coat, 'you are sounding like a parent. Which of course you are. But not mine,' she patted her coat pocket for her car keys. 'So don't wait up. I'll see you both later.' And with that my mother-in-law turned on her heel. Not before either of us had copped the small overnight bag she was clasping in one hand. Seconds later, there was the sound of her Micra starting up.

'Well I'll be–'

'Not a word Cassie,' Jamie grimaced. He leapt to his feet. 'My God! My mother has just left the house,' he peered at his wristwatch, 'in the dead of night–'

'Oh hardly darling–'

'To go to another man's home,' Jamie raked his hair, 'and do heaven only knows what. It's outrageous. She's seventy-two years old! What on earth is she thinking about?' he spluttered.

'Having a nightcap,' I said. I had a mental picture of Arthur and Edna tucked up in bed together, wearing identical nightcaps and looking like a pair of elves. I batted the vision away. Standing up I pointed the remote control at the television. The screen instantly went black.

'She's not coming home!' Jamie exhorted.

I chucked the remote control on the sofa. 'Darling, let's go to bed.'

'I won't sleep a wink,' Jamie began pacing the floor in agitation. 'What do you think they might do?'

'Come on,' I took his hand and led him across the hall. 'They've bought a boat together darling. What did you think they were going to do?'

'Sail the ruddy thing!' Jamie gasped.

'Y-e-s,' I led my husband up the stairs and across the landing to our bedroom. 'And when they've thrown down the anchor at the end of a day, then what?' I quietly shut our bedroom door.

'Then they go to sleep. In their separate berths. They're too old for shenanigans Cassie.'

'Does that mean that when you're seventy-two you will no longer be up for it?' I gave Jamie a playful push towards our bed.

'No!' he gasped. 'I would hazard not.'

'Why?' I began to unbutton his shirt.

'Darling I'm sorry but I really cannot even begin to think about doing anything sexy when my mother has just–'

'Shhh,' I put a finger over Jamie's lips and felt for the belt on his trousers. 'Sometimes you think too much.'

'Is this my wife talking?'

'No. It's your lover talking.'

'My lover eh?'

'Yes,' I shoved him backwards and he fell onto the bed. 'Your lover who does unspeakably rude things.'

'Tell me more,' Jamie whispered.

My hand snaked out for the bedside light. Seconds later the room plunged into darkness.

'So,' Morag chortled, 'old Edna is a bit of a goer on the quiet eh?'

She reached for the coffee pot and topped mine and Nell's cups up. The three of us were seated in Morag's bright sunny kitchen. Eddie and Henry were gurgling together in Henry's playpen. Through the kitchen window I could see Matt talking to an owner whilst stable girls scurried about seeing to hay nets and water buckets.

'Jamie was beside himself,' I reached for a Hob Nob. 'By the way, not a word about this to Matt and Ben okay?' I bit into the biscuit. 'I'm not sure my husband would be thrilled to know I've been gossiping with the pair of you about his mother's love life.'

'Blimey,' said Nell, 'and there was me thinking Ben and I were pretty much past it,' she shifted baby Rosie onto her other breast, 'just goes to show that there's potentially life in an old dog yet.'

'And talking of dogs,' said Morag, 'I do wish you'd left Rocket at home Nell. She keeps drooling all over my clean kitchen floor. Oh for goodness sake,' Morag rolled her eyes at Rocket. Ribbons of saliva were hanging from Rocket's jowls. 'Give her a Hob Nob.'

Nell leant forward, shifting Rosie slightly, and tipped half a packet of Hob Nobs on the floor.

'Not like that!' screeched Morag. 'I'll have to anti-bac the floor now.'

'For goodness sake Morag,' chided Nell, 'your floor is so clean I could eat my dinner off it.'

'Not after your dog's bottom has been all over it,' Morag protested.

'You have strong OCD tendencies, do you know that?' Nell reached for another Hob Nob.

'Girls, girls,' I clapped my hands.

'So what did Jamie think about Selina spiking your drink?' asked Nell, tactfully changing the subject.

'He thought it was an absolute load of tosh and nonsense,' I took a sip of coffee. 'Nor was he best pleased that I'd spent the afternoon filming Stevie and Selina at Maxwell's Equestrian Centre.'

'Did you show him the evidence?' asked Morag.

'Er, it didn't film quite the way I'd hoped. Initially Jamie pooh-poohed Stevie being involved with Selina, but later said it was none of our business.'

'Well he's got a point,' said Morag. 'Doesn't alter the fact that we all think Selina is up to no good though.'

'I followed her again yesterday,' I lowered my voice conspiratorially.

'What?' Nell sprayed biscuit crumbs over Rosie.

'Selina threw a sickie from work. And it just so happens that Stevie did too. I accidentally stumbled across the pair of them whilst I was out shopping for an evening dress–'

'Well you could have told me Cass. I'd have loved to have done a bit of shopping.' Morag looked incredibly put out.

'Sorry,' I placated, 'but it was totally spur of the moment.' Morag looked slightly mollified. 'Anyway, when I was reversing my car out of its space, who should be walking behind it?'

'Stevie and Selina,' breathed Nell.

'The very one and same,' I nodded picking up another Hob Nob. 'He is such a slippery snake.'

'That reminds me of a joke,' said Nell, 'you'll like this.'

'Spit it out Nellie-Wellie,' Morag groaned. We both propped our elbows on the table, chins cupped in palms.

'There once lived, deep in a forest, an orphaned bunny and an orphaned snake. Both were blind from birth. One day the bunny was hopping through the forest when he tripped over the snake. "I'm sorry," said the bunny, "I'm blind. And because I'm also an orphan, I don't even know what I am." "It's okay," replied the snake, "I too have been blind since birth and never knew my mother. Maybe I could slither over you and work out what you are." "That would be wonderful," replied the bunny. So the snake slithered all over the bunny and said, "You're covered in soft fur, you have long ears, your nose twitches and you have a cottony tail. I'd say that you must be a bunny rabbit." The bunny said, "Maybe I could feel you all over with my paw and help you too." So the bunny felt the snake all over and reached his conclusion. "You're smooth and slippery. You have a forked tongue, no backbone and no balls. So you're either a team leader, supervisor or possibly someone in senior management."

'Stevie to perfection,' I giggled.

'So,' Morag turned the conversation back to Selina, 'what happened after you spotted the pair of them in the car park?'

'I waited for them to drive off, and then I followed them.'

Morag's eyes widened. 'And did you manage to keep up?'

'Yes,' I beamed, 'I'll make a getaway driver yet!'

'So where did you follow them to?' asked Nell.

'To Selina's bachelorette pad. A swanky building in Blackheath. They'd obviously gone back to hers for a bonk.'

'And then what happened?' asked Morag.

'Well,' I grimaced, 'then I realised I was behaving rather ridiculously, and went and fetched the kids from school. But one thing is certain. Selina is messing about with my ex-husband. So much for Jamie insisting she's loved up to the eyeballs with Ethan.'

'Loved up,' Morag sneered. 'The woman sounds like a mercenary gold digger.'

'Of that there's no doubt,' I nodded.

'So what's all this about shopping for an evening dress?' Morag once again topped up our coffees.

'Oh don't remind me,' I groaned. 'The bank's annual ball. This Saturday. Me and Jamie. With Ethan and Selina.'

Nell blew out her cheeks. 'Well I don't care what Jamie says Cass. You watch your grub. And your glass. I wouldn't want that woman around anything that's going near my mouth.'

'Don't worry,' I nodded, 'her card is marked. I might just lean over her dinner and drop Senakot over it.'

'That reminds me,' said Nell unlatching Rosie from her breast, 'I must get some laxatives. Haven't had a good pooh since my daughter was born.'

'Thank you for sharing Nell,' Morag rolled her eyes.

'Well it's true,' said Nell hoiking up her maternity bra. 'Much as I love my darling daughter, she is definitely the last baby I shall be having. In the first flush of pregnancy you suffer morning sickness. I'd completely forgotten you can keep vomiting long after you think you're finished. And then when you're nearing the end of the pregnancy, it completely wrecks your fanny. Not to mention your backside. Do you know–'

'Nell I do *not* want to know about your haemorrhoids,' Morag waggled a finger.

'Why not?'

'Because I want another baby and I don't want you putting me off. So,' Morag turned her attention back to me, 'tell us both about the evening dress you bought.'

When I went downstairs the following morning with Eddie on my hip, Edna was already at the kitchen range. The aroma of sausage and hash browns filled the air.

'Good morning Cassandra dear,' she trilled. Just like that. As if she'd been in our house all night long tucked up on the pull-out bed in the study. Not knocking back nightcaps – or whatever it was that seventy-two year old women did in the privacy of another pensioner's home.

'Hello Edna,' I smiled. 'No Arthur this morning?'

'No dear.' My mother-in-law gave the frying pan a vigorous shake. 'He'll be coming over a little later.' She didn't quite meet my gaze.

At that moment Jamie came in. There was a shift in the atmosphere. As though a chill wind had blown in. 'Morning Mother,' he said bleakly, before sitting down at the table.

Edna didn't bat an eyelid. 'Good morning Jamie dear.'

'So,' Jamie did a spot of noisy throat clearing, 'did you discuss whatever it was you wanted to discuss with Arthur?'

'Yes thank you dear.'

'And that warranted you staying out all night did it?' The words were out before Jamie could stop them.

'Um, I think I'll just take Eddie's bottle up to the nursery and leave you two–'

'Good idea,' said Jamie curtly. I hastened out of the kitchen. Seconds later the door closed after me. Oh God. Please don't let my husband get stroppy. It was bad enough trying to stop him from losing his cool with the children sometimes, never mind a lovesick pensioner.

I went upstairs and into Eddie's nursery. Picking up Eddie, I plonked myself in the rocking chair. Settling my baby boy into the crook of one arm, I gave him his bottle. I could hear the children scampering about in their rooms as they sorted themselves out for school. Petra's radio burst into life. Seconds later Dave Berry and Lisa Snowden were clashing with the boys listening to Radio 1. The sounds of a family home. I rocked away contentedly while Eddie guzzled from his bottle.

Minutes later a shadow fell across the doorway. I looked up to see Jamie standing there. He looked white-faced. Shocked.

'Whatever's the matter darling?' I asked in alarm.

'It's Arthur,' Jamie whispered.

I paled. 'Has something happened?'

'Yes. He's asked Mum to marry him.'

Chapter Nineteen

I stared at my husband. He looked devastated. As though the bottom of his world had fallen out.

'Jamie?'

'She can't marry him Cassie. They've only known each other five minutes.'

'Has Edna accepted Arthur's proposal?'

'Not yet. She said she'd think about it.'

'Well there you go then,' I said, rocking Eddie. 'Your Mum isn't daft darling. She's not the type to rush into something without thinking it through.'

'Actually, I disagree.' Jamie moved over to the window. He gazed out at the Common below. The ground was smothered in glittering frost. The bare trees added to the bleak look at this early hour of the morning. 'If she thinks things through properly, how come there's a scaled-down ocean liner in our garage?'

'Well,' I blustered, 'granted that was a bit uncharacteristic but–'

'Uncharacteristic!' Jamie spluttered. 'It was totally impulsive, reckless and irresponsible. I know my mother's always been a bit eccentric – brandishing an egg whisk in one hand and a power drill in the other – but there's a world of difference between knocking up a bookcase for the kids and buying a shipwreck with a man she hardly knows. Do you think Arthur's after her money?'

'No, of course not! Why are you so against Arthur all of a sudden? I thought you liked him.'

'I'm not against him. And he seems perfectly affable. I just don't want him–'

'As a step-father,' I finished Jamie's sentence.

Jamie turned his back to the window and leant against the sill. 'No, no, it's not that,' he sighed. 'I guess I've been so used to Mum being single for decades, I just assumed she'd always be on her own. It just seems strange, after all these years, to think of her being romantically involved with someone.'

'She had to get used to you being romantically involved again Jamie. After you were widowed.'

'Hardly the same thing though, is it? I'm younger than her.'

'Oh my God,' I crowed, 'you sound like a typical Neanderthal man. Sexist. Ageist. Utter prejudice!' I stood up and put Eddie over my shoulder. Rubbed his back. 'Whatever the future holds for Edna and Arthur, I'm sure it will be a very companionable one – whether they marry or not. They clearly have common interests.' Eddie emitted a man-sized belch.

'Well I'd just like to see a long, old-fashioned courtship. That's all. There's no need to rush into things.'

'Of course, darling. I mean, we didn't eh? We had the longest courtship in history.'

'That was different,' Jamie huffed.

'Absolutely,' I nodded. 'We were never like Edna and Arthur. They are only in their seventies after all. They've all the time in the world, right?'

Jamie opened his mouth to say something, but then appeared to change his mind. 'I'd better get ready for work. Selina is apparently going to be off for the rest of the week.'

My head jerked up. 'What's the matter with her?'

'Haven't a clue. But Ethan is concerned. He said she's very out of sorts. Pre-occupied and distant. And periodically behaving quite oddly. He confided that Selina still sees a psychiatrist and counsellor routinely. Apparently she hasn't kept her last two appointments, but won't talk about it.'

'I hope he knows what he's doing taking her on,' I grimaced. 'He could do miles better than an unstable basket case like–'

'Now who's showing prejudice?'

'Not without due cause.' I pursed my lips. How had the conversation shifted from Edna and potential wedding bells to Selina and her mislaid marbles? I placed Eddie down on his changing mat and set about topping and tailing him. Blasted woman. All she seemed to have done recently was invade my life. And now, even though she wasn't in my house, somehow her very name had conjured up the ghost of her presence, upsetting the harmony within my home. I snapped Eddie into a clean romper suit and stood up.

'Let's not argue.' Jamie moved towards me. Moments later his arms encircled Eddie and me. 'I know Selina will never be your best friend. And I'm sorry you've recently seen so much of her.' Jamie kissed the tip of my nose.

I shrugged and sighed. 'I shall look forward to dancing with my husband at the bank's ball. You'd better get ready for work, or you'll be late.'

'Yep,' Jamie took Eddie from me for a quick cuddle. 'And by the way Cassie, don't mention anything to Morag and Nell about Mum's marriage proposal.'

'Of course not,' I replied.

'So when do you think Edna will make up her mind about marrying Arthur?' asked Nell.

'I really don't know.' I set three mugs on the table and moved a screwdriver out of the way. Clearly Edna had left it behind. Nell, Morag and I had congregated, this time in my kitchen, for one of our regular coffee mornings. 'Edna hasn't even mentioned the marriage word to me. Only to Jamie.'

'So Mum's the word,' said Morag, tapping her nose.

'Discretion is my middle name,' Nell assured.

Outside the sounds of Edna and Arthur banging and crashing about on the boat filtered across the driveway. In between bashes, a blaring radio could be heard.

'Just think Cass,' said Morag reflectively, 'all that wasted time we spent looking for potential husbands. Trawling wine bars. Nightclubs. Not forgetting speed dating. And what we should have done was visit our local B&Q and loiter around the paint aisles. And then we'd have been up to our elbows not just in boats, but dreamboats. Funny old world.'

Nell picked up her coffee and blew on it. 'Didn't you two also try out The Lonely Hearts column in the local rag?'

'Oh God,' scoffed Morag, 'all those pitiful specimens who advertised themselves in print. Do you remember, Cass, going on a blind date with that Granddad who tried to make out he was only forty-something years old?'

I put some Hob Nobs on the table. 'Don't remind me. Certainly there were a few who told porkies about themselves.'

'Like what?' Nell stretched a hand across the table and palmed a Hob Nob.

'Well, there was one guy who waxed lyrical about himself. Said he was passionate, open-minded, adventurous and emotionally secure.'

'Sounds too good to be true,' Nell pulled a face.

'And was,' I agreed, helping myself to a Hob Nob. 'He turned out to be a desperate, pathological liar, on medication with stalker tendencies.'

'Or what about that guy who insisted he was thirtyish, athletic and large framed?' Morag giggled.

'Bit of a hunk?' Nell raised an eyebrow.

'If you like hugely fat sixty year olds with bigger boobs than me. The women were just as bad,' said Morag. 'You can bet your last fiver that if a woman described herself as a fun, new age feminist it actually meant she was an annoying whinger with body hair in the wrong places.'

'Well you both found your soulmates in the end,' Nell brushed crumbs off her hands before reaching for her mug. 'And with a bit of luck, Edna has found hers too.'

'Found my what?' said a familiar voice.

I froze. Christ, I hadn't heard the back door open. How long had she been standing there listening to us gossiping? Long enough to hear me indiscreetly talking about marriage proposals that I wasn't even meant to know about, never mind repeat?

'Um, your screwdriver,' I snatched up the forgotten implement and waggled it at Edna.

'Thank you Cassandra dear,' Edna wiped her feet before coming over to me and retrieving it. She slid the screwdriver into the folds of a leather tool satchel strung around her waist. 'Don't mind me girls, carry on talking. I've just popped in to make Arthur and myself a quick sandwich.' Edna washed her hands at the sink before removing the breadboard from a cupboard.

'I must say, you're a dark horse Edna,' Nell chirruped. 'I didn't even know you'd bought a boat, never mind found yourself a bloke. So you're shacking up together on an ocean wave. Nifty work! What's this Arthur like then?'

Morag and I stared at each other, appalled. I caught Nell's eye and made a slicing motion across my throat. All that tripe about discretion being her middle name. Nell looked perplexed. 'What's the matter?' she hissed, 'I'm only making conversation.'

There was a pregnant pause. Edna sliced up some bread. Morag was suddenly very interested in the contents of my fruit bowl. I studied my fingernails.

'Arthur is indeed a very nice *bloke*,' Edna eventually said. 'Nice enough for me to share the expense of a boat restoration project and,' she reached into the fridge for some butter, 'whilst I wouldn't term it as *shacking up together on an ocean wave*, it is true that we are seriously thinking about committing to each other.'

'How do you mean Edna?' I asked.

Edna returned the butter to the fridge and pulled out some thin slices of rare beef. My stomach gave a sudden growl of hunger. 'I might as well tell you, Cassandra dear, that Arthur has asked me to marry him.'

'Ooooh how exciting,' Nell shrieked. 'Cass said–'

I kicked Nell hard under the table. 'That's absolutely *wonderful* Edna,' I gushed. 'Let me be the first to congratulate you.'

Edna blushed. 'Well thank you Cassandra dear, but I haven't yet accepted Arthur's proposal. We've only known each other for a brief time. Committing to a boat restoration is one thing. I can extract myself from that any time I like. Signing up for marriage is something else, and will need thinking through. Carefully.

Morag cleared her throat. 'Well you must have some good vibes about Arthur to have made such a financial commitment with the boat.'

'Of course. But the boat can be sold. For a tidy profit too. Whereas a marriage,' Edna cut the crusts off the sandwiches, 'well that's a completely different ball game.'

'You can say that again,' Nell laughed smuttily.

'Well whatever decision you reach,' I glared at Nell, 'I'm sure it will be the right one.'

'Thank you Cassandra dear. Now if you'll excuse me girls, I must take these sandwiches out to Arthur. Grafting is hungry work.'

'Laters Edna,' Nell waved. The back door shut. 'Aw, your mum-in-law looks quite loved up. I wonder what it's like getting your leg over at seventy-two.'

'For heaven's sake Nell, talk about royally dropping me in it! And fancy referring to Arthur as a *bloke*. He's quite refined. Ex-Merchant Navy stock. Not Uncle Albert from *Fools and Horses*!'

'Oh keep your hair on Cass. I was just joshing with Edna, and she knew it. So what if she's seventy-two? She's still a woman like the three of us. With emotions. And dreams. And unfulfilled urges.'

'Speak for yourself,' Morag sniffed. She shifted on her stool, straightened her back and stuck her chest out. I instantly recognised the body language. Morag was revving up to tell us her latest sexy shenanigans. And under no circumstances was she to be interrupted. 'Last night we did something very different.'

'You mean you didn't go to the stud farm?' I muttered.

'What stud farm?' Nell frowned.

'Last night we went in the car,' Morag nodded, eyes wide.

'To the stud farm?' asked Nell.

'For a drive Nellie-Wellie,' Morag said irritably, 'keep up. We went for a drive and parked in a lonely, dark lane.'

'Why?'

'For fun!' Morag trilled. 'I was the driver. Matt was in the passenger seat. Blindfolded and handcuffed. He was my hostage.'

'Did anybody see you?' I asked. I wasn't quite sure what the Old Bill would have made of a female driving along with a blindfolded man sitting next to her.

'No!' she sighed, 'It was dark remember? So I parked up, dropped the back seats down and ordered Matt into the back of the car. Then I demanded he strip off.'

'What the heck would you have done if somebody had come along Morag?' I shook my head incredulously.

'All part of the thrill. But in reality that wouldn't have happened. It was an uninhabited country lane.'

'No stud farm?' asked Nell.

'It was my Ford Galaxy Nell,' Morag enunciated.

'Blimey, all that fuss you made when you took me to hospital,' Nell fumed, 'insisting on towels in your car, and there you are rogering your husband senseless on the upholstery.'

'Slightly different. Matt was on his back. And I climbed on top of him. No spillages.'

I groaned. Too much information.

'So,' Morag continued, 'I then whispered to Matt that he was my sex slave, and I could do to him whatever I pleased.'

'And what did Matt say to that?' I picked up a Hob Nob, but held off biting into it for fear of choking.

'He was whimpering. Absolutely begging me to let him go. He said he had a wife who would be furious with him.'

'But that's you,' Nell looked puzzled.

'Yes. We were *pretending* Nell. You know. Fantasising.'

Nell shook her head slowly. 'I see.' She clearly didn't.

'And I called him a bad boy for rising – literally – to the charms of another woman.'

'Who was that?' Nell frowned.

'Me of course! We were still pretending, yes?'

'And then what happened?' I risked biting into the Hob Nob.

'We both had the noisiest most incredible climax at exactly the same time. Matt was going, "Guuuh-guh-guh-guh," and I was going, "Aaaaaaaah ah ah ah."'

I began to choke. Nell thumped me on the back.

'And after you'd made all this noise, how did it end?' she asked.

'Well unfortunately my leg jerked out and crashed against the steering wheel setting the airbag off. It didn't half make us jump.'

There was a pause while Nell and I tried to understand the need for car sex.

'So what's all this got to do with a stud farm?' Nell eventually asked.

At that precise moment my mobile announced a text message. I leant sideways. Making a long arm to the worktop, I grabbed the handset. A message from Stevie.

Going away. Catch you later.

I stared at the text. Odd. Where was he going? And would he be back in time for the weekend? I knew Stevie had purchased top dollar tickets to take the twins to Billy Elliott the Musical on Saturday night. Surely he wasn't going to cancel after nearly bankrupting himself? I tapped a message back.

Will you see Billy?

Rosie began to wail. Nell heaved herself upright and went over to the playpen. She lifted Rosie out. 'I suppose I'd better get you fed Madam and then head back home. There are a million chores I should be doing. Shame on me for guzzling coffee and listening to stories about debauched sex and pensioners being proposed to.'

Morag stood up and stretched. 'All that talk about sex has made me quite up for it. I think I shall find my husband. Have another go at making a baby.' She smirked in satisfaction. 'I can't wait to be pregnant again.'

'More fool you,' said Nell.

My phone announced another text message.

Yes, staying at Billy's for a few days. Talk soon.

I stared at the text message. What on earth was Stevie talking about? Something didn't stack up here. I hit the ring button. Stevie's voicemail immediately kicked in. Oh for goodness sake. I hung up irritably. I'd give him a call later. When Nell and Morag had gone, and the air wasn't filled with the sound of wailing babies. I tossed the phone onto the worktop, and went to the playpen to pick up my son.

By the time I'd fed Eddie, cleared up coffee cups and plates, and made myself a quick sandwich, it was time for the school run. I spent the rest of the afternoon working my way through manky PE kits and scrubbing football boots, before starting on a pile of ironing. It was gone nine when I had the next window of opportunity to talk to Stevie without interruption. But, as I reached for the telephone, it rang.

'Cass?' asked a tremulous voice. 'It's Charlotte.'

Now there was somebody I hadn't expected to hear from again.

'Hello Charlotte. Is everything all right?'

'No,' she replied breathlessly. 'No, things are not all right.'

'Whatever's the matter?' I asked.

There was a pause. When she next spoke, her voice crackled with emotion.

'I think Stevie is missing.'

Chapter Twenty

'Missing?' I gripped the handset. 'What do you mean you think Stevie is missing?'

'I mean he's not around. He's disappeared. Without a trace.'

Ah. Whilst Charlotte might believe Stevie's absence to be worrying, thanks to my brief role as detective, I knew Stevie wasn't far away. And quite possibly with Selina by his side. The fact that she'd absented herself from work for an entire week probably meant the pair of them were holed up in some quaint inn with a roaring fire and personal service in hot tea and crumpet. With Selina being the crumpet.

'Charlotte, I don't know how to tell you this, but–'

'Oh my God. What's happened to him?' she squawked.

'Absolutely nothing. He's fine. Really. But the reason you can't find him is – well there's no other way of telling you. He's met somebody else. And he's probably with her.'

There was a pause while Charlotte digested this. 'B-but I don't understand. He's not gone into work.'

'Well he's probably taken the week off as holiday.'

'N-no,' I sensed her shaking her head. 'I was meant to meet Stevie in London today. For lunch. But he didn't turn up. And he'd been adamant about us getting together to talk. You see, I've taken legal advice about staking a claim on half his house.' Ouch. 'Well I've co-habited with him for long enough,' Charlotte said defensively. 'Paid my share towards bills and maintenance. Made the place look nice. I don't see why I shouldn't walk away with a few thousand pounds so I can start all over again.'

'Well obviously I can't comment on that Charlotte. It's between you and Stevie.'

'I appreciate you're going to take his side,' she said stiffly.

'Charlotte, your relationship with Stevie is none of my business. So there is no side for me to take. And if Stevie failed to turn up today, that's more likely because he's feeling aggrieved rather than anything sinister happening to him.'

'I'm telling you Cass, something isn't right. After work I drove round to his house. I still have a key. I let myself in and tripped over a pile of mail.'

'That's because Stevie has been with this other woman. At her place.'

'So why hasn't he taken his toothbrush and wash bag with him?'

'Because he's a slob?' I ventured.

'I went through his wardrobe Cass. Everything is still there. All untouched. He's taken no spare clothing. In fact I can probably tell you what he was wearing when he last walked out of his house. I checked his underwear drawer, and also the laundry bin. He hasn't even taken a change of underpants with him.'

'Did you find his wallet in the house?'

'No. He must have that on him.'

'So, if he'd left on a whim, theoretically he could buy himself a fresh change of clothes?'

'Well, put like that, I suppose so. But the other thing is,' she took a shaky breath, 'nobody at Stevie's work knows his whereabouts either. He's not telephoned to explain his absence Cass. He's not taken annual leave. And other than phoning in sick on Monday with a bad back, nobody has heard from him since. He told the Personnel Officer he'd return to the office on Tuesday. Tomorrow is Thursday, and so far Stevie has been a complete no show.'

I paused. For all Stevie's womanising faults, and lack of responsibility in a relationship, one thing he wasn't apathetic about was work. Okay, so he'd pulled a sickie on Monday pretending he'd had a bad back. But he wouldn't have done that unless his diary had been quiet. And he certainly wouldn't have neglected to telephone the office without some sort of further explanation for any prolonged absence. Even if it was just to dish out more lies!

'I don't know what to say Charlotte, other than I had a text message from Stevie earlier on today. So I know he's okay.'

'What did it say?'

'Nothing much. Just that he was going away. He's cancelled seeing the twins this weekend. So there you have it. I'm sorry. Stevie must have this woman really bad to forego his kids and neglect his employers. I hope he doesn't lose his job.'

There was a pause. I sensed Charlotte trying to absorb the body blows one by one. A failed relationship. A man who had moved on from her without a backward glance – and stood her up without even a text by way of apology.

'Did Stevie say where he was going?'

'He mentioned he was staying with somebody called Billy.'

'Stevie doesn't know anybody called Billy,' Charlotte sounded puzzled.

'Billy probably doesn't exist. He was meant to be taking the twins to see Billy Elliott the Musical this Saturday. When I asked if that was still on, he texted back saying he was staying at Billy's for a few days. It was probably the first name that came into his head Charlotte. Honestly, Stevie tells so many lies when it suits him, I don't think he can always keep track of the porkies he's telling. You really are better off without him you know.'

'Yes,' she sighed miserably. 'And I am ready to move on. Promise. I was just concerned. But if you really think there's nothing to be alarmed about. Well, I guess I'll stop worrying.'

'Tell you what, give me your mobile number and I'll send you a text when I next speak to him. Just to put your mind at rest. How's that?'

I duly scribbled down Charlotte's number before ringing off. I felt desperately sorry for somebody so young and beautiful being passed over for the likes of a manipulative, lying bitch like Selina. But then again, Stevie wasn't exactly squeaky clean himself. In fact, the more I thought about Selina and Stevie as a couple, the more well-suited they appeared to be. Although God help that woman if she had designs on being my children's step-mother. Calm Cass. Take deep breaths. That would never happen. The woman was a user. She'd use both Stevie and Ethan for her own purpose. Ethan would provide the fantastic job and lifestyle. Stevie would provide the sex. I retrieved my mobile from the kitchen, and tapped in Charlotte's number.

'Who was that on the phone?' Jamie wandered in. He opened the fridge and peered inside. 'I'm feeling peckish. What can I nibble?'

'It was Charlotte. And come out of that fridge. You're as bad as the children constantly grazing between meals. You'll get a tummy if you're not careful.'

'Well thank you for your concerns about my waistline Mrs Mackerel,' Jamie reversed out of the fridge, 'but perhaps you should worry about your own tummy before you comment on mine,' he prodded me gently in the abs. Or where my abs would have been had I bothered to do stomach crunches.

'What?' I looked down my gently rounded abdomen. 'Are you telling me I look fat?'

'No! I was just saying–'

'That I'm overweight. Well thanks a bunch darling. You certainly know how to make a girl with a post-baby figure feel good about herself. I suppose you think I should be skinny?'

'All I said was–'

'Perhaps you'd like me to be like Victoria Beckham? Stick thin with a lollipop head. And when pregnant, look like a pipe-cleaner but with one of David Beckham's golden balls under my oh-so-cute poncho.' I could feel a rant brewing. How dare Jamie say I look fat! I was well aware of the need to lose a few pounds. But I didn't need my tactless husband reminding me. Typical – just when I had an evening dress to slither into. And had to stand around hob-nobbing with the likes of another stick thin creature. God life was so unfair. 'You're a typical man Jamie Mackerel. You think women should swan around looking gorgeous, even when they're up the duff. And when they've finally popped a sprog, they should shimmy back into their size zero jeans before picking up a duster and flick it in time with their hair extensions. HOW DARE YOU!'

Jamie flattened himself against the fridge, hands up in a gesture of surrender. 'I never said any such thing Cassie. It's you that's just gone off on a wobbly. Is it your time of the month or something?'

'POSSIBLY,' I roared, 'But DON'T think you're getting away with telling me I'm FAT.'

I turned on my heel and stomped off to the lounge. Bloody men. Bloody waistline. Bloody Hob Nobs. I'd eaten way too many of late. Bugger McVities for inventing the blasted things. Didn't companies like them realise they were playing havoc with women's silhouettes? I picked up the remote control and pointed it at the television. I'd take them to Court. What a brilliant idea! In this day and age of compensation-madness, I'd probably succeed too. A mental picture of the Daily Mail floated through my brain. WOMAN SUES BISCUIT MANUFACTURER – OH CRUMBS! Or The Sun: FAT WOMAN GOES CRACKERS OVER HOB NOBS.

Jamie peered around the lounge door. 'Is it safe to come in?' He stuck out one arm and began waving a white tea towel. 'Sorry if I sounded tactless darling. You're not fat. You're perfect.'

I sighed and leant back against the sofa. 'Sorry too. I over-reacted. Probably hormonal. Period's a bit late.'

Jamie sat down next to me. He slung an arm around my shoulders. 'I haven't had a chance to talk to you properly all evening. So, why was Charlotte calling?'

'She was worried about Stevie, and thought he was a missing person.'

'And is he?'

'No, of course not. Just buggering her about. As usual. Causing problems. Wrecking relationships. And not just his own. I know you don't believe me about him seeing Selina–'

'Oh Cassie, please. I don't want to discuss Selina. Every time her name is mentioned in this house, we go to war.'

'I agree,' I said quickly. 'I don't want to talk about her either. But Stevie was meant to meet Charlotte today, and he stood her up. He also sent me a text cancelling seeing the twins this weekend. And he's absented himself from work with no explanation. Charlotte was initially anxious about his whereabouts. I told her he'd met someone else and was probably with her.'

'Well wherever Stevie is, I can promise you he's not with Selina.'

'Oh?'

'She came into the office this afternoon. Looked a bit pale. But assured she was ninety per cent better and would be firing on all cylinders by tomorrow. She later went home with Ethan who was all over her like a rash. Selina was lapping up the attention. I'm afraid where Stevie is concerned he's just an old dog. And it's a shame he's cancelled seeing Livvy and Toby, but leopards don't change their spots. The sooner Charlotte realises that, the better. She's a great kid and lovely looking. No disrespect to your ex-husband darling, but she can do miles better than him.'

'Yes, I more or less told her the same thing.'

'Charlotte will find somebody else. This time next year she might even be married.'

'Mmm. Talking of marriage, your mum told me and the girls that Arthur had proposed.'

Jamie shifted in his seat. A regrouping gesture. This was a topic he wasn't comfortable with.

'Oh yes. And did she say whether she's going to accept his proposal?'

'No. But she did say she was going to give it careful consideration.'

Jamie nodded. 'Good. Well at least she's not rushing into anything. However, there's a distinct absence of my mother this evening. Is she at Arthur's again?' At that moment the front door clicked. 'Talk of the devil,' Jamie muttered. He hauled himself up from the sofa. 'Is that you Mum?'

Edna walked into the lounge. She unbuttoned her coat. Her eyes looked very bright. I wondered if she'd been crying.

'Everything all right Edna?' I asked.

'Yes thank you, Cassandra dear. I want you both to know I've turned down Arthur's proposal of marriage.' Jamie looked visibly relieved. 'However, I have agreed to stay periodically at Arthur's house and we will, of course, be sailing the boat together just soon as she's ready.'

'Why did you turn him down Mum?' Jamie asked quietly.

'Because we've only known each other five minutes. But that's not to say I'll turn him down again, if he asks me in six months time.' Jamie arched an eyebrow. 'Anyway, I won't intrude on your evening. I'm going to have a bath and get myself off to bed. Goodnight dears.'

Jamie stood up and kissed his mother goodnight.

'Goodnight Edna,' I called after my mother-in-law. I stood up too. It was gone ten and I did feel tired. Time to hit the pillow.

'Going up darling?' asked Jamie.

'Yes. Shall I leave my bath water in?'

'Please.'

I wandered back out to the kitchen and picked up my mobile. I'd give Stevie a call while the bath was running. But upon calling his number, the phone rang unanswered. Eventually it went to voicemail. I hung up. Perhaps he was in the bath too. Half an hour later I tried him again. I listened with growing impatience to the ringtone. Stevie's voicemail once more kicked in, inviting me to leave a message.

'Where the devil are you?' I barked irritably. 'I've had Charlotte on the phone wanting to know if I'd seen you. I'm annoyed that you've cancelled seeing the twins this weekend, and I think you're playing with fire skiving off work. Also I want to discuss Billy. I've had an idea. What about the kids see Billy with me? Can you give me a call tomorrow? If it's not *too* much trouble,' I added sarcastically. I pressed the disconnect button. Wretched man.

Hours later I surfaced from sleep aware that something had awoken me. My ears strained to catch any untoward noises. Eddie's baby monitor was faintly buzzing but otherwise silent. Jamie slumbered beside me, his breathing slow and steady. I turned over and was immediately aware of my mobile phone glowing on the bedside table. I picked it up, squinting slightly at its bright light. A text message. From Stevie. At three o'clock in the morning?

Don't leave me snotty voicemails again you stuck up bitch. And don't contact me either.

I blinked. Was I dreaming? I turned the bedside light on. No, I was definitely awake. I read Stevie's text again. Well clearly he was up. And yes I would most definitely contact him again. Who the hell did he think he was! I tossed back the duvet, and padded silently across the carpet to the en-suite bathroom. Shutting myself in, I rang Stevie's number. Once again it went to voicemail.

'Stevie, you've just this second texted me. So why aren't you picking up? Have you been drinking? I can think of no other explanation for the tone of your text message. There's no need to be rude and unpleasant. Regarding Billy – tell you what, to hell with him. Why should I care about you wasting money? And as for not contacting you again – *hellooo*? You're the father of my children, so of course I'll be contacting you again!'

God's sake. Blasted man. I hung up and went back to bed. Annoyed, I grabbed my pillows and gave them a vigorous plumping before flopping back against the mattress. But I felt angry. And rattled. I thought Stevie and I had a good relationship. Having a pop at me and referring to me as a stuck up bitch was bang out of order. I'd give him another call tomorrow. And if he didn't answer his phone next time around, then I'd be blasting his voicemail with both barrels.

Chapter Twenty One

The twins were unimpressed that their father had cancelled his weekend with them. They were also disappointed to be missing Billy Elliott.

'I was really looking forward to it,' Toby whined over the Cocoa Pops.

'Whaddya wanna see that musical for?' Jonas jeered. 'Are you planning on being a ballet dancer?'

'Shut up Jonas,' Toby said good-naturedly. 'I just happen to think it was an ace film and wanted to see the musical.'

'Rather you than me, bud. I can't be doing with pirouettes. Not unless they're being done by Diane Cooper. And preferably in a tutu.'

I bent down and wiped some squashed Cocoa Pops from the floor. 'Who's Diane Cooper?'

'The most gorgeous girl in Year Ten,' said Toby wistfully. 'She's in Petra's class.'

'Take it from me,' said Jonas, 'Diane Cooper has not even registered your existence.'

'Actually I have a plan to make her notice me,' said Toby smugly.

'Oh yeah?' Jonas goaded. 'Are you going to imitate Billy Elliott and pirouette past her?'

Petra came into the kitchen and caught the tail-end of the conversation. 'You're not twelve yet Tobes.' She ruffled Toby's hair affectionately. 'Diane Cooper isn't interested in little boys.'

'She will be,' Toby assured with supreme confidence.

'You better let me in on your plan,' Jonas winked at Toby, 'and leave the big boys to do the flirting.'

Livvy rolled her eyes. 'You might be nearly thirteen and six feet tall Jonas, but you're like a piece of string, and as unappealing as Toby. Plus you both have voices squeakier than a door hinge.'

'If my plan is successful,' said Toby, 'then my voice will have more gravel than our driveway.'

Jonas sat up straight. 'Spill the beans Tobes.'

'Laters,' said Toby. He jerked his head in my direction.

I pretended not to notice, and set about loading the dishwasher with bowls. The likes of Toby and Jonas trying to impress a girl called Diane Cooper were not of interest to me right now. I was far more concerned about making contact with Stevie. I'd give him another call shortly.

'Good morning everybody,' Jamie came into the kitchen. 'And what have we here for breakfast? Oh. Cocoa Pops. Any chance of something hot?' my husband glanced hopefully at the range.

'Certainly.' I reversed out of the dishwasher. 'I can put your Cocoa Pops in the microwave if you wish.'

'Ah. I see you're not a sunny bunny this morning darling.'

'I'm perfectly sunny thank you.' I hunkered back down to my stacking. 'I'm just a bit tired.'

Not to mention queasy. That was why everybody had cereal for breakfast. The thought of standing at the range and frying bacon turned my stomach. Unusually Edna wasn't up and about. Most mornings she straddled an industrial-sized frying pan like a cello player. I hoped my mother-in-law was all right. It was unlike her to not be having breakfast with us all. My mind wandered back to last night, and her over bright eyes. Again, I found myself wondering if she'd been crying. I sighed. Did the path of true love ever run smoothly? Even when seventy-two? Jamie sat down. His face looked as bleak as the weather outside.

'Sorry darling,' I smiled apologetically. 'I'll cook you something nice tonight. Promise.'

'Mum,' Livvy piped up, 'you shouldn't make promises you can't keep.' My daughter got up from the table. 'Not unless it's something like fish fingers and chips.'

The kids scraped back their chairs, and peeled off to bedrooms to sort out school bags. Seconds later Edna came into the kitchen. Jamie perked up. His expression said it all; any chance of a plate loaded with a few sizzling somethings?

'I must have overslept,' said Edna. 'Are you all right Cassandra dear? You look a bit peaky.' Edna pulled the frying pan from a cupboard and immediately began cracking eggs into it. And now a saucepan was making an appearance. A tin of baked beans were being opened. Jamie was looking as though he'd died and gone to heaven.

'I do feel a bit rough actually Edna. I think I'll borrow Rocket later on, and get some fresh air with Eddie.' I paused. Studied my mother-in-law. She didn't have quite her usual buoyancy. 'No Arthur this morning?'

'Oh, he'll be along in a bit,' Edna assured. 'I think he's,' she focussed on the bubbling eggs, 'licking his wounds. He was a bit upset about me turning down his marriage proposal. And I felt somewhat distressed at causing him hurt.' Ah. 'Do you want some eggs Cassandra dear?'

I mentally shuddered. 'No thanks.'

'Is everything all right between you and Arthur?' Jamie asked.

'Right enough. He's a good man. A nice man. He's just feels somewhat discomfited that he – you know – allowed himself to be prematurely swept away by the M word.'

'Is that all it is then Edna – a friendship?' I asked gently.

'Well,' she flipped eggs onto plates and ladled on beans, 'I can't deny that I don't think of Arthur romantically. Because I do. But marriage is a big leap of faith. And not one I can make just yet.'

'Do you want me to have a word with him Mum?' Jamie picked up his knife and fork. 'I can take Arthur out for a few beers if you like.'

'Oh no, Jamie dear. He'd die of embarrassment. Probably best he didn't know you are even aware of his proposal, much less it being declined. He's a proud man. And rightly so.'

Jamie and I glanced at each other as Edna pulled out a chair.

'So,' Jamie nodded his head in the direction of the garage, 'does that mean the boat project is still on?'

'Oh yes! Most definitely. We aim to be sailing around the coast this Spring. There's not a moment to lose with the restoration.'

I went over to the playpen where Eddie had been gurgling happily. Leaning over the safety rail, I picked up my little boy before turning back to my mother-in-law. 'Well I'm glad to hear it Edna. And I'm sure everything between you and Arthur will be fine. Just give him a day or two to recover his pride. You know what men are like,' I smiled. 'And talking of men, I must sort this young man out.'

I hastened upstairs. En-route to Eddie's nursery, I grabbed my mobile phone and punched out Stevie's number. Clamping it to one ear, I deftly set about topping and tailing my little boy, whilst listening to unanswered ringing. Once again my call went to voicemail.

'Hello Stevie. Me again.' I wrestled Eddie into a nappy. 'I'm not going to prevaricate. I know exactly what's going on. You're having an affair with Selina. Of all the women in the world, I don't know why you have to mess around with that one. She's an absolute bitch. And if you want my honest opinion, I think she's a bit of a basket case too. She's an ex-girlfriend of Jamie's and has a major axe to grind with me. She's under the impression I took him off her, when I did no such thing. Before we married she tried to split us up by making out she was having an affair with him. And now she's shacked up with Jamie's boss, who's a very decent bloke. He doesn't deserve the likes of Selina mucking his life up, and I'd be mortified if he found out his fiancée was messing around with my ex-husband. It's embarrassing Stevie. Embarrassing for all of us. And what if the kids found out? Don't you ever stop and wonder what they think of you constantly tom-catting around? And why the heck haven't you been in touch with your employers to let them know where you are? I know you're a reprobate Stevie, but I didn't have you down as irresponsible where work was concerned. Anyway,' I posted Eddie's arms and legs into a romper suit, 'could you please call me. Apart from anything else, I said I'd let Charlotte know you were okay. She was worried about you.'

Without further ado I ended the call. Popping Eddie over my shoulder, I charged back downstairs, grabbed my coat off the banister and pocketed my keys.

'Kids?' I stopped and yelled back up the stairwell. 'I'll see you outside in the car.' Going through to the kitchen, I plucked my holdall from the back of a chair. Edna had gone off to get dressed. I gave Jamie a fleeting kiss on the cheek. 'You're going to be late darling.'

'Thankfully there's no rush this morning.' Jamie caught my hand and pulled me back to him. 'So I'll have a second kiss. Preferably not on my right eyeball.'

I leant in and kissed my husband gently on the mouth. 'Like that?'

'Not bad. You can carry on tonight.'

I gave a lop-sided smile. I felt so dog-tired, by this evening I'd probably be snoring for England. Hurrying out to the car, I strapped Eddie into his car seat. Whilst waiting for the children, I rang Nell. She answered on the seventh ring, and sounded harassed. Rosie was yelling lustily in the background.

'Blimey,' I gave a wry smile, 'I thought World War Three only occurred in my house.'

'I'm going bonkers here Cass. I need to get out of these four walls. Most babies have colic in the evening. But Rosie seems to start in the morning and go on until lunchtime. I can't stay in listening to this, or I'll go potty.'

'I was going to suggest taking Rocket for a lovely long walk. What about we take the babies too? Some fresh air and a stroll in her pram might soothe Rosie.'

'I'll try anything. How cold is it outside?'

'Not too bad. No rain, so that's good. Wrap her up warm. She'll be fine. I'll see you after the school run. I'll give Morag a ring and see if she wants to join us.'

I ended the call and then rang Morag who seemed to be having her own difficulties with Henry.

'I think he's teething,' she said. 'He's grumpy and grizzly. Not to mention producing more dribble than Rocket. Where shall I meet you?'

'At Nell's, in about half an hour.' The kids finally made their appearance and hopped in the car. Doors slammed. 'See you soon,' I said to Morag before disconnecting. 'What's that funny smell?' I sniffed the air.

'Oh no,' groaned Livvy, 'I hope it's not Eddie. He'll make us late if his nappy needs changing.'

'No. It's not a stinky smell.' I sniffed again. 'It's a smoky smell.'

'I can't smell anything,' said Toby. 'You're imagining things Mum.'

I gave a few more sniffs. 'It's gone now. Oh well. Right, are we ready? Everybody got everything? Good. Let's go.'

I reversed the car out of the drive, and pointed the bonnet towards Boxleigh Grammar.

On the journey there was more talk of the delightful Diane Cooper. Every boy in the school apparently wanted to date her. I zoned out and cracked the window down a little bit. Fresh air trickled in and I gulped at it greedily. Why was I feeling so queasy? As I drew up outside Boxleigh Grammar, Eddie began to protest. He was clearly unimpressed at his siblings piling out of the car and going off to school without him. By the time I pulled up at Nell's, he was screaming his head off. Morag's car was already on the drive, but empty. She was obviously inside the house. I carried Eddie – avoiding contact with his wet face and twin snot trails – to Nell's front door. It took several rings of the doorbell before Morag answered. Henry was on her hip and parodying Eddie. The sound of Rosie bawling her head off filtered along the hallway.

'Flaming Nora,' Morag rolled her eyes, 'what the heck's the matter with our kids this morning?'

It was at times like this I was so glad we were all in it together. Our husbands were good fathers, but once they were at work they had respite from teething, colic, tantrums and temperatures. Morag stepped to one side and let me in.

'Eddie's having a paddy because his brothers and sisters have left him,' I said. 'I think he was enjoying listening to the boys' chat-up techniques over some girl they both like. Perhaps Eddie was making mental notes for when he falls in love with Rosie,' I grinned and shut the door behind me.

'Eddie is welcome to Rosie,' said Morag. 'With lungs like that, she's going to make an excellent fishwife one day.'

'Still feeling broody?' I quipped.

'Yes,' Morag assured.

As we pushed open the kitchen door, Rosie's howls assaulted our eardrums. Nell looked like she was at her wits' end. And Rocket, in her basket, bore a look of long suffering.

'Hello Cass,' Nell shouted above the din. 'Where shall we go?'

'I think the park is the easiest option.' I raised my own voice to answer.

'Do you want a coffee first?' Nell asked.

My stomach still felt fragile. 'No. Maybe later. Let's take our brood out first. A bit of stimulation and fresh air, and hopefully they'll be shattered by the time we get back. Then we can have a drink in peace.'

'I'll be hitting the gin at this rate,' Nell threatened. 'Pass me Rosie's jacket Morag. It's behind you. On top of the fridge.'

'Naturally,' said Morag handing her the tiny pink coat. 'Where else would one put one's baby's clothes.'

'Well we can't all be domestic goddesses,' Nell sniffed. 'I'll bet you have Henry's wardrobe arranged in days of the week, colour coded, accessorised and in seasonal order.'

'Of course,' said Morag. 'And then you can find what you're wanting like that,' she clicked her fingers. 'I can't be playing hide and seek with items. And why are Rosie's bootees in Rocket's basket?'

Nell stopped posting Rosie's arms in her coat and glanced at the basket. 'Oh Rocket. You naughty girl,' chided Nell. She stooped down to retrieve the footwear. 'You mustn't take things that don't belong to you. Oh and look. You've chewed one of them. Mummy is very cross.' Nell waggled her finger in the dog's face. Rocket had the grace to look ashamed.

'Surely you're not going to put that bootee on Rosie's foot!' Morag looked repulsed. 'It's been slobbered on by your dog.'

'There's nothing wrong with a bit of slobber.' Nell looked affronted. 'It builds up a baby's immunity.'

Morag visibly shuddered. 'Rather you than me. Right, are we all ready? I'll just get Henry's pram out of the boot.'

'Likewise.' I followed Morag to the front door.

As winter walks went, it turned out to be a pleasant one. The three of us wheeled our babies along, enjoying the scenery and bracing air. Henry had stopped crying. Eddie was nodding off. Only Rosie still grizzled, although her cries were softer now. She was clearly exhausted. We trundled along a path flanked by immaculately turned flower beds, the earth hiding thousands of bulbs. Spring always brought a lovely show of daffodils along this section, and it was a pleasure to watch golden trumpets nodding in a warm breeze. But right now it was chilly. Towering oaks waved their bare branches, awaiting the emergence of green buds and acorns. Rocket ran ahead, nose down. She meandered from side to side, seeking out squirrels. Nell glanced inside Rosie's pram. The baby's eyelids had fluttered shut.

'Thank Gawd for that,' Nell sighed. 'I'm bleedin' knackered. I could do with pulling up on that park bench and going to sleep right here and now. You look a bit worse for wear too Cass. Did Eddie give you a bad night?'

'On the contrary.' I took in a lungful of fresh air. Thankfully the earlier nausea was starting to recede. 'Since I actioned Morag's sleep plan, Eddie is sleeping like the proverbial log. No, my sleep was interrupted by something else.'

'Ooh, I sense a sexy story coming on.' Morag momentarily removed her hands from the stroller handle of Henry's pram. She clapped them together with glee. 'So come on Cass. Spill the beans. Can you beat my car sex story?'

'Morag, I don't need car sex to make my life complete,' I tutted. 'I'm quite happy with conventional sex, preferably in a double bed with a duvet over my body and the light off.'

'There's nothing wrong with adding spice to one's love life,' Morag lectured. 'Last night we had food sex. It was a major turn on. And scrumptious too.'

'Don't tell me,' I sighed. 'Sausage and chips in bed – and Matt's todger was the sausage.'

'Very good Cass.' Morag nodded approvingly. 'Now you're letting your imagination flow. Although you're wrong about the sausage and chips.'

'So what food was involved?' asked Nell.

'Melon,' said Morag.

Nell and I glanced at each. '*Melon?*' we mouthed simultaneously.

'We chopped some chilled melon into chunks,' said Morag. 'Then, in bed, Matt placed them over different parts of my body. Juice ran over my skin, and Matt licked it all off. Obviously two pieces of melon were impaled on my nipples.'

'Yes obviously,' I murmured. I mean where else would one put melon? God forbid in a fruit bowl. Too boring for words.

'I think I missed my vocation,' said Morag.

'What do you mean?' I asked.

'Instead of being a solicitor, I should have been a sex therapist. I think I'd make a damn good counsellor. I can see me now, sitting in a swivel chair, tapping my pen against my teeth whilst listening to a couple lamenting about their boring sex life. I'd soon have them breathing fun back into their relationship. Perhaps I should write a book on it,' said Morag thoughtfully.

'You'd frighten the pants off potential clients,' said Nell. 'Not to mention give them raging complexes. If I greeted my Ben with two melons on my knockers, he'd have me carted off to the funny farm.'

Morag shook her head dismissively. 'You don't know what you're missing Nell. Anyway, back to you Cass. You were about to tell us your sexy story involving,' she posted quotation marks in the air, 'a duvet over your body and the light off.'

'Actually there was no sex involved at all,' I said apologetically. 'Instead I had a text at three in the morning from Stevie. He's gone AWOL. Not even bothered to let work know either.'

'What do you mean AWOL?' asked Nell. 'He can't be. Not if he's texted you.'

So I told them both about Charlotte's phone call, and her anxiety about thinking Stevie was missing. And my telling Charlotte that Stevie had met somebody else, followed by Stevie standing Charlotte up after arranging a lunchtime meeting, and concluding with my ex cancelling his weekend with the twins. 'Oh. And he also sent me a charmless text asking me not to leave him snotty voicemails, and told me I was a stuck-up bitch.'

'Stevie said that!' Morag was incredulous.

'Yep. I think he's lost the plot this time. Total mid-life crisis. He's obviously so enthralled with Selina he's gone doolally. I hope he doesn't get the sack from work. He has a mortgage to pay at the end of the day.'

'So what did you do after receiving his text?' asked Nell.

'Well I tried contacting him again earlier this morning, and this time I really did leave him a snotty voicemail. If I'm going to be accused of such a thing, I might as well go ahead and commit the crime. I told him I knew he was having an affair with Selina, and that she was borderline lunatic in my opinion.'

'And has he got back to you?' asked Morag.

'Not yet.'

At that moment my mobile, buried deep within the depths of my coat pocket, announced a text message. I stopped dead in my tracks. Curling my cold fingers around the phone, I withdrew it.

'Who's your message from?' asked Nell.

I touched the screen. 'Talk of the devil. It's from Stevie.'

'Well go on then,' Morag urged. 'Open it.'

I tapped the envelope icon. And blanched.

Chapter Twenty Two

'What does the text say Cass?' asked Nell.

Morag took the mobile from me. 'Here. Let me. *You always had a vivid imagination Cass, and now you are excelling yourself. I am not having a relationship with Selina. She is the sweetest girl I have ever met, whereas you are the biggest (in every sense of the word) cow I've ever had the misfortune to know. So fuck off.*' Morag passed the phone back to me. 'I'm flabbergasted. I always thought you two had an amicable relationship. This is completely out of character.'

'I agree,' said Nell. 'Even when you were going through divorce, the pair of you always managed to be friendly enough. What's got into him?'

I stared at the mobile phone and re-read the message. It didn't ring true. Particularly the words *you are the biggest (in every sense of the word) cow*. Stevie might well have called me a cow in the past, but only because I refused to take him back after one affair too many. But to say *biggest (in every sense of the word)*. Well! The words kept leaping off the mobile's screen and walloping me in the face. That wasn't how a man spoke. It was bitchy talk. Words that a woman might say. A woman with an axe to grind. I let out a shaky breath and looked from Nell to Morag. 'This isn't Stevie's text.'

'What do you mean it isn't Stevie's text?' Nell frowned. 'It says his name there!' She tapped the contact name. 'Of course it's Stevie who sent you the text.'

'It might be Stevie's phone that sent the text, but Stevie isn't the author. He didn't write this.'

'Well who the bloody hell did?' asked Morag. Her eyes widened. 'You don't think–'

'Yes. Yes I do think.'

'Am I missing something here?' Nell puckered her brow.

'This is Selina's work.' I waggled the phone at Nell. 'Charlotte was right. Something *is* going on. I think Stevie really is missing.' I smacked my forehead with my palm. 'Everything makes sense now – why he's not telephoned work, and why he stood Charlotte up. Charlotte said Stevie hadn't taken as much as a change of underwear from his house. Not even his toothbrush! And he hadn't been home for days, because there was a pile of mail on his doormat.'

Nell's eyes were like saucers. 'What do you think has happened to him?'

'Well,' I blustered. 'It sounds utterly preposterous. But I suspect kidnap.'

There was a resounding silence as we all stared at each other. The word *kidnap* hung in the air. It sounded incongruous. Ludicrous. Here we were standing in the middle of an ordinary park, on an ordinary winter's day. Three mothers with our babies in prams and a dog peeing on an empty Mars bar wrapper. And yet the conversation was not so much ordinary as extraordinary. The abduction of a strapping great man. By a woman no less.

'And you truly suspect Selina is his abductor?' Nell was the first to speak.

'I know it sounds absurd.' I shrugged my shoulders helplessly. 'But yes. I think that woman knows his whereabouts.'

'Cass, before we all let our imagination run away with us,' said Morag, 'let's just think this through for a moment.' We pushed off with the prams again, slowly this time. Our brains whirred with unanswered questions and possibilities. Rocket headed along the tow path by the geese and swans. We followed her. 'If Selina really has abducted Stevie, what would be her motive?'

'God, I don't know. The woman isn't all there. Ethan told Jamie in confidence that Selina had recently been behaving rather oddly. He confided that she sees a psychiatrist and counsellor routinely, but hadn't kept her last two appointments and wouldn't talk about it. Who knows what her motive might be.'

'Sex,' suggested Nell. 'There was a story years ago in the paper about a woman who used mink-lined handcuffs to kidnap and ravish a burly missionary.'

'But hang on a moment,' said Morag. 'We know that Stevie is more than willing to bonk Selina. She doesn't need to hold him prisoner for that. If she's kidnapped him, then I suspect the motive would be,' she gave a worried look, 'somewhat more sinister.'

We all stopped walking again. I felt a chill wash over me. Like a premonition. But not quite able to put my finger on what it was.

'Morag, are you hinting that Selina might want to kill Stevie?' I whispered.

'This is madness.' Nell rolled her eyes. 'What would that daft bint gain by killing Stevie?'

'That,' said Morag, 'is the sixty-four thousand dollar question. Why indeed.' She looked at me. 'Any ideas Cass?'

'No!' I shook my head. 'This is crazy. We sound like frustrated women who have overdosed on too many detective movies. It's nonsense. Rubbish.' I straightened up. 'I have to face facts. I've simply received a nasty text from my ex. He's spent so much time bonking a bitch, he's turned into one. Hence his propensity to write bitchy texts.'

'Let's put that theory to the test,' said Morag.

'What do you mean?' I asked.

'Reply to that text. Send a message that appears to be playing along but,' she held up a finger, 'tests who we're really talking to. A message which – for the real Stevie – would make no sense whatsoever.'

'That,' I breathed, 'is a brilliant idea.' I hit the reply button. 'What shall I write?'

'I know!' Nell chirruped. 'Why don't you text, "If you are the real Stevie, what are the middle names of our children?"'

Morag and I stared at Nell in amazement. 'No Nellie-Wellie,' Morag enunciated. 'We need to be discreet. Without arousing suspicion. Comprendez?'

'But Nell does have a point.' I smiled kindly at my old neighbour. 'Firstly, discussing the twins is a legitimate reason to text. Secondly, using the twins as the topic should reveal whether it is Stevie reading my messages. I have an idea.' I began to tap.

Sorry to offend. Your private life is none of my business. Regarding the twins' birthday next week – any preference on which restaurant to book for celebrations? Thanks. Have a nice day.

'Perfect!' I hit send. 'That message is apologetic. And a little bit contrite. Also totally inaccurate. The twins' birthday is not for another six months.'

'Very good Cass,' Morag nodded approvingly.

We resumed our walking but had barely gone five paces when my mobile tinkled the arrival of another text. Once again we all stopped and huddled over the phone. I opened the message.

Apology accepted. Let twins choose restaurant.

'OH MY GOD!' squawked Nell. 'He's been kidnapped. Call the police. Call an ambulance. Get the Fire Brigade too.'

'Phone Jamie,' said Morag urgently. 'Phone him now.'

I stared at the message in shock. It was one thing to suspect I'd not been communicating with Stevie, but quite another to have it confirmed. I suddenly felt a bit strange. A little wobbly.

'Hurry up Cass,' said Morag. 'Ring Jamie.'

'Yes,' I whispered. With shaking hands, I found Jamie's number on speed dial. It rang three times before connecting.

'Hello?' said a female.

My mouth dropped open. Selina! Why the bloody hell was that woman answering my husband's mobile? How many mobile phones belonging to other men did she have in her possession?

'Er, it's Cass.'

'Hi Cass,' she greeted me warmly. For a moment I felt wrong-footed. What if it wasn't Selina sending fake messages from Stevie's phone? What if it was another fanatical female? It wasn't unfeasible that Selina was the only woman Stevie was seeing. Two-timing wouldn't trouble Stevie's conscience. For all I knew he might even be three-timing. Stevie was like a dog on a scent where women were concerned. 'How are you?'

'Yes, I'm good. Thanks for asking. Um, is Jamie there?'

'Sorry, no. Both he and Ethan are in a meeting with James Powell. James is the bank's big cheese. The men want absolutely no interruption for the next couple of hours, hence me having their mobile phones. Can I give Jamie a message?'

'I was ringing to ask, er, what he wanted for his dinner,' I said lamely. 'Nothing important.'

'Shall I get him to call you?'

'No, that's fine. He can take pot luck.'

'Okay, I'll tell him that,' she laughed. 'So, are you looking forward to the ball this Saturday?'

Gordon Bennett. Now she wanted to make friendly small talk. This couldn't be right. Selina sounded so natural. So unfazed. Not remotely like a person with a screw loose. Jamie's words suddenly reverberated around my head. *Can I just say Cassie, you're not just coming across as neurotic, but certifiable.* If I told Jamie about this, he'd immediately declare it was me with the screw loose.

'Yes!' I replied. 'I've bought my dress and accessories. Can't wait! And you?'

'Well, it's business really for me. But I'm hoping for some romance!' She gave a throaty laugh. 'Ethan has booked us into a fancy boutique hotel for the night – deluxe king room with river view no less. I'm one lucky lady.'

'Sounds fab,' I chortled.

Morag and Nell stared at me. Both women were clearly baffled by my friendly conversation with a kidnapper.

'One small hitch though Cass,' said Selina.

'Oh?'

'It's looking like Jamie and Ethan will have to go into work this Saturday. James Powell has done wonders for Fareham & Mackerel, but boy does he want his pound of flesh.'

'That's a nuisance. Is James Powell expecting you to be there too?'

Nell tugged at my sleeve. 'What the hell's going on?' she whispered. I flapped my hand at her.

'Fortunately James doesn't need all three of us.' Selina gave a sigh of relief. 'But it does mean the boys won't have time to go home prior to the ball. Therefore, when they've finished work, they'll head straight to the hotel in Oxford. Ethan has suggested I pick you up and we travel to the hotel together. From there, we'll later take a minicab to the ball.'

I hesitated for a moment. My heart wasn't skipping with joy at spending the best part of an hour in the car with Selina.

'Oh. Right. Would you like me to drive?' I asked. 'I'm more than happy to do so.'

'Can't unfortunately. Sunday morning Ethan and I are expected in Abingdon to have lunch with his parents. We'll need a car. So I'll pick you up at six, or thereabouts.'

'Okay.'

'Lovely chatting Cass. I'll look forward to seeing you Saturday. Bye.'

'Bye.' I hung up.

'What on earth was all that about?' asked Morag incredulously.

'You heard,' I sighed. 'A bit of chit-chat about Jamie and Ethan in an important meeting – without their mobiles, hence Selina answering. And then an exchange of pleasantries about the bank's ball this Saturday. All four of us are attending. And joy of joys, on Saturday evening Selina will be my driver.'

'So,' Nell splayed her palms out in a gesture of bewilderment, 'is Selina a kidnapper or not?'

I raked a hand through my hair. 'I would hazard not. She was as cool as a cucumber.'

'So who,' asked Nell, 'is sending those texts from Stevie's phone?'

'I really don't know,' I shook my head. 'We're going around in circles. I'm not sure about anything anymore.'

'Well something isn't right,' said Morag. 'That last text about the twins choosing a restaurant for a fictitious birthday was utter tripe.' She paused and looked thoughtful for a moment. 'I have an idea. What about we take a drive right now to Selina's bachelor apartment and check it out? You said you followed her the other day Cass, so you know where it is. Let's have a bit of a sniff around. See if it yields any clues.'

Nell pulled a face. 'You mean like hearing a man shouting, "Help! Help!"'

'Yes,' said Morag firmly.

'Actually that's not a bad idea,' I said. 'At least we can potentially rule out Selina being a kidnapper. If she *has* abducted Stevie, then her flat is the most likely place to keep him prisoner.'

'I'm not up for this.' Nell shook her head vehemently. 'What if Selina turns out to be a kidnapper after all? What would happen if she unexpectedly showed up and found us peering through her letterbox? We'd be brown bread.' She made a slicing motion across her throat.

'Selina is at work,' I pointed out. 'We're safe for hours.'

'I don't get a good feeling about this,' Nell protested. 'You two go. Leave Eddie and Henry with Rosie and me.'

'We'll take you up on that,' said Morag. 'If there were any danger – I said *if* Nell – then we certainly wouldn't want the babies with us. Come on.' Morag spun Henry's pram around. 'There's not a moment to lose.'

Forty-five minutes later I stood in Morag's bedroom. The bed was covered in a collection of wigs.

'So tell me again what you use these for?' I picked up an afro wig. It was like an early Jackson Five hair-do. Except in pink.

'These are my sex wigs,' Morag purred. She picked up a shoulder-length brunette jobbie. 'Matt particularly likes me in this one. I wear it with these.' She rummaged in a drawer and produced a pair of black geeky spectacles. 'Et voila!' Morag pushed the specs on her nose and plonked the wig on her head. 'Now I'm Secretary Susie. Susie loves taking down dictation and her boss's trousers.'

I picked up some waist-length blonde tresses. 'Don't tell me,' I sighed. 'Barbie.'

'How did you know?' Morag clapped her hands together gleefully.

'Combined with your chest measurements, it doesn't take much working out.'

'Matt adores playing Barbie and Ken,' confided Morag. 'And I particularly like this one.' She reached for a wild ringletty affair. It wouldn't have looked remiss on Cher.

'Pop icon?' I asked.

'Wrong!' Morag trilled. She rummaged briefly in the drawer before slinging a stethoscope around her neck. 'Does this give you a clue?'

'Ah yes. Doctor Do-Anyone.'

'Nope. Nurse Knockers!' she smirked. 'Nurse Knockers is *very* naughty. She wears an old-fashioned uniform with a hem line around her bum. She particularly likes using her stethoscope to check out pulse points near the penis.'

'Oh for heaven's sake Morag.' I snatched the wig from her. 'We're meant to be looking for Stevie, not playing dressing up.'

'Au contraire.' Morag suddenly looked grim. 'If we're going snooping, we need to be suitably disguised. I don't think for one moment Selina will turn up. But she must have neighbours. If we bump into anybody, I want to be sure we look very different. So both of us are wearing wigs and specs.'

'Are you serious?'

'Deadly. Hurry up and choose one.'

I picked up the shoulder-length brunette wig and put it on my head. A few adjustments and it looked surprisingly passable. Picking up the geeky spectacles, I slotted the arms behind my ears. Good heavens. I didn't recognise myself. Morag put on a dark heavily fringed number. She instantly morphed into Jessie J. Seconds later she'd teamed it with sunglasses and a trench coat.

'Don't you think the sunnies and mac are a bit obvious?' I asked. 'You look like Inspector Clouseau's sidekick.'

'Nonsense,' said Morag. She belted the coat and stuffed her mobile in one pocket. 'If anybody asks what we're up to, we tell them we're from the Council. Let's go.'

With Morag behind the wheel, the drive to Blackheath didn't take long. As the Galaxy swung between the gateposts to Selina's apartment, I found myself pulling my coat collar up and putting my chin down. I hoped to God we were both right in assuming Selina would remain at work. The last thing we needed was her pulling another sickie and turning up here.

'Okay,' said Morag. 'Let's investigate.' She grabbed an official looking clipboard from the backseat. It had been swiped from Matt's office at the yard. The clipboard actually held various horses' diet sheets. 'Now remember. If anybody asks, we're investigating a noise complaint.'

We slid out of the car. For a moment we stood uncertainly on the forecourt. Morag peered at me over her sunglasses, and then jerked her head at the building. I nodded and swivelled my eyes to the front door. Morag signalled her understanding. Suddenly joined at the hip, we shuffled as one to the entrance. My heart was starting to speed up. It wasn't a pleasant sensation. The wig was making my head feel uncomfortably hot. Seconds later my face had broken out in a fine sheen. The specs slid down my nose. I pushed them back up with one finger and looked at the door in front of us. It was a mix of wood and glass. It was possible to see inside the hallway. We peered in. The foyer was high-ceilinged and stylish. The floor was marble. An elegant wrought iron staircase swept upwards. Nobody was about.

And then a shadow fell across the doorway.

Chapter Twenty Three

'Can I help you?' asked a voice behind us.

Morag and I let out ear-splitting screams. If the residents hadn't been aware of our presence before, they certainly were now. We spun round and came face to face with a tall silver-haired pensioner. He wasn't unlike Victor Meldrew. Hell, this was all we needed. A nosy neighbour. Morag was the first to recover.

'I'm so sorry. You rather startled us. We're from the Council and investigating a noise complaint. We were asked to pay a visit by Miss Selina–' Morag hugged the clipboard to her chest whilst pretending to consult it.'

'Selina Hadley?'

'The very one.'

'That's strange. Miss Hadley is rarely here these days. Although,' he frowned in concentration, 'I did see her recently. With a gentleman. But they didn't stay long. She'll be at work right now. I have her mobile number. Do you want me to call her for you?'

'No!' we trilled together.

'Thank you,' Morag said, 'but that won't be necessary. However, it would be helpful if we could go inside and listen for a bit before making an official report.'

'I'm sure that won't be a problem. And your name?'

'My name?' asked Morag.

'Yes,' said Victor. 'It's just for the purposes of Neighbourhood Watch. I'm the co-ordinator for this building.

There are only three tenants here. But I always ask visitors for their name if a resident isn't at home.'

'Of course,' Morag said briskly. Her eyes darted to the clipboard. 'I'm Mrs Dobbin. And my colleague here is–'

'Marple.' I straightened up. 'Miss.'

Victor nodded. 'Thank you.' He produced a notebook and pen from the inside pocket of his jacket. He wrote the names in carefully. 'So that's Mrs...Dobbin and...Miss...Marple.' He snapped the notebook shut. A second later it had disappeared back inside the jacket. Fishing in another pocket, he produced a key and unlocked the entrance door. 'After you ladies.'

We stepped over the threshold and strolled over to the centre of the hallway. Victor made his way to the only door on the ground floor. Clearly this was his apartment. However, he didn't go inside. Instead he hovered.

'Thank you very much for your help,' Morag said dismissively. Victor inclined his head graciously. And stayed put. Bugger. Morag peered at her clipboard before addressing me. 'It says here,' she stabbed a finger at Dobbin's feed proportions, 'that prolonged industrial sawing is occurring within the premises.'

I peered dutifully at the clipboard. Dobbin was to have two scoops of bran, one of pony nuts and absolutely no oats whatsoever. 'How utterly inconsiderate,' I said to Morag. We appeared to be talking very loudly. And woodenly. As if on a stage. Victor would have no trouble catching what we were saying. 'I suggest we stand very still and listen.' My voice bounced off the walls of the hollow hallway.

'I quite agree,' Morag enunciated.

'I agree too.'

'Good. So we are both in agreement.'

'We are indeed,' I articulated.

There was a pause while we stood, still as statues, and listened for prolonged industrial sawing. You could have heard a pin drop. I contemplated the floor. Rocked back and forwards on my heels for good measure.

'I think I just heard something,' Morag cried. She cupped one ear.

'I think I did too,' I shouted.

'And it seemed to be coming from upstairs,' Morag yelled.

Victor moved away from his apartment door. He walked carefully towards us, hands folded behind his back.

'Mr Dawson lives upstairs,' he said quietly. 'He's a retired school teacher. He doesn't own a screwdriver, never mind an industrial saw.'

'Nonetheless,' Morag waggled a finger authoritatively, 'we are duty bound to investigate. I insist Miss Marple and I check out the first floor.'

Victor looked at us without saying anything. Eventually he gestured toward the staircase. 'Please, do go up.'

'Thank you,' said Morag. 'Our investigation won't be complete until we have also examined the top floor. Would you like us to let you know when we are finished?' Morag stared unblinkingly at Victor. Her unspoken message was clear. Leave us alone.

Victor again regarded us silently. The seconds began to stretch towards a minute. I could feel my nerves starting to frazzle. Just when they were at screaming point, he cleared his throat. 'I will be in my apartment.' Victor indicated the door behind him. 'You know where to find me.'

'Indeed. We won't be long. Come with me please Miss Marple.'

As Morag took to the staircase, I scampered along behind her. I risked a quick backward glance at Victor. He was in the process of opening his apartment door. Thank heavens for that. The man was an absolute nightmare. A professional busybody. We reached the first floor landing. And walked smartly past the door to Mr Dawson's flat. The second flight of stairs was straight ahead. Fortunately the staircases and landings were carpeted. As we wound our way to the top floor, our footsteps were silent and stealthy. Suddenly we were standing outside the door to Selina's apartment. I was feeling inexplicably edgy. A part of me was terrified the door would fly open. That Selina would swoop down on us like an avenging angel, her head rotating three hundred and sixty degrees. But the door remained shut. All was quiet apart from the thud-diddy-thud of my heart, and slightly ragged breathing from climbing two staircases.

Morag put one ear against the door. She listened intently. 'I can't hear anything,' she whispered. 'Shame these apartments don't have letterboxes, otherwise we could peer into the hallway.'

'Somehow I don't think we're going to find Stevie in Selina's hallway,' I sighed. 'I know. Why don't we knock? If he's in there – but unable to get to the door – he could call out.'

'Cass, I'm quite sure if Stevie was being held prisoner he'd be yelling his head off,' said Morag.

'Not,' my eyes widened, 'if he was bound and gagged.'

Morag shuddered. 'Don't say that Cass. That sounds horrible.'

'Well that's why we're here isn't it,' I hissed, 'because we suspect dodgy circumstances! Go on. Knock on the door.'

'No, you knock on the door.'

'Oh for goodness sake,' I huffed. 'We'll knock on it together. After three. One...two...three.'

We rapped on the door and instantly sprang backwards, as if the wooden panels were red hot. It remained shut. No sound came from within.

'Oh my goodness. Look,' I pointed down the landing. I'd initially assumed it was a window set in the wall. In fact it was a glass door. A fire exit. 'Let's see if it's unlocked. We might be able to peek into Selina's apartment from a mezzanine platform or something.'

We scuttled over to the door and peered out. Sure enough there was an open steel floor that wrapped around one part of Selina's apartment. It connected up to a series of staircases that criss-crossed all the way down to the communal gardens. A fire escape. We were at the rear of the building. I levered down the door handle. It creaked open. So much for Victor's Neighbourhood Watch. Any wannabe burglar could simply jump the garden fence, climb the fire escape and walk right in. Cold air blasted our faces as we stepped out onto the platform. It was windy up here, and the long brown tresses of my wig whipped about. I put a hand up to stop the wig from taking off. Turning, I indicated that Morag should follow me. Together we eased our way along the platform. It ran straight past a window of Selina's apartment.

'That must be her kitchen.' I indicated an extractor fan and vent set into part of the wall.

'Let's check it out.'

We darted across the platform and ducked below the window sill. Crouching down, we eyeballed each other anxiously.

'Come up slowly,' I said to Morag. She nodded by way of response. Together the pair of us peered over Selina's window ledge and gazed into a modest kitchen. It was nothing like the contemporary granite and steel jobbie in Ethan's penthouse. Plain white cabinets and a matching worktop ran the length of one wall. On the other side was a sink, washing machine and ancient fridge. In the centre of the kitchen was a small table with two chairs on either side. I pressed my nose up to the glass. Papers were scattered across the table. Three small bottles of liquid stood side by side. There were labels on them, but I couldn't decipher the writing. They looked like the sort of bottles I had in my medicine cabinet at home, full of liquid vitamins for the children.

'Can't see anything unusual,' I said. 'Can you?'

'Well, Stevie's not in the kitchen that's for sure.' Morag stood up. Lowering her sunglasses, she peered through the window pane. 'What's that on the table?'

'Vitamins I think. And notes of some sort.'

Morag stared hard. 'Not vitamins Cass. I would hazard a guess it's something medicinal. Something you'd get on prescription.' She squinted hard. 'I can't read the label properly. Whatever it is, it begins with G. Let me take a picture.' She whipped out her mobile phone and switched it to camera mode. 'You never know, it might come in handy later.'

Another gust of wind tugged at my wig. 'Come on. Let's go. We've been on a wild goose chase. Stevie's not here. Whoever sent that last text, it would seem we're going to have to rule Selina out. I might mention it to Charlotte though. Just in case she can put her finger on anything. Perhaps she can go back to Stevie's house. Have another look around for any indications of Stevie having an affair with a second woman.' My stomach let out a growl of hunger. I'd had no breakfast and it was coming up to lunchtime. At least the earlier nausea had disappeared. 'Come on. Let's get out of here and back to Nell's. She can make us a couple of bacon butties.' Suddenly I was ravenously hungry.

'Sounds good to me,' said Morag.

We clanked back along the steel platform. I pulled open the fire escape door and stepped back onto the carpeted landing. After being out in the bright winter light, for a moment I couldn't see a thing. I blinked rapidly at the shadows and waited for my eyes to adjust. And when they did, my heart sank. Victor was standing there.

'Ah. Miss Marple. Mrs Dobbin. I wondered where you'd both gone. So, did the fire escape yield any industrial saws whirring away at distressing noise levels?'

The sarcasm was unmistakable. I felt a rush of anxiety. Victor was giving off a bad vibe. I had a feeling we'd been rumbled. If Morag felt alarmed, she was doing a good job at hiding it. She peered into the gloom over the top of her sunglasses. Her eyes found Victor's.

'I am very pleased to report that no saws, industrial or otherwise, have been located. I've made some notes.' Morag stood up to her full height and indicated the clipboard. 'It's all here, and I shall be reporting back to the Council immediately.'

'Very good,' said Victor. He was blocking our access to the stairs. 'And what Council did you say you were from?'

'I didn't,' said Morag crisply. My eyes had now fully adjusted to the internal light, and I was horrified to see Morag's wig askew. Pale blonde hair poked out from the Jesse J hairpiece. 'I merely said I was from the Council.'

'Well I'm asking you now. Which Council?'

'That is classified information,' said Morag.

Suddenly Victor's hand shot out. For a moment I thought he was going to hit Morag. Instead he grabbed her clipboard. His eyes scanned the equine diet sheet.

'Cuthbert – two portions of hay, must be damped down. Bramble – bran mashes with a handful of sugar beet. Matt – sex food until further notice.'

'Give me that.' Morag snatched the clipboard back. 'I'll have you know this is a confidential report.'

'Mrs Dobbin – if that is indeed your real name – I don't know who you are or what you are doing here. But I will be giving a full account of your visit to Neighbourhood Watch. And the same information will be passed on to the police. It is quite apparent to me the pair of you are casing the building for burglary and–'

We didn't wait to hear the rest of Victor's suspicions. Morag shoved him to one side. Grabbing me by the hand, she yanked me after her. We fairly flew across the landing, and almost hurled ourselves down the entire flight of stairs. By the time we'd reached the ground floor, our wigs had flown off. I was aware of Victor coming after us. For an old boy he could certainly shift. But not as quickly as us. Morag shouldered the entrance door open and sprinted, hand out, key fob extended, to the Galaxy. She popped the central locking and we threw ourselves into the vehicle. The engine burst into life and tyres squealed as the vehicle shot backwards – nearly knocking Victor over in the process. Hell's bells. That was all we needed. Not only arrested on suspicion of burglary but wanted for flattening a pensioner in the process.

'Oh my God Cass,' Morag gasped. 'He's making a note of my registration number. I'll be arrested.'

'Don't panic,' I clutched my chest, convinced I was about to have a coronary. Morag swerved out into traffic and blaring horns. 'It's our word against his. We'll say we popped round to see Selina and he got the wrong end of the stick. He's a doddery pensioner at the end of the day. We'll make out he has senile dementia or something.'

'And I've lost my lovely wigs!' said Morag. 'How are we going to explain the wigs if we get questioned by a police officer?'

'We don't,' I gasped. 'We make out we know nothing about them.'

'From now on Cass,' Morag said as we hurtled onto the dual carriageway, 'we leave Stevie to his own devices. Whatever is going on, he's a big boy. I'm sure he can handle himself.'

I gripped hold of the door handle for support as Morag shot into the outside lane. I didn't know where Stevie was or what had happened to him. But one thing I did know. If Morag and I had the police knocking on our doors, we were going to have our work cut out explaining ourselves.

Chapter Twenty Four

Nell set the bacon butties before us, tutting loudly.

'So in a nutshell,' she paused briefly to search out tomato sauce from the fridge, 'your investigation of Selina's apartment backfired. And any moment now the Old Bill could descend and cart you off to the local nick for questioning.'

'That's pretty much the gist of it.' I took the sauce from Nell and squirted liberally over the bacon. 'Mmm. Delish.' I took a massive bite. Grease slid down my chin. I'd better make the most of this. I didn't know if the food in jail ran to bacon butties. When I was a child I'd listened, round-eyed, to my parents telling me about prison. That should I ever break the law, my doom would be a dungeon-like abode with only bread and water to survive upon. At the grand old age of eleven, I'd been outraged to discover this was a huge untruth. Indeed, these days it seemed there were more rights to be had on the inside than the outside. Why, only last month I'd received a ticket for parking illegally whilst giving Eddie an emergency change on the car's back seat. I'd been watched by a sadistic traffic warden who had gleefully fed my car registration details into his machine. What about my son's human rights for a clean bottom, eh? I took another chunk out of the bacon butty and sighed. Time would tell whether we'd be eating more butties in Nell's house, or languishing in a cell dressed in pyjamas covered in arrows.

'It was a disaster,' Morag agreed. 'I hope Matt doesn't find out. I can't begin to imagine how he'd react. Bonks might be suspended by way of punishment.'

'A whole new meaning to going bonkers then,' Nell arched an eyebrow.

'Jamie would go ballistic.' I gave an involuntary shudder whilst imagining my husband's reaction. 'He works in security! Can you envisage client reaction? How would Jamie explain the little matter of his wife tootling off in a wig to case a colleague's joint and being party to knocking over a pensioner? That would be the end of Fareham & Mackerel. Well, the Mackerel bit anyway. Definitely not the career move he's looking for.'

'Regarding our husbands, I think we'd better keep Mum for now, don't you?' suggested Morag.

'Definitely.' I nodded my head vigorously.

'And as for Stevie,' said Nell, 'can I suggest you try getting hold of him one last time. If you don't speak to him, leave a message saying that unless he properly returns your call, you will report him to the police as a missing person.'

'I think the last thing I need right now Nell is to flag myself up to the police.' I licked one finger and ran it around my plate, gathering up butty crumbs. 'However, you've made a good point. If I don't get hold of Stevie, I'll give Charlotte a ring and suggest she phones the police. She's still pretty much Stevie's partner as such. There's the house to sort out after all. Plus she has some stuff to collect. I think Charlotte is the most appropriate person to report any unexplained prolonged absence.'

'Great idea,' Morag nodded her head. 'The Old Bill can investigate Stevie's whereabouts, and we can be left firmly out of the equation. Then I can get back to normal life. And bonking my husband instead of being celibate behind bars.'

'And talking of bonking, why was Matt and the sex food diet mentioned on that clipboard?'

'Oh it was just a joke. You know, to tease Matt the next time he consulted his beloved horses' diet sheets. He's always tweaking them about.'

'I thought that pensioner was going to swallow his dentures.'

'Pity he didn't,' Morag grimaced, 'and then he'd have been too busy giving himself the Heimlich Manoeuvre to take down my registration number.'

I drained my coffee. 'Time to go home. And do normal things. Like ironing. And housework. I will never again complain about chores being boring. From now on it's the quiet life for me.'

'Me too,' Morag agreed. 'We will leave you in peace Nell. At least Rosie's colic has stopped.'

'Yes,' Nell sighed. 'For now.'

With a sigh of relief, I set off on the afternoon school run. It was bliss to be pootling along at twenty miles per hour, instead of roaring away from furious pensioners or getting entangled with Astravan drivers suffering road rage. One way or another, the last few days had seen rather a lot of drama on the roads.

The kids were in high spirits when they piled into the car. Livvy and Petra were talking nineteen to the dozen about a new physics teacher. Male. Fresh out of uni by all accounts.

'Mr Boardman is gorgeous,' Petra gushed. 'I just know I'm going to love studying physics from now on.'

'He can explain Newton's laws of motion to me anytime,' Livvy sighed dreamily.

Jonas was intent on teasing Toby over his crush on Diane Cooper. 'How's the grand plan coming along Tobes? You know, the one to deepen your voice. I can't wait to see Diane faint clean away the next time you pass her in the corridor.'

'All in good time,' Toby assured. 'One day I'm going to marry Diane Cooper.'

'Ha ha ha!' Jonas let out a raucous laugh. 'That's the funniest joke I've heard all year.'

'I've heard a funnier one,' Toby retorted. 'My wife to be – Diane Cooper – sat down next to me as I was flipping channels. She asked, "What's on TV?" so I said, "Dust". Although that's probably the sort of thing Jamie would say to you, isn't it Mum!'

'Very droll,' I smiled. There probably was a fair sprinkling of dust on the telly, indeed throughout the entire house. But not for much longer. I would give the place a good bottoming. Just as soon as I'd barricaded myself into a handy room with my mobile phone. I wanted to speak to Charlotte away from wiggling ears. The last thing I wanted was the kids worrying about their father.

The Muck Truck bounced into the driveway of Lilac Lodge. I was relieved to catch a glimpse of Arthur and Edna working away on the boat. Their body language indicated they were perfectly at ease with each other. It would seem Arthur had recovered from his marriage proposal being rejected. They both put up a hand and waved as we emptied out of the car. I waved back. The kids charged through the front door. Dumping their coats over the banister, they thundered upstairs and disappeared into their rooms.

'I'll be coming around with the Hoover shortly,' I called after them. 'So pick things up off the floor please.'

I went into the kitchen with Eddie on my hip. He started to grizzle, so I made up a feed before popping him into his playpen. Two minutes later he was under his mobile and guzzling contentedly. Shutting the kitchen door, I went over to my holdall. Rummaging inside, I extracted my mobile. First things first. Call Stevie. I touched the screen, selected his number and waited for it to connect. Seconds later it began to ring. And ring and ring. Once again the voicemail kicked in. I took a deep breath.

'Hi Stevie. It's Cass. I was really hoping you'd answer the phone. Can you call me back please? I haven't spoken to you for a few days. Frankly I'm concerned. Concerned enough to report you to the police as a missing person. So call me. As soon as possible.'

I hung up. Wallace and Gromet appeared through the cat flap. They set up a cacophony of howls, demanding their tea. I opened a tin of cat food and was just doling out some particularly pongy meat, when my mobile signalled the arrival of a text. Setting the cats' dishes on the floor, I snatched up the phone. The text was from Stevie.

For God's sake Cass, get off my back. I told you I was going away. Stop looking for drama and making a crisis where there is none.

I stared at the message. Well, that had told me hadn't it! Or had it? Why couldn't my ex have simply telephoned to say the same thing? Stevie wasn't the most thoughtful of men, but I really didn't think he'd deliberately not wish to put my mind at rest.

I touched the screen and Stevie's message disappeared. This time I scrolled through my contacts looking for Charlotte's number. She answered on the second ring.

'Hi Charlotte, it's me.'

'Hello Cass,' she inhaled sharply. The breath caught in her throat and she coughed slightly. She was clearly anxious. 'Have you heard from Stevie?'

'Yes. And no.'

'What do you mean?'

'Well, he's texted a few times. But when I ring he never picks up. Frankly I've had doubts that it's been Stevie texting me at all. I've even wondered if his phone has fallen into somebody else's hands. His messages have been both inaccurate and downright rude. I rang him ten minutes ago and left a message on his voicemail to call me, or else I'd be reporting him as a missing person.'

'I've been going out of my mind all week with worry. And I've tried calling him myself. Several times. But despite all my messages – voicemails and texts – I've heard absolutely nothing from him.'

'Well I had a text from Stevie's phone just five minutes ago. The message was to get off his back. Why he couldn't phone to say that is a mystery. It's out of character. So in all honesty, I think his absence should now be reported to the police.' There was a silence at the other end of the phone. 'Hello? Charlotte, are you still there?' And then I heard a gulping noise and realised Charlotte was sobbing. 'Charlotte, please don't cry.'

'Sorry Cass,' she hiccupped. 'I'm just so concerned.'

'Try not to be. Stevie's a pretty solid chap. I'm sure he could pack a punch if needed.'

'So when are you going to phone the police? Now?'

'Ah.' I raked a hand through my hair. 'Actually, I think it would be better if you phoned the police. After all, I've been hearing from Stevie by text. Whereas you've heard squat diddly. You can truthfully tell the police you've had no communication whatsoever. That you know for a fact Stevie did not inform work of his absence, nor taken a change of clothes from his house – not even a toothbrush. I think the police are more likely to get a move on with things if they hear from you. Whereas if I speak to them and say I've been having texts, I'm pretty sure they would delay things. Especially if they saw the contents of Stevie's last message.'

'Y-yes,' Charlotte wept. 'I-I'll do it now. Thanks Cass. I-I'll let you know how I get on.'

We said good-bye to each other and hung up. For a while I stared pensively at my mobile. Where the heck was my ex-husband? I chucked the phone back into my holdall. In his playpen, Eddie had pulled himself upright and was making mum-mum-mum noises. Meanwhile I needed to do some vacuuming.

'Come on little man.' I bent over the playpen's rails and scooped up my baby boy. 'Let's go and see if one of your sisters will keep an eye on you while I push the vacuum cleaner around.' Eddie responded by reaching up and grabbing a fistful of my hair. He tugged hard. I winced with pain. 'No darling – argh! – let go.' My son squealed with laughter. Six months old and already displaying sadistic tendencies. After a bit of tussle, I disentangled chubby fists from my tresses and hastened up the stairs to Livvy's bedroom. I knocked on her door. On the other side, a great deal of chuntering was going on. I pushed the handle down. My daughter was on her mobile phone.

'I knew this would happen,' Livvy huffed. 'Do you think? Ah, my bad. Really? I told Lucy there would be beef. What a beg. Yeah. Peak times. You're kidding? Oh that's reem.'

I hadn't the faintest idea what language my daughter was talking. It made no sense whatsoever.

'Can you look after Eddie?' I mouthed.

'Hang on a minute Emma.' Livvy moved the mobile away from her ear. 'You won't be long will you Mum, only I have homework to do. Just as soon as I've finished talking to Emma,' she winked.

'I will ensure the vacuum cleaner goes flat out,' I grinned, 'and will screech around all corners and skirting boards on two wheels.'

'Okay.' She held her arms out and took Eddie from me.

I was half-way down the stairs when I stopped dead in my tracks. And sniffed. That smell again. The same whiff as this morning – when the boys had climbed into the car. A smoky smell. Like – I stiffened – cigarettes. I spun around and re-traced my steps, sniffing the air like Rocket on a trail. Outside Jonas's bedroom, my nostrils went into overdrive. Yeuch. Definitely ciggies. I flattened one ear against Jonas's door. Low voices. Every now and again Diane Cooper's name was mentioned, followed by sniggering. I rapped on the wooden panels. There was a sudden frenzy of activity from within.

'Hang on a minute,' Jonas bellowed.

More noises. Darting footsteps. The squish-squish of a canister spraying the room.

'Can I come in?' I asked. And didn't bother waiting for a reply.

Toby was playing nonchalantly with some alien goo. He threw the gelatinous gunk repeatedly up in the air before catching it. Jonas had prostrated himself across a bean bag near the sash window. Which just happened to be open. Both boys were chewing gum, jaws rotating noisily. I narrowed my eyes. An open window – in January?

'What are you both up to?' It came out as an accusation.

'Nuthin',' drawled Jonas. 'Take it easy man.'

Man? *Easy* man? More teen speak. Toby continued playing catch with the alien goo. He caught it deftly in the palm of one hand. Then up, up it went. Higher and higher. A change of tactic was required.

I cleared my throat. We could all do the silly teen talk thing. 'I'm cool,' I shrugged. 'So cool in fact that I'm chilled. *Real* laid back and easy. Peasy. So,' I strolled into the room, 'howzit goin'? Wassup an' stuff?'

Jonas's eyebrows shot up into his hairline. There was a stunned pause.

'Kay,' he replied eventually.

Kay? Who was Kay? I looked suspiciously around the room for a female of the same name.

'We're both 'kay.'

Ah. *O*-kay. More silly teen speak.

'Thass good buddy. So you're all cool an' chilly willy too?'

Jonas and Toby glanced fleetingly at each other before swivelling their eyes back to me. I strolled across to the window. Sniffed deeply.

'What's with the little ol' pongo then dudey?'

Jonas produced a canister and waggled it about. It was a body spray for men.

'Just road testin' my new stuff.'

Again I sniffed deeply. 'That's a hip hop smelly you got a-roarin' there. Sorta limey lime with *smoky* undertones.'

My mouth seemed to have slipped into spaghetti western lingo. And now my legs were swaggering up and down the bedroom. Even my thumbs were doing strange things, currently wedged in imaginary twin gun holsters. Clearly I'd turned into a cowboy. Any second now I'd lasso Toby's alien goo and holler *yee-ha.*

'S'cool,' shrugged Jonas.

I stared at him. He looked cocky. Insolent. He blew a gum bubble. My blood began to boil. Where were the fags? At that moment Toby's constant throw-and-catch with the alien goo backfired. The sticky blob flew up in the air and hit the ceiling. It stuck fast. It was, regrettably, a gesture which tipped the balance of my mood.

'For God's sake Toby, look what you've done to the ceiling,' I shouted.

Annoyed, I grabbed Jonas's computer chair. Wobbling precariously, I clambered up. The chair creaked ominously as I plucked the alien goo from the ceiling. A bright green patch remained on the otherwise spotless paint.

'Look at that!' I snapped.

'Oh man, keep yer hair on.'

Toby's attempt to parody Jonas sent me rocketing into orbit.

'Keep my–? Watch!' I bellowed furiously. 'Watch carefully now!'

I jumped off the chair and, with all the force of a javelin thrower, hurled the alien goo through the open sash window. The blob sailed through the air, straight into next door's garden. And hit our neighbour – who just happened to be inspecting his winter patio pots – slap on the forehead.

'Shit!' I squeaked in horror, and ducked behind the curtain. 'Right you pair of Herberts. Give them to me.'

'Give you what?' asked Toby, eyes as round as saucers.

'Don't come the innocent with me. I want your cigarettes.'

'I didn't know you smoked Cass,' Jonas said flippantly.

'I don't!' I howled. 'And I'm not having you two puffing on cancer sticks either. Now hand them over this minute, or I'll tell Jamie and the pair of you will be in the biggest trouble you've ever–'

Jonas instantly produced a packet of Silk Cut. 'Please don't tell Dad, Cass. He'll go ape.'

'How long has this been going on?' I looked from one boy to the other as, ridiculously, the soundtrack by Van Morrison began to play in my head.

Toby cleared his throat. 'It was my idea Mum. I wanted to impress Diane Cooper.'

'What, by smoking? No girl is going to be impressed by a boy humming like an ashtray Toby.' I now had a mental picture of several ashtrays humming a tune. God, I must be incredibly stressed. Clearly the events of today were starting to get to me.

'But I heard cigarettes make your voice gravelly. And I want a deep voice. So Diane Cooper might fancy me.'

'Oh man,' sighed Jonas.

I stared at these two children of mine. One on the threshold of puberty, the other a man-boy in a six foot body. Trying to impress girls. Smoking. Doing stupid things. It was all part of puberty and growing up.

I glared at them. 'Promise me you won't do it again.'

'Promise.' They nodded solemnly.

'Okay, I won't tell Jamie. *This* time.' Crushing the box of cigarettes, I stalked out the room.

Back downstairs, I tossed the mashed cigarettes into the bin. And then fished them out again. If Jamie saw them languishing amongst the potato peelings, questions would be asked. I found a Tesco's carrier bag and carefully wrapped them within. Only then did I put them back in the bin – right at the bottom and buried underneath household detritus.

Irked, I marched into the utility room. Opening the tall cupboard, I yanked out the vacuum cleaner. Bending down to plug the cable into a socket, I paused. My mobile phone was ringing. I straightened up and hastened to my baby holdall. Pulling out the mobile phone, I was amazed to see Stevie's name flash up in the caller display. Hitting the green handset icon, I put the phone to my ear.

'About flippin' time!' I said.

'Cass,' Stevie gasped. 'Help me.'

Chapter Twenty Five

At some point in everybody's lives there comes a defining moment. When, for whatever reason, time stands still. Clocks stop. Noises cease. All movement of objects and people in your feeling world come to a standstill. Even your heart feels like it skips a number of beats. Briefly you are aware of your existence, but not actually *living* life. Instead you're stuck in a moment. And right now that was happening to me.

Stevie sounded so scared. Desperate. And...odd. Like he was – my blood ran cold – *drugged*. From the other end of the phone there was a sudden scuffling. A kerfuffle of sorts. And then the call disconnected. I stared at the mobile in horror. My heart gave a lurch and began beating again. Blood whooshed around my body, and my ears roared with the return of everyday noises.

'Mum!' Livvy was screeching down the stairs. 'When are you going to take Eddie? He's driving me nuts!'

I chucked the phone down and ran up the stairs two at a time. My daughter was standing on the landing holding Eddie out as far as her arms would extend. 'And he's done a number two. So his nappy needs–' Livvy broke off and stared at me. 'Whatever's the matter?

'Nothing.' I took Eddie from her. Livvy was right. He stank.

'But you're as white as a sheet.'

'I'm fine. Go and do your homework.' I took Eddie and went into his nursery, my mind whirring. I'd ring Charlotte in a minute. I stripped Eddie off and whizzed some wipes over his bottom. And I'd have to tell Jamie now. Not about casing Selina's flat, but about Stevie's phone call. I reached for the Sudocrem. But I definitely wouldn't be telling the twins. I didn't want them upset and scared for their father. For once Eddie lay still while I strapped him into a clean nappy. In no time at all he was dressed in his romper suit. Swinging him onto one hip, I flew down the stairs and into the kitchen. Leaving Eddie in his playpen, I settled down at the table with my mobile phone.

'Charlotte? It's Cass. I've just heard from Stevie. Properly this time.'

'Oh thank God,' she squawked. I could hear a car engine in the background. She was clearly on the road. 'Is he all right?'

'No. Not as such anyway.'

'What! Why?'

'I don't know,' I cried. 'He said–' my brain struggled to remember Stevie's exact words. 'I think he said "Help". Or "Help me". Something like that. And then there was a scuffling noise in the background, as if somebody was trying to get the phone off him. And then the line went dead. And his speech was slow. Like he was disorientated or something.'

'Cass, you're going to have to tell the police about this. I've already phoned them and given them as much information as I possibly can. They've asked me to pop into the station with all Stevie's bank and credit card details. They're going to check if he's made any cash withdrawals or spent money anywhere. I've also got to give them some photographs, along with his toothbrush.'

'His toothbrush?' I asked incredulously.

'Yes.' She stifled a sob. 'It's to provide a DNA sample for forensic examination.'

I blinked. And felt slightly sick. Stevie's absence was taking a whole new turn. One that had fear curdling in the pit of my stomach.

'Shall I meet you somewhere?' I asked.

'I'm on my way over to Stevie's house,' Charlotte said. 'I need to collect the information the police want. And the toothbrush. Shall I meet you there? Perhaps you can have a look around with me. See if I've missed any clues to his whereabouts. And then we'll drive to the police station together.'

'Yes,' I whispered. 'Okay. I'll see you shortly.'

I disconnected the call just as the back door opened. Cold air blew into the kitchen as Edna came in, Arthur bringing up the rear. He smiled by way of greeting. I put up a hand in response.

'Hello Cassandra dear,' Edna said. 'We're calling it a day out there,' she jerked her head in the direction of the boat. 'Time for a cup of coffee while I get some dinner going. I thought I'd do shepherd's pie tonight. Would that be all right?'

'Lovely,' I nodded.

'Are you all right Cassandra? You look terribly pale.'

'Um, no. Not really. The twins' father has gone missing. The police are investigating. Charlotte is on the way to Stevie's house to collect some bits and pieces for the police, including his toothbrush for DNA purposes.' Edna and Arthur stared at me in horror. 'And to cap it all, I've just had a peculiar telephone call from him. Stevie sounded dazed. He begged for help. And then the line disconnected. Something is very wrong Edna. I haven't told the twins. I don't want them to know.'

Arthur was the first to recover. 'This is terrible Cass. Is there anything we can do to help?'

'Can you possibly look after Eddie for me, until Jamie gets home? Charlotte wants me to go to the police station with her.'

'Of course we will,' said Edna. 'Eddie's no trouble at all. You go and do what you have to do Cass. Don't worry about a thing. And if you're not home by the time Jamie gets in, I'll discreetly bring him up to date. Try not to fret. The police will find Stevie. You'll see.'

An hour later, Charlotte and I were at the local nick. We were holed up with PC Thomson and PC Smith. The former looked like Humpty Dumpty's brother. The latter was a woman with thin lips. For a moment I couldn't think who she reminded me of. And then it came to me. Popeye's girlfriend. Olive Oyl.

I couldn't imagine PC Thomson pursuing criminals. He looked more like the sort of chap you'd find in a department store in December. Wearing a jolly Father Christmas outfit. On the other hand, PC Smith had a body that matched her lips. No doubt she would be extremely agile if chasing law-breaking offenders. However, I had a feeling PC Smith had never hitched up a hemline in order to pursue a felon. She didn't need to. All she had to do was look at them. And then the offender would instantly drop down dead. Her eyes were hard. The colour of flint. I was pretty sure she'd taken every psychology course under the sun. That she could suss guilt in a nano second. Her eyes flicked from Charlotte to me. And eventually came to rest just on me. I met her gaze. And inwardly shook. She finally looked back at Charlotte.

'So, Miss West. Let me confirm. You are Mr Cherry's partner. But you don't live at his house.'

'That's right.'

'So how can you be his partner?'

'Because I did live at his house, but currently I'm not. But I might go back. But then again I might not. So Mr Cherry might say I'm not his partner. But in actual fact I still am.'

PC Smith closed her eyes. For a moment she looked pained. 'Miss West. You aren't making this very easy for us. Why did you move out?'

'Because Stevie won't let me have a baby. We had a big row about it, and I stormed off.'

PC Thomson and PC Smith looked at each other. PC Smith wrote something down. 'A big row,' she repeated. 'So was the row violent?'

'Not as such. I didn't throw crockery at him if that's what you mean. Not this time.'

'So you've had violent rows in the past?'

Charlotte screwed up her face. 'Well, I suppose they have been a bit physical from time to time. But he's never beaten me up, if that's what you mean.'

PC Smith gave Charlotte a level look. 'Miss West, have *you* ever beaten Mr Cherry up?'

'No! I've chucked things about. And waved my arms like windmills. That sort of thing. Why?'

'I'm just trying to get a handle on the situation, Miss West. Sometimes people disappear because they don't want to be found. Other times they disappear because they've been murdered. You'd be surprised how many folk report their partners as missing. Some even make national television appeals for witnesses to come forward. Yet all the time the missing person has been languishing under the patio.'

'Except,' I interrupted, 'I heard from Stevie less than two hours ago begging for help. And I think your insinuation that Charlotte would be capable of such a thing is bang out of–'

'Ah yes. Mrs Cherry.' PC Smith's eyes swivelled my way. They remained on me. Unblinking and cold. 'Stevie's wife?'

'No! Ex-wife. I thought I'd made that clear at the start. My name is now Mackerel. I'm re-married.'

'Ex-wife. Interesting.' She exchanged another look with her colleague. PC Thomson was now leaning back in his chair, hands folded across his ample tummy. 'And what sort of relationship do you have with your ex-husband, Mrs Mackerel?'

'A very good one,' I snapped.

'So good that he sent you a series of extremely unpleasant text messages.' Her mouth twisted into a thin smile as she consulted her notes. 'Telling you to – and I quote – fuck off, and also get off his back' I could have crowned Charlotte when she'd accidentally mentioned me receiving text messages from Stevie. I hadn't wanted PC Smith to know about that. In my opinion, the only thing that was relevant was Stevie's telephone call pleading for help. If these two plods started digging in other areas, it could open up a can of worms. 'Mrs Mackerel, these text messages are not evidence of an amicable relationship. Are you sure you haven't some sort of axe to grind with your ex-husband?'

My mouth dropped open. 'This is preposterous! What exactly are you implying?'

'I'm not implying anything Mrs Mackerel,' PC Smith said evenly. She put her elbows on the table and steepled her fingers together. 'I'm simply trying to piece events together. And how people fit into them. Which brings me to another person in this jigsaw. Who is Selina?'

I knew it! The can of worms was now in PC Smith's hand, the relentless line of questioning acting as the tin opener. Soon the worms would be spilling all over her desk, no doubt influencing the warped report she was hell-bent on making. I wondered if Selina had already been in touch with the police about Morag's car on her premises. Did PCs Thomson and

Smith know all about two wigless women screeching away from Selina's Blackheath apartment? And did they know that one of those women matched the description of Selina's ex-boyfriend's wife and just happened to be sitting right here, right now, on the other side of this desk? Were these two coppers playing some sort of cat and mouse game with me? I let out an involuntary whimper and stared at PC Thomson. Wasn't it *his* turn to ask questions? Ideally some nice ones? But PC Thomson was staring at the ceiling, apparently fascinated with a patch above my head.

I cleared my throat. 'Selina is – I believe – Stevie's horse riding friend.'

I was aware of Charlotte, in my peripheral vision, looking amazed.

'But in one of the text messages, Mrs Mackerel, you imply there is a relationship going on between this woman and Mr Cherry. A physical relationship.'

'Well it would seem I got the wrong end of the stick. Stevie denied there was any such relationship. He insisted they were just good friends.'

'And why, Mrs Mackerel, should it even bother you who Mr Cherry has relationships with?' asked PC Smith.

'It doesn't bother me!' I protested. 'I just didn't want him messing Charlotte about,' I added lamely.

'But Miss West had already left Mr Cherry,' PC Smith pointed out. 'It seems to me that Mr Cherry regards himself as a free agent. So much so, Mrs Mackerel, that he sent you a text. A text that said he was going away for a few days. And most definitely without you, Miss West.' PC Smith's eyes returned to Charlotte. She promptly burst into tears.

'Stevie and I are always busting up,' Charlotte said tearfully. 'And then we get back together again. It makes no difference whether he went away on his own or with someone else. In the long run, we'll get back together.'

'I don't agree. This time it strikes me your separation has a flavour of permanency. After all, you say you were due to meet him during your respective lunch hours. That you wanted to discuss legal action. Indeed, a claim for half his house. That doesn't smack of reconciliation, Miss West. Not to me.'

Charlotte didn't reply. But that was due to being engulfed in a spasm of sobbing. She sounded as though her heart was breaking. PC Thomson tore his gaze from the rafters. Leaning to one side of the desk, he picked up a box of tissues. Silently, he placed the box in front of Charlotte. I put an arm around Charlotte's shoulders and patted her ineffectually. PC Thomson's gaze was back on the ceiling, so I addressed PC Smith instead.

'Charlotte and I have absolutely nothing to hide about my ex-husband's apparent disappearance. Stevie telephoned begging for help! And we're here trying to see that he gets some! Now are you going to get out there and find him, or not?' I was aware my voice had gone up several octaves. One might even say I was shouting.

Suddenly PC Thomson leant forward. His bulk seemed to fill the entire space in front of me. How had I ever thought of him as unassuming? He no longer looked like Humpty Dumpty? More like Hagrid. And he was giving off all the rancour of Professor Snape.

'My colleague is asking the very questions that will enable us to find your ex-husband Mrs Mackerel. So I'd ask you to co-operate. Do you understand?'

'Yes,' I said in a small voice.

'Mrs Mackerel.' PC Smith took up the reins of the conversation again. 'I find it somewhat odd that Mr Cherry telephoned *you* in his apparent request for help. Most people would call the police, don't you agree?'

'I suppose.'

'There's no suppose about it,' PC Smith snapped. 'I also find it strange that a man who has categorically told you to leave him alone and clear off – and that's putting it politely – telephones, allegedly distressed, imploring you to help him. Do you have any comment to make about that Mrs Mackerel?'

'Yes,' I cleared my throat. Ah! That had her attention didn't it! 'I don't think my ex-husband was the author of those previous texts.'

Humpty and Olive did another eye meet. I tried to work out what they were conveying to each other. They were obviously communicating in some sort of secret code:

We've got a right one here Humpty.

You're not kidding Olive. Guilty as hell in my opinion.

I agree. Not sure about the other one though. What do you think?

She's innocent Olive.

Any other thoughts Humpty?

Yes. The ceiling needs painting.

'Look,' I implored, 'my ex-husband and I have had our difficulties in the past, but we have two children together. We maintain civility for our kids' sake. I do not believe for one moment Stevie would cancel his weekend with the children without proper explanation, and certainly without the unpleasantries. It's completely out of character.'

PC Smith gave me an assessing look. 'So any thoughts on who else might be behind the texts, Mrs Mackerel?'

This was my opportunity to spill the Selina beans. That Selina was in fact Selina Hadley, once PC Hadley and very probably a former colleague of Humpty and Olive's. But if I did that, I'd have to justify why I had initially suspected her involvement. And bearing in mind that Selina was no longer off sick from work – indeed had answered Jamie's mobile earlier on – I had no evidence for such an accusation. I'd found nothing untoward at her apartment block. Heard nothing from within. Nobody had answered her door. Indeed, the place had appeared empty when peering through a window. Telling PC Smith that Stevie and Selina had been out horse riding one Sunday afternoon, or gone shopping at Fairview, was not hard evidence of abduction and bizarre text messages.

'I don't know who sent those texts PC Smith,' I said quietly. 'However, I *can* prove it wasn't my ex-husband. I deliberately asked Stevie about a choice of restaurant for the twins' impending birthday. He texted me back suggesting I let the children choose the venue. The fact is, their birthday is months away.'

This time it was my turn to gaze at PC Smith levelly. Put *that* in your Sherlock Holmes pipe and smoke it! But instead PC Smith gave a sardonic smile.

'Mrs Mackerel, I think there are a goodly proportion of fathers out there that make the same error as Mr Cherry. And they do it year in, year out. Men are notoriously bad at remembering dates – be it birthdays, anniversaries, or family events. You are not the first woman to experience this male phenomenon. And you certainly won't be the last.'

'I can assure you that's not the case with–'

'Meanwhile,' PC Smith cut across me, 'I have enough details to let us get started on an investigation. You've both given me names of friends and relatives, places Mr Cherry is known to frequent, and of course bank details. We will be checking to see if any sums of money have been withdrawn from his account and, if so, what area. We also have photographs and,' she picked up a plastic bag containing Stevie's toothbrush, 'this. What I would ask,' PC Smith turned to Charlotte, 'is that we have permission to search Mr Cherry's home. This is normal procedure and nothing to be unduly alarmed about. Is this okay with you, Miss West?'

'Yes,' Charlotte gulped.

'Good.' PC Smith stood up. 'We will be in touch.'

Charlotte and I also stood up. I couldn't believe we were being dismissed. For a moment I'd half expected Humpty and Olive to slap handcuffs on us and put us in a holding room on suspicion of kidnap. Or murder. Or whatever else had been flitting through their brains. But of one thing I was fairly sure. Either Victor hadn't yet seen Selina to pass on the details about Morag and me visiting, or else Selina had chosen not to pursue the matter.

In which case, why?

Chapter Twenty Six

I arrived home cold and hungry. I also felt worn out. My mood was swinging between irritation and immense worry. Humpty and Olive had exasperated me beyond belief. I also realised that keeping secrets from the twins and trying to remain cheerful would be testing. My worry for Stevie's safety and whereabouts was nothing, you understand, to do with old feelings or regrets. Absolutely not. But it was everything to do with wanting my kids to grow up with their biological father on the scene, alive and kicking.

Jamie greeted me as I came in through the front door. He took my hand, led me into the study and shut the door.

'Mum's brought me up to date Cassie.' Jamie put his arms around my shoulders and drew me close. I snuggled into his chest. It felt warm. Solid. Utterly dependable. 'I've been on the phone and spoken to my old Super. Harry. He's already been in touch with the local nick and is pushing things along. Before the night is out, some of the boys will have paid a visit to Stevie's house. Charlotte is probably liaising with them right now about access. And all hospitals are being checked. Just in case any lone, white, middle-aged male has been admitted – concussed or unconscious. Finally, Stevie's bank details are being tracked. Any transactions and the location will instantly show up. They'll find him. And soon.'

I nodded. 'I just don't understand how he could simply disappear.'

'I'm sure all will be revealed very shortly.'

'I'd better go and bath Eddie.' I went to pull away, but Jamie caught hold of me.

'Mum's doing it as we speak. You go and have some dinner. We've kept something hot in the oven for you. And I agree that we don't say anything to Livvy and Toby for now. No need to worry them eh?'

'Definitely not.'

'Want me to keep you company while you eat?'

'Yes please.'

We walked into the kitchen and I flopped down at the table. The smell of shepherd's pie made my stomach growl with hunger. I was also aware of another part of my stomach contracting in revulsion. Oh no. The earlier nausea seemed to be making an unwelcome return. Perhaps I was coming down with something? Jamie set a steaming plate before me.

'Dinner is served Madame. Glass of wine?'

'Why not,' I smiled. Perhaps a drop of alcohol would quieten the queasiness. I forked up some mince. 'How was work today?'

'Busy. I gather you spoke to Selina earlier. You know Ethan and me are required at the bank this Saturday for a few hours.'

'Selina did mention it, yes.'

'I'm sorry work has been getting in the way of things so much lately Cassie. But the good news is the contract is almost complete, and James Powell has generated some fantastic contacts for us. Business is booming!'

'Which surely means we'll see even less of you,' I pointed out.

'Not necessarily. We'll be recruiting again very shortly. And between you and me, I think Selina will take a lesser role in due course. She's not up to the pace.' Jamie massaged his chin and looked thoughtful.

'What do you mean?' I picked up my glass and took a sip of wine.

'She's not herself. Very distracted. Snappy. I don't think she can cope with pressure. When Ethan and I came out of the meeting with James Powell, Selina happened to have a neighbour from her old apartment ring her. From her reaction, you'd have thought there had been some sort of catastrophe.'

My hand froze mid-air, wine glass suspended. 'And had there been?'

'No! The neighbour was just letting her know he'd signed a delivery on her behalf, and to look in on him at some point. But her concentration was shot to pieces for the rest of the afternoon. What's the matter Cassie? Your expression is the mirror image of how Selina was looking.'

'Nothing,' I said quickly. I flung some more wine down my throat. 'I'm just a bit, you know, distracted. About Stevie.'

'Of course. Well with a bit of luck, by this time tomorrow Stevie will have been found, safe and sound. And the twins will be none the wiser. Then we can get on with having a nice weekend. Are you looking forward to the ball darling?'

'I wanted to talk to you about that.' I swallowed some mashed potato and put my fork down. It was too hot to eat properly. 'You know, I'd rather not have Selina give me a lift. I have a better idea. What about I come into work with you on Saturday? Keep you company and,' I shrugged, 'you can show me what you do. It would be interesting.'

'Hardly Cassie! You'd be bored to tears in five minutes.'

I blew on my dinner in an attempt to cool it down. 'No I wouldn't. Please let me come in with you.'

'And what about getting the kids to and from the stables? Not to mention seeing to Eddie? I know Mum has been here pretty much twenty-four seven, and she'll be here Saturday night while we're out, but I don't think we can just presume she'll step into the breach all the time. Not to cover you coming into work with me on a whim.'

I took a deep breath. 'Look Jamie. I'll put it bluntly. I don't want to travel with Selina.'

'Why?'

'Because,' I shrugged.

'Because what?'

I tossed the last of my wine down my throat. The alcohol had emboldened me. Just spill the beans Cass and be damned. 'Okay Jamie. I'm going to level with you.'

My husband looked exasperated. 'About what!'

'I haven't told the police this because I have no evidence. But I think there is a possibility that Selina knows where Stevie is.'

Jamie stared at me. I could tell he was annoyed. He refrained from reminding me that I liked to blame Selina for everything. From tampering with my dinner, to spiking my drink, to being involved in the disappearance of my ex-husband. Instead he just sighed heavily in a here-we-go-again manner. 'And you base this theory on what?'

'Because I've seen her with Stevie. Twice now. Recently they were shopping together at Fairview. It was on the day she rang in sick from work. And I happen to know he was skiving too. He told his employers he had a bad back.' Jamie regarded me silently. 'I saw them quite by chance when I was shopping for my evening dress for the ball. They didn't see me. The two of them hopped into her sports car and roared off together. I refrained from telling you because you were adamant she was loved up with Ethan, and wouldn't mess him around. And I realised that if I told you, you might feel awkward with Ethan.'

Jamie raked a hand through his hair. 'Yes, yes possibly I would. But Cassie, even if Selina did have something going with Stevie, how does this tie in with him going missing?'

'Because I don't trust her!' I cried.

'Cassie, you are absolutely right.' Hurrah! At last my husband believed me. 'You are absolutely right there is no evidence to tie Selina in to Stevie's disappearance. No listen,' he put up a hand to stop me. 'So Selina and Stevie did what thousands of Brits do every day. Skived off work to play hooky. And they did whatever they wanted to do together. And then Selina went home to Ethan. She's back at work. And after work she's been going home with Ethan. Therefore, at what point has she had an opportunity to magic Stevie into thin air? Apart from anything else, what the hell would be her motive?'

'Because,' I waved a hand around, 'she's jealous of me. And wants to upset my world in whatever way she can.'

'Cassie,' Jamie's eyes bored into mine, 'Let's examine your theory together. You're saying Selina wants to impact upon you. Am I right?' I nodded my head. 'Okay. Now if your theory is correct, put yourself in Selina's shoes for a moment. She wants to upset you. Rock your world off its axis.' I nodded my head vigorously. 'Now forgive me for pointing this out, but if Selina wanted to majorly upset you, wouldn't it make more sense for her to arrange *my* disappearance instead of Stevie's?'

I stared at Jamie. He was right of course. My head knew he was right. But my heart also knew he was wrong. Oh so wrong. I held back telling him about tailing Selina to her apartment with Stevie. And kept quiet about later visiting the place with Morag. I had a feeling there was only so much I could tell Jamie without him majorly losing his rag with me.

'Look,' Jamie took one of my hands, 'if it makes you feel any better, I'll talk to Harry about it. I'll leave your theories out of the equation though. But I'll tell Harry it's possible Selina was the last person to have seen Stevie. Harry can decide what line to take. Just remember Ethan has police connections too. How the heck would it look if Ethan discovered I'd been talking to our old Super about his fiancée being involved – even loosely – with the disappearance of your ex-husband? So this is absolutely between you and me. Okay?'

'Of course. And thanks Jamie.'

'In the meantime, we just carry on as normal.'

'What do you mean?'

'I mean you drive to Oxfordshire with Selina.'

'But I don't want–'

'Enough Cassie.' Jamie stood up. Clearly his patience had run out. 'Finish your dinner. I'll go and get Eddie off Mum.

An hour later Eddie was in bed. I then spent a bit of time with the children. My impromptu visit to the police station was passed off as seeing Nell over a domestic emergency. Jonas and Toby were playing on the Wii. I joined in with their fun for a while, before popping in on the girls. I found them deep in conversation about the pros and cons of buying a Lady Gaga wig.

'Whatever do you want a wig for?' I asked.

'Because,' said Petra, 'we can enjoy the benefits of being platinum blonde without wrecking our hair.'

'I suppose,' I nodded.

'The downside is that a decent wig is expensive.'

'But cheaper than umpteen visits to the hairdresser,' Livvy pointed out. 'Do you like the idea of wigs Mum?'

'They're not for me darling.' No need to tell my daughter about a recent venture with brunette tresses. I wondered if Victor had picked the wigs up and shown them to Selina. And whether he'd regaled her with the tale of two unlikely visitors peering through her kitchen window. 'That reminds me, I need to phone Morag about something.'

I left them gossiping, retrieved my mobile phone and slipped along the landing to the master bedroom. Jamie was still downstairs watching television. I shut myself into the en-suite and started a bath running. Whilst waiting for the tub to fill, I rang Morag's home number. I put the loo seat down and perched, waiting for the call to connect.

'Hello?' It was Joanie, Morag's sweet step-daughter.

'Hi Joanie. It's Cass. Is your step-mama around?'

I sensed Joanie smiling. 'Hey Cass! No, sorry. Morag's out with Dad. They've gone to check the horses. They usually take a while.'

I bet. No doubt Morag was, at this very moment, cantering around the indoor riding school totally starkers.

'When she's back, please could you give her a message Joanie?'

'Sure.'

'Tell her,' I chewed my lip, 'that I will be over tomorrow morning after the school run. And that we need to discuss Dobbin's diet.'

Joanie laughed. 'You know about him do you? He's one fat pony! Keeps breaking into the feed room and stuffing all the oats. He was charging around the riding school last week completely off his head.'

Dobbin clearly had much in common with Morag.

We made some small talk before saying good-bye. I hung up and turned off the bath taps. There was a sick feeling in my stomach. It had nothing to do with the earlier nausea. More a sense of foreboding. And that things were coming to a head.

Chapter Twenty Seven

Friday morning dawned. When the alarm went off I'd been in the middle of a terrible dream. PCs Thomson and Smith had come a-knocking on the door with a warrant for my arrest.

'But why?' I'd quaked.

'For the manslaughter,' Humpty had announced, 'of Victor Meldrew, the neighbour of Miss Selina Hadley.'

'B-but,' I'd stuttered, 'h-he's a fictitious character!'

'That's where you're wrong Mrs Mackerel,' Olive had interrupted. 'And you are also under arrest for harassing Miss Hadley and for abducting your ex-husband, Mr Stephen Cherry.' And then Humpty had stepped forward and snapped a pair of pink fluffy handcuffs on my wrists, the likes of which you might find in a sex shop.

'I want a solicitor!' I'd yelled at them. 'I know my rights!'

'Ah, but do you know your nursery rhymes?' PC Thomson had sneered. 'You can only have a solicitor if you sing Humpty Dumpty. Backwards,' he'd added.

'Cassie!' Jamie nudged me with his ankle. 'Turn the alarm off.'

My hand shot out from under the duvet and groped for the switch on the clock radio. I groaned and turned over. And as I did so a feeling of nausea rushed into my throat. I couldn't take much more of this anxiety. It was literally making me ill. I flung back the duvet and padded into the bathroom. Maybe I'd feel less queasy once I'd cleaned my teeth. I squeezed out some toothpaste and began brushing, staring at my reflection in the overhead mirror. A grey-skinned woman with frightened eyes and dishevelled hair stared back. I couldn't wait to get the school run out the way and see Morag.

An hour later, the Muck Truck came to a halt outside Matt and Morag's house. I suppressed a dry heave and unstrapped my seat belt. Matt was coming down the pathway, en-route to the equestrian centre.

'Good morning Cass,' he trilled as I clambered out of the car. 'Quick, give me a hug and a kiss now. Before I disappear down the yard and end up stinking like the dung heap!' He grabbed me in a bear hug and planted a smacker on my cheek. I hugged Matt back. He was always such a cheerful soul. 'What's up?' he asked. 'You look a bit peaky.'

'I'm feeling a bit peaky,' I nodded. 'But it's nothing to worry about. And anyway, you're a fine one to talk. You're looking somewhat jaded yourself Mr Harding. What's Morag been doing to you?'

'Ah. You might well ask.' Matt tapped the side of his nose. 'But where my wife is concerned, sometimes there are secrets that cannot be shared.' I understood entirely. God forbid if Jamie knew some of the secrets I was keeping. 'Go in Cass. Morag's expecting you. See you later!' Matt turned, waving briefly to Eddie through the car window, and ambled off to the yard.

I opened the car's rear door and unstrapped my boy. Swinging him onto my hip, I leant back inside the car and grabbed the baby holdall before walking up the path to the front door. Matt had left it on the latch, so I pushed my way inside.

'Yoo hoo!' I called. Henry's grizzles floated along the hallway. I followed the noise into the kitchen. My godson was in his playpen, clearly upset that his Mummy wasn't giving him the attention he wanted. Morag was slumped at the kitchen table.

She was surrounded by little packets which I initially mistook for toothbrushes. 'What's all this?' I asked.

'Hi Cass.' She looked up. 'They're ovulation kits and pregnancy tests.' She waved a hand at the paraphernalia. 'I picked up a load in the chemist a little while ago. We are officially trying for another baby and my period is late. I was absolutely convinced I'd scored a bingo.' She stood up and retrieved a stick from the rubbish bin. 'However, according to this,' she waggled the stick in front of my eyes, 'there are no buns baking in my oven.' She chucked the test kit back in the bin before washing her hands at the sink.

'Well never mind,' I soothed, jiggling Eddie on my hip. 'It's not the end of the world.'

'You don't understand Cass.' Morag dried her hands on a tea towel. 'I feel absolutely gutted. And now I have to wait another twenty-eight days before I find out if Henry is going to have a little brother or sister. That's *four weeks*.' She flopped back down at the table.

I remembered how Morag had been when she was trying to conceive Henry. Words like *obsessed* and *neurotic* sprang to mind. Morag had spent months carting around a handbag stuffed with ovulations kits, pregnancy tests, charts and graphs, not to mention every kind of multi-vitamin under the sun. Wherever Morag went, so did the test kits. Seeing all the scattered packets gave me a feeling of déjà vu.

I walked over to the playpen and popped Eddie inside. Henry immediately ceased grizzling and stretched out a little hand. My son squealed with delight and began blowing bubbles. I left the boys to it and pulled out a chair at the table. Now was a good time to tell Morag that plans for another baby might need to be suspended. Certainly for the foreseeable future.

'I think,' I cleared my throat nervously, 'that a negative pregnancy test might be a blessing in disguise.'

'What do you mean?' Morag straightened up.

'There have been some developments since I last saw you.'

'I only saw you yesterday. What developments?'

'Police developments.'

Morag blanched. 'Is it to do with that ruddy pensioner I nearly knocked over?'

'And some,' I nodded.

'You mean there's more to tell?' She stood up and went to the kettle. Picking it up, she moved over to the tap and blasted water inside.

'Unfortunately,' I sighed, 'it is possible that shit might soon be hitting the fan.'

'Specify shit,' said Morag, flipping the kettle lid down and flicking the switch.

And so, over coffee, I brought her up to date. From Stevie's dazed phone call begging for help, to ringing Charlotte, to visiting the police station and being grilled by PCs Thomson and Smith, to updating Jamie with a doctored version of events.

'And later, when Jamie and I were talking about his work, he happened to mention Selina hasn't been herself. Apparently she's been very distracted and snappy. Ethan said it was pressure of work. However, Jamie noted Selina's concentration was shot to pieces when a *neighbour*,' I rolled my eyes meaningfully, 'rang Selina on her mobile. Jamie said that from her reaction you'd have thought something truly awful had happened.'

'And did Jamie ask Selina what had made her react that way?' Morag prompted.

'Yes. Apparently the neighbour wanted Selina to look in on him and pick up a delivery. Do you think that's a truthful explanation?' I fiddled nervously with my cup.

'Christ,' said Morag nearly spilling her coffee all over the table. 'Of course not! That interfering busybody clearly rang her to give her a Neighbourhood Watch update. No doubt Selina is now in possession of my wigs. Forensics might be analysing them this very moment. Looking for our DNA. And – oh my God!' Morag clutched her mouth. 'Selina probably now has my car registration number!' She stood up and began pacing around the kitchen. 'This is catastrophic news Cass. Selina used to be a police officer. She's going to have her own connections, isn't she! Why, she's probably already fed my car registration details into a police computer somewhere. She could turn up on my doorstep any minute now! Demand to know what the hell I was doing snooping around her apartment block! What if she goes to the police herself?'

'Um, yes, the thought had occurred to me.' I took another sip of coffee. 'That's why it *m-i-g-h-t* not be a good idea to have another baby just yet.'

Morag narrowed her eyes. 'I'm not sitting here waiting for the Old Bill to come knocking.'

'But maybe they won't. Well, hopefully not anyway. Selina had plenty of time to get the police involved following that pensioner's tittle-tattle. In which case, how come the coppers didn't ask about my movements yesterday? Or whether I knew somebody called Morag Harding? They had plenty of opportunity to ask those questions while Charlotte and I were at the police station. As you say, Selina has connections. But so does Jamie. He's been in touch with his old Superintendent whose influence will speed things up. Charlotte texted me late last night to say the police have checked out Stevie's house and car. If Selina is so innocent in all this, why hasn't she been pulling her own strings to have our guts for garters?'

'True,' Morag considered. 'Do you still have a key to Stevie's house?'

'Yep.' I held up my key ring and gave it a little shake. 'Ever since I had to let in decorators after Charlotte took a spray can to Stevie's walls and generally wrecked the place.'

'Ah yes. Wasn't that revenge for Stevie dumping Charlotte for a well preserved marine biologist?'

'That's right.' I drained my coffee.

'You know,' Morag frowned, 'one way or another, your ex has led Charlotte a merry dance.'

'I know.'

'And she's forgiven him time and time again.'

'She has,' I agreed.

'You don't think that this time Stevie pushed Charlotte too far. And she knows more than she's letting on?'

I looked at Morag and let out a sigh. 'I agree she could have a motive – and the police made inference of such when they were talking to us. But then they also implied the same with me. They asked me outright if I had an axe to grind with Stevie because of the unpleasant text messages he supposedly sent me. So,' I shook my head, 'no. No I don't think Charlotte knows where Stevie is or has had anything to do with his disappearance. She was absolutely distraught when I told her he'd rung me begging for help.'

'She could be a good actress,' Morag didn't look convinced.

'Yes,' I acknowledged, 'she could. The police also made sarky comments about that too. Said it was amazing how often relatives of missing people went on national television appealing for witnesses, sobbing their hearts out, when all the time they'd hidden Uncle Tom's body under the patio.'

Morag shuddered. 'Those two plods sound like a right ball of fun.'

'Believe me,' I pushed my coffee cup away, 'they weren't.

'Well I suggest,' said Morag draining her own coffee, 'that if the police have finished doing their stuff, we nip over to Stevie's place and do ours. Let's see if we can't perhaps find something of Selina's to link her in some way to Stevie. If nothing else we could then ring up Jamie's old Super–'

'Harry,' I interrupted.

'Harry, and tell him that his former colleague is having an affair with the missing person and should, at the very least, be questioned about when she last saw Stevie.'

'Sounds like a plan,' I nodded.

'Well I can't think of anything else to do in the present circumstances.'

I stood up. 'Come on then.' I rummaged in my big holdall and dug out my mobile. 'In the meantime, I'll let Nell know we're on our way over. As she's only a few houses down from Stevie's place, we'll leave my car on her drive.'

'Let me just clear up.' Morag began shifting cups from the table to the dishwasher. 'And anyway,' she turned back to the table and scooped up the test kits, 'I'm not going in your car. It's a tip.' She dumped all the little packets in her own enormous baby holdall. 'So go and get Eddie's car seat, because we're going in mine.' Morag slung the holdall over her shoulder and then picked Henry up from the playpen.

'Oh for goodness sake,' I sighed. 'A bit of dirt never hurt.'

'Dirt is dirt Cass,' Morag arched an eyebrow, 'but your car is pure filth.'

'I'd have thought you'd have been well at home in it then,' I quipped. 'Joanie did tell me where you were last night. I don't need to be Einstein to work out what you were doing.'

Morag smirked and led the way out of the house.

'So let me get this straight,' said Nell as we stood in her hallway. 'You want to leave Henry and Eddie here and go for a snoop in Stevie's house.'

'Clever girl Nellie-Wellie,' said Morag as she bent down to pat Rocket's head. The red setter stood at Nell's heels, optimistically wagging her tail in hope of walkies. 'And I'll leave my car on your drive if you don't mind. Don't want to draw attention, as such, to Stevie's house.'

'You couldn't draw any more attention to Stevie's place if you tried,' Nell huffed. 'There was quite a bit of activity over there last night. Three plods visited. Two went inside and one stood outside, as if guarding the place. They were obviously giving the house the once over. Fortunately Dylan didn't see anything. He was in bed and asleep, otherwise he'd have been asking what was going on.'

'Thank God for that,' I said with feeling. The last thing I wanted was Dylan asking the twins at school why their dad's house had been visited by the law.

'Well bring the boys through.' Nell shut the front door. 'They can go in Rosie's playpen. Would you both like a coffee before you go super sleuthing?'

'We've just had one,' said Morag.

'We could have another,' I said hopefully.

'Let's search Stevie's house first,' said Morag. 'There will be time for coffee later. And anyway, if you have too many you'll only be weeing for England. You know what your bladder is like if you overdose on caffeine.'

'Charming,' I grumbled. 'Well put the kettle on anyway Nell. We won't be long.'

'Will do.' She took Eddie and Henry from us. 'Come with me boys. You can keep Rosie company.'

We let ourselves out of Nell's house and walked the short distance to Stevie's. When I was married to Stevie and living next door to Nell, Stevie had had an affair with a neighbour at the other end of the cul-de-sac and moved in with her. Weeks later, when their relationship had gone pear-shaped, the woman had wanted to move away and start afresh. Stevie had ended up buying her house. In the early days of our split, it had meant the children were never far away from either of their parents. As we walked up the pathway, I was surprised to see the place looking perfectly normal. Somehow I'd been expecting the house to be wrapped in red and white caution tape with police signs prohibiting access. But then again, no accident had occurred. Nor burglary. There was no crime to investigate. Just a person who had seemingly disappeared into thin air.

I slotted my key into the door's barrel lock. Inside, post had been picked up from the doormat and stacked neatly on the hall table. The house had a stillness about it. Despite its nooks and crannies being prodded and poked about, the silence signified nobody had lived within it for days. Morag brought up the rear and shut the door behind us. I looked around.

'What exactly are we looking for?' I asked.

'Who knows? Just peer into every cupboard, pull out every drawer, and be on the lookout for anything...odd. And anything belonging to a female,' Morag added.

'You're forgetting this was Charlotte's home too,' I reminded Morag. 'And she still has some bits and pieces here. Who's to say that a hair clip in the shower isn't hers rather than Selina's?'

'We'll evaluate everything we come across. Let's check that pile of mail for starters.' Morag began sifting through envelopes.

'I doubt you're going to find a letter addressed to Selina,' I shook my head. 'I'm sure the police have already examined the mail anyway.' I moved away from the hall table and took to the stairs. 'I'll check the bedrooms. You search the downstairs.'

'Okay,' said Morag, and moved down the hallway towards the kitchen.

I walked along the landing. Straight ahead was the master bedroom. I might as well start in that room. I paused in the doorway, surveying the functional rectangular space. Everything was neat and tidy apart from a pair of Stevie's jeans slung across the bed. Picking them up, I automatically went to one of the fitted wardrobes to put them away. Sliding back one of the wardrobe doors, I found an empty hanger. Clothes hung in a regimental line. At the bottom, shoes were placed in an organised arrangement. Every single pair belonged to Stevie. I slotted the jeans' hanger onto the rail and shut the wardrobe door. Walking around one side of the bed, I stopped to investigate the bedside table. Nothing looked out of the ordinary. I brushed some dust from my hands. Ahead was the master bedroom's en-suite. Going into the small shower room, I explored the fitted storage system that housed the sink and ran the length of one wall. Deodorants. Shampoo. Bottles of hair conditioner. Hair-dye. I picked up the carton. *Black* hair-dye. Interesting. Charlotte was blonde, so my hunch about Stevie colouring his hair was correct. A part of me felt intrusive going through his belongings. Like I was violating his private space. But then again, I told myself as I opened the cupboard over the sink, if the boot were on the other foot and I was missing, I'd be wanting everybody sifting through my stuff for whatever clues they could come up with. I stared at the shelves before me. Toothpaste. A toothbrush. Pink. Not Stevie's. Quite apart from the fact that he wouldn't buy himself a pink toothbrush, I knew that Charlotte had taken his toothbrush to the police station for DNA purposes. But surely this particular toothbrush wasn't Charlotte's? When a woman moved out, the first thing she'd chuck in her suitcase would be her make-up, skin care products and most definitely her toothbrush. Was this Selina's toothbrush? Should I pop it in a plastic bag and go off to the police station waggling it at PC Thomson and PC Smith and say, 'Look! See what I've found?' Or – hang on – maybe it would be best to leave it here. As proper evidence. If I removed it, then it might not be construed as proof of her having been here. Perhaps I should ask Morag's opinion. I retraced my steps to the landing.

'Morag?' I leant over the banister rails. 'Come up here a minute!'

Morag appeared in the hallway. 'Have you found something?'

'Possibly.'

She took the stairs two at a time and followed me into the bathroom.

'Look!' I pointed at the cabinet.

Morag's eyes widened. 'Oh my goodness! Clever girl Cass.' She leant across the toilet bowl and whipped a bit of tissue off the loo roll holder.

'What are you doing?' I asked. 'I was referring to this.' I pointed to the toothbrush. 'I think it might be Selina's.'

'Bugger the toothbrush.' Morag covered her finger tips with the toilet paper and reached into the cabinet. 'Don't you recognise this Cass?' She began carefully nudging a small bottle around on the shelf. 'When we were peering through Selina's apartment window, she had identical bottles to this on her kitchen table.'

I frowned. Flipped back through the pages of my memory. 'You're right,' I nodded.

Morag kept gently turning the bottle until its label was facing us. She straightened up. Let out a shaky breath. 'Bloody hell. How did the police miss this?'

'What is it?' I asked.

'I do believe,' she pointed at the bottle, 'that this is the sort of thing some unscrupulous individuals use to spike drinks.'

My mouth dropped open. My recent spectacular pass out at the Oxo Tower was still very much to the forefront of my mind. I stared at the label. In neat black typeset was the inscription *Gamma-Hydroxybutyric Acid.*

Chapter Twenty Eight

'What shall we do?' I asked Morag. 'I mean, we can't exactly prove this stuff belongs to Selina. The Old Bill will think it belongs to Stevie.'

'What the hell is GHB doing in his cabinet?' Morag frowned.

'I've no idea. You know, when he phoned me he sounded so dazed. Like he was drunk or drugged. And now we've seen this, I'm wondering if Selina used it on Stevie to drug him. But why would she leave it in his cabinet?'

Morag fished in the pocket of her jeans and took out her mobile phone. 'Heaven only knows. But I'm going to take a picture of it on that shelf next to the pink toothbrush. Get out the way Cass and give me some space. This shower room isn't big enough for the two of us with my elbows sticking out at right angles.'

I left Morag to it and returned to the master bedroom. I wandered over to the window. Looking out at the cul-de-sac below, I wondered where Stevie was right now. And then I froze. A car had turned into the road. A bright green Mazda MX-5 convertible. And it was coming this way. I watched in horror as Selina's car bounced gently over the road's sleeping policemen.

'I do not believe it.' I paled and stepped smartly back from the window.

Morag stuck her head out the bathroom doorway. 'What's the matter?'

'We have a visitor.' I jerked my head at the window. 'Selina.'

Morag strode over to the window and peered carefully around the curtain.

'Oh buggerations,' she hissed. I risked a peek over Morag's shoulder. Selina's car had now slowed to a stop outside Nell's house. A pair of eyes were studying Morag's car. And the number plate. 'Oh double buggerations,' Morag groaned. The Mazda began to move again.

'What are we going to do?' I squeaked, panic rising. We didn't have time to make an escape out the back door. Selina's car was now on Stevie's driveway.

'Nothing,' said Morag calmly. 'Just be quiet and don't let her see us. She can't get in after all. She doesn't have a key.' With that Selina extracted a bunch of keys from her coat pocket and extended one towards the lock. 'Triple buggerations. She *does* have a key.'

'Shit!' I yelped. And nearly did. 'What are we going to do?'

'Hide.' Morag shoved me towards the fitted wardrobe.

'No! Don't make me go in there – it will be dark. I hate small dark spaces.'

'For God's sake Cass,' Morag hissed, 'now isn't the time to get claustrophobic. Get under the bed then.'

'I don't think I'll fit,' I bleated. There was the sound of a key slotting into the barrel of the front door's lock.

'Well take a deep breath and do your best. With my bosoms I've no hope of getting under there. I'll be in the wardrobe. Now hurry up!'

I flung myself onto the carpet and wriggled with all my might under the bed. Downstairs I heard the letterbox rattle as Selina pushed against the door. I twisted my neck sideways, laying awkwardly on my stomach, chin at a sharp right angle to one shoulder. Tucking an arm behind me, I hoped my feet weren't sticking out the bottom of the bed. My heart was crashing about in my ribcage, my pulse thudding in the ear that was squashed into the carpet. I couldn't hear Selina's footsteps for the noise my cardiovascular system was making. I gulped, and prayed to God she would clear off again very soon. I held my breath in an attempt to be as quiet as possible. It was dusty under the bed and my nose twitched involuntarily. Please God, don't let me sneeze. But all thoughts of sneezing fled my mind as a pair of slim ankles appeared in the bedroom doorway. My eyes widened in horror. She was here! Just feet from where I lay. The tension was unbearable. I was half expecting Selina to stoop down and peer under the bed. Or cover the short distance to the wardrobe opposite the bathroom, yank the door open and exclaim, 'Ah ha! You must be Morag Harding. Mind telling me why you were snooping around my apartment block yesterday? And why are you hiding in my lover's wardrobe?' Morag would have her work cut out trying to explain she was from the Council whilst nestling amongst Stevie's suits and shirts.

But Selina didn't go to the wardrobe, or look under the bed. Instead she went into the en-suite. Seconds later there was a clicking noise – the bathroom cabinet opening. Then a tinkling as a glass bottle chinked against another glass bottle. Another click – the magnetic lock on the cabinet snapping the door shut. Seconds later, the ankles briefly re-appeared and crossed the distance from bathroom door to bedroom door. And then they disappeared along the landing. My ears strained to hear further movement. There was a brief pause followed by the sound of the front door opening. Moments later it banged shut, the momentum reverberating through the floor on which I lay. I didn't dare move. Not until I knew for sure she was gone. My neck was aching from the awkward position I was laying in, and my right arm had gone to sleep. There was the sound of an engine bursting into life followed by grinding as reverse gear failed to initially engage. And then the car's engine slowly receded.

Morag's head appeared sideways, inches from mine. 'She's gone. You can come out.'

'I don't think I can move,' I said. My breath disturbed a little flurry of dust and I finally sneezed. My body jerked, catching my head on the underside of the bed. 'Ouch,' I yelped. 'Lift the bed up Morag. I can't get out.'

Morag obliged and I wiggled out, brushing my clothes off. 'Geez,' I gasped as I straightened up. 'My legs are like jelly.' I rubbed my arm as pins and needles briefly took hold from the earlier lack of blood supply. 'So what the hell was she doing in that bathroom?'

'What do *you* think!' Morag blew out her cheeks. 'She took the bottle of GHB. She knew what she was looking for and where to find it, so it's obviously hers. I cracked the wardrobe door open and,' Morag thrust her mobile phone at me, 'look! I've managed to film her removing it.' Morag touched the mobile's screen and played it back to me. The picture was a bit grainy and the wardrobe door partially encroached on the picture, but it was good enough.

I sat down on the bed. My legs were starting to tremble violently. 'And another thing,' I looked at Morag, 'she let herself into this house – and not with just a single key. She had a bunch of keys. And they weren't hers because she was holding her own keys! I saw her extract a second bunch from her coat pocket. Clearly those were Stevie's house keys. She simply has to know where he is. Do you think we should arrange to meet her and, you know, *confront* her?'

'No.' Morag shook her head and sat down next to me on the bed. 'She's dangerous Cass. We have to tell the police what we know.'

'What – that we were trespassing in a missing person's house, and then hiding in wardrobes and under beds? Those two plods down the station will have us in custody before we can say *parole*. You have no idea how they turn the tables with their words.'

'Then tell Jamie. He'll know how to handle it.'

'Will he?' I gave a mirthless laugh. 'You're forgetting that he doesn't know about our little jaunt over to Selina's apartment, or subsequent entanglement with the nosy neighbour. Not to mention the delicate matter of him being in partnership with Selina's fiancé. But you're right, the police should know. And they will be told,' I nodded. 'But anonymously.'

'Brilliant idea Cass!' Morag nodded approvingly.

'We'll get hold of Jamie's Super – Harry.'

'What will you tell him exactly?' Morag asked.

'Oh I'm not going to tell him anything.' I shook my head. 'If they end up recording the call, they'll have my voice on record. And I'm not risking Selina with her,' I posted quotation marks in the air, '*connections* getting tipped off that a caller rang in accusing her of kidnap and abduction. If she listened to the recording she'd know it was me. However, she hasn't a clue what you sound like. She's never met you. So you're going to make the call instead.'

'Me?' Morag's eyes widened.

'Yes, you! And you might as well do it now, before we go back to Nell's and have babies screaming in the background or Rocket woofing away. Ring Directory Enquiries and ask for the number of the local nick. And when you get through, tell the operator you want to speak to Harry. And don't forget to withhold your number.'

'Don't the police have fancy equipment that can work out where the caller is ringing from, even if the number is withheld?' Morag frowned.

'I don't know,' I considered. 'What about we use Stevie's landline then. Just in case.'

'Good idea,' said Morag. She stood up and went to the bedside cabinet. A telephone handset nestled against the lamp. 'You keep a look-out by the window. Just in case Madam makes a second appearance. We don't want to take any chances.'

'Okay.' I positioned myself discreetly behind the curtain. The cul-de-sac was quiet. Not a natty green sports car in sight.

A few minutes later and Morag was connected to the local police station.

'Hello? Hello! Can I speak to Harry please? Yes. Harry. Well I'm not sure. All I know is the Harry bit. Oh hang on, it's Super Harry. Yes, I'm quite sure. *Sooper Har-ree,*' Morag enunciated. 'No I'm not being ridiculous. No I don't know Superman. What? No I don't want to talk to any other super heroes. Hello?' Morag stared at the receiver. 'The bugger's hung up!'

'Oh for heaven's sake!' I cried. 'Give me that phone.' I snatched the receiver and pressed the redial button. Placing two fingers over the bridge of my nose, I pinched my nostrils together. 'Heddow? I want to deport a didnap. A man called Devie Derry-'

The phone was snatched out of my hands.

'Hello. It's me again. Yes I spoke to you a minute ago. Now listen here. So far you've wasted six minutes of precious police investigation time. I want to speak to Superintendent Harry Somebody-or-Other about a life threatening matter. Harry's not there? Well who can I speak to? Yes I'll hang on. Hello? Who's that? PC Smith, I see.'

I paled and nudged Morag. 'It's Olive,' I whispered. 'She's that horrendous female officer I was telling you about. She and Humpty questioned me and Charlotte. They both tried to tie us up in verbal knots and–'

Morag put up a hand to hush me. 'Now then PC Smith – never mind who I am, that's not important. The important thing Olive – I hope you don't mind me calling you that – is that I have some information regarding the disappearance of Mr Stephen Cherry. Yes, *very* important information. And I'd like you to share it with your colleague, PC Humpty. Stevie Cherry has been kidnapped. He was drugged with Gamma-Hydroxybutyric Acid prior to his abduction. No I am not the kidnapper! No I am not asking for a ransom! Look Olive, will you listen to me please because this is a matter of life and death. The kidnapper is Selina Hadley. She's an ex-cop. Oh you know her do you? Jolly good. Highly respected? Ha! More like highly dangerous. She's a total fruitcake. Well Olive why don't you ask her eh? Just pop along to her swanky Greenwich apartment that she shares with Ethan Fareham who – incidentally – she's cheating on, and pop the little old question at her. Ask her if she knows Stevie Cherry. And how she comes to be in possession of his house keys and a few nifty bottles of GHB. No I can't tell you my name, because if I did my life would be in danger. Although,' Morag blanched, 'I've just realised my life already is in danger because,' the blood drained from Morag's face, 'Selina knows I nearly killed Victor.'

I made hand swiping motions in front of Morag. 'No!' I hissed. 'Don't say that or Selina will put two and two together!'

'Hello Olive? You won't tell Selina it's me will you? Only I don't want her paying a visit and–' Morag paused, her expression stricken. Suddenly her face drained of colour, her eyes rolled backwards and she crumpled to the floor. The handset flew out of Morag's hand and clattered against some skirting boards.

Oh bloody marvellous. Morag had fainted. I roughly shoved my friend into the recovery position before snatching up the phone.

'Heddow? Dust do it Olive. Arrest Delina.' I disconnected the call and slammed the handset back into its cradle. Morag's eyes were fluttering open.

'What happened?' she groaned.

'You keeled over. It's shock from the realisation that we're both dealing with an unstable, kidnapping, drug-inducing, nutcase who–'

'Thank you Cass,' Morag interrupted. She sat up carefully. Her hands fluttered up to her temples and she massaged them gingerly. 'My bonce is making strange buzzing noises.'

'Stay still for a minute.'

'No thanks. I want to get the hell out of here and back to Nell's.' Morag hauled herself upright. 'We better put Nell in the picture. Selina spotted my car on her driveway. We need to warn Nell and Ben to be vigilant. Thank God they have Rocket who will bark the place down if Selina pays a visit.'

'We need to keep a level head on us – the last thing we want is to frighten Nell. Hopefully everything will be fine now. We've put Olive and Humpty on the trail. They're probably zooming off to Greenwich at this very moment to question Selina. I'm one hundred per cent sure that woman will be out of our hair by tomorrow morning,' I said confidently.

Which goes to show how little I knew.

Chapter Twenty Nine

When we returned to Nell's, our friend raised her eyebrows at Morag's pale complexion and me covered in flick and dust.

'What's the matter with the pair of you?' Nell scrutinised us as we piled into the hallway. 'One of you looks like you've seen a ghost, and the other looks like she's impersonating one.'

'We're fine,' Morag assured. 'It was just a bit odd seeing the house so,' she paused to find the word she was looking for, 'still. It made Stevie's absence seem, you know, a lot more ominous. It just shook me up a bit. And Cass managed to trip over and get flick on her clothes.'

'I see.' Nell didn't look convinced as she shut the door behind us. We followed her through to the kitchen. 'Let's have that coffee and you can tell me if you found anything of interest.' She reached for the kettle.

'Actually I'll pass on the coffee,' I said. I was very aware of Morag twitching violently next to me, desperate to remove her car from Nell's drive. 'I'd really like to get home and change these clothes.'

'I need to get back too,' Morag said quickly. 'I've just remembered the window cleaner is coming.'

'But I've not seen anything of you both!' Nell protested. 'The babies are asleep, and I was thinking we'd have a nice gossip about your snoop around.'

'There's nothing to tell,' Morag assured. 'The place looked perfectly normal.' Morag walked over to Rosie's playpen and peered over the side. 'Ah, look at them. Three little cherubs all fast-a-bye-byes.' She leant over the safety rail, picked up Henry and then turned to face me. 'Come on Cass. Take Eddie. We'll leave you in peace Nell.'

Nell was looking thoroughly short-changed. 'When will I see you both again?'

'Soon,' I assured as I scooped up my little boy. He was out for the count. I placed Eddie gently over my shoulder. 'After we've gone Nell, make sure the door is firmly shut. In fact I'd lock it if I were you.'

'And put the safety chain on for good measure,' Morag added.

'Whatever for?' Nell asked.

'Because you're a woman on your own with a baby. You can't be too careful these days,' said Morag. 'You never know who's going to come a-knocking on your door.'

'It's only ever the Born Again brigade. And I quite like chatting to them actually,' Nell sniffed. 'There's nothing like a bit of spirituality in one's life. You should try it some time.'

Morag and I gave each other a look. Not so long ago Nell had had a deep flirtation with the local church. Which had been nothing to do with wanting to follow Lord Jesus but everything to do with an unrequited crush on the gay vicar.

'Well just watch out please Nell,' Morag said. 'They're not called Bible Bashers for nothing.'

'Are you absolutely sure nothing happened in that house?' Nell frowned.

'Quite sure.' Morag grabbed her baby holdall. 'Come along Cass. The window cleaner beckons.'

I reached for my own holdall. 'See you soon Nell.' I gave my old neighbour a hug. 'And don't forget to put that chain on after we've gone.'

'Well,' said Morag as we sped along the main road, 'I think we got away with that quite lightly.'

'What – not getting found by Selina?'

'No, I mean not arousing Nell's suspicions.'

'Oh come off it,' I snorted. 'She thought we'd lost the plot.' I looked out the window at the scenery rushing by. Houses. Somebody mowing a front lawn. A man walking into a newsagent. A park full of children playing in the chill winter air. People doing normal things. Not hiding under beds or worrying about police investigations. 'I wonder if Olive and Humpty have caught up with Selina yet. Just think,' I shifted in my seat and turned to face Morag, 'she might be in a patrol car right now. Sitting on the back seat and shaking like a jelly. Shouting that she knows her rights and demanding a solicitor.'

'Well let's hope so,' said Morag gripping the steering wheel, 'because I'll sleep a lot easier once I know she's not on the loose. Either way Cass, I'm going to tell Matt everything.' Morag lifted one hand off the wheel to silence me. 'Hear me out please! Things are looking a bit different now. And not in a good way. Selina's on the warpath. And I don't want to be the next person to vanish into thin air. I need Matt by my side, looking out for me.' Morag slowed down for some traffic lights on the change to red. 'And if you've got any sense, you'll tell Jamie too. Ideally before my husband gets on the blower to yours and spills the beans on what the pair of us have been up to. Matt will go ballistic to begin with. Hopefully he'll calm down when he knows the police are now properly involved.'

'I understand,' I sighed. 'But could you ask Matt to refrain from calling Jamie until tomorrow? Just until I've spoken to Jamie myself. I'm going to have to pick my moment. He's not going to be too impressed when he hears what we were doing this morning. It's very likely that this is going to put a spanner in the works regarding the bank's ball tomorrow. If Selina's arrested, she won't be attending. In which case Ethan will be too frantic about his fiancée to attend himself.'

'I doubt any of you will be going,' Morag glanced at me.

'What do you mean? Jamie will insist the pair of us still go. It's business! So I'll carry on as normal – get ready and drive myself up to Oxfordshire.'

'Cass, I know you can be a bit ditzy, but you seem to be forgetting something.' Morag looked away from me as the lights shifted through their colour change to green. Shoving the car into gear we lurched forward. 'Stop and think. What will happen when the truth comes out?'

'Well, Selina will go to jail,' I replied. 'Obviously.'

'Y-e-s. But you seem to have suffered a memory bypass on the other *obvious* matter.'

I frowned. And then gasped. 'Stevie!'

'Yes! Stevie! I don't think Jamie is going to agree to waltz off to some ball – business or otherwise – when your ex-husband, father of your twins no less, is finally found and probably in need of a hospital.' Morag gripped the steering wheel again. 'Hopefully Stevie will only be drugged up to his eyeballs, and not in a body bag from whatever that bitch has been doing to him.'

'Oh God Morag,' I let out a shuddering gasp. 'Don't say that. I just assumed that once Selina was in for questioning all would be well. You know – Stevie would be found safe and sound. Selina would go to jail. Stevie then goes home. And we're not looking over our shoulders all the time. Happy endings all round.' Suddenly the earlier nausea made an unwelcome return. I clung on to the door handle, closed my eyes and willed it to pass. 'Anyway,' I opened my eyes again and took a deep breath, 'I'd better give Charlotte a call. Have her on standby.'

'No. Not yet. We don't want her getting hysterical and turning up on your doorstep. Not until you've put Jamie in the picture. For the moment, just let events take their course. All the chess pieces are in place. We just sit tight and wait.'

When Jamie came home that evening, he looked absolutely knackered.

'Hi darling.' I pecked him on the cheek. 'Arthur has taken Edna out for a romantic candlelit dinner, so you have my cooking tonight.'

Jamie pulled me into his arms and gave me a hug. 'Please tell me you've not attempted anything adventurous.'

'You're safe tonight.' I hugged him back. 'Omelette and chips.'

At that moment the girls came down the stairs. Livvy was holding Eddie on her hip and letting him play with her mobile phone.

'I've been trying to get hold of Dad for two days now,' she grumbled, 'and he's not picking up. Hello Jamie,' Livvy waved Eddie's hand at her step-father. 'I suppose he's taken off with a new girlfriend and is all loved up at the moment.' She rolled her eyes.

Jamie and I exchanged a look. 'Ah ha ha ha.' I gave a strangled laugh. 'Good old Dad!'

'I suppose one day he'll grow up,' Livvy sighed.

'Hey Dad,' Petra pecked her father on the cheek.

'Hello girls. What are you both up to?' Jamie shrugged off his suit jacket and slung it over the banisters.

'We're about to watch The Only Way Is Essex,' said Livvy, opening the door to their TV room.

'Isn't that reality rubbish?' Jamie asked.

'Certainly not!' said Petra haughtily. 'It's a documentary. And anyway, Eddie loves it.' And with that the door to the TV room briskly closed.

'Wonderful,' Jamie sighed, and followed me into the kitchen.

I went to the range and retrieved a plated dinner while Jamie settled himself at the table.

'Et voilà!' I set the meal before my husband. He was suddenly looking rather glum. 'Sorry about the omelette.' I followed his gaze to the scrambled mess on his plate. 'It got stuck to the pan.'

Jamie smiled ruefully. 'The omelette isn't the problem Cassie.'

'What's up?' I pulled out a chair and sat down.

'Ah, you know,' Jamie sighed.

'No, I don't know. Enlighten me.'

Jamie picked up his knife and fork, but didn't tuck in. 'Work. It's crap at the moment.'

I straightened up. 'I thought everything was rosy in the garden with the business.'

'Oh the business is rosy all right. It's the staff that aren't.'

'What do you mean?' I asked.

Jamie put down his knife and fork again. 'Look Cassie. I know you don't like me talking about Selina, but I need to get a few things off my chest.'

I shifted in my chair. 'Like what?'

'Some grumbles. Well I can't moan to Ethan can I? He's my business partner and the majority shareholder. But his fiancée is really starting to be a burden with her unreliability. I told you that Selina's not been herself recently. Up one minute, down the next. One day she's in the office. Then you don't see her for dust. Well she didn't come in today. Ethan was very tight-lipped about it. Said *Lena* had car problems. Again.' Jamie picked up his fork and speared a bunch of chips. 'And that excuse didn't ring true. Selina has just had her car fixed by the garage – what could be wrong with it? And if she really did have car problems, why didn't she travel in with Ethan? Why the need to absent herself?'

'Well perhaps they'd had a row.' I reached for the salt pot on the table. Fiddled with it. 'Why didn't you ask Ethan the question?'

'He wasn't in the mood to answer questions. He's not been himself either. Not for the last couple of days. Very preoccupied – mind elsewhere. Something's wrong. Very wrong.'

I nudged the salt pot around with my index finger. Took a deep breath.

'I saw Selina this morning.'

Jamie's fork froze mid-air. 'You saw Selina?'

'Yes.'

'Do you mind elaborating?'

'I was at Nell's. Selina drove past.'

'Let me get this straight.' Jamie put his fork down again. 'You were at Nell's and just happened to be standing by a convenient window, when you saw Selina drive past in a car that Ethan told me is defunct?'

'That's about the gist of it,' I nodded.

Jamie stared at me. 'And why would Selina be driving past Nell's house?'

'Well funnily enough I didn't rush out and flag her down to ask. But I watched her. She parked outside Stevie's house. And then she pulled out a bunch of keys and let herself in.' I fiddled with the salt pot, this way and that, not liking myself for bending the truth. 'Look Jamie, there's a few things I need to tell you.'

'Like what?' Jamie stared at me.

The salt pot fell over with a clatter making us both jump. I set it right and folded my hands in my lap. 'I did try and tell you that I thought Selina and Stevie had started an affair, but you told me it was none of my business and that I had an obsession with the woman.'

'Well she can hardly be having an affair with Stevie right now! The bloke's done a disappearing act.'

'Jamie you're an ex-copper. You should be able to put two and two together. Ask yourself these questions: why is Selina absenting herself from work so frequently? Why did she drive to Stevie's house this morning? Why is she in possession of a missing person's house keys? And why is she letting herself into the missing person's house?'

'I don't know Cassie. But before you put two and two together and come up with five, I'm going to give Harry a ring. He said he'd push things along regarding finding Stevie, and be in touch if there was anything to report. Well obviously Stevie's not languishing in any hospitals, nor made any cash withdrawals from banks, otherwise Harry would have been in touch. So let me give him a call and see if his boys have come up with anything.' Jamie pushed his dinner plate away and stood up.

'Hang on a minute Jamie.' I grabbed my husband's hand. 'Sit back down a minute. Finish your dinner. I have something else to tell you.'

Jamie paused. He gave me a considering look. 'Why do I get the feeling that I'm not going to like what you're about to tell me.'

I squirmed in my seat. Oh God. Perhaps I should backtrack. Before it was too late. But then again it was very likely Morag was at this moment bringing Matt up to date. And what if Matt ignored Morag's wishes not to tell Jamie, and rang my husband to say their respective wives had been doing stupid things and consequently alerted a dangerous fruitcake to come after them? I took another deep breath. At this rate if I took too many I'd start hyperventilating.

'I wasn't in Nell's house when I saw Selina drive into the cul-de-sac.'

Jamie sat back down again, but his plate remained untouched. When he spoke his voice was dangerously quiet. 'So where were you?'

'In Stevie's bedroom.'

Jamie blinked. 'Alone?'

'With Morag.'

My husband closed his eyes. I could see him struggling to maintain patience.

'Why?'

'To see if we could find any clues about Stevie's whereabouts.'

'I see. Well actually I don't see. So let me get this straight. Even though I've been in touch with my old Superintendent about Stevie missing, and asked Harry to speed things along, for some reason my wife and her friend deem it necessary to pay their own visit. Tell me Cassie, were you both calling each other *Cagney* and *Lacey* again?'

I ignored Jamie's sarcasm. 'You may mock, but I'll tell you one thing our detective work threw up.' I leant forward and crossed my arms on the table. 'A bottle in Stevie's bathroom cabinet. And not any old bottle,' my eyes blazed triumphantly, 'but one with a label on it. A label that read Gamma-Hydroxybutyric Acid. Known as GHB. Also known as the date rape drug.'

'Cassie, before you leap to conclusions, GHB is regulated in most of Europe and used to treat a number of things – sleep problems, depression, also fibromyalgia symptoms. In short, anything from experiencing pain to having an irritable bowel. There might be any number of reasons why Stevie's GP prescribed GHB for him.'

'I don't believe this!' I slapped the table with the palm of my hand. 'Why do you refuse to see what is so obvious to me?'

'Cassie, right now nothing is obvious to me. You've told me that Selina had a bunch of keys to let herself into Stevie's house, and that you and Morag were in Stevie's bedroom. Leave Stevie's medicine cabinet out of the equation for a minute. What happened when the three of you came face to face?'

'Nothing. Because Selina didn't see us.'

Jamie took some deep breaths. Clearly it was now his turn to flirt with hyperventilation. 'So *why* didn't Selina see you?'

'Because we hid. Morag climbed in the wardrobe and I wriggled under the bed.'

Jamie rubbed the heels of his hands into his eyes. 'Could you tell me why on earth you felt it necessary to hide, when you could have simply taken the option for straight talking? If it had been me I'd have asked Selina what the dickens she was doing letting herself into your ex-husband's house.'

'Oh no,' I shook my head, 'we couldn't do that. Not after that Council business and losing our wigs and Morag nearly killing Victor who tipped off Selina who sussed out Morag's car and checked out her number plate and found it on Nell's driveway and–'

Jamie held up both hands. 'Enough!' My husband scraped back his chair and stood up. Began pacing the kitchen. 'Let's go back to the bedroom bit. Morag's in the wardrobe. You're under the bed.'

'Yes.'

'And then Selina comes into the house?'

'Yes.'

'And from your superior vantage point, what did you see?'

'Her ankles. And they went into the en-suite shower room. But Morag filmed it all.'

'Selina's ankles?'

'No! Selina removing the bottle of GHB of course.'

Jamie ceased his pacing and turned to stare at me. 'Selina took the bottle of GHB?'

'Yes!' I cried. 'It's what I've been trying to tell you all along. Morag and I think it's hers. It was in the apartment too – bottles of the stuff on the kitchen table. Morag took a photograph.'

'You went to Ethan's apartment?'

'No! Morag and I paid a visit to Selina's *Blackheath* apartment and–'

The phone rang. There was a moment where both of us just stared at the handset all lit up on the kitchen worktop. I couldn't see the caller number display from where I was sitting. My stomach contracted with nerves. Was it Matt? Calling to tell Jamie the full extent of what Morag and I had been up to?

Jamie stared at the handset. 'That's Ethan's number.'

The knot in my stomach tightened. 'Aren't you going to answer it?' I whispered.

Jamie picked up the handset. 'Ethan! Good evening.'

There was a pause. I stared at my husband and tried to read his expression. I wondered what Ethan was saying. 'I see,' Jamie eventually said. 'Is there anything I can do? Right. Don't worry about work. No problem. Yes of course I'll sort tomorrow out. It really couldn't matter less. You see to Selina and look after yourself. Okay. Goodnight.' Jamie put the handset back in its cradle and turned to face me.

'Well?' I asked.

'Selina's ill. Ethan doesn't think she'll be going to the ball tomorrow. And apparently he's not feeling so fab himself. So it's unlikely he'll be going either. He's not going to cancel his room at the hotel just in case, but it's not looking promising.' Jamie sat back down and stared at his cold omelette and tepid chips. 'Somehow I get the feeling I've just been fed a load of bullshit.' He looked up at me. 'And I presume you know exactly what's happening in Ethan's household. Am I right?'

'I've got a rough idea,' I murmured.

'Right Cassie.' Jamie shoved his dinner plate to one side. 'How about you tell me exactly what's been going on. From the beginning please.'

Chapter Thirty

As anticipated, Jamie was furious that Morag and I had taken it upon ourselves to snoop around Selina's Blackheath apartment.

'It's one thing to bump into Selina and Stevie shopping together and follow them out of curiosity Cassie,' he'd raged, 'but it's quite another to take yourself off with Morag and poke around Selina's apartment block. What if the pair of you had knocked over and killed that old boy?'

Jamie had then tried getting hold of his old Superintendent, Harry, only to be told he was unavailable. Nobody would tell Jamie anything about the investigation or what progress, if any, had been made. It was as if a wall of silence had suddenly sprung up. Frustrated, Jamie had slammed the telephone back into the receiver muttering oaths about confidentiality, bureaucracy and red tape.

'Are we still going to the ball?' I'd asked timorously.

Jamie had raked his hands through his hair. 'For now, yes. You'll have to drive yourself up to Oxfordshire. I've left a message for Harry to call me immediately if things break on the investigation. Until then we carry on as normal. Mum's looking after the kids, and Ethan has told us to make free with his hotel room. I'll square it with Mum for us to stay overnight. We might as well take advantage. Before my wife finds herself in Court for false impersonation, trespass and manslaughter.'

We'd gone to bed not on a row exactly, but certainly things had been very strained. And now, Saturday morning, I had awoken to find Jamie's side of the bed empty. I had no idea what time he'd taken himself off to James Powell and the bank.

I stretched and turned over. The clock radio said a little after eight. The baby monitor emitted a few noises indicating Eddie was stirring. Seconds later a cry went up.

I flung back the duvet and shivered. Gosh it was chilly. Wrapping my dressing gown around me, I crossed the landing to Eddie's nursery. I could hear activity from the other children in their rooms. Moments later Livvy shot out of her bedroom.

'I don't have any clean jodhpurs,' she wailed.

'In the airing cupboard,' I called after her. I picked Eddie up, sorted out a smelly nappy and then went downstairs to start on the breakfast. In the kitchen I found Edna had beaten me to it.

'Good morning Cassandra dear,' my mother-in-law chirruped. She was looking quite radiant. And there was no mistaking the spring in her step as she moved between fridge and hob, cracking eggs into one pan and frying a mountain of bread in another. From nowhere a wave of nausea hit me.

'Hi Edna.' I strapped Eddie into his highchair and set about mixing up some chocolate Ready Brek.

'Will you be having a slice of fried bread?' Edna asked.

'Um, I'll pass thanks.' I popped the Ready Brek in the microwave and twiddled the dial. 'So how was your meal with Arthur last night?'

'Most enjoyable dear.' Edna paused long enough in her frying to go slightly dewy eyed. 'We visited that new Italian trattoria in Boxleigh. You and Jamie must try it. I had a tender sirloin steak with herb roast potatoes and cherry tomatoes. Absolutely delicious.'

The thought of sitting down to an eight ounce jobbie, tender or otherwise, had me fluttering a hand over my mouth.

'Jolly good,' I mumbled. The microwave pinged. Removing Eddie's Ready Brek, I gave it a quick stir and made sure it wasn't too hot. 'So how's the boat restoration progressing?' I snapped a plastic bib around Eddie's neck and set about feeding him.

'It's coming along a treat dear.' Edna slotted a stack of fried bread into the range to keep warm, and began plating up the fried eggs. 'She's now structurally sound, so we can move on to the cosmetic bit. This morning we're prepping the underside of the boat ready for painting. This afternoon we'll be taking ourselves off to sort out other bits and pieces. We also need to buy some anti-fouling paint.'

'Anti-fouling paint?' I repeated. 'Whatever's that?' I let Eddie take the spoon from me and have a go at feeding himself. The spoon found his cheek and left a cereal trail before disappearing into his mouth. My son gave a chocolaty grin.

'It's a special paint to inhibit marine growth,' Edna explained. 'Meanwhile, Cassandra dear, I know you'll want to get ready for the ball this afternoon. Eddie can take a ride with his nanny and Arthur. You'll like that won't you darling?' Edna cooed at her grandson. 'Nanny will make a fine workman out of you one day.'

Eddie rewarded his grandmother with a gummy smile before picking up his bowl and sticking his face in it.

'Well as long as he won't be any trouble to you and Arthur, that would be absolutely fab.' I gently prised the bowl out of Eddie's curled fists and set about wiping his face clean. 'Jamie suggested I meet him at the hotel about half five.'

'I saw him very briefly before he left this morning. He put me in the picture about Selina and Ethan not being well. Never mind. It will do you both good to have a bit of a break on your own.'

'That's very thoughtful of you Edna,' I smiled. Not for the first time I realised there were hidden advantages to a mother-in-law that never seemed to go home.

Later, I ferried the children to the stables. Hugging them hard, I told them to be good for Nanny Edna while Jamie and I were away overnight. I then popped in on Morag for a very swift coffee. Blow-by-blow accounts were exchanged regarding our husbands' respective reactions to our confessions.

'Matt calmed down eventually,' Morag said. 'My husband thinks I need to get back to work. That I'm bored, and needing more mental stimulation.'

'And how do *you* feel?' I asked.

Morag shrugged. 'My maternity leave finishes in six weeks. I've been in touch with Hempel Braithwaite about doing a three day week. But we'll see. They're keen to get me back on the treadmill, preferably full time and with a partnership.' She stared out the window of her large kitchen. Winter sunlight was pouring in, making it look a lot warmer outside than it actually was. 'A couple of years ago I'd have jumped at it. But now–' she trailed off.

'Now the invisible umbilical cord is tugging,' I smiled.

'Not half,' Morag sighed. 'I can't bear the thought of leaving Henry with a nanny while I go off to stress myself out over some commercial takeover. Having a baby was all I ever wanted. And relinquishing the daytime care of Henry to a person who isn't even related to him, isn't what I want. What if I missed his first step? Or his first proper word? You can't press a rewind button – once it's happened the moment has gone forever.' She sighed and stared into the depths of her coffee. 'Apart from anything else, I want another baby. A partnership isn't going to mix well with anti-natal appointments.'

'You've got a few more weeks to think about things. Anyway,' I drained my cup and stood up, 'I'd better be heading back. Edna has things to do, and she's taking Eddie with her while I titivate.'

'I'm surprised at Jamie going ahead with this function. I thought he'd want to be closer to home for the next twenty-four hours.'

I grabbed Eddie's holdall and stood up. 'At the moment there's no official news. Harry hasn't responded to Jamie's calls. The police refuse to comment on the investigation. All we have so far is Ethan ringing to say that Selina is unwell. Ethan was apparently very anxious about James Powell being looked after, and asked Jamie to take care of things today. Without any info from the police, Jamie can hardly refuse Ethan. So we're just carrying on as normal until circumstances dictate otherwise.'

'Well have a great time in Oxford.' Morag walked me and Eddie to the door. 'I know what I'd be doing tonight if I were in your shoes.'

'Hmm. I don't think there are any indoor equestrian centres near the hotel.' I gave my friend a wry smile, before hugging her good-bye.

On returning to Lilac Lodge, I transferred Eddie's car seat from The Muck Truck to Edna's Micra. Letting myself into the house, I cleared up a fur ball one of the cats had sicked up, and then gave Eddie some lunch. My earlier nausea had subsided, so I munched on toast while Eddie worked his way through a jar of Mr Heinz. Edna and Arthur appeared soon afterwards for a bite to eat, and then took Eddie off with them.

Suddenly I was alone. I couldn't remember the last time I'd been in the house without somebody around. Even the cats had naffed off to chase mice. I found my mobile phone and gave Jamie a ring. Hopefully his time spent with James Powell today hadn't been compromised by Ethan's absence. However, upon connecting, my call went straight to voicemail.

'Oh, hi darling.' I started to leave a message. 'Um, I hope you're not having too many problems without Ethan being with you and, well, I'm going to get ready now. I'm looking forward to seeing you later. Love you.'

I disconnected the call and headed off for the shower. Fifteen minutes later I blew my hair dry, but decided to do my make-up at the hotel. I chucked everything required into an overnight bag along with my mobile phone, and made sure my expensive evening dress and a soft pashmina were zipped safely into a protective cover.

Grabbing a coat, I took everything downstairs. I lay the dress over the banister. Leaving my bag and coat by the bottom stair, I did a final security check. Peering into each room, I ensured no windows were left on the crack, that the ovens and hobs were off in the kitchen, and the back door was locked. Everything was as it should be. The house was so quiet it was almost eerie.

Suddenly the doorbell drilled into the silence making me jump. Oh no. I hoped it wasn't the Born Again brigade. I really wasn't up for debating what would have happened had Adam and Eve not eaten the forbidden fruit. Picking up my car keys, I went to answer the door. No doubt there would be a little apple dumpling of a lady standing on the doorstep, holding a bible and inviting me to find God. But as I released the catch, the breath whooshed out of me. For there on the doorstep, in all her malevolent glory, was Selina.

Chapter Thirty One

It was probably only a nano-second that I stood, framed in my own doorway, with my mouth hanging open. But the brevity of the moment, for me, stretched into a lifetime. Several questions crashed through my brain, the most pressing being: why wasn't Selina in an interrogation room with Humpty and Olive? Selina was the first to speak.

'Hello Cass.' She smiled, showing a row of even white teeth. I was reminded of Lucifer the cat in Walt Disney's *Cinderella*, beaming at Jaq the mouse before tormenting him. 'You look quite bemused to see me.'

I re-arranged my gaping mouth into a hasty smile. 'Selina! Well yes, actually I'm exceedingly surprised.' Exceedingly? Steady Cass. Don't overdo it with the astonishment. This wasn't a Mr Kipling commercial. 'Ethan telephoned Jamie last night to say you weren't at all well. We understood Ethan wasn't feeling fab either. And that neither of you would be attending the ball.'

Selina rolled her eyes and made a dismissive gesture with her hands. 'Trust my darling Ethan to make a mountain out of a molehill. Honestly Cass, it was nothing. One of those annoying little bugs that lower your equilibrium for two or three hours, before leaving you wondering what it was all about. Certainly nothing a good night's sleep couldn't put right.'

'Great,' I nodded, but my mind was whirling. 'So Ethan went into work this morning?'

'Eventually. He didn't want poor Jamie coping with that horrendous James Powell all on his own.' Selina rolled her eyes again. 'Boy, does that man want his pound of flesh.'

'Yes,' I agreed. 'So–'

'But never mind James Powell and banks and security and heaven knows what!' Selina bared her teeth again. 'Let's get ourselves off to Oxford. I see you haven't put your make-up on yet.'

'Well I–'

'Ethan wants the four of us to have champagne cocktails together before heading off to the ball. So there really isn't a moment to lose if you need the luxury of time to dolly up.'

'Oh, right. Well I'll just do a final sweep of the house before locking up.'

'Okay. I'll pop your stuff in my car. Hurry up.' Selina pushed her way into the hall and picked up my overnight bag and coat. Spotting my dress over the banister, she flung it carelessly over one arm. She noticed my horrified expression. 'Don't worry,' she assured. 'I'll fold it flat and put it in the boot with mine.'

Selina headed off down the driveway to her car. I had an urgent, overwhelming need to speak to Jamie. I decided to try his number one more time before leaving the house. Disappearing into the study, I picked up the handset on the desk and quickly tapped out Jamie's number. But once more the voicemail kicked in. Damn and blast my husband for not picking up!

'Hi Jamie. Me again. Look, Selina's here. She is apparently fit and well, but presumably you know that, because Ethan is now with you? I can't say I'm happy about this Jamie. I really don't have a good vibe, and–'

A shadow fell across the study door. I looked up and blanched. Hell's bells. How much had she heard?

'Come on Cass.' Selina tapped her wristwatch.

I disconnected the call. 'I'll just double check the back door is locked.' I walked into the kitchen. Selina promptly followed me.

'Did you just speak to Jamie?'

I pulled down the back door's handle. It held fast. 'No. It was his voicemail. Why?'

'Just wondered. Let's go then.' Selina trailed me out of the kitchen and back through the hall.

'I need to put the alarm on,' I said. 'I'll be right behind you.'

Selina said something I didn't quite catch. I watched her walk out the front door and towards the Mazda MX-5. Clearly the business about her second lot of car trouble had been a pack of lies. Either that or she frequented a garage with the quickest mechanics in history. A chill went down my spine, which was nothing to do with the cold winter air filtering into the hallway. I went to the cupboard under the stairs where the burglar alarm was housed and tapped in the security code. Shutting the front door after me, I scampered across the drive to Selina's car. Moments later I was seated, most reluctantly, in the passenger seat.

'Buckle up Cass,' Selina started the engine. 'The seatbelt is a bit stubborn. Here, let me help you.' She leant across the handbrake and yanked at the strap. The belt flowed into her hands before something caused it to resist. 'Breathe in,' Selina instructed. God, how embarrassing. The wretched thing hardly stretched across my abdomen. Surely I wasn't that fat! Selina hauled on the strap until it skimmed my tummy and then quickly snapped the buckle home.

'It's awfully tight,' I ventured, and gave it a little tug.

Selina shrugged. 'It will probably loosen up in a while.'

Ramming the gear into first, she shot forward so quickly the sensor on the electric gates didn't have enough time to let us off the driveway. Selina hit the brakes so hard I lurched forward. The seatbelt tightened to the point where the simple act of breathing was almost a challenge. I pressed the release button. But nothing happened.

'Um, the seatbelt seems to have jammed and–'

The words died on my lips as the gates rolled back and Selina once again hit the accelerator. I found my neck whipping backwards. We shot along the unmade up lane, bouncing uncomfortably over the potholes. At the end of the private road, the Mazda swerved out onto Lavender Common and roared off. I clung on to the edge of my seat. Clearly Selina was a bit of a girl racer. But then again, anybody driving a sports car was hardly going to emulate my style of nervous driving.

The Mazda roared towards the M25. As it powered along the slip road to join the motorway, I began to wonder what Selina was playing at. There was fast and there was, well, faster. And her speed was definitely out of my comfort zone. I glanced at my chauffeur and felt a frisson of alarm. She was staring through the windscreen looking strangely elated. Her eyes flicked sideways and snagged on mine.

'Are you sitting comfortably Cass?'

'Well actually, no.' I tried releasing the seatbelt again but it was having none of it. 'This belt is really cutting into me.'

'Good.'

'Sorry?'

'You heard.' The Mazda sailed past a lorry hogging the middle lane. 'Oh how I've waited for this moment Cass! And at last it's come. I have you right where I want you.'

For a moment I tried to kid myself we were at cross-purposes. That her words had simply come out wrong. 'Lovely,' I smiled brightly. 'I've been looking forward to this opportunity of girly bonding. Having a nice chat and wotnot!'

'Oh we're going to have a chat all right Cass.' Selina's tone clarified there was no misunderstanding. Her voice was filled with loathing. 'We're going to chat all the way to Oxford. So what shall we chat about eh?' There was a pause before she thumped the centre of the steering wheel. I jumped at the sound of the horn blaring. An ancient Renault that dared to be in the outside lane at seventy-two miles per hour, winked its left indicator and made the transition to the middle lane. 'I know! Let's talk about me overhearing a voicemail meant for somebody else. A message where you referred to me as a *bitch* and a *basket case.*'

I clung on to the sides of my seat as the Mazda whooshed along. Right. Clearly it was cards on the table time and pointless pretending otherwise.

'Look Selina. Can we just leave the past in the past?' I was amazed at how steady my voice sounded. Inwardly I was cacking myself.

'I think not.' She pursed her lips. 'There are times where I might have been a bit of a bitch Cass, but I'm not a basket case. Understand?'

Was she kidding? After everything she did to Jamie and me last year? I felt my face flush with anger. 'That's your opinion,' I shrugged – not easy in the stranglehold of the seatbelt. Suddenly I was seeing stars as the back of her hand connected with my temple.

'DO NOT FUCKING DISRESPECT ME!' she screamed.

Something warm was trickling down my face. I put up a hand and touched my cheek. When I took my fingers away they were covered in sticky blood. Selina's massive engagement ring had split skin.

'So Cass,' Selina took a deep breath and calmed herself. 'Now that we've cleared that little matter up, let's cut the crap and be honest with each other.'

I took a deep breath. 'Okay. Where's Stevie?'

Selina let out a high-pitched squeal of laughter. 'Excellent! Now we're both talking the same language. Stevie is a bit tied up at the moment,' she sniggered. 'Literally. Get my drift?'

Suddenly my mouth was devoid of saliva and I had a horrible urge to throw up. A detached part of me wondered if it were possible to projectile vomit over her face, blind her with puke and wrestle the steering wheel from her hands. We were now right up the backside of a Mini. The speedometer said eighty miles per hour.

'Is Stevie alive?' I croaked.

'For now.'

'What – are you going to kill him?'

Selina smirked. 'A man committing suicide is nothing to do with me.'

I cleared my throat. 'And how is that going to happen? Would it be in conjunction with Gamma-Hydroxybutyric Acid by any chance?'

Selina laughed. 'Aha! Methinks you sussed out your drink was spiked at the OXO Tower! That was such fun to watch. Did you also realise I'd tampered with your food too when you came to dinner at Ethan's apartment?'

'I suspected,' I said through gritted teeth. 'What special ingredient did you use that night?'

'Nothing fancy. Just a tasteless liquid laxative bought from the local health shop and drizzled over your food. Call it my naughty sense of humour,' Selina chortled. 'But regarding the GHB, forgive me for using you as a guinea pig. I wanted to test it out prior to giving it to Stevie. In time I'll overdose him. But not until I've killed you first.'

I felt the hair stand up on my head. Selina uttered her last sentence so matter-of-factly I felt as though I were caught up in some frightful movie. The thought of dying didn't bother me as such. But the timing most certainly did. To leave this world right now was simply not on. I had children. Two of whom had already lost their biological mother. I wasn't going to let them lose a second mother.

'If you want me dead, why didn't you kill me at the OXO Tower?'

'Couldn't,' Selina sighed. 'A post mortem would have revealed the cause of death. That would never have done. So when the time comes for you to die – which will be in about an hour or so – it will look like an accident.'

'W-What do you mean?' I stuttered. 'Are you going to cause a car crash?'

'Sort of,' Selina nodded.

'Then surely you risk dying too!' I cried.

'No,' Selina shook her head with supreme confidence. 'I've checked out the spot where it's going to happen. And I have a crafty plan,' she promptly convulsed.

I waited for her mirth to subside. 'Would you mind sharing?'

'Of course. Wilsham Road. It's in Abingdon – a lovely part of Oxford. There's a very pretty stretch of road right by the Thames – and not a safety barrier or set of railings in sight. So that's where the car is going to end up. In the river. With you in it. Trapped, due to a dodgy seatbelt. You will drown.'

I began to frantically press the seatbelt release button. Nothing happened. The strap was so tight I couldn't even wiggle my way out of it.

'Selina you can't just career off a road. There will be questions by the police – an investigation!'

'Of course. And I'll say how very sorry I was Officer – I should have known better being an ex-copper myself. But reflexes are reflexes. And when that damned cat ran out from nowhere, I found myself automatically throwing the wheel to the right and – SPLASH!' Selina shrieked with laughter.

'So why won't you be drowning?' I quavered.

'Because I will wind the window down, let the sinking car fill with water, and then simply swim out of the window. It *is* possible to survive these things Cass, provided you don't panic. And you're not wearing a seatbelt!' Selina gave another screech of amusement.

I stared out of the window as we overtook a Tesco truck. Calm Cass. Keep calm. You have an hour to talk yourself out of this situation.

'Look Selina. Can we start all over again? I apologise for calling you a bitch and a basket case. There's time to stop this. We can put things right.'

'I don't want to *put things right*.' Selina blared her horn at the Mini that was still resolutely hogging the outside lane. 'As far as I'm concerned, everything is going just swimmingly. Oh I say - *swimmingly*! Ah ha ha ha!'

'Look, I know you don't care for me, but–'

'Oh that's an understatement Cass.' The laughter stopped abruptly. 'Make no mistake about it. I absolutely *detest* you.'

'Fine. You detest me. So why implicate Stevie?'

'Because I need him out of the equation.'

'But why?' I cried. 'Just what the heck is this all about?'

'What's it all about? WHAT'S IT ALL ABOUT?' she screeched. Some spittle flew from her mouth and dotted across the steering wheel. 'In a nutshell Cass, it's all about wanting what you've got.'

'But I'm not with Stevie anymore!'

'Funnily enough,' Selina said through clenched teeth, 'I'd worked that out for myself. And I'm hardly surprised you divorced Stevie. The man is a total letch. Very good between the sheets mind you. But definitely not husband material, and certainly not for me. Oh no. The husband I want Cass, is the one you're married to right now.'

Well what a surprise. 'Selina, Jamie is married to *me*. He loves *me*.'

'Don't kid yourself Cass. That man is deeply unhappy.'

'Now you listen to me–' My head momentarily buzzed as Selina lashed out a second time. 'If you do that again,' I said hoarsely, 'I'll–'

'Shut up BITCH,' Selina spat. 'You're not doing anything other than sitting there and listening to me. And you might as well give up trying to get that seatbelt to release, because it isn't going to happen. My car hasn't been with a regular mechanic, know what I mean?' she gave a high pitched laugh. 'Now, where was I? Oh yes. Jamie. I was absolutely devastated when he left the police force. Bereft. And then I heard he was going into partnership with a man called Ethan Fareham. So I asked around – a few questions here and there. Did a bit of digging. And I succeeded in finding Ethan – and set my cap at him. It was so easy. Like taking candy from a baby. A whirlwind romance, an engagement, plus a new job. And *da-daaaa*,' she made a sound like a fanfare of trumpets, 'suddenly I was seeing Jamie again. Bliss! And now it's just a short hop, skip and a jump to being back by his side. You see Cass, Jamie might have been enthralled by you in the beginning, but he's not anymore. Since you had Eddie and let yourself go, he's been miserable as sin.'

'He's told you all this has he?' I mumbled.

'Jamie doesn't need to Cass. His face is an open book. I've seen the way he looks at me. With so much longing,' her voice softened, 'and regret.'

'So why doesn't he leave me?'

'Because he's an honourable man Cass. *Too* honourable. So I'm taking charge of the situation. I'm going to bump you off and give the grieving widower – grieving out of guilt you understand, not because he actually misses you – a shoulder to cry on. And once he's in my arms, he'll never want to leave.'

'Right,' I nodded. 'But I still don't understand why you have to *bump* Stevie off too Selina.'

'God you really are thick Cass,' Selina tutted theatrically. 'Stevie is the father of your twins, yes?'

'It's his name on their birth certificates,' I confirmed. Where was this conversation going?

'And if Stevie is dead – and you're dead too don't forget – then legally, who is your twins' next of kin?' Selina prompted.

I didn't have any other living relatives. My blood ran cold. 'Jamie,' I whispered.

'Correct!' Selina crowed. 'So I'll have not just your husband, but your kids too!'

I lunged for her. 'OVER MY DEAD BODY!' I screamed. The too tight seatbelt held me back but my right arm managed to grab a chunk of her hair. I pulled hard, almost yanking her head off her neck.

The knife appeared from nowhere. Instantly I recoiled, tucking myself into the curves of the passenger door as much as was physically possible.

'Yes Cass,' Selina hissed. 'Over your dead body. And if you try that again, I will hurt you. Not enough to kill you – yet. But enough to make it look like an injury sustained in the crash. Do you understand?'

I nodded mutely. Every fibre of my being was screaming silently for a way out of this situation. Seeing Selina holding the knife was like a small window of opportunity. If I could get hold of that knife, maybe I could hack through my seatbelt?

'So,' I exhaled shakily, 'you seem to assume that even if you walk off into the sunset with my husband, my children will scamper after you. That won't happen.'

'Yes it will,' Selina said dismissively. 'Your children absolutely adore me. And little Eddie will grow up probably thinking I'm his real Mummy. And of course I'll be having one or two little ones of my own,' Selina smiled indulgently. 'And Jamie will be so happy. He'll look at me and think to himself, "Selina! Why was I so blind to the woman who was there all along? She's so right for me – the perfect business colleague, the perfect mother for my children, the perfect wife!" And I will live happily ever after Cass, with my husband and children in beautiful Lilac Lodge. Forever and ever. Amen to all that.'

The hand that was holding the knife came down hard on the steering wheel as Selina once again beeped the Mini in front of us. The driver was still obstinately refusing to move over.

'You're never going to get away with this,' I quavered, mindful of the knife. It was about the size of something I'd peel the vegetables with. Nonetheless, I was acutely aware of the damage it could do. 'The police are on to you. They know that you kidnapped Stevie.'

'Oh the police,' Selina scoffed. 'I've already spoken with them. And most apologetic they were too. But they said they had to check out every lead, no matter how ridiculous. They explained two women gave the tip off that I'd abducted Mr Stephen Cherry. You don't have to be Einstein to work out which two women gave that little gem of information to the police. The same two women who happened to snoop around my apartment block and tell a resident they were from the council. Thank heavens for neighbours like Gerald. Retired and with nothing better to do than sit on every committee and avail himself to the local council – a man who likes to make other people's business his own. And then he managed to secure the registration number of your silly blonde friend – the one with a bust size bigger than her IQ.'

'I don't know what you're talking about.' I stared resolutely out the windscreen. The Mini was finally alive to the fact that Selina was almost touching its bumper. It edged into the middle lane. The Mazda leapt forward.

'I used to be a policewoman Cass. I have contacts. It took only a second to check out that registration number and find a picture of the owner. And Jamie, innocent lamb, unwittingly confirmed that Morag Harding was your mate. That she used to be your boss when you worked at Hempel Braithwaite. And coincidentally went on to marry Matt Harding, who I met when I dated Jamie. Small world, eh?'

'Leave Morag out of it. She's nothing to do with this.' I refrained from telling Selina that Morag wasn't so silly to have photographed bottles of GHB in Selina's apartment, and had filmed Selina removing the same from Stevie's house.

'If Mrs Harding stays out of my hair, then she'll be safe. After all, it's not her husband or life that I want.'

'Do you mind telling me how Ethan fits into your grand plan?'

'Well unfortunately he's going to be a jilted fiancé.' Selina shrugged. 'These things happen.'

'And I take it he was quite calm about you speaking with the police yesterday – seeing how you were being asked about a kidnap?'

'Ethan knows nothing of it Cass!' Selina hooted with laughter. 'We've not been getting on too well lately. I've had things on my mind – obviously – which has unsettled Ethan. I've absented myself here and there at work. When I disappeared in the evening to talk to the police, Ethan just thought I was having one of my blue moods. So when I finally got back home – a little on the late side admittedly – I just did my dying swan act. And Ethan was all over me like a rash. Said he'd look after me. Wouldn't go to the ball without me.'

'You think you have it all worked out Selina, but you don't.'

'Shut up Cass. You're starting to bore me.'

'Do you mind me asking where Stevie is?'

'Not at all,' Selina said magnanimously. 'He's in a disused warehouse by the docks rented by my mate Charlie Phillips. When I was in the police force, I rubbed shoulders with a few naughty boys on the wrong side of the law. It's easy to come to an arrangement with most of them. You know, "I'll keep my gob shut Fred if you pay me a few grand," or "I'll turn a blind eye to your little *project* Bill, but it's subject to you doing me a favour."'

'I see,' I nodded. 'So you were a corrupt police officer.'

Selina shrugged. 'Call it what you will. I prefer to call it a mutually agreeable arrangement. Charlie is the one who supplied the GHB to me. He also assisted in,' she smiled maliciously, '*persuading* Stevie to write a suicide note.'

'There is no reason on this earth for Stevie to commit suicide,' I assured.

'Ah, but then you don't know about his little drug problem do you?' Selina looked at me with wide eyes. 'I planted a bottle of GHB in Stevie's bathroom cabinet hoping the police would find it. They didn't. What a pitiful shower they are! However, I had to borrow it back again because I was running low, and Charlie is awaiting a fresh supply via his own source. Anyway, Stevie has written all about his drug problem and that he can't cope with it any more. And when the deed is done, Charlie will take care of posting the suicide note to Stevie's ex-girlfriend, Charlotte. The note explains where Stevie can be found and–'

A red Vauxhall Astravan suddenly shot into the outside lane, almost clipping the wing of the Mazda. Selina automatically hit the brakes and the pair of us lurched towards the dash and then back again. She sounded the horn long and loud. For a moment I thought she was going to lose her grip on the knife. The Astravan reacted furiously to the angry blasts by jamming his brakes on and off, so that we nearly ended up impacting into its rear bumper. I had a sudden flash of déjà vu. The same thing had happened when I'd been in the car with Morag recently, on our way to Fairview. And it had been a red Vauxhall Astravan! Oh my God. If this was the same van, I didn't like to think how this bit of the journey was going to pan out.

'What a fucking prat,' Selina hissed. She drew back and let rip with the horn again. When the driver once more hit his brakes, she was prepared. 'I can't stand arseholes like this. Think they own the motorway. As if his tin pot van can keep up with *this*!'

She floored the Mazda. The vehicle leapt forward and took the van on the inside. As we drew level, Selina suddenly buzzed her window down. We were travelling at over one hundred miles per hour. Air roared in through the open window whipping Selina's hair around her face, and playing havoc with our eardrums.

'What are you doing?' I screeched over the wind noise.

Selina had released her seatbelt. Instantly an alarm went off warning the driver to buckle up again. But Selina was now leaning out of the driver's window. Her left hand was clamped on the steering wheel, her right arm stretched towards the van's passenger window with the knife raised. As soon as the Mazda drew level, she brought the knife down hard. It smacked against the centre of the glass and instantly caved in. Cackling manically, she once again floored the Mazda. The vehicle whooshed forward. She had both hands back on the wheel, but the knife's blade was now sticking up vertically in the air. The window remained down, and I thought my eardrums would surely burst. And then several things happened at once.

I was aware of the Mazda being propelled forward, as if a small rocket had gone off behind us. I deduced that the van had deliberately shunted us. But peculiarly, despite registering the surge, everything slipped into slow motion. And something was happening to sound, as if somebody had taken control of the volume and couldn't decide whether to turn it up, or switch it off, or turn it back on again. I initially assumed my eardrums were in the process of perforating from the hurricane coming through Selina's open window. Roaring engines, wind noise and metal upon metal were punctuated by fat full stops of silence. And then there was the most almighty bang. Suddenly the Mazda lifted off the M25 and spun gracefully towards the crash barrier. Vision was now frame by shocking frame. I could see vehicles on the opposite side of the carriageway hurtling towards us, and horrified expressions of drivers as the scene ahead of them registered in their eyes. Pupils widening. Mouths silently forming a perfect O. Arms stiffening on steering wheels and dashes as they braced themselves for impact – a middle-aged mother with a teenager plugged into an iPod...a young executive illegally talking into a mobile...a car full of young lads.

Bit by bit I tore my eyes away from this endangered audience, and turned my attention to Selina. Her beautiful face wore an expression of surprise. Her dark hair flowed out like a Vogue model with a wind machine upon her. Without her seatbelt she was free-falling towards the steering wheel – and a sharp blade. The knife, still firmly in the grip of one white-knuckled hand, was sticking up and pointing towards her neck. Little by little I managed to squeeze my eyes shut, but not before witnessing the knife plunge into Selina's throat, followed by the airbag inflating, and Selina's body rising upwards and forwards so that her skull fractured against the windshield. I was aware of the Mazda landing with a jolt on the other side of the carriageway. And suddenly the air was filled with the screeching of tyres and the stink of rubber being left on tarmac.

Chapter Thirty Two

Six Months Later

The bride stood framed in the church hallway. She looked absolutely stunning. But then all brides do. Her father looked very dapper, his face a mixture of both pride and anxiety – hardly surprising given the track record of the bridegroom.

Charlotte smiled at her father reassuringly. Mr West's eyes welled. A series of rapid blinks pushed tears back into ducts. The organ gave a succession of staccato notes before bursting into tune. And they were off! Charlotte glided down the aisle, a cloudy veil making her beauty almost ethereal. The silk of her ivory gown swish-swished as she passed by my pew. Mr West's eyes brimmed again, but this time he lost the battle with emotions. Tears coursed silently down his cheeks. Behind Mr West and Charlotte came Livvy, self-conscious and sweet in her taffeta bridesmaid's dress. She was clutching her posy as if her very life depended upon it. At the altar stood Stevie, handsome in morning suit. He turned to watch his bride's progress, and looked blown away by the vision coming towards him. I hoped to goodness he'd look after Charlotte. Love and cherish her. Properly this time. I had a feeling he might well do so after his experience with Selina. There was nothing like a brush with death to make you appreciate everything, and grab life with both hands. Next to Stevie stood Toby, looking tremendously self-important in his role of best man.

The organ swelled to a crescendo. It crashed out its final bars of music as Charlotte reached Stevie's side. There was a brief pause. For a moment the only sounds were that of the Order of Service sheets, flapping backwards and forwards as members of the congregation fanned themselves on this warm June afternoon.

Clive, the incredibly camp vicar, was dressed flamboyantly in a pink-hemmed cassock. He cleared his voice to address the congregation.

'Good afternoon ladies and gentleman. We are here to witness the marriage of Charlotte and Stephen.' Clive promptly launched into a little homily about love being patient and kind. When Clive went on to advise the congregation that love should not delight in evil, Stevie visibly flinched. As well he might. He'd had a close encounter with wickedness. Although Ethan preferred to call Selina's spectacular meltdown into madness as *issues*.

'She wasn't well,' he'd whispered, face pale, hands trembling as the police had broken the news of his fiancée's road rage antics leading to her demise.

The driver of the red Vauxhall Astravan had ended up in intensive care. It had transpired he had a record of reckless driving and had been on a driving ban at the time of the accident. Miraculously nobody else had been injured in an accident that had brought one side of the M25 to a standstill for the best part of two hours. Several drivers had tweeted just minutes after the crash to warn other road users that the carriageway looked like being closed for a long time. The police and ambulances had hurtled up the motorway hard shoulder, sirens blaring and lights flashing. The London Air Ambulance had also shown up, whisking the van driver off to hospital. Part of the central reservation had been cut away so the police could turn drivers around.

And me? Thanks to the stranglehold of the tampered seat belt, I'd escaped with nothing more than bruising and a broken finger nail. I'd been taken to hospital and kept in overnight for observation after a doctor informed me I was pregnant.

I gazed down at my whopping great bump, and smoothed the folds of my maternity dress. Jamie caught my hand and gave it a squeeze. He'd been beside himself after the accident, not to mention furious with himself for not heeding my misgivings about Selina way back when she'd first reappeared in our lives.

'All right?' he mouthed.

I smiled and nodded back. He winked and gave my bump a pat. Being told I was pregnant had been a surprise. Being told we were expecting twins had been an all out shock. Jamie didn't want to know the sex of the babies. But I knew. Two identical little boys.

'Looking forward to getting your udders out again?' Morag had quipped upon learning of my pregnancy.

'Don't,' I'd groaned. 'My boobs will rival Katie Price's feeding two babies.

'I don't envy you Cass,' Nell had declared.

'I do,' Morag had sighed. 'I'm insane with jealousy.'

Despite six months of visits to *the stud farm*, so far Morag had not achieved fulfilling her ambition of providing another sibling for Henry. Her attempts to get pregnant were not for wont of trying. Everywhere Morag went so did a supply of pregnancy tests, ovulations kits, graphs and plots. She'd been to her GP twice, and even forked out to see a private gynaecologist – the highly esteemed Mr Rafferty.

'Patience, Mrs Harding,' Mr Rafferty had sighed. Which wasn't one of Morag's virtues.

Forty-five minutes later we filed out of the church. A handful of wedding guests peeled off from the main party to light up cigarettes. A photographer, resembling a harassed sheepdog, began rounding up family members for photographs. A videographer with an enormous camera and fluffy microphone proceeded to get under everybody's feet. The new Mrs Cherry beamed adoringly at her husband of twenty minutes.

Stevie had made all the national papers when the story broke of how Selina had periodically drugged him, bound him, raped him and kept him prisoner. Inevitably comparisons were made to a not dissimilar tabloid sensation three decades earlier. Selina had confiscated Stevie's mobile, but on one occasion had unwittingly left it at the bottom of the bed to which he was tied. Using his toes he'd managed to operate the phone, but only succeeded in contacting the last caller – me. Stevie had begged me to help him, but seconds later Charlie Phillips had returned with his GBH stock-up and angrily disconnected the call.

In due course PC Thomson and PC Smith had wrapped up the case. Stevie's house keys had been found in Ethan's apartment. On the key ring was the key to the warehouse where Stevie was held captive. I'd passed on Charlie Phillips' name to Humpty and Olive. They'd put it through their database and duly picked him up. Charlie had promptly squealed like a pig and told the police where Stevie was.

As for Stevie, the whole traumatic episode had left him a reformed rake. As far as he was concerned, he never wanted to flirt with another female again – other than Charlotte. And if that meant giving in to Charlotte's desire to start a family, then so be it.

The photographer clapped his hands for attention, calling friends to join the bride and groom for the obligatory group photograph. Jamie and I mingled with the crowd and stood next to Matt and Morag. Nell and Ben joined us. Our babies were all at home in the capable care of Joanie, Matt's sweet daughter. Our other children were on the far side of the group, collectively disowning their parents, as kids of a certain age do.

Edna and Arthur broke away from chatting to Ethan and joined the swelling crowd. Both of them were looking incredibly smart in their respective suits, which certainly made a change from the overalls they'd worn almost daily following the restoration of *Lady Love*. The boat was now moored at Medway Bridge Marina. But not for much longer. Edna and Arthur were chartering *Lady Love* for Stevie and Charlotte's honeymoon, which would encompass the Solent and Isle of Wight.

The photographer put out a final call for stragglers to join the group. Ethan stood uncertainly on the outskirts. Charlotte caught his eye and signalled for him to join everybody. He smiled in acknowledgement and took the hand of a thin bespectacled woman standing by his side. She looked up at Ethan adoringly. Her name was Stella. She was the PA to James Powell at the bank. It was early days yet, but romance was clearly blooming.

'Look this way please,' shouted the photographer, his voice almost drowned out by the peel of church bells. 'The gentleman at the end! Take a couple of steps to your right please. Perfect. Everybody smile!'

With the last group shot in the can, the crowd disbursed. Some drifted off to the car park weaving through gravestones, heels pegging in soft grass. Others, including myself and Edna, followed Stevie and Charlotte's progress through the lychgate to the awaiting Rolls Royce. The bride and groom paused briefly to have confetti thrown over them. An upward breeze lifted the colourful whirling flakes where they split and fire-worked outwards, raining down on the newlyweds and covering the dark shoulders of nearby morning suits. A uniformed chauffeur materialised and opened one door to the vintage Roller. Charlotte stooped to climb into the car, but then hesitated.

'Wait!' Charlotte straightened up and turned to the crowd gathered around her. 'I haven't thrown my bouquet.' There was a sudden jostling as a bevy of beauties – Charlotte's girlfriends no doubt – stationed themselves like cricket fielders. 'Are you ready?' she bellowed.

A second later the bouquet was soaring skyward, caught in a backdrop of blue as it tumbled over and over upon itself. Hands stretched upwards, fingers reaching to catch the free-falling ball of petals and blooms – which were sailing straight towards me. From nowhere my mother-in-law's arm shot out and plucked it from the air. Edna smiled triumphantly and waved the bouquet like a flag. A small cheer broke out. Instantly Arthur pushed his way forward and whirled Edna round to face him. She looked up at him, but Arthur suddenly disappeared from view. I jostled sideways and was astonished to see Arthur down on one knee. And judging from the gobsmacked expressions around me, I wasn't the only surprised witness.

'D-Darling Edna,' Arthur stammered, 'we've been courting for several months. My first proposal was too soon and you turned me down. But I'm desperately hoping I've now truly captured your heart. I love you Edna. Will you marry me?'

Suddenly sound was suspended. Even the ringing bells seemed to quieten as everybody collectively held their breath.

And then Edna's face broke into a grin. 'Yes. Yes I will marry you Arthur!'

The crowd whooped and hollered as Arthur stood up and scooped Edna into his arms, squashing the bouquet in the process.

Jamie pushed his way over to Arthur's side and pumped his hand.

'Congratulations,' he laughed. 'Does this mean I have to call you Dad?'

Five hours later, suit jackets had been discarded and ties loosened. Disco lights flashed and music pounded out of vast speakers. The floorboards beneath me fairly bounced from the frenetic activity of guests dancing, self-consciousness discarded along with the crates of empty champagne bottles. I did my best to bop with Jamie but it began to get a bit farcical when he bounced off my bump for the third time. Nell was just feet away from me and showing off her Ceroc skills with Ben. Morag, close by, was grinding suggestively against Matt and clearly the worse for wear. The twins within me weighed upon my bladder, and I signalled to Jamie that I needed to find the rest room. As I headed out of the function suite and into a carpeted corridor, I realised Nell and Morag had fallen in behind me.

'God I'm blinkin' rat-arsed,' Nell giggled as she swayed into the Ladies.

'I think this is the first time I've ever gone to a wedding and remained sober,' I smiled ruefully.

'Lucky you,' Morag sighed. 'I'd give anything to be up the duff.'

We stood in a line against the washbasins, our dainty clutch bags open as we rummaged for make-up to repair shiny faces. As Morag extracted a lipstick, something fell out of her bag and dropped onto the floor.

'What's that?' asked Nell.

'A pregnancy test,' said Morag. 'I never leave home without one these days. That or an ovulation test kit,' she sighed.

'You must be spending a fortune,' Nell tutted. 'Why don't you just forget about it all and let nature take its course.'

'Yep,' Morag nodded. 'I'm not buying any more. This is my last pregnancy test.' She picked it up and waggled it about. 'I meant to widdle on it earlier, but everything has been such a rush today I haven't had a chance.'

'Is your period late?' I asked.

Morag shrugged noncommittally. 'My period is due today. So far it's a no-show.'

'Well what are we waiting for?' asked Nell.

'What do you mean?' Morag frowned.

I nodded towards a cubicle. 'Go on. In. And take your pregnancy test with you.'

Morag's shoulders drooped. She looked almost defeated. 'What's the point? Every time I do a test, it's negative. There's a part of me that wonders if I'll ever be pregnant again.'

'Stop being ridiculous.' Nell gave Morag a little push towards the cubicle. 'Now hurry up.'

Morag sighed and walked in. 'Here, what are you doing?' she yelped as we pushed in with her. The loo was generous enough in size, but it was a tight squeeze with my baby bump and Morag's chest. 'I'm not weeing in front of you two,' said Morag indignantly, 'so you can both get out right now!'

'Payback time,' I said firmly. 'You insisted on once doing the same to me – remember?'

'Oh all right!' Morag rolled her eyes. 'But the pair of you can bloomin' well turn around. At least spare me some dignity.'

Nell and I giggled and dutifully faced the door. There was a rustling noise as Morag hitched up her skirt.

'Well?' asked Nell.

'Give me a moment,' Morag huffed.

There was a brief silence.

'Well?' I asked.

We turned around to see Morag, knickers at half-mast, staring at the stick.

'Well?' Nell and I prompted together.

Morag looked up, her face wreathed in smiles. 'Well, well, well.'

THE END

ALSO BY DEBBIE VIGGIANO

Stockings and Cellulite

As the clock strikes midnight on New Year's Eve, Cassandra Cherry's life takes a turn for the worse when she stumbles upon husband Stevie lying naked, except for his socks, on a coat-strewn bed with a 45-year-old divorcee called Cynthia. Suddenly single, Cass throws herself into the business of getting over Stevie with gusto. Her main problems now are making her nine-year-old twins happy, juggling a new social life with a return to work and avoiding being arrested by an infuriating policeman who always seems to turn up at the most inopportune moments. Then, just when Cass is least prepared, and much to Stevie's chagrin, she crashes head over heels in love with the last person she'd ever expected.

AVAILABLE NOW AS E-BOOK AND PAPERBACK

ALSO BY DEBBIE VIGGIANO

Flings and Arrows

Steph Garvey has been married to husband Si for 24 years. Steph thought they were soulmates. Until recently. Surely one's soulmate shouldn't put Chelsea FC before her? Or boycott caressing her to fondle the remote control? Fed up, Steph uses her Tesco staff discount to buy a laptop. Her friends all talk about Facebook. It's time to get networking.

Si is worried about middle-age spread and money. Being a self-employed plumber isn't easy in recession. He's also aware things aren't right with Steph. But Si has forgotten the art of romance. Although these days Steph prefers cuddling her laptop to him. Then Si's luck changes work wise. A mate invites Si to partner up on a pub refurbishment contract.

Son Tom has finished Sixth Form. Tom knows where he's going regarding a career. He's not quite so sure where he's going regarding women and lurches from one frantic love affair to the next.

Widowed neighbour June adores the Garveys as if her own kin. And although 70, she's still up for romance. June thinks she's struck gold when she meets salsa squeeze Harry. He has a big house and bigger pension – key factors when you've survived a winter using your dog as a hot water bottle. June is vaguely aware that she's attracted the attention of fellow dog walker Arnold, but her eyes are firmly on Harry as 'the catch'.

But then Cupid's arrow misfires causing madness and mayhem. Steph rekindles a childhood crush with Barry Hastings; Si unwittingly finds himself being seduced by barmaid Dawn; June discovers Harry is more than hot to trot; and Tom's latest strumpet impacts on all of them. Will Cupid's arrow strike again and, more importantly, strike correctly? There's only one way to find out....

AVAILABLE NOW AS E-BOOK AND PAPERBACK

ABOUT THE AUTHOR

Prior to turning her attention to writing, Debbie Viggiano was, for more years than she cares to remember, a legal secretary. She lives in leafy Swanley Village in Kent with her husband, children and a food-obsessed beagle.

www.debbieviggiano.com

###

Printed in Great Britain
by Amazon

16523806R00217